Right Dreams

jay gee heath

Cover photograph design of rudbeckia by Susan E. Jameson

Library of Congress Control Number: 2014900213
Jay Gee Heath, Naples, FL

Dedication

Sam, of course!

Also by jay gee heath

Right Talents
Right Skills

Acknowledgements

Thanks for all your help and support.
Vivian Horak who keeps demanding I write another
book for her to proof
Janet Benjamins who keeps those pesky commas and
semi colons under control
Jo Anne Sullivan who makes the finishing corrections
Jean Smith whose picky, picky comments work so
well

PhysioFit, Niki and her very able crew
who challenged me to exercise and got me fit and
where most of the last quarter of the book was
created

Susan Jameson had the perfect cover photo design

The errors are mine, all mine

Then

She could deal with the pain. Knew how to work around it. Had worked through pain often enough before. It was the timing that sucked. These wounds were going to be career ending. Just great. Monday she breaks up with her lover; Friday she kills her career. Hopefully, not herself too.

She didn't really break up with him. She'd decided she didn't want the sleazy affair; she wanted more. Love. She wanted to love and be loved. Maybe he was the one. After all, he was the one she was having the affair with. She knew she liked him. Otherwise she wouldn't be sleeping with him. This whole love thing was her sister's fault. It started with her sister's wedding. Penney's wedding. Penney was so happy. Had met the guy two weeks ago for God's sake. Agreed to marry him after five days. They hadn't even slept together then. But it was obvious to everyone that the two were in love. The two belonged together.

Her other sister, Sarah, was also in love. But she and Michael were taking a more traditional route. A long engagement. Because they were setting up a business and didn't have the time for a wedding. Huh?

Becca wanted that love. Wanted to feel that happiness in a man's arms. Wanted to share a life with him. She wanted that dream for herself. Wanted to look forward to a future that included more than herself and a cat maybe. Even for that, she'd have to get a cat first. Wanted more than this sleazy affair. She wanted to try, anyhow. See if she could love someone.

Her brother, John, had found the man of his dreams. It was the first time Becca had seen John relaxed, content. She was happy for him. Theirs was to be another long engagement. Her brother, Kevin, was still single and happy. And her other sister, Cilla? Her marriage had hit a rough spot for a few months. Now she was back with Jake and seemed, well, besotted was the only word.

Cilla had told her, *take a chance; trust your feelings.* Cilla had trusted that her own love for Jake and his for her would be strong enough to carry them through the rough time. That, if their love was real, they would make it together. Looked like they had.

Becca trusted Cilla. Cilla had saved her. Cilla and her family. Not a family of blood relatives; they were a family created out of necessity and hardship. Created for survival. Her sisters and brothers by adversity. The Gang of Five: Penney, Sarah, John, Cilla, and Kevin. They had saved her. The gang had saved her and then she had helped save The Boys.

Only one of The Boys had made it back for the wedding; the other was still on some secret assignment. Otherwise the whole family had been there. Both of The Boys were still single so she and Kevin were not the only ones.

It was funny in a way. The gang members were all methodical, logical, and deliberate in their work. None of them made decisions on the fly. Yet Sarah and John had met their partners in the last four months. Cilla had met and eloped with Jake after knowing him barely a month. And Penney? Well Penney had met and married within two weeks. But Penney did live in the moment. That was Penney. It appeared that members of the gang loved impulsively.

Not her though. She wasn't sure she could love. Let alone fall in love at first sight. Could she fall in love? Was Tom the one? Tom, her lover? How could she tell? How could she be sure? Spend more time with him? She liked him; she knew that.

She had gathered all her courage and with her heart in her throat, she had propositioned him. Ha. Like that worked.

She could remember the words. She had practiced them over and over.

"I know we agreed that this was just a sexual relationship. But I would like more." She could see she had guessed wrong already. He stared at her as if she were speaking Russian. But she continued anyway, hoping.

"I want it all. Husband, house, kids. Yellow sunflowers in the front yard. We could start easy. See if we could work. Maybe meals together. I don't want sneaky afternoon sex anymore."

He was shaking his head and backing away. "No." That's all he said.

What did that mean? Didn't he feel something? Anything? He was still shaking his head.

"Has it only been sex between us?" Please say no; please say you at least like me. Please say it's not just sex. She pleaded silently. Though why did she want him to say that when she wasn't sure herself? But he was turning away.

"I guess that's it then," she said quietly. He turned back toward her, puzzled. "I'm done. I'm not going to settle for just sex. Even if it is great sex." He suggested adding a meal or a night out and she'd declined. "No, all or nothing. I'm done."

"You're leaving?"

"Yes," she whispered.

"If that's the way you feel. I can always find another willing woman to take your place and keep my bed warm."

Well, that hurt. He wasn't even going to make an effort to talk her into staying? Just replace her. So it truly was over. She had hoped that he felt a little something for her. She had been watching him closely since the wedding. And now he had confirmed her worst fears. He didn't love her. Probably didn't even like her much. Not enough to let her down gently. Or even offer an alternative.

"I'm taking a shower. Get your stuff and be gone when I get out. Or get back in bed. Your choice." He turned and left her there.

My choice? This was a choice? She had already made the choice when she had decided to confront him. She was with a man who couldn't or wouldn't deal with commitment. Who'd have thought? A man who couldn't commit. He had just kicked her out. No, he would say it was her decision to leave. And he was right. She could stay and settle, or go and find the future she wanted.

She hadn't needed much time to gather her few belongings and then she was gone.

Timing is everything. If she had waited one more week, until she got shot, he would have just walked away and she could have saved herself the embarrassment of confessing she wanted a traditional life. Of course, if she hadn't been thinking about her messed up love life, she wouldn't be on the ground bleeding now. She hadn't been paying attention. Her own fault.

She tried to remember. When was the last time she'd called in? Had she told them where she was? Would anyone find her in this alley? The answers were too long ago, no, and no. No one would find her here in the alley or yes they would, when it was too late.

Her radio was busted. It had flown out of her hand when she took the first hit. She could see it in multiple pieces. Her cell had no bars. Why was it that whenever you really needed a cell there were either no bars or the battery was dead. Better turn it off until she got out of the alley. And better not think about dead right now.

She took inventory. Her chest ached. The vest had stopped that bullet. The right shoulder wound didn't feel like much, but she couldn't move the arm, so muscle damage at least. But the gut shot could have done some damage and she couldn't stop the bleeding. That slug had snuck under the vest when she'd been going down. She had heard stories about the pain. They didn't even come close to what she felt, an agonizing, burning pain. If the slug hit any internal organs she was dead; she wouldn't have to worry about bars on her cell. She wasn't sure about the leg. Couldn't reach it. Or feel it. That was the only part of her that didn't hurt. The silver lining? She didn't know a person could feel so much pain at one time.

So she could stay here and die or drag herself out to the mouth of the alley and hope her cell found some bars or that some early morning riser found her before she bled out.

Choices. Not really any choice at all.

She used the pain to focus, and rolled over, screaming. OK. That worked. Screaming helped, even if she did sound like a girl. No one could hear her. She tried to take a deep breath. That wasn't a good idea. Short breaths. Get ready, reach out with your one good arm, pull, and scream. And repeat. She dragged herself. Actually the blood made it easier. Made the ground slick. What is it they say about silver linings?

Short breaths, get ready, reach out, pull, scream. And repeat. She felt herself getting weaker. Drag and scream. That would be her new mantra. Drag and scream. So she did, until she couldn't anymore.

She hadn't made it to the street. Wasn't going to. Maybe she had bars on her cell now. She turned the phone back on.

Waited.

Two. Two bars? Pushed a button.

"911," the operator said.

Whispered, "Officer down. Corner Waters and First."

"Can't hear you, speak up please," she was instructed.

Louder this time, all her energy, "Officer down. Corner Waters and First."

"I understand, Officer down? Corner of Waters and First? Is that correct?" was the calm question.

Yes she thought, that's right. And that was the last thing she remembered.

Now six weeks later

"What are you going to do?" Cilla asked her again.

Becca had given it a lot of thought. Six weeks in a hospital bed gave you a lot of time to think. "Don't really have a lot of choice." Choices again. This time not hers, though. "They won't let me go back to work. Not the work I was doing. They won't even let me take a desk job. They retired me on a full disability. At 28, retired. They didn't even wait for my prognosis. They will pay me not to work; they are going to pay me not to work. Though the terms of the disability let me get another job. Anywhere, doing anything, even the same job. Just not this job, here. And I not only get paid to stay home, but my pay is tax free. Some more of my silver linings it seems." She stopped whining.

"I am coming back home. Which is one thing you are asking." Home, being the town where they both grew up. Because she couldn't climb one step let alone the three flights of steps to her one room apartment.

She had made a lot of progress in the hospital's physical therapy program. She could walk, stand, and sit. Slowly. With minor pain. Well, minor compared to six weeks ago. She hadn't realized before how every single effing motion was connected to her abdominal muscles. Made her want to scream. Hah. From both the pain and the frustration. Sometimes she wondered if she would ever get well. Whining again, she thought. She could take a deep breath now, without pain. That was progress. And she could walk with the crutch. She had come a long way. Besides, she must be better because the hospital was kicking her out.

Cilla had volunteered to clean out Becca's apartment; pack up and move her things. Pay off the lease. And she hadn't been happy when she came back to Becca's bed side. "No wonder you always met me at restaurants. You knew what I'd say if I saw how you live. Your apartment is a disappointment. One room. Bleak. Sad. Rental furniture. Bare walls. Just one picture. A small one of the gang, on a dresser. Nothing personal or pretty or soft or comfortable."

"This isn't right. You should have pretty stuff. Things to make you happy. This isn't living; this is barely existing. We didn't rescue you so you could simply survive. Subsist. You should be flourishing, happy, enjoying life."

So the discussion then became about where she would live. Cilla had suggested her vacant condo. "We just finished with the redecoration in the condo and it screams Becca. Come on Becca." The gang had never called her Rebecca. It had always been Becca. That year when they had saved her, rescued her, they had rescued Rebecca Anne Travis. They had welcomed Becca into their family, their geek gang. They'd been poor, homeless, alone. Well, Kevin wasn't poor, but he might as well have been for all the attention he got from his parents. The housekeeper, Annie, raised him. Though they had all pretty much raised themselves.

Becca fit into the requirements of abandoned and abused. The gang recognized her as one of their own; they knew the signs, the symptoms, and pulled her in. Protected and hid her. For a year.

"Come on, Becca," Cilla coaxed. "I don't know if I should rent the condo or sell it. So do me a favor and move in so I don't have to make a decision. You know how I hate to make decisions. And you know I don't need the income from either a sale or a rental. Come on, it will be fun, Becca. You'll be right across the hall. And you can help take care of Tiff." Her cat, another outcast and rescue.

"I really don't want to stay with you and Jake, or move into your other condo. And I don't need charity."

She didn't get a chance to finish. "So stay at the gatehouse," Cilla suggested not giving up. The gatehouse, Kevin's gatehouse

"I'm not sure I could go back there." She'd lived there, hidden out there more like, most of her last year of high school.

"I don't know if I could go back there. I was so helpless then." She could go back physically. But not emotionally, she couldn't go back to that time when she was helpless.

"You weren't helpless then," Cilla said angrily. "You were in control. We all were. We made it happen. Don't you dare let me hear you say you were helpless. You were strong and brave. You were making your first step toward independence and success. That step led you here."

Yeah, here to this hospital bed, Becca thought.

"It's different now, though," Cilla cajoled. "Cleaned up. Pretty and warm. You saw it at the wedding. You wouldn't be alone; someone is always coming or going. We all work there still and sometimes even spend the night. It will be fun."

She could picture the room in her mind. It was one huge room furnished in five different styles, one for each of the members. The front door led to the simple functionality of the plain Shaker woods of Sarah's space. Across were the floral pastels of Cilla. The loud bold colors that were so Penney were next to Cilla's. And the black leather and glass of Kevin's in the center, next to John's beanbag scheme, a holdover from his wanna-be-a-hippy days.

A central common area had additional couches and a long dining room table with chairs for twelve. A full kitchen was along the back behind a counter with stools which faced a wall of cabinets and appliances. Two corridors, one each side of the back wall, led to the bedrooms and baths.

She would be living in the eclectic sea of styles and colors. Maybe she could find one of those areas soothing or cheering.

Cilla had made the suggestions earlier, when they had been talking about where Becca should live. "A move to the gatehouse will be an opportunity to start over. You started over there once, you will do it again." An order, Becca thought.

"OK. I'll live at the gatehouse, just like I did before," she agreed. She didn't have anywhere else to go. "But only until I get better. Then I'm going to find a job. I want to work, not sit around and watch the world go by. Just not sure what I should do. I want to do what they're paying me not to do. Be a cop." She was nodding to herself.

"I need to be around people. The activity at the gatehouse will be good for me. Take my mind off my problems. That's another reason to move to the gatehouse and not your condo where I would be alone. I know you're right next door, but you'll be working. And being at the gatehouse will almost be like I'm home." And she had another reason. She was going to find the person who shot her. Her Captain was calling it a random shooting, but she didn't believe that. She believed she was purposely led into that alley and she was going to find out why. And who. So she had to go to the gatehouse where she could use the computers. Where no one could track her. She couldn't do the searches at the hospital and leave traces all over their server. They'd be no tracks at the gatehouse.

"While you are convalescing, you can consider different ideas for your future. Do you want to work for yourself? Private investigator?" Cilla was still talking to her.

"No. I don't want to be on my own. Like I said, I need people. A gang. A team. A partner."

"How about investigative reporter? Body guard? Building security? Mall cop?"

They both laughed at that. No, not mall cop.

During her stay at the hospital, Cilla or one of the other members of the gang had been with her almost every day. Each member had visited frequently. Bringing flowers and toys. And, thank goodness, a tablet. Her lover, ex-lover, though, had never shown up or called. She shouldn't have been surprised, but she was disappointed. They'd been involved, that should have meant a visit. Or at least a floral arrangement. It really had been just sex and the affair was over. She stopped her pity party. And the private nurses Cilla had hired? They looked a little bit like bodyguards. Bodyguards with medical experience. Cilla hadn't said anything, neither had Becca. She knew Cilla would get around to explaining when she was ready. Most days Cilla sat quietly by Becca's bedside, busy writing code or doing some geek thing.

Cilla had listened sympathetically when Becca had talked a little about her love, lust affair. Not mentioning any names. Partly because

Cilla would probably go over and beat him up if she knew who he was. Partly because the affair had been a secret. A secret affair, just between the two lovers. Becca should have known. Secret affair? That always meant just sex. She had been too much in lust to realize or care.

Cilla brought her back to the present again; she was still talking.

"You wouldn't believe the confusion after you got shot. I saw Cav walk in the door all serious and somber. He looked right at me with such pain in his eyes. But he went over to Jake. He told him. I guess he thought that Jake could break it to me gently. I saw Jake shake his head."

"I got curious and walked over and heard Jake say, *She doesn't have a sister. Doesn't have any family. Just the gang. The gang is her family.*"

"Cav pulled a piece of paper out of his pocket and said "Rebecca"? Jake started to shake his head and then I saw it register. His face turned bleak and I heard him say 'Becca'."

Cilla shook her head, "If I hadn't told Jake about you, at Penney's wedding, I might never have known you were hurt. Scary. I mean, I told him about you and The Boys. I guess I never told him we were sisters. I had to explain to both him and Cav. Not everything. Just that we were blood sisters, like blood brothers. They don't understand what it means to have a blood sister or brother. That we vowed to always be sisters and mingled our blood." And that was why Cilla was listed as Rebecca's next of kin, her sister. And that's what Cilla called herself when the hospital staff asked. "They're guys. You would think they would have done that." She was laughing.

"I don't think they approve that you lied on the next of kin line." She shook her head.

Cilla had been the first person Rebecca saw when she woke up.

"Cav brought us here with lights and sirens. Even though it's way out of his jurisdiction. And he got updates on your condition on the way. You'll like Cav."

"How do you know him? A cop? The Sheriff? Why would he notify you himself? And bring you here?" Becca asked.

"Long story. Maybe on the ride back." She paused, "No, I don't think I can tell that story in front of Jake. I mean, he knows it. He was there. It's just that it would feel funny telling you some things in front of him. My feelings. His feelings. It's all tied up to him leaving and then coming back."

Jake, the ex-estranged husband, had come by the hospital a few times with Cilla. Becca wasn't sure she liked him. He had hurt Cilla. Last year Becca had spent long hours trying to comfort Cilla after Jake had walked out. It was a new role for Becca because it had always been Cilla doing the comforting. Now Jake was back. Cilla was happy. But Becca was a cynic. He would have to prove himself to her.

"So I will tell you," Cilla was saying. "But later, after we get back, on some rainy afternoon. You helped me through that whole ugly episode; you deserve to know what happened. I can't tell you everything. Some of it is still officially secret, so I can't talk about it. You could write a book about it. Hey, maybe that's what you should do. Write about enforcing the law."

"I want to do what I was doing." Becca heard the whine in her voice again. She hated that.

"Now you are just being defeatist. Jake did that you know. He went through the poor me. I've ruined my life. I have a bum leg. I'm a failure phase. You know I think I will get Daffy in here to talk to you. Have him make an intervention. He helped Jake see reality."

She pulled out her cell. And Becca was on her. "No, don't call him. I don't want to talk to him. A guy named Daffy? How can a guy be named Daffy? He should be gay. Like John." Their brother. He was a child advocate attorney and a serious geek. He was engaged to Peter Conrad.

Cilla laughed. At least she had gotten Becca out of the poor little me syndrome.

"Don't want to talk to any guy named Daffy."

Now Cilla really laughed. "You can ask Penney if he's gay. After all, she married him."

Penney was a finance investment guru. She handled all of the gang's finances. Both individually and for their business. In addition to being family and friends, the five had formed SC Digital to raise money for Sarah's Child, a charitable foundation. A safe haven for kids like themselves. Because their sister, Sarah, wanted it. She was a child psychologist. Her new beau, Michael, would be the pediatrician for

Sarah's Child. The gang had raised millions of dollars by creating and selling an online computer game. Hundreds of millions. Enough to fund Sarah's Child forever. The gatehouse was SC's office. The place where they wrote and collaborated on the game.

While Becca was learning to walk again, she could learn how to live, not just exist. Was that something you learned? Could she put her past behind her and heal both physically and emotionally? Find happiness? Put color and light back into her life? Become whole?

Friday

Jake and Cilla came back at the end of the week to bring her home to the gatehouse. Cilla hadn't asked Jake, or even suggested that he might give Becca a job. She would be a good addition to his security business. But on the drive to pick Becca up at the hospital, Cilla tried to figure out the proper way to broach the subject with Jake.

While she was dithering he said, "I can watch Becca, observe her, see how she handles herself during therapy. I can talk to her and feel her out. If it seems that she would be a good fit, I can offer her a job."

She looked at him in surprise. "How did you know I wanted to ask you? That's why I love you because you always know what I'm thinking. That should be scary, but in a way it's kind of comforting."

"Don't get your hopes up," he cautioned, "There are a lot of other issues involved."

"I know. And some of them scare me. She will need to find her own self. Her own place. She won't let you just give her a job. She will want to fight for it, earn it, and win it. That's one of the reasons I didn't ask you." Aside from the very personal reason of being afraid to ask. "She's dealing with a love affair gone bad. She needs to heal. From the physical wounds and the emotional wounds. From her childhood. And all the residual psychological scars."

"Yes, there's a lot to deal with. Fortunately, the convalescence will give her time to get a handle on most of them. And we can be close to her and help her through it. You helped me; you know how to do it. And I learned from you. At least I can identify with and understand the convalescent parts."

"I expect her to hunt down whoever shot her. Her Captain isn't going to pursue it. But she will," Cilla stated the fact.

He glanced at her and said, "I have already checked into the shooting and her case. I can't find anything."

"We have too. The Gang. Same results. And she isn't talking about it yet. She keeps everything so close. We can't even find the lover. Probably a good thing. She might think that us examining her personal life and mistakes is a betrayal." Cilla didn't know if she should be proud that Becca was so good at keeping secrets or annoyed that Becca kept them from her. Both probably.

"Cilla? You'd share wouldn't you? You'd let me know if you found anything? We should work together on this. We're both involved and we each have our area of expertise." He was worried that she wouldn't want to share her family with him. Their trust was still too new. They were both still feeling their way. It had seemed so simple in the beginning, but there were so many shades of gray it was confusing. Would she trust him enough to let him help with her sister?

"You want to?" she asked, surprised.

It hurt him that she could still be so unsure of him as to be surprised that he would want to help. "Of course, she's your sister, she's in trouble. Of course I want to help."

"Great. That's a relief. I kind of wanted to ask you to help and I wasn't sure I should. And I wanted to ask you about a job for her too and I wasn't sure if that was something I could ask. Because of the secrecy angle of your business." His business kept a low profile and used a cover as consultants who helped startup companies. "I didn't want to put you in the position of having to refuse me. I had just decided to ask you if I could ask you," she admitted. The trust issues. She was glad she had finally laid that out for him.

"You can ask me anything, anytime." He smiled. That was so like her. Not the confusion, but admitting she was confused. "We made that deal, to trust, when you let me back into your life. Everything.

You can talk to me about everything. Even my job. I will never again assume you don't need to know."

**

At the gatehouse, Becca insisted she could walk on her crutch herself. She was a little embarrassed that she had slept for most of the drive. And surprised and happy to see the gang was waiting. Even Michael and Peter, the almost in-laws were there. It was almost a party. Annie, Kevin's housekeeper and the gang's mentor, had made Becca's favorite although it was late afternoon, not breakfast. Scrambled eggs with ham chunks. Sausage links and English muffins on the side.

They told tall tales on Becca. Sounded like tall tales, but most of them were true. Smart, pretty, tall. Abused and always in trouble, till the gang rescued her. Cilla always claimed she was jealous of the tall, and the sleek, and the lithe. Cilla complained she could only pull it off with five inch heels. And then only for a few minutes.

Becca talked with Peter some more. He was an interesting man. Medium height, solid. Warm. And so obviously in love with John it both hurt her and made her happy for both of them. John deserved a lot of happiness. They were heading to Europe to visit with Peter's family.

And Sarah's Michael. There was a real surprise. Sarah falling in love and getting herself a doctor. And the doctor couldn't help himself from checking Becca, surreptitiously. Becca laughed at him and said, "I'm fine, they wouldn't have let me out if I wasn't."

"Even so, I'm going to keep an eye on you," he said. "And Jones's sister is one of the best physical therapists in her field. It shouldn't take you long to be fully recovered with her help."

Penney was there. Alone. Daffy was on assignment, no one saying what type of assignment or where or what he actually did for a living. He would be back sometime, soon, maybe. Becca noticed the vague details but didn't comment. Another puzzle the gang would explain when they were ready. She brushed the back of her index finger across her brow. Sometimes the gang just made her tired.

Annie finally broke them up saying Becca looked tired and Becca couldn't deny it; she was tired. And she ached. She had stopped taking the pain medication. She knew she could handle her current level of pain and the meds made her brain lazy and sluggish. It had been a long day for her. She got a hug from each of them as they left. Annie reminded her she'd left individual meals in the refrigerator. Cilla told her, again, that an assortment of people would be using the gatehouse and Becca shouldn't be surprised if one or two of them wandered in. "You met them at the wedding, so it will not be a complete stranger coming to the door. And the security system will stop and check anyone who comes through the gate. Video will show you who it is with text identifying them by name." She made sure the system was on and then she left too, after a kiss.

Penney asked if she should stay. But suddenly, Becca wanted to be alone.

She breathed a sigh of relief when they were all finally gone. Got herself a glass of milk, turned out the lights, sat down in a soft rocker and put her head back. Alone. The first time she'd been alone since she was shot. She loved her family but, oh, this moment alone was glorious. She was almost too tired to enjoy it. She felt guilty that her family was spending so much time with her. She knew they were worried. And would stay worried until she was back on her feet, figuratively and literally. So she would just have to get better. Physically, she thought, would be easier then emotionally. She was having nightmares. Taking those hits and almost bleeding to death in a dark alley had brought them back. The ghoulish, grinning face woke her in a sweat. She was hoping the bad dreams with the horrid face would go away now that she was home and healing. She hadn't told anyone, but if she didn't get better, she might talk to Sarah. Sarah could help; childhood nightmares were her specialty.

Becca sat there a long time just thinking. She still couldn't figure out who had shot her or why. But someone had certainly wanted her dead. Somewhere she had missed something. She fell asleep rocking gently.

A chirping woke her. She was disoriented, confused for a moment. The gatehouse, she was in the gatehouse. The chirping was the security system. Someone was coming through the gate. Cilla had turned on the system when she left and the image was on the big screen. Older man, familiar from the wedding she thought. Her gut quivered. She reached for the remote and turned on the text. Ryan Gibbs. She had met him at the wedding. Her gut had done the same quivering then. A friend of Daffy's, his best man. And Jake's friend too. She was trying to remember what more she knew. Friendly guy. Laid back. Soft. Quiet. Had a son about Cilla's age. Yeah, that was the guy. She waited.

He carded the door and stepped in. Threw his duffle on the floor. Locked the door behind him. She switched on the light. He turned quick and was reaching behind his back when his eyes adjusted and he saw Becca in the chair and stopped, brain finally kicking in over instinct.

"I didn't realize anyone was here; I didn't see a car," he said. "I was just going to crash here for a while," he was explaining his presence. He had planned on a couple of days down time at the gatehouse. It had been a tough week and the gatehouse always calmed and renewed. "I didn't know you were here. Annie didn't say when I texted. Rebecca? Right? We met at the wedding?" When he had stood up for Daffy.

She did remember him. She also remembered her physical reaction because her body was still doing it to her again. A physical shock of recognition had slammed through her when he'd turned around. She'd discounted it at the wedding. So much was going on. And he was too old for her. He was still too old for her. She'd have a talk with her body later. She had to deal with the man, now.

"Yeah, and you're Ryan. Were you just reaching for a weapon?" she asked. Hers were in the bedroom with the rest of her stuff. Might as well be on the moon if she needed it.

"I better go to the hotel." Reaching for his bag.

"Why? Why do you have to leave? And you didn't answer my question."

He was caught, a little embarrassed, and wasn't sure what to say. "I've been spending some of my off time here. Guess I've been out of touch with the gang or I would have known you were here. I don't want to impose." He followed his explanation up with a question, "You don't mind? I can stay?" because she seemed to imply it was okay.

"There's plenty of room. I don't mind. Just not my room, I'm in Cilla's room. And you didn't answer my question." Which was kind of an answer in itself she thought.

"Can I sit down? Get a drink?" he asked playing for time. Trying to remember what he knew about her, besides that his body had recognized her before his brain kicked in with her identity. The same way it had responded when he met her at the wedding. A way that had only ever happened with his wife. The '*I'm ready. You're mine. Let's get to it*' demand of his lower body. His little brain. He was cataloging. Rebecca. Cop. Not a member of the gang, but a later rescue. Probably not the politically correct term, but an accurate term. Rebecca was older than the original five gang members. Younger kids saving an older kid. He didn't know anything more. Cilla had only said that Becca had lived in the gatehouse for a year.

"Just make believe I'm not here. I'm used to sharing the place with other people and Cilla said there would probably be people in and out. Were you reaching for a gun?"

"Can I get that drink?"

"Just answer the question."

"Yes, I was reaching for a weapon," he finally acknowledged.

"Tell me why you're carrying. I thought you were from Florida. An innkeeper someone said." Older innkeeper she reminded her body.

He inspected her closely. "You look tired."

Becca just shook her head. He was going to be one of those. Pull the answers out one by one. She wasn't swearing, but in a minute she was going to get up. Slowly, because that was all she could manage. Go get her gun, and come back and shoot him.

"I am tired. I was shot. I'm recuperating. You probably know all that. I hurt and I'm sore and you are making me testy. You won't like me if I'm testy."

She saw his lips twitch.

"Don't laugh at me. I'm a cop. I'm not going to forget I asked you a question. Why are you carrying?"

He sighed; she would know soon enough and it really wouldn't need to be a secret much longer. "I'm sort of an innkeeper. Was sort of an innkeeper. I was on a leave of absence, helping my daughter-in-law run her inn while my son was on assignment."

"OK. That's a start. Leave of absence from?" waiting.

"FBI."

She hadn't been expecting that. "Funny you don't look like FBI."

"We have a look?"

"Yeah. Now you're just funning me. Black suits, stick up the ass, don't ever share." She heard herself. "Well, apparently you do have the 'don't ever share' gene."

He laughed. He liked her. He could see her wondering how he fit in. With Jake. With Daffy.

"There are going to be a lot more questions, aren't there?"

"Oh yeah. Okay, go get a drink. Pour me a glass of milk."

He poured himself coffee form the carafe and handed her the milk. Sat across from her and waited for her questions.

"Tell me how you fit in. With the gang."

"What do you know about the events surrounding Sheri?"

"Not much. Sheri tried to kill Jake. She got killed. Jake and Cilla got back together. I know there's more. I know they aren't telling me everything. But they will eventually. So you tell."

He was considering how much he could tell. The last week had pretty much tied it all up. They would put the bow on it Monday. Wouldn't hurt to share some.

She watched him deciding and waited.

He could give her an abbreviated outline of part of the investigation. "About a year ago, Jake bumped into Sheri and stumbled onto her white slavery ring, trafficking children. He was instrumental with busting the ring and sending Sheri to jail. She broke out and came after Cilla and Jake. Killed a few people before we took her down. Cilla sort of took her down. We were backup. I can't talk about Jake or Cilla; you need to get that story from them. The Sheri case opened up two other investigations which are still active. I can't go into those right now. Your friends were asked to keep everything confidential; that's why they haven't told you."

She thought about that while sipping her milk.

He watched her think, waiting for the next question. This was another strong woman. Penney, Cilla, Sarah. Each had proven themselves. And he had been there when Cilla had gone after Sheri. Almost slowed him down he was so amazed at her courage. And later, after Daffy's wedding, he had looked over Cilla's shoulder as she went through her scrapbook with Jake. Explaining how the gang had started. Short thumbnails on each of the members. He shook his head. He'd heard Becca had been shot on the job. An injury which had ended her career. Was she bitter? Maybe resigned?

He didn't know anything else about her. Beyond what his gut thought. Abused, like the rest he was sure. And that was all he was sure of. Older than the rest but protected by the gang. The gang members were about thirteen or fourteen when they rescued Becca, who was then about sixteen, and The Boys were about fourteen.

Becca decided to let it go for now. She was tired. "Well I guess Cilla has a lot of 'splaining to do. Thank you. I think I'll go to bed now." It took her a minute to stand pushing up with her hands. One arm more help than the other. Then she had to make sure her feet were under her before she grabbed her crutch, and headed for her bedroom. He hadn't tried to help her; she appreciated that.

She spoke from the door to the bedrooms, "See you in the morning. And I'll warn you now; I don't do mornings too well before coffee."

He laughed out loud. It had taken all his will power not to help her out of the rocker. "Testy?" he asked with a smile.

"Testy and cranky. Promise."

"Well then I better get up first and make coffee. Eggs? Toast too?"

She smiled at him, "After coffee. Goodnight."

Saturday

She woke up smelling coffee. And bacon. It was nearly nine o'clock. She never slept until nine. And she hadn't slept through the night since she woke up in that hospital bed. She wanted to jump out of bed and eat bacon, but she settled for sitting up slowly and doing the leg and arm exercises she had learned at the hospital rehab. Skip the shower, she thought, maybe after bacon. He must have heard her because he knocked on the door, snuck a hand in with a cup of coffee, and waved it around. She hobbled over and grabbed it.

"Breakfast in fifteen. You have time for a shower."

She didn't have much to wear, gray cotton sweat pants, and a t-shirt. Maybe tomorrow she'd check Penney's closet. She sort of felt like color. She left her hair down to dry after her shower and made it out to the kitchen in ten minutes.

"I like a woman who is prompt," he said smiling, "Hand me your coffee and I'll refill it."

She pulled herself up onto the high counter chair, at one of the two place settings he had put out. It was just a good thing she still had some upper body strength. "And I love a man who cooks." She watched him drop his whipped eggs into butter and scramble them. "And cooks in butter. A man after my heart."

"Yes, that's what they all say. Except that part about the butter. Most of you ladies don't like butter. But you don't get the flavor without it."

She watched him finish cooking breakfast. On a closer look, she thought not soft - dangerous. This was a dangerous man. He had it covered by a thin layer of soft and friendly. That had fooled her. That layer. She remembered his eyes, sharp piercing gray. Eyes that saw right through you. Cop eyes. She remembered how quickly he had moved last night when she had turned on the light. And just as quickly he had realized that there could be no danger here in the gatehouse. How come she hadn't noticed how quick he was? She'd been tired. That was her excuse.

A cop. A Fed. How had Cilla met up with a Fed? One who felt comfortable using the gatehouse? How come she knew he was older, but not that he was a fed? And just what was her system trying to tell her?

She hadn't really seen him last night or at the wedding either, except to note that he was older. Could be her father, he was old enough. So she hadn't really noticed that he was built, though apparently her system had. She could see the muscles ripple through his t-shirt. That was the difference. He had been wearing the standard long sleeve white shirt both times before. And now that she thought of it, he'd looked pretty good in that too. Medium height, medium build, with the broad shoulders, slim hips. And the cutest butt. A good-looking man.

"What? What did you say?" she'd gotten lost in her new evaluation. Get real girl.

"I asked if you wanted orange juice or jelly with the toast." He turned around with both those items in his hands. Laughing at her. A nice laugh. She had a feeling he knew exactly where she'd been gazing and what she was thinking. God, he was old enough to be her father.

She wouldn't turn red. "Both."

He poured juice for both of them, freshened their coffees. Spooned the eggs into their dishes, took a platter of bacon from the small oven, and put that on the counter with a plate of buttered toast. "Butter on the toast already. Add your own jelly."

He sat beside her and dug in. They ate in silence.

She savored every bite. No one ever cooked for her. "No one's cooked for me since I was a kid," she admitted. "And this is great, thanks." She smiled. "I could really get to like having you around."

Had she really said that? She went on hurriedly, "How long will you be here?"

"The weekend, if that's all right with you." He was surprised to find that he wanted to spend time with this woman, on a personal level. Learn more about her.

"Sure. This has always been a place for anyone who wants to be here. You cooked, I'll do cleanup," she offered.

"I'll help. It will go quicker."

While they worked she asked some questions she thought he might answer. It was like wading through quicksand. He deflected most of her queries. She didn't give up but gave him a small smile and a slight shake of her head and said, "You are actually telling more by the questions you're not answering. Which is making me even more curious. Do you really want me drawing conclusions based on your half answers and then doing my own research? Isn't that dangerous for you?" she asked sweetly.

He considered his options and then pulled out his cell and hit the speed dial. He was watching her when he said, "Ryan," into the phone, identifying himself.

He got an immediate demand from Jake. "Ryan, do you guys have this wrapped up yet? Cilla is getting anxious. She doesn't like leaving Becca out of the loop. Especially since she's now living in the gatehouse."

"That's why I'm calling. I'm at the gatehouse."

"Becca's there," Jake told him.

"Yes, I'm looking at her. She's asking excellent questions and drawing her own conclusions. We are close enough to the end that I can tell her some. How much can I tell her about you and your business?"

Becca wondered who he had on speed dial. Someone who knew she was here apparently.

"All of it. Tell her everything," Jake said.

"OK, but she'll be coming to you for more. I'm not getting into personal stuff, just the case. How about Pretty Boy?"

There was a pause while Jake did a quick review and then said, "You need to ask him. Or Penney. I doubt if there is a problem, but check with them."

He hit the off button and, still watching Becca, ran through the contact list on his cell, and made a selection.

"Hey, sweetheart," he said in a warm voice. "How you doing?"

"Ryan, where are you? Are you here?" Penney asked warmly.

"Yes, in the gatehouse."

"Oh, gee, Becca's there."

"Right. I'm getting ready to tell her about everything. It was wrapped up yesterday. Can I tell her about Pretty Boy?"

"Is she right there?"

"Yes, watching me talk to you."

"Let me talk to her."

He passed the phone over. Becca didn't know who would be on the other end. Sweetheart and Pretty Boy? She spoke into the phone tentatively, "Hello?"

"Becca, its Penney," Penney? Ryan was calling Penney, sweetheart? What in the world? Penney was talking. "Becca, we wanted to tell you; they wouldn't let us. We begged. But they used National Security on us. Used it on Ryan too. It's not his fault we couldn't tell you. OK? Don't blame him. But I want to be the one to tell you about Daffy."

Becca was still back at national security and not Ryan's fault. Daffy? Penney wanted to tell her about Daffy? Becca didn't have a chance to speak even if Penney had given her an opportunity.

"I know you wondered, but we couldn't explain his occupation without getting into the secret stuff. He's a professional bodyguard. That's how I met him. He was working for Jake. And protecting me."

Jake? Jake hired bodyguards? Daffy was a bodyguard? She thought back. That felt right. It fit with her impression of a powerful man. Even if he did have a sissy name. But Jake? He didn't seem the type to know bodyguards. Why would he be hiring bodyguards?

Penney was still talking, laughing, "Daffy was guarding my body. Which I must say he did very, very well. Listen to Ryan. Call me if you have more questions. OK?" And she was gone. In the moment Penney.

Becca handed the phone back to Ryan, a little stunned. She thought her mouth might be hanging open. Reached her hand up and closed it. National security? And bodyguards? This was a whole lot bigger then she'd imagined. Why did Penney need a bodyguard? What was Jake?

Who exactly was Ryan? She took a breath getting ready to ask. And then remembered her therapy. "I have therapy in fifteen minutes. I have a feeling this is a long story. I have some quick questions."

He waved her off. "Let me tell it my way. I can do a quick outline. Even the sweetened condensed version will be too long. I think I can hit the points that interest you the most and give you the basics."

"You think you know me that well?"

"No. But I can debrief that well. First Jake. His business is a cover for corporate protection, bodyguard service, and background checks on new employees. A number of his clients are under contract to the federal government, secret contract, through Munson. Munson is Jake's FBI contact. You met him and his family at the wedding."

He gave her a chance to digest that and added, "Cilla didn't know about Jake's real work."

"Cilla didn't know? He didn't tell her?" Becca was outraged. She knew how much that deceit would have hurt Cilla. "Ooh, I hate him. I hated him when he walked. When he left her. Now I hate him even more. Keeping secrets."

"He has a story," Ryan said gently. "You need to hear it before you condemn him."

"Tell me," she demanded.

"No. It's his story, not mine. Not part of our current debriefing. And he needs to tell it, not me. You need to hear it from him or Cilla. He was my first call because most of this revolves around him. Two of his federal clients were hacked and sensitive breaking edge weapon schematics were stolen. The trail led to Peter."

"Peter? John's Peter?" was all she could manage to say.

"Yes. The gang proved to Jake that Peter was innocent and followed a trail to the real culprit. That part is need to know and confidential, still." He looked at her and waited for her to nod understanding.

"Next, second, Sheri. Jake originally stumbled onto Sheri when he was doing a job for Munson. I told you some last night. Sheri was sent to jail but busted out. Jake and Munson both believed that Sheri had help busting out. Someone high up, a top level FBI agent. Jake contacted me to help. Then he called in his people because Sheri went after Cilla to get at Jake. She went after Cilla's gang to get to Cilla.

Daffy was one of the bodyguards Jake brought in to protect them. He is one of the best in the protection trade. Sheri is dead. Shot by one of her own thugs"

Becca felt a silly pride that Penney had married one of the best.

"Third, Penney discovered a money laundering scheme linking the mob to our guy and Sheri. Jake was right about an inside guy. We had the local cops, FBI, Homeland Security, and FinCEN working together for about three days. Homeland finished mopping up Wednesday. FinCEN and the FBI busted the mob guys yesterday. That is for your ears only until it makes the papers. Probably Sunday, Monday at the latest. Did I hit all your questions?"

She took a couple of breaths and said, "You missed one."

"I don't generally miss. What didn't I address?" he was puzzled.

"You. Who are you?"

And he was saved by the security system chiming the arrival of the therapist.

"OK, you're off the hook. But you'll have all weekend to tell me the stories and how they tie together. Right now, one more question, tell me who is Jones and what is his sister's name? She's the therapist Cilla hired for me. Well, that's two questions."

"Jones is a Deputy Sheriff; he works for Cavanaugh. He was new on the job and baptized under fire during the Sheri take down. The kid did OK. Better than OK. His sister's name is Lori. She was at Penney's wedding."

Lori turned out to be a cute girl. Well, maybe not a girl, she was at least as old as Becca. But she acted like a teenager. About 5'4" with a halo of curly blond hair. Dark flashing eyes and a wide smile. She bounced in. Exuberant. Vibrant. The energy just rolled off her. Becca had felt stiff and sore before Lori walked in. Now she also felt old and dull too.

Lori gave Ryan a hug and a kiss on the cheek. She got a warm smile in return. She turned to Becca and said, "I know you're Rebecca. I can tell by the crutch and we met at the wedding. I'm Lori," she said giggling. "I have to make friends quick, because as soon as my clients start therapy they decide they hate me and end up cursing me well before the end of our sessions. But they get better. And I'm tough enough to take a few curses."

Becca liked her immediately. "If cursing you out and calling you vile names is all it takes to get better, I'll be happy to do that," Becca offered with a smile. "I have a feeling, though, that it isn't going to be that easy. Call me Becca."

"Okay Becca, we'll start with an evaluation which will help me decide on your protocols. I have copies of your medical records and the physical therapy you completed at the hospital. But I need to see for myself where your body is so I can set up a plan to manage your pain while we get you back to full strength. Seems you did a little extra damage dragging yourself out of the alley, but since that's the only reason your still alive, I think I'll forgive you." She didn't mention that the medical records went back to childhood and told a horrific tale. She had been around the gang of five long enough to know they'd all had bad childhoods. It was a past they each shared and one of the glues that kept the gang together, made them family.

Ryan thought he noticed an anxious look on Becca's face and interrupted to say he was going for a run. "How long will you be?" he asked Lori.

"Give us an hour. I might still be finishing my write up, but we'll be done with the physical work by then."

"OK. Back in about an hour," he told them as he went out the door.

They watched him leave. "I like him, makes me think of my Dad," Lori said wistfully. "Well let's get started. Ground rules. You need to let me know when something hurts, when you feel pain or stretching. It's only you and me. You don't need to be tough or macho or proud. If you overdo, your recovery will take longer. Can you do that?"

"Sure," Becca said not meaning it for a second.

"I need to determine your strength and range of motion. Those govern how long and how often we meet and the length and intensity of our sessions. As you get stronger, we'll modify the schedule to reflect your progress. We might have to go to the rehab center a couple of times for specialized treatments but I can do most of what we need here. But first I need a cup of coffee," she finished as she went over and got herself one. "None for you because I'm just mean. And you need your hands free. I'll watch how you sit, stand, walk, bend, stoop. Then there will be some range of motion and flexibility exercises.

An hour later, when Becca was thinking, but not saying, bitch, bitch, bitch, Lori finally called a halt to the session.

"Sit. Rest. You didn't fool me. I went easy on you and gave you extra rest breaks. You cops all think you're so tough. You need to learn and remember that if you do too much too quickly, you will slow the healing and can, in some instances, do some more damage and reverse the healing. Let's meet again on Monday. We'll do Mondays and Thursdays because your body needs to recoup between sessions. I'll give you additional exercises for your off days. Don't overdo!"

Becca was chagrined; she had thought she was fooling Lori. "Easy on me?" she disputed irritably. "You did not go easy on me. Look at me. I'm soaked with sweat. And I'm not going to sit if you are going to make me get up again. I don't think I can get up one more time. I can hardly move. You call that easy on me? I can barely catch my breath." Testy now.

"That means we did exactly the right amount. Especially if you are too tired to swear at me. I heard the 'bitch'. I'll work you as hard as your body will let you work. Not how much you think you're ready for. Sit down, I'm getting more coffee. Can I get you some water?"

They settled down and Becca asked, "Tell me how Cilla decided you would be my therapist."

"We met through my brother. He works for the Sheriff's department and met Cilla and the gang on the job. He recommended me as the best, which I am, all modesty aside. And she apparently looked me up on line and talked to some of my patients. Who immediately told me she had called. They are very protective. She hired me to work with, um, a man, to improve his mobility, relieve his pain, and restore complete function. He was actually pretty well along that path when I got to him. I just added the finishing touches. She liked what I did. We became friends in the process. Actually, the gang took us both in. My brother and me. Like lost dogs. Like family. When you got hurt, shot, she asked me to work with you."

"Cilla has a track record of finding good people. She has a sixth sense. It's a little spooky. Jake was her only failure. Oh, I shouldn't have said that."

"It's okay. I know part of that story. It's a sad one. Do you know it? No, you don't or you wouldn't be thinking she failed with him."

"You're the second person to tell me there's a story I need to hear. One that will let me forgive him for what he did to her. I guess I'll have to hear it. So you're the best in the business?"

"Yes. Follow my instruction and you will be ready to take on the world. I am really good at what I do. My only weakness is that I read trashy romance novels."

Becca just looked at her. "Only old maids read romance novels. For those steamy sex scenes. That's what I hear anyhow." Becca would never admit that she read them.

"Yes, that's a typical reaction of people who don't read them. Even some who do. Put us down as frustrated, sex starved old maids. I love the stories. I love the happy endings. I know that is just like a guy saying he reads Penthouse for the articles, not the pictures. I don't care what people think. I like to mention my addiction early in my relationships so you can get your judgments out of the way."

"Guilty. That's exactly what I was thinking. That was my first thought. My second was can you bring me some? Please? I haven't had a romance to read since I got shot and I'm frantic for a fix. I can't shop, no car. I can go online, but shipping takes time and I hate eBooks. I'm afraid to ask anyone to buy me a romance. Please?"

Lori laughed and high fived her. "Got some in the car I was taking back to the used book store. I'll bring them in. And bring you a dozen more when I come back. But these are all romance suspense and romance adventure. Might be a science fiction or straight contemporary romance mixed in. No Scottish or British lords. You have some favorites?"

"What you say sounds perfect. My favorites too."

"Let me get those now," she said as she got up and walked out. She was back in a minute with a sack full, which she put on Becca's lap.

Becca peaked inside and read some titles and almost sighed. "These are brand new. They're on my want to, must read, list. Thank you, thank you. Go away now. Leave, I'm gonna read."

Lori laughed again as Becca pulled out a book and checked the back.

"Before I go I'm going to finish my notes while I can still read my scrawl. You can sit and read."

Ryan knocked on the door and peeked in. "You all done? Safe to come in?" he asked. Lori motioned him in and he saw Becca putting a sack down on the far side of her chair. Hiding it?

"I'm just finishing my notes and writing exercises for tomorrow for Becca to do on her own. If you're going to be here, you can make sure she doesn't overdo."

"Hey, I can follow orders," Becca complained. "Now I need a shower."

Lori jumped up, "I have great exercises for the shower. I'll come in with you and show you how to do them safely." She waited while Becca got up and slowly hobbled to the back room saying, "Do these only until you feel them. Don't push it."

The vision of Becca in the shower flashed through Ryan's mind. And froze there. Picturing her in the shower made his insides tighten. Huh? What was that all about? He hadn't been interested in a woman since his wife died. Five years now he realized. There never had been anyone else for him, but her. Now he was picturing this girl, who was young enough to be his daughter, naked in the shower? Not just picturing her, his body was reacting to the image. Like it did the first time he saw her at the wedding. And again last night. He had a grand kid for Christ's sake! Get ahold of yourself he thought. He tried to erase the image from his mind and the reaction of his gut. This wasn't going to happen. He needed a distraction. He edged toward the sack she had tried to hide and peaked inside. Romance novels? She was hiding romance novels? He remembered that Jones said his sister read romance. Her reading had been instrumental in the discovery of a safe room hidden in a wine cellar and the rescue of a woman and her two children. She'd told Jones about the scenario of a hidden room; he had told the Sheriff.

Ryan heard Lori coming back and moved away from the books.

"I told her to take a nap and she's tired enough to do it. So you won't see her for a few hours. I gave her some exercises for tomorrow and, if you're here, make her take it easy and not over do. I have another appointment or I'd stay and talk. I'll be back Monday."

He saw her out and then looked for something to do. He realized he was restless, waiting for Becca to get up.

**

Just as Becca finished dressing in one of Penny's bright red shirts, her cell went boink. A text. She looked and saw it was from Cilla. It said 'johnsdog'. One word, no caps. Nothing else. Unlike Cilla who was meticulous about her grammar and spelling, even in her text messages. Something they all gave her a hard time about. And John didn't have a dog. So this was code. For what? Mysterious. Becca would think on it. She knew that Cilla expected her to decipher the message.

Meanwhile she finally had a chance to start her search for the person who shot her. Finally had a safe network where no one could track her. She sat at Cilla's computer and woke it up. Got sidetracked with Cilla's message. Typed johnsdog in the search box. Found a folder by that name. Opened it. There was one picture, untitled. She opened that. A cute stuffed gray dog with long ears. Curious. Tried a right click with her mouse for the picture properties. It was tagged "Dos Chdiri 8 years old". Now what? Was that Spanish? Dos would be 2. 2 chdiri? That didn't make any sense. Tapped her fingers on the desk top. Dos, Dos, DOS!!! Disk Operating System. The original code for running a computer. It was DOS. Cilla wanted her to go into the Disk Operating System. It was underlying the Windows Operating System. Cilla knew Becca was in the gatehouse and in Cilla's room. Cilla's computer in the bedroom used Windows. Now it made sense. Go into DOS and chdiri meant change (ch) directories (dir) to i.

Was there an i directory on this computer? She opened Windows Explorer and Computer and saw no i drive listed. Well of course not. She had to go into DOS. She went to DOS and typed in chdir (i). There it was. With an unnamed folder.

Why so circumspect? Why send it to me here? Why hide the files? Why not just tell me? Or put them on the desktop? She opened the folder. More files, unnamed.

She opened one and gulped. Looked around to make sure no one was watching her. *Of, course no one's watching you, idiot. You're alone,* she told herself. She shook her head. She realized she was holding her breath. She opened another file at random, then two more. These were her case files. All her case files. Official case files! Cilla! Cilla why did you do this? The names were scrambled, but it looked like her whole career was here. She checked properties again. They were all taken from the official network. The final version of her cases. Oh my God. Oh my God. Cilla. What have you done? You hacked into the system?

She closed them all down and just sat. Cilla had hacked into the Sheriff's files and copied all of Becca's cases. Cilla could do it; she was a computer hacker almost from birth. Cilla, John, Sarah, they could get into most any network. Past all kinds of security. The Sheriff's network probably didn't give Cilla any trouble at all. And no one would ever know. Cilla could cover her tracks. And no one would find these files. Even if they were really looking. Searching the hard drive partitions. They wouldn't find it.

Becca rearranged it in her brain and now that she thought about it, it made sense. The gang wasn't going to let the shooter get away with hurting one of their own. This was Cilla's way of telling Becca, they were going to help her find him.

She closed everything down. She needed to think more before she did anything else. Because Cilla had to know that Becca had her own copies of her cases. So why did Cilla hack into the Sheriff's network? Becca gave it up and went into the great room.

It was empty, but she saw Ryan outside on the glider.

He hadn't heard her moving around and was caught reading one of her books when she opened the door. He copied her movements from the day before and tried to hide the book beside him. "Come on out," he said. He almost asked her about her nap, but thought better of it and said, "Pull up a seat," motioning to the bench. She raised an eyebrow at him and pointed toward the not quite hidden book. "What are you reading? You were pretty engrossed in that. Didn't even hear me. And did I see a guilty start?"

She lowered herself slowly and sat stiffly on the bench. She thought she saw a little pink in his face.

"Oh, no, you're not reading porn are you? Show me," she ordered.

He really was embarrassed now and could see no way out and guiltily turned the book so she could see the cover.

She laughed out loud. And then gasped. "Stop, that hurts. You're reading romance. Jane Ann Krentz? Running Hot? You're not. Men don't read romance." She noticed he was still holding his place in the book. When he saw her looking he checked the page number quickly and closed it.

"Want me to go inside and come back when you're done?" she offered.

Then she saw the other book on the swing. Had he already read that one? "Oh, my God, the dust bunnies. You didn't read about the dust bunnies? Did you?" Now she really was surprised and he turned a bright red. She was laughing again. "Please, don't make me laugh, it still hurts. Say something serious."

He covered his face with his hand and then owned up, "I just picked it up to pass the time. Got started and got hooked. And, yes, this is the second one. Both have some pretty explicit, steamy sex scenes. No wonder you women read them."

"We read them because they're love stories. I am so hooked on happy endings; there are so few of them in real life. The women are all smart, and strong, and stunning, the men tough and tender. They almost always fall in love immediately. Have a few problems and then live happily ever after. Romance gives me happily ever after. The sex is a perk. You are just being a typical male."

"You just spoiled this one by telling me the ending," he complained.

"Bah, it's a romance novel. The rule is it ends happily ever after. Give me that one beside you, I haven't read it yet. I want my own dust bunny."

He handed it to her. "I'll deny I ever touched either of these books. After I finish this one. Later. I'll finish it later. It will give me something to look forward to. It's not manly to be caught reading romance."

God he was so sweet, she thought. Honest about his intention to finish the book. "You got into the bag that Lori left for me huh? She and I bonded over romance suspense and adventure. She brought those in when I told her I was in withdrawal. Haven't been able to read one since I got shot. Had to fall back on straight adventure or suspense. Couldn't ask anyone to bring me a romance novel. I too have an image to uphold. So I guess we're even here. I won't tell if you won't tell."

He nodded.

"Where did you go?"

He didn't bother to misunderstand; he knew she meant where did he go when he left for a run. "Coffee shop. How did you know?"

"You don't look like a runner." He looked like an older model Prince Charming she thought. Someone you would be happy with, comfortable with, for a long, long time. She pulled herself back from that thought. "You weren't dressed for running. And you smelled faintly of … strawberry, I think."

He was impressed she had caught all of that. She must have been a good cop. "I'm impressed, you must have been a good cop."

He saw the fleeting distress cross her face, and then it was gone.

"Yes, I was. And I will be again too. Just not with the same department." Pointed to her crutch and said, "Sidelined for now."

"Sorry."

"Not as sorry as me," she said. "But one door closes, another opens. Or maybe a window." She changed the subject. "Tell me about Ryan Gibbs. How does he fit into the tale you told me this morning?"

"FBI, like I said."

She waited.

"OK. Twenty two years with the FBI. Hired right out of law school. Now, high enough up the food chain to pick my assignments. High enough now to ensure the separate departments of the bureau work with me and work together. High enough to liaise between all the agencies. I've worked with both Munson and Jake before. And Daffy. That's why they called me in with Sheri. Because of the FBI connection. They knew I could manage all the separate departments and control all the egos."

"Wife? Kids?" Why had she asked that?

"High school sweetheart." He got a soft smile on his face. "Married right after graduation." He paused, "She died five years ago. Still miss her. One kid. Boy. About your age now, with a wife and little girl. I was with them when Jake called me in on the Sheri thing. I was on leave, vacation, but had just helped close two cases while I was Innkeeper."

"Girlfriend?"

Now he looked at her, his head tilted. Was she flirting? "No. Not yet. But maybe soon," he finished, considering her.

She was sure she must be red. "That was a little nosey. But I wanted to know so I decided to ask. I think me too. Boyfriend. Maybe soon. Come as close as I did and have to wonder about dreams, goals. Priorities. Been rethinking my options. I was already rethinking my priorities actually. That's how I got shot."

She didn't know why she was telling him this. He was almost a stranger.

"Rethinking you goals, got you shot?"

"Wasn't paying attention. Thinking how I had really screwed up my life with the wrong man. A jerk. Was just walking my beat by habit, I wasn't looking. Listening."

"Tell me what happened."

"Night shift rounds, just part of the job.'

"I thought Cilla said you were a detective."

She laughed at that. "Well, when they need a detective, there's me and another guy. But most of the time, we just do the regular, routine, deputy stuff. I had just wrapped up a big case and night shift was on my rotation.

"You weren't wearing a vest?"

"Yes. Of course I was wearing a vest. We all wear vests." She paused there and frowned. "Well, we did until I got shot. Now maybe we wear different vests. Some of the guys blame me. Like it was my fault I got shot. And maybe it was."

"Stop. Nothing makes it your fault."

"I know it's not my fault that some guy shot me. I'm not that dumb. But it did feel personal. My gut says he was waiting for me. Waiting for me specifically. Some creep hiding in the dark waiting to shoot me."

"If it was personal, who gains? Who benefits if you die?"

"No one. And no one in my personal life hates me enough to shoot me."

"Why didn't he finish you off?" Ryan asked, wondering what her answer would be.

"I've been thinking about that," she said slowly. Hearing it out loud for the first time. Would it still make sense? "The killer, no, the shooter, didn't know I was wearing a vest. He hit me four times. He knew I was hurt. He could shoot me in the dark but wasn't brave enough to get close. Couldn't look at me. He thought I would die there and he was almost right." Was relieved it still sounded reasonable when she said it out loud. And Ryan was accepting it.

"Could it be the jerk with whom you had really screwed up your life?"

"No, not him."

He just looked at her and she decided to tell him. "He gave me up without a moment's hesitation when I suggested getting serious. He forgot me before I was out the door."

"He really was a jerk then to let you go. Just the same, someone should look at him."

"Someone will." She did need to know, at least to cross him off her list. Wasn't going to go through life wondering if it could have been Tom who shot her. "Are you offering?"

He nodded again.

"Go for it," she said. "You have my permission." She gave him Tom's full name and address. Then just shook her head. "It's not him. Even if he did care, it's not his style."

Ryan had written the information in his note book. He had it out; he ought to write more in it. He was an interrogator after all. "What about before him? Anyone serious? Any other boyfriend? Ex-boyfriend?"

Now Becca looked at him. "No. It was a long time before the jerk. I was with him about three months. Not really with him. Didn't live with him. Didn't date him. Just sex. You can look at Tom because I do need to be able to cross him off my list. But it wasn't him."

"Was he married?" He would be surprised if she fooled around with a married man. He hadn't pegged her as that. She had asked if he was married up front. As if it made a difference.

"Lord no, I don't do married. How can you even ask?" She heard herself and added, "Oh, sure, tawdry sex with no intimacy. Got it. That's what I just told you. No, he wasn't married," she repeated.

He was silent for a moment, thinking. "How about at work? Any conflicts?"

"No. We worked well together. I got along with everyone."

"What about the case you just closed?"

"No. Everyone was happy with how that turned out. You know crooks don't really hold cops accountable. They like to blame someone close to them. This guy blamed his wife not me. But I plan to look at all my cases." She was still wondering why Cilla had downloaded the official files. "I've got plenty of time. Lori thinks I'll be able to walk without the crutch in a couple of weeks. And my arm will be functional. Until then, I can do digital checks. Keep me busy and occupied."

He decided not to push. He'd come back to it later maybe. And he did have the jerk, he wasn't going to call him a boyfriend, to check into.

"I'm curious, how you're going to do it. Check Tom."

"Don't know yet. But I'll let you know the results." He changed the subject because he was getting hungry. They had both missed lunch.

"Hungry?"

She hadn't realized until he asked and her stomach growled. She laughed. "Kind of like Pavlov's dogs." She started to stand up. "You did breakfast, I should do supper."

He immediately felt guilty. "I was thinking peanut butter and jelly."

She stopped. "You're afraid of my cooking? Someone warned you?"

"I don't know anything about your cooking. PB&J sounded easy. And it's still too early for dinner."

"You would be smart to fear my cooking. I was going to do take out. That's one of my specialties."

"Chinese?"

"Pizza."

"Chinese. Has to be Chinese. It's gotta be Chinese. Pizza tomorrow."

"OK."

Her cell chirped, Cilla's chirp. She pulled it out, "Hey Cilla." She listened a minute and checked with Ryan, "Cilla and Jake are coming over with Chinese in about an hour? Hour and a half? To answer my questions. And Jake wants to talk to you"

Got his nod again with a smug grin.

"Sure. Come on over. You and I need to talk about johnsdog. But make it an hour, we missed lunch."

"Chinese, in an hour," she said to Ryan when she disconnected. "Just like you ordered."

"Apple to tide you over," he said tossing it to her from the fruit bowl. She caught it one handed, barely.

"Sorry, forgot you had that bad wing," he said embarrassed.

"It's okay, I've had lots worse," she said and was instantly sorry. She wasn't doing any more confessions even though he looked receptive. "Better hide the books if we don't want to be tormented forever. Let's put them in your room. No one will be going in there."

Lots worse? Lots worse than being shot four times and nearly dying? Another issue he would come back to. He got himself an apple, "I'll hide the books. Then I think I will Google the jerk."

"I already did that. Before. You will not get to see another side of him. He is not there. And there are no pictures. No Facebook or social media either. At least not back then. Maybe I'll come help. See if there's anything new." Reminding herself to Google Ryan when she was alone.

"Let me get my laptop," he said.

"Work laptop or personal?"

"Oh, right. Work laptop." Neither of them would want a record of his search on an FBI computer. "Which one of these should I use?" he asked waving around at all the computers.

"Here, my tablet. Fetch me some pillows from Penny's area, one of those bright ones," she said pointing. "Come sit on the couch beside me. We can project our results on the large screen."

He thought about that a minute deciding if it was a legitimate request when she added, "I'm tired and a little sore. This will be easier for me then leaning over you while you work."

Had she really read his hesitation so accurately he wondered? Picked out two pillows he liked and settled in beside her.

First he Googled Tom Farwood.

"See. Nothing. Try Facebook," she instructed.

He clicked on the login and paused. Again she read his hesitation. He couldn't use his work alias and didn't have a page of his own. "Use my alias, Andrea Y. Norton, password fisci57. And do the same with linkedin"

Still no results. "OK. You're right, he isn't here. That's a problem."

"How come?" she asked.

"Well, there are really only two reasons not to show up in the public databases. Either he has never done anything or…"

"He's a crook. He lied to me. He's not Tom Farwood," she completed his thought. "Wait. Google me."

He did but said, "Of course you are going to come up. You're a cop." There were multiple hits for her.

"Those part way down. That's the case you just wrapped up?" he asked considering. It was two days before she was shot. He'd have to come back and read the comments. He didn't want to do that in front of her. The online protection of anonymity brought out the meanness in some of the commenters. He wondered if any of them might be angry enough to follow up physically.

"I didn't realize it got so much press." She had another idea. "Google you."

Again he hesitated, but did as she asked.

She sat forward, "Nothing. Nothing about you? You're not there? What you just said about Tom? Right back at you. What about those two cases you solved in Florida? And the ones you just finished here? Why?" she paused for only a second, her brain working fast, "Because you're a cop. Because you keep a low profile."

She sat back following the reasoning. "If Tom isn't here, you're thinking he's a crook. Only a crook would use an alias." That meant that he had used her in more ways than one. It was devastating. She hadn't even realized he might be lying to her. Where were her gut instincts? Why had she never noticed? She looked at Ryan with horrified eyes.

He was backing out returning to the search page on Tom. He stopped and grabbed her hands. "Don't. Don't go there. Your gut, your instincts aren't always right. Sometimes sex clouds things and we just go with the moment. You had no reason to suspect that he might be lying. We don't know. We have to look further. We don't know he's a crook." He could give her some hope, some thread, to hang onto. "He could be a cop." She wouldn't be so devastated if he were a cop.

She wanted to put her head in her hands, hide her face, but he wouldn't let her. She looked up at him. "It's all right. You liked him. You slept with him. You enjoyed him. Be he jerk, crook, or cop. That's all there was to it. You can't run a background check on everyone. You have to trust, have faith. Otherwise you will always be alone, and that is far worse then maybe being deceived by a lover. Are you hearing me?"

She could almost laugh, he was so serious. So intent on stressing positive excuses for her. Finally she nodded. 'Yes, you're right. But I am still an idiot. My intuition never even tinged."

"No, maybe that's why you ended it. You sensed something off."

She did get a hand free then and cupped his face. "You are so sweet. Trying to make me look good. I didn't know I was ending it. Asking him for commitment ended it. Because I saw how happy Penney was. I wanted that."

"What I said still holds. You forced the end and you can't tell me you didn't know what would happen when you asked for commitment," he insisted.

"Maybe you're right. You make me feel better anyhow. I'll hope he turns out to be a jerk and a cop."

The security system chimed then. Showed Jake and Cilla driving in.

He stood, offering her his hand, "Come on, let's put this aside, and eat."

Conversation during dinner centered on the sequel to Midnight plus One, the digital game John had designed and for which the gang had created and enhanced the visuals. The one SC Digital had sold for hundreds of millions of dollars.

"Jake wants to buy a house on the beach. Right near Penny and Daffy," Cilla laughed. "I thought we should be next door, but Jake convinced me that there might be such a thing as too close. He's buying it with the money he got from SC Digital," she said referring to his half of her own share, the money she set aside for him. "You both will have to come and see. Maybe tomorrow. We'll talk."

After dinner, Jake asked for an update on the cases as Ryan helped Becca back to the couch. Sitting down she juggled the tablet and the large screen came to life with the results of the search for Tom.

"What's this?" Jake asked.

Becca looked at Ryan who was sorry he hadn't shut it down completely, but he'd been distracted by the desolation on Becca's face. While he was trying to think up an explanation, Cilla said, "It's him, isn't it?" looking at Becca. Then she turned to Jake and said, "Let it go, Jake."

"OK. Never mind. What about the cases, Ryan? You said they are wrapped up?"

"No," Becca said cutting him off. "Ryan said he was going to check out my ex. Make sure it wasn't him who shot me. This was the first step. We can't use official channels." Then she turned to Cilla and added, "Cilla, you leave him alone. You can't go over there and use any of your dirty fighting moves on him. No one beat up Jake when he left." Mostly because no one knew he was gone or where he went she thought.

Ryan brightened at the idea of Cilla using her moves on the jerk. "Hah. That might be fun to watch though," he said.

Jake chimed in, "Yeah, I want to be there too if she does that. I never saw a move like the one she used on Sheri. Reminded me of a pit bull I used to know. Be interesting to see what else she has before she tries them on me," laughing. Then he got serious, "Becca, I can do an in depth background check on the guy. That's my work and I'm good at it. Just say the word." He was waiting for her answer and added, "I'll keep the pit bull off of him too. Unless we all agree to let her loose."

"It's a good idea, Becca. He can do more than either of us. He has the resources and doesn't have the restrictions we have. I'll work with him," Ryan offered.

Becca hugged one of the pillows. Cilla was nodding to her.

"Okay, I'll hire you to do the background check. You tell me before you tell Cilla. I'm going to go through all my case files while I'm recuperating." She looked at Cilla and asked, "Why did you get me the official files?" She didn't realize what she had said until she saw Cilla's horrified expression and realized Jake and Ryan had gone quiet.

She looked at Ryan. "Ooops."

"You hacked into the police department files? You hacked the Sheriff's files?" Ryan asked incredulously.

"Well, maybe." Cilla smiled at him. "I might have. If I did, I certainly wouldn't admit it to the FBI," she admitted. She looked around smiling and said, "If anyone doesn't like it, I can put the, uh, purloined files back."

Ryan's lips quirked; he wasn't going to pursue that. Jake was smiling proudly.

Cilla turned to Becca and said pointedly, "I probably didn't get you anything. But if I did it's because I want you to compare your notes on your files with the final official resolutions. That case with Sheri? There were discrepancies between the original data and the official final data. I want to be sure there aren't any discrepancies with your cases."

Ryan coughed; Jake laughed out loud and said, "Yup, that's my girl."

Ryan attempted a stern expression and admonished, "You really shouldn't do that. If you did do anything. I didn't hear anything about hacking."

Becca took the pressure off her. "I'll do them side by side Cilla," she promised, referring to the files. "I want to be sure too. I don't really think I'll find anything out of line. Gut feeling," she said. "But I have to check all my cases anyhow and I have the time."

Ryan nodded once and returned to Jake's question. "Homeland wrapped everything up Friday. It will be on the news tomorrow." He turned to Cilla, "None of the gang is mentioned. Homeland and FinCEN were happy to take credit for everything."

"That's a relief. After all the repercussions with Sheri. I'll tell the Gang. Now I'm going to clean up the supper mess and Ryan's going to help me. Jake why don't you take Becca out in the garden."

"Oops," Becca said. "Someone is going to the tool shed. Better get it over with. Help me up." Cilla clearly was separating them. Was it Ryan she wanted to talk to? Or did she want Becca with Jake?

Jake answered her unspoken question as they walked outside. "Cilla left us alone, so I could talk to you. Try to explain why I left." Jake waited to see if she would listen. When she nodded, he continued. "I screwed up. No excuse. There is no excuse for what I did to her. I was undercover. I'd infiltrated Sheri's white slavery ring. I had to hurt Cilla to keep my cover and to protect her. I couldn't deal with that. I took the coward's way out and walked. I wasn't brave enough, didn't trust her enough, to talk to her. I was scared she wouldn't forgive me, would hate me, so I didn't give her the chance. I took on a lot of blame and guilt that wasn't mine. I let Sheri and the situation mess me up. I was wrong."

"Ron, my partner, tried to talk to me, and Munson. Didn't do any good. I just saw myself as a screw-up. Being near Cilla again … Well that and Daffy. Daffy finally reached me. Helped me come to my senses. Gave me the courage to talk to Cilla. If I had just talked to her ten months ago, I could have saved us both a lot of pain. She's forgiven me, thank God, but I will spend the rest of my life making it up to her." He stuck his hands in his pockets and continued.

"Becca, you mean a lot to Cilla. She wants us to be friends. I need you to give me a chance, to prove to you that I deserve her. That's all I'm asking."

Becca thought about that. "I'm going to hold a grudge because you really hurt her and you deserve to suffer for that."

"I did hurt her. I do deserve to suffer, you're right," he agreed. That surprised her.

"Where were you for ten months that you couldn't call her or write her?" How could he possibly justify that?

"Sheri didn't just mess with my head. She shot me. I spent most of that time in a hospital. I could still have written or called, but I didn't want Cilla to feel obligated. Stupid, I know that now. She's angry because she couldn't be with me and help me through that." He paused a moment but then added with a grimace, "She paid me back for that though; she hired Lori to put me through hell for two months. So I might have an inkling of what you are going through now."

Becca thought about that. Cilla had forgiven him. Maybe she had to give him a chance too. "I can be neutral. I can do that. Only because Cilla has forgiven you."

"Thanks. That's all I can ask." He changed the subject. "Would you like to see how we do our background checks? Maybe work with us?" he offered. Before she jumped on that, he added, "There will be some rules if you say yes."

"What rules?" She knew she was going to say yes even before she heard the rules. Exercise and romance novels weren't going to keep her busy. She'd be reviewing her files, but she couldn't do that all day long. She'd need more.

"You'll be working with Ron. Used to be my office manager, now my partner. His wife, Jen, will pick you up tomorrow afternoon and bring you to the office. She is one of my body guards and she'll be with you whenever you leave the gatehouse. You go nowhere by yourself."

"OK. But only because I can't drive."

"Not just because you can't drive. This isn't up for debate. This is mandatory. You go nowhere without a bodyguard. Until we find out who shot you or if it was really random. Can you agree to that?"

A bodyguard. That need made her feel weak and helpless. But a bodyguard would also give her mobility. Allow her to do some of her own footwork.

Slowly she agreed, "Yeah. OK. I've never seen the civilian side of background checks. It should be interesting."

"Keep you off the streets and out of the bars?" he asked.

Was he kidding? Had Cilla told him? No Cilla could keep a secret. What was he implying? "You think I'm going to do some bar pickups?"

"What? What? No. That's a joke. A family joke. I wasn't implying anything. Where did you get that?" Where had she gotten that? Was there more to Becca's background then Cilla had described? And then he realized that, yeah, of course there was. She was a rescue.

Becca hastily backtracked. Didn't want him going there. No, she didn't want Jake thinking about her childhood.

"Sorry. Guess I'm still not quite neutral." She hoped he would think it was him she didn't trust. See if he would accept that as her explanation.

"Okay. Sorry. I'll leave out the jokes from now on." He really had touched a nerve. She had made a good save, but he knew there was more to it. Should he ask Cilla? "Jen will pick you up around one Monday."

"How about after my therapy. About ten?"

"No. You need at least an hour of downtime after therapy when you're starting, and then you need to eat lunch."

"I'll be OK at ten."

"Don't forget, I've been where you are. You'll need at least an hour. Your body will. If you want to get better, you'll give your body the rest it needs."

"You guys are all treating me like a baby."

"You're acting like one. Take your medicine and stop whining." He held his breath, hoping he hadn't pushed too far.

She paused, "I was whining, wasn't I? One sounds good. After my nappy." She couldn't resist getting in the last word.

He shook his head. "You're just like Cilla. Even when you lose, you still fight."

They went back inside where Cilla was watching anxiously.

"We're going to declare a truce. And Jake is sending Jen for me Monday so I can help with the background checks." She looked at him and added, "After my therapy and nap."

"That's all right with you Becca? Having Jen?" Cilla asked apprehensively.

"I don't like it. I mean I don't like that someone might be trying to kill me. But if someone is, then a bodyguard is a good idea, I guess. It's what I would recommend to someone in this situation, so yes, it's okay. And while we are on the subject of bodyguards, I wondered about those nurses in my hospital room."

Cilla looked at Jake smiling and said, "Turns out Jake knows some EMTs and medics who double as bodyguards. You just won me ten bucks. I bet Jake you'd know they were guards. Does it get any better than that?" she joked.

"I pay for them. And I pay for Jen. I have plenty of money saved and I'm still getting paid. I pay for Lori too," Becca insisted.

Cilla looked at Jake again and saw the slight shake of his head. So he hadn't told Becca about the trust fund they had set up for her. The gang had set aside a portion of SC Digital income for her. And Jake had contributed a portion of his share. Becca had a lot more money than she knew. Cilla would deal with it another day.

Jake covered the moment with, "Jen works for me. Ron too. They both get paid whether they're on a job or not. Family discount."

"OK. Family discount." She gave Cilla a hug and hesitantly went over and hugged Jake too.

"We better be going. Becca, call me if you want to talk." Cilla hugged Ryan. Becca watched them drive out the gate and then asked Ryan, "What kind of cop are you? My sister admits she hacked into a law enforcement site and you smile."

"I did? I thought I hid that." He laughed now. "She looks so innocent. Naïve. It was all I could do not to laugh out loud. She's amazing."

"Yeah, she is."

"I don't imagine there's anything she wouldn't do to protect any of you."

They looked at each other for a few moments. Becca thinking, oh, you are so right. But most of Cilla's transgressions were past the statutes of limitations. What Cilla did for her that she knew about anyhow. She wasn't so sure of what Cilla might have done for The Boys. "If you will go get me my books, I think I'll sit here for a while and read. I love this pillow; will you bring me the matching one too? And I'll just get comfy." She did like Penney's pillows. The bright colors. She was going to enjoy them. It was a start.

Wondering, he smiled at her, she had just changed the subject. He did as she asked.

But she couldn't concentrate on her reading. He confused her. Didn't seem to mind Cilla's hacking. A cop, but a gentle cop.

He got his laptop. He had reports to write and forms to complete. The forms should have been simple. Just a summary of events and actions. But his eyes kept wandering over to Becca. He kept sneaking glances at her, curled up reading. She looked so, why did he think, sweet? She was anything but sweet. He smiled to himself and got back to work.

It took him an hour and a half to write a simple report. Give it up he said to himself and looked over to see her sound asleep.

He touched her arm to wake her and send her to bed. She just curled up tighter. He scooped her up and carried her to the bedroom. The bed was made, he hadn't thought of that. He couldn't hold her and pull down the covers without waking her. He knelt down on one knee and rested her hips on his thigh. Threw back the covers and laid her on the bed. Take off her clothes? No. He wanted her awake and responding when he took off her clothes. The thought didn't even surprise him. He had been aware of her all day. What surprised him was that these feelings hadn't died with his wife. He gently caressed her cheek, pulled the blankets over her, and quickly left the room.

Sunday

Again she woke to the smell of coffee. And sausage? She lay there just enjoying the idea of a man cooking. For her. Suddenly, she couldn't remember coming to bed. She peeked under the covers. She was still in her clothes. How did she get here? And more important, since she was still dressed, could she just go out and get a cup of coffee? Maybe snatch a sausage? Yes. She sort of jumped up out of bed and went out to the kitchen.

She watched him turn the sausage for a minute. No law said she couldn't enjoy the sight of a good looking man in the kitchen.

"Good morning," she said. "I smelled coffee."

He turned around smiling. "Sleep well?"

"Yes. Um. I don't remember going to bed?" it was a question, inviting an answer.

He poured a cup and confessed, "I carried you. You fell asleep on the couch and didn't even wake when I picked you up and carried you to bed. You were out like a light."

"Well, that's embarrassing."

"Why? You were tired. Physical therapy is hard work. I have a feeling it won't be the last time I carry you to bed." Let her figure that one out. He handed her the coffee.

She took it, pretty sure he didn't mean the next time she fell asleep on the couch. She found that she wanted to be awake the next time.

Participating. But she chose to ignore the innuendo. "Um, can I grab a sausage? I'll get a quick shower."

He stabbed a sausage with a fork and handed that to her and was rewarded with a bright smile as she grabbed it and then padded back to her room. *Gonna carry me to bed again?* She tingled all over during her shower at the thought. She got dressed. Today in Penney's multi colored tee. She put on her cop face for breakfast.

"Eat up. Then we'll do your off-day therapy. Then quiet time, rest. Maybe repeat yesterday."

"You have my day all planned?" Should she be angry? She should be angry, but she thought it was kind of cute.

"Yes, breakfast, exercise, nap. Sounds exciting."

"What were you and Cilla talking about last night?"

He considered for a minute and then said, "She wanted Jake to talk to you. Explain why he left, why he came back. Wanted you to know. Wanted him to tell you. She thinks that the more he says, the healthier he will be. He still has some dark pockets of pain. Emotional pain. Her words, not mine. Cilla thinks that he can cleanse those pockets by opening and sharing them."

"Tell me about Jake. What happened to him," she said. And waited while he thought it over. "Why are you hesitating? Do you think he might have lied to me?"

"Huh? No. He didn't lie. But he might have left some things out. I was hesitating because it's not manly to talk about feelings or weakness. Men don't talk about those things. Here is what I know from observation and from the records. Jake stumbled onto the sex trafficking. He's a manager, not an undercover cop." He waited for her to acknowledge that.

"Undercover work requires a special type of personality. Jake doesn't have it. That was the problem. He called in Munson and the locals as soon as he realized what he had. They decided to leave him in there. Jake was operating blind. He had to hurt Cilla, not physically, emotionally. He had to renounce her, demean her, to protect her from Sheri and protect himself. It twisted him up. Made him unworthy. He left."

"Fast forward to the take down. Just before they auctioned off the children, just before the bust, Jake stepped in to protect one of the girls. She'd tried to escape. They were going to beat and rape her as an example to the other children. When Jake tried to protect her, Lenny, Sheri's brother, shot him. Jake took the girl with him when he went down and covered her with his body. Sheri shot him while he was lying there, then she grabbed a pitchfork and staked his leg to the ground. Laughed about how she was going to get Cilla and bring her back for the same treatment the girl would get. They left him there, bleeding."

"Jake got the girl, Juanita, to use his cell to call Munson and tell him the location of the auction. Then Jake passed out. Those are the facts. Maybe I inserted a little unmanly emotion. I think, well I know, that Jake interpreted his inability to save Juanita and himself as a weakness. That he blew the operation. Something fried in his circuits. That would be my manly way to describe feelings."

"Anyhow, later, his need to protect Cilla when Sheri came back helped mend him somehow. Of course Daffy helped too. Daffy seemed to know the right buttons to push to make Jake step back and take a fresh look at reality. Kind of like replacing a breaker or a blown fuse."

"He said he was in the hospital?"

"The leg. The pitchfork was dirty, the leg was infected. They thought he might lose it. That was another reason he wasn't going to come back. He didn't want to saddle Cilla with an invalid." He shrugged his shoulders and continued before she could interrupt, "I know it's all stupid, but that's the way his brain was functioning."

She couldn't help it; she was impressed by the story, but covered it with, "I didn't know a man could discuss subjects like feelings."

He was relieved that she wasn't going to ask for details and changed the subject.

"I'll walk you through your regimen and then clean up the dishes."

"You're telling me what to do again," she accused him.

"No, just getting you started. I promised Lori I would work with you today."

He didn't allow her to sneak in any extra repetitions but by the time she was done, she was too sore and too weak to argue when he sent her off to shower. "I'll set up the couch for you and you can rest and read for a while; you don't actually have to go back to bed."

She thought about it in the shower. She wasn't sure how she felt about the way he took charge. She was achy and tired and the couch and a book sounded good. She must still be in hospital mode where everyone had charge of her. That explained why she was letting him get away with it. She'd be stronger tomorrow; she would argue with him then. Except he'd be gone tomorrow. She was surprised at her sense of loss at the thought. Huh, you are in bad shape girl. Letting a man boss you and being sad that he was leaving. She shook her head and got dressed. New clean clothes. Penney's bright colors again.

He was waiting for her. "Coffee? Milk?" he asked.

"Both," she said.

He motioned her toward the couch. "I'll bring them over."

She limped over and settled into the cozy nest he had made her with Penney's quilt and bright pillows. This was so where she wanted to be right now. He had her tablet and the bag of books on a table he had pulled over to the couch. It warmed her all over. She looked at him in amazement as he brought her drinks.

"What? Something wrong?" he asked. "Want me to get something else?"

"No, this is fine. You surprise me. This," she motioned around, "This nest you made for me, doesn't seem to be a very manly action."

He turned a little pink. "Not a nest," he argued, "It's a cave." He went over to the desk nearby and went to work on his laptop so he couldn't see her laugh at his discomfort.

She read; he typed.

**

She woke with a start and caught him watching her with a strange expression. Not pity. Tenderness? Affection? "I was resting my eyes," she lied. Secretly pleased to notice he had covered her over.

"Yes, for about an hour now." It was his turn to laugh at her.

"You put a quilt over me," she accused.

"You looked cold and that's what a quilt is for." He wasn't uncomfortable at being caught, but he changed the subject. "How do you feel?

I finished my reports and I thought we might go out for an ice cream?" he asked uncertainly. "Get you out and give you a change of scenery."

"Yes, I'd like that." She really wanted to go for ice cream with him.

"We'll have ground rules," he reminded her. When she appeared puzzled, he added, "Body guard?" It distressed him to see the delight fade from her face and he tried to cheer her up again.

"You must do what I say, without question." Now he was really laughing at her.

"No way," she said. "You're just saying that."

"Jen will tell you tomorrow. Stay on my left side, leave my right hand free." For his gun, she would know that. "I check a room before you enter. You sit where I say. Do exactly what I say. If I say drop or down, you go down. Simple rules. You get to choose the flavor and type of ice cream you want, though."

"I can do that. Except the drop bit. That will take time. I'm not too limber right now." She tried to joke.

He had to lift her into his truck. She couldn't manage the step up. "Finally I get a manly job." He leaned over and kissed the tip of her nose, surprising both of them. She covered her confusion by saying that she hoped that Jen didn't have a manly truck.

"I want a black raspberry, double dipped, cone with chocolate sauce. And lots of napkins." She smiled when he came back with an extra dish for her and water. He had a single vanilla cone.

He kept her entertained with stories of his time as an innkeeper, helping his son and daughter-in-law. She told him some early tales about the gang and some of the antics of The Boys. They didn't talk shop. He wished he didn't remember how it felt to lift her into and out of his truck. He was still embarrassed he had kissed her on her nose. He was aiming for her lips when he'd stopped himself at the last second. He wasn't sure where that would have led. She had covered nicely. In fact she had been a good sport about all of it.

When they returned, he offered to help her look over her cases. "It will be fine as long as you don't tell me where they're from. I'm sure your Captain gave you access," he added.

"That's the funny part of it. He would have."

"I can look them over and give you an objective perspective. Another cop's take," he offered.

She considered his offer. She really didn't know what kind of cop he was. Must be pretty good to have reached his level in the FBI. She knew that Jake and Daffy respected him. And Cilla liked him. That alone was enough for her to accept his help.

"I'll shoot them over to that desktop. Right now they are set up as chapters in a book. One chapter, one case. Better yet, why don't I send them to that tablet and you can take the tablet with you? That way they won't show up on your work machine." If he did take the tablet, it would mean that she would hear from him again. "You can flag any that you think I should review again."

"Sounds good. Let me have them and I'll get started."

They spent the rest of the afternoon working together. He found one case he had questions about. "This Jerome Wilson? How did his family take him going to prison?"

"Happy. Lucky to get rid of him. If he held a grudge, he would go after them first. But he's dead. Got in a fight with the wrong guy in jail." She wiped the back of her index finger across her brow.

He saw that. She didn't realize it was a tell. She did it when she was tired. "Let's have supper. What do you feel like?" he asked.

"Shrimp scampi and pasta," she said immediately and then laughed at herself. "Annie keeps some in the freezer for me. It's a weakness."

He opened the freezer and found four different kinds of scampi, "Which kind?"

"Any. Can you do pasta?"

"Scampi, pasta, and salad. Half hour, go wash up."

He was telling her what to do again. It was what she had planned to do anyhow so she didn't argue.

He had everything ready when she came out. All she had to do was sit down. She could get used to this.

"This is wonderful. I'm going to miss you when you leave."

They ate and she went back to her couch and her files while he cleaned up. She didn't fight with him over the clean-up; she was tired.

At ten pm he called a halt. "We don't need to do them all tonight. Save some so you have something to do tomorrow," he suggested.

"You're right. I am tired. I better go to bed before I fall asleep and you have to carry me again."

"It's okay. I don't mind carrying you to bed."

"I think I want to be awake the next time you do though," she admitted. She heard what she said and immediately added. "I am going to miss you. And not just because you take good care of me. I like you." She thought about that for a while. "I like that you take care of me, but I like that you seem to want to. Am I reading too much into this?"

He had never met a woman quite so direct, who said exactly what she felt. Put him on the spot. Equally blunt, "No, you're not. I like you too. I like taking care of you." Then he took a chance. "I'll be gone before you get up tomorrow. May I come back?"

He wants to come back. To see me. "Yes, I'd like that. But you should know that I'm not going to be easy. You are not seeing the real me because I'm hurt. My normal isn't nice, it's testy."

"And that's different how?" he was laughing at her again. "You think I haven't noticed testy? How you bristle each time I make a suggestion? Or, okay, give an order? I know you're just going along because it's what you want to do."

She limped over to him and straightened her arm, putting her hand on his shoulder. She leaned in and kissed him lightly on his mouth. Backed up quickly before he could respond, holding him away with her arm. "I just wanted a taste. To help me sleep." But she knew it was a lie, she wasn't going to sleep. The simple, quick, kiss had surged through her, awakening all her nerve ends. She walked unsteadily toward her bedroom. "Yes, I'd like you to come back," she said over her shoulder.

He stood there a long time. Watching. A simple kiss. A shock through his system. A huge promise. Maybe he would come back before the weekend.

Monday

When she awoke the gatehouse felt lonely. Something was missing. Someone. How could that happen in just two days? The gatehouse had never felt empty before. And she had never felt lonely; she had always enjoyed her own company. It wasn't just the coffee and the meals she missed, it was him. His smile, his presence. She missed waking up to him in the kitchen, his gaze when he gave her coffee. The desire and fondness behind the gaze made her warm all over. He looked at her as if she were a fast car or race horse. Yeah right, hobbling around on one crutch.

She missed the repartee, even though he always seemed to win. She didn't mind, which surprised her. Well, he did have the benefit of age and experience on his side.

Did she mind his age? He was probably twenty years older. Should age be a factor in a relationship?

She missed talking to him and, surprise, she missed watching him. She laughed at herself. Get a life. He's gone. Make coffee. Decide if you should shower before therapy or after. Eat now or later? She decided exercise, shower, and then eat. She had a plan.

She found Annie in the kitchen when she came out dressed. Annie's back was to her so she had time to hide her disappointment. Annie had breakfast ready. She accompanied it with some funny tales of Joey's latest predicaments. Joey, one of the boys. One of the kids Becca had helped rescue. Danny was the other. Becca was pretty sure Danny was in some specialized military force. He had always been the more physical of the two. Joey though, had apparently landed a geek job.

"He's a nice man, our Ryan," Annie said.

"Yes. I like him."

Annie smiled at her, waiting. Becca knew she'd get the story sooner or later anyhow.

"I think he likes me too. He asked if he could come back. To help me find the guy who shot me." She felt her face get red and added, "Well, he also said he wanted to see me. I know he likes me. How do you know when it's real?" she asked Annie. She saw the answer on Annie's face and got it. The smile. The smile Annie always got when anyone mentioned love. "That's it isn't it. You're thinking about that man. You still love him, whoever he is. You get that look on your face whenever you think about him. Talk about him."

Annie seldom spoke about her life before she came to work for Kevin's parents. But the gang all knew that there had been a man. One very special man. No one knew what happened or why. Or even if the relationship was still ongoing.

"Do I look that way when I talk about Ryan? I feel my mouth smiling. No." She was adamant. "This is just like. I like him. Am I that pathetic? It's only been two days. Can it happen that quickly?" She said all that in one breath and only stopped talking because she needed to breathe.

Annie came and sat beside her. "Well, yes, if you can judge by Cilla and Jake. Or Penney and Daffy. We know it took Penney four days. And I hear that maybe with Ron and Jen it worked even quicker. Though I think there was danger involved in that relationship and that sometimes speeds everything up. And you do look like a woman who might be falling in love. My advice? The same as Cilla's. Enjoy it."

"But what if it doesn't last?" Becca whined. "What if it's only me who feels this way?"

"Then it will end. And we'll help you pick up the pieces. But while it lasts, it will be good. Don't skip happiness today because of what might happen tomorrow. Grab today."

"Did you? Did you grab today Annie?"

"Oh, honey, you bet your life I did. I enjoyed every second we had together."

Becca could see that in Annie's face. Not a doubt. "But what about Tom? How do I explain Tom?"

"Think back girl. You never said love or feelings when you spoke of Tom. You seldom smiled when you mentioned him. I never saw love in your face. Or the hope I see now. This, what I see now? This looks real to me."

"But I don't know what love is," Becca moaned.

"Yes, you do. You remember your parents and their love for you."

"But that's different."

"It's a different kind of love. You love Cilla. You love me. We love you. It's not the love between a man and a woman, but it still reaches the same depths. Grabs you just as hard. Makes the same demands. You need to give it a chance."

Lori was announced then; Annie gave Becca a hug and said she would be back with supper and left.

Becca confronted Lori as soon as they were alone. "I want to change our time."

"Why?" Lori asked.

Annoyed, Becca said, "Do I need a reason?"

"Yes, you do. A good reason. It's important that we have a schedule that we both follow. Why do you want to change the time?" she repeated.

Aggravated, Becca explained about Jake's offer. "I can do my exercises as soon as I get up. I am generally up by seven thirty or eight o'clock and that's when I like to exercise. Then I can get my shower, and then my breakfast. Rest for an hour. That makes more sense to me. And then I can work with Jake's crew at a reasonable time. I can come home and rest all afternoon when my body rests normally." She hadn't realized she had all those reasons. And they were all true.

"Okay. All good reasons. We can do it. I'll be back Wednesday and again on Saturday at eight and you'll do your off day exercises at eight. Wednesday and Saturdays will work. Let's get started. I brought more books; you get them when we're done."

When Becca could breathe normally again she thanked Lori for the books. "I haven't really had time to read them, but it's a comfort knowing I have them. I have started one. It's like a fine piece of chocolate. I'm taking it slow and savoring it, while reviewing my case notes."

After Lori left, she decided she was tired. A good tired. She stretched out on the couch to rest and woke up an hour later. So Jake was right. She barely had time to shower and dress and grab a bite, before the security system announced Jen, who apparently had her own code. Seemed everyone had a code, but Becca knew that only the gang and a few others would be able to get into the complex.

And this was not the conservative Jen she had met at the wedding. This was a biker chick. Black leather pants and vest. Tattooed arm sleeves. Becca gawked. Realized she was gawking. Why? Cilla drew no lines. None of the gang did. They wouldn't judge a person by how they dressed. By tats. It was her cop training. A cop would look at Jen and see a dumb, possibly dangerous, bimbo. Becca knew to look beyond the costume.

Jen gave her time by saying, "Hey, I'm your new escort and driver. Jake says to bring you to the office and stay with you whenever you're out of the compound." She noted that Becca was using a crutch. "You need a wheelchair?"

"No, I'm slow, but I can manage. Don't I rate a limo? I gotta ride in an old faded, paint peeled SUV?" she complained looking out the door. She was trying to be funny, but the SUV, an old rusted, puke green, Land Rover, looked on its last legs.

"Don't let the outside fool you," Jen said. "This car turns on a dime, zero to sixty in a flash. The doors stay locked until you decide to open them. And it's armored." Locked doors were important. Those agents were killed in Mexico when their armored vehicle was forced off the road. The vehicle stopped and the doors automatically unlocked, a nice family friendly option. But deadly for the agents. "It has a step so you can walk into it and it looks like you really need that, because I'm not going to lift you into a vehicle unless you're shot and you won't be shot on my watch."

The second time in as many minutes that Becca knew she'd slipped. She had to get her brain back into shape, the same as her leg and shoulder. Maybe she should talk to Sarah. "You brought an armored vehicle for me?"

"Yeah, Jake doesn't take any chances with clients; he's certainly not taking any with family."

"Sorry, I'm an ass. I'm going to blame it on my recuperation. My mouth opens and words come out. I love the car."

Jen laughed, "Come on, you can get yourself in. But first, you know the rules. You do what I say as soon as I say it. No arguments, just act. Always stay on my left side, away from my gun hand. I go out first. You'll be behind me. I open your door, you get in. Same procedure when you get out."

"How far are we going?" Becca asked as she maneuvered into the car which was plush on the inside, and comfortable. She'd never been in an armored vehicle. Never even been in a Land Rover. She had assumed it would be minimal.

"About a mile. You can walk it. Well you can't walk it." She laughed at her joke.

"So what is it exactly that Jake does?"

"The business is called Safe Keeping. Our motto is 'you work; we worry'. The name is meant to be ambiguous and yet on the mark. We set up security for businesses, complete background checks on employees, and keep clients safe. This car is one of our newest purchases. This is a special paint job. The Escalades draw attention. Jake wanted a nondescript safe vehicle for you, one that is low profile."

"How many employees?"

"Lots. Trouble shooters, bodyguards, investigators, security experts. Now we are adding online and network security. The gang is helping us get started. Safe Keeping has four offices around the country. We pretty much work in the U.S., though Jake does accept some work out of country on rare occasions."

"What do you do?"

"I'm a bodyguard. All I do is keep the client safe, alive, and unharmed. My husband, Ron, you met him at the wedding, used to be a trouble shooter. That's how we met, on the job. He does the scheduling, organizing, planning. He realized that was his strength when some asshole didn't plan ahead."

Becca was surprised again when they stopped in front of a fenced facility at the end of a side road. There was an old faded sign spelling out Industrial Park with the letters 'dust' missing. The building looked to be in disrepair. A one story masonry building with office space and warehouse. Loading docks and closed garage bays. Wonder what those are for? Show? Eight garage doors on this side. Probably for the employees. The place looked totally deserted. She didn't see any sign that a business occupied the deserted site. But she realized this was a cover and smiled. "This is your cover right? Run down building and parking area. But the fence is good. Lots of land too."

Jen was delighted with her reaction. "We moved in last month. Jake's had it in the works for over a year. It's totally secure, state-of-the-art. We also have an office in town. Ron had this building painted. Left the parking area with the grass growing through the cracks. I love it. The front door and bays are reinforced steel; the windows are bullet proof. It's probably overkill, but Jake decided to test out some of the products on his own place before using them for customers." She keyed them through the gate and through one of the remote controlled garage doors.

"We all park inside. There are four more armored vehicles here. The Escalades. There are sleeping quarters for employees and the occasional client. Jake incorporated some of the gatehouse ideas here. This building wasn't ready when Sheri was loose. Though Cilla wouldn't have stayed here anyway." She led Becca into the building.

"It's a perfect location for New York, Washington, and Philly. Come on, I'll show you around and take you to Tony."

Becca liked Tony immediately. Maybe because he was a geek. And a really well built geek. He looked like the body guards she had met. Tall, broad shoulders, well-muscled under his t-shirt. Cute, blond and blue.

"Jake got me started on this Saturday," he told her. "I understand you're a cop. We don't do checks quite the way you do. We start with name and address, just to confirm those. We found your guy right where you told Jake he would be. No phone, but utilities are in his name. We talked to the landlord and got a copy of his rental references. We don't lie; just say we're checking his address and how long he lived there. Either for employment or loan or car rental. This time we pulled out the big guns; inheritance. We told his landlord that he might be the Tom we are looking for who has come into an inheritance and that we need to go back and see if he was in Philly in 1999. It was that easy. Well, that and the fact that we sent Mary Lee, our own version of Miss America. People tell her all kinds of things. They even volunteer what they ate for breakfast. Maybe you'll get to meet her.

"We'll complete a background check on the current landlord and Tom's references. And Tom's current employer, who rents limousines. We check for relatives. Even though you say there are none, we'll look anyhow. You can help with the online parts. Later we may call people or contact them in person if we need to.

"We go back as far as we can. Look at three employers. We check each location where he lived and how long he lived there. We go back three residences or ten years. We look at the prior landlord, references, job and so on. We look at any references he used for that rental or employment. Who they are, how he knows them, where they live and work. Then we go down one more level on each of those names, locate their family, contacts, jobs."

"We check online sources and databases, though we don't consider them complete or accurate. We try to check date of birth, credit history, if there are any liens filed. Education, we can check dates and graduation. And yearbooks, they sometimes have pictures and more references, classmates. Driving records, DMV, civil court records, and criminal history. We use all the normal databases and reverse directories. We subscribe to everything. We also check Google and the social networking sites." He walked her around the room.

"We do have access to NCIC if we are investigating for a government contract. We can't use it for you, but we can work around that.

"We'll also do a face to face check, a visual. Maybe get fingerprints. Though we can't run them, we'll have them. We'll follow him for a week or as long as you want. Check to see if he works where he says he works. If he works nine to five. Where he has lunch, drinks. Who he meets. Decide if we can talk to them. Follow them. However deep you want us to go. If we find something, or notice something out of whack, we follow that up of course. The landlord shared Farwood's references. I was just getting ready to check those. But I'll show you how to do it.

You can start on them and I'll contact the prior landlord. Sit here, I'll show you the procedure." He sat her down and walked her through the steps.

"First you run them through our online databases, then through the social media networks. Follow each hit, drill down to the next level. Fill in this form as you go along. It tracks everywhere you have been, everywhere you have looked. Don't leave any line blank. If you look at something or someone, you record what you find. If you find nothing, you record that. Sometimes nothing is more important than something."

"How do we know any of this social network stuff is real?" she asked.

"We don't, we assume nothing is, until we get backup."

Tony had said they would go in person to some of the references when they finished the online work. Meanwhile someone would be following Tom to double check employment, hangouts, bars, and friends. Not her. Poor Tom. She hardly felt he warranted this depth of investigation. She had never met any of his friends. He had said he didn't have any family. But then she had never introduced him to any of hers either."

"Some people find it tedious. Can barely manage to follow one lead down one level. No fault with that. We are all built differently. I'm always looking at the pattern and it's rather like an ancestry genealogy for me. The target's lineage."

Becca said, "I'm pretty good with a computer but I prefer the field work. I can do this though. Better then staring out the window." And even romance novels get boring.

Tony's research was all done online and stored electronically. She was surprised with the thoroughness. Tony was right; it was just like a genealogy tree.

"Just follow the form, filling in the blanks. See how far you get."

He watched her for a while, the forms automatically opening for her to fill in as she found information. Once she got started, she could see Cilla's handwork all over the software. She specialized in the creation of user friendly applications for specific tasks. This was typical of her thoroughness and simplicity. The data entry forms and split forms.

The blank content boxes for landlords, references, friends, coworkers. Once a blank was filled in, a split form opened for dates, check boxes, drop down lists, photos, memos. Entering a zero opened a box for the next name. Intuitive and user friendly forms. Simple to start a new branch for the new landlord form.

Becca worked all afternoon, checking off the references on the rental application. She filled in the data on the landlord. Both of Tom's references. Their social networks, business, friends. She located each name on Facebook; put that information on the form. Next did the same with the Facebook 'friends'. In this case the references were each other's friends. Hmm. Both references had each other as friends on Facebook, plus one new name that they shared. That was curious. She thought about that for a minute. She didn't know enough. Maybe all Facebook people shared the same friends. Made sense, in a weird way. Tom wasn't on Facebook and wasn't 'friends' with his references. She lost herself in the search. It was a little boring, but the hits kept her attention from flagging.

She half listened as Tony contacted the prior landlord, the second level, using the story about the inheritance again, wheedling out the information he needed for the third level. Then contacted the third landlord and references. She was surprised what some people would tell. As a cop, she couldn't get information without a warrant. Everyone watched TV. But a man giving away money on the phone? Or a strange, beautiful woman? No problem. What kind of sense did that make?

Tony posted his new information in her tree. She took a quick look and saw that this second rental form, level two, had the same two references with the same addresses. Tom had used the same ones, which was reasonable. But he had a different place of employment, which also made sense. The software recognized she had entered a name already and asked if it was the same. When she checked yes, it filled in all the information. That was different from what she'd used at work where everything had to be reentered. Cool. Cilla again, she was sure. The third landlord again had the same two references. As soon as she entered the dates the software calculated the length of stay. Ten months at his current employment so far. Eight months at level two, and seven months at level three. About two years of undercover or covert work? She hoped. Not a long con.

She slogged through the new information. Was surprised when Tony stopped her. "Jake says take a break. Enough for one day. Jen will take you home." She thought about arguing but she was tired and she still had her own files to work through.

"Can I take a copy of what we have so far?" she asked. There was something there. Something off. Kinky. She'd think on it.

"Only to study. Work on it in this office only," he instructed as Jen came for her.

"What did you do all afternoon?" Becca asked Jen when they were in the Rover.

"Cataloged and cleaned weapons. Paperwork. It was only a few hours. When we get back, I go into the gatehouse first. Clear it and come back out for you.

Becca almost rolled her eyes but then remembered the crutch and how much she couldn't do for herself. "Sure, go for it; make coffee while you're at it."

"After I clear the building."

Becca wasn't going to apologize. Just sat and silently watched as Jen cleared the building and came back and got her. Jen started the coffee, opened the refrigerator, and got out chunked cheese, celery, and strawberries. Put them on a platter with the crackers and brought them over to the table and couch. Then went back for coffee cream and sugar.

"You take cream and sugar?" Becca asked surprised. Didn't fit her image of Jen.

"No, you do. It will take away the afternoon cranky sulk you got going."

Now Becca was embarrassed.

"Don't worry; it's pretty normal for my clients to be frustrated by the restraints dictated by protection. Besides, I'm hungry."

Becca realized she was also, and put cheese on a cracker. She leaned back on the couch, took a bite and said, "No one can get in here you know. The security is above state of the art."

"Someone can get in anywhere. Suppose, someone takes Annie when she is in town and forces her to use her code to get in. Say he beats the distress code out of her too. Knows the camera will recognize Annie so it has to look like Annie entering the code. He makes her do it. You aren't notified of a breach because security doesn't see one. Or the bad guys could jam the signal." She waited to see that Becca understood. "Not to mention the whole perimeter. And what if they dropped a guy in from a chopper? Not reasonable from what we know. But that could change. If we thought that could happen, we would have a team in place here. Right now we think, and you believe, that we are looking at one person. An amateur. A coward maybe, who attacks from ambush in the dark. Right now that is what I am protecting you from."

"OK. OK. I give up."

"Jake wanted me to remind you, ask you, to please only use his office computers for the back ground check on Tom." Jen said politely.

"Yes. I have enough other stuff to do here. To keep me busy."

Jen stood and said, "Same time tomorrow," as she left.

Becca limped around the couch twice just to limber up. Tony had made her stop every hour and walk around her desk, but she was still stiff and sore. She wasn't quite ready to go back to work on her cases and stretched out on the couch. Realized her book was in the bedroom, groaned as she went to get it. Made sure she could reach the quilt before she sat back down.

**

The phone woke her. And she was chilled. The quilt was within reach and she grabbed it thinking, Ryan would have put it over me. Her cell was still ringing. 'Not provided'. Well she knew a lot of cops and a lot of 'not provided' phone numbers. Though most had names and ring tones attached. She noticed it was after seven. She'd slept two hours.

"Speak," she said.

"Hi, Crip," Ryan said.

She was surprised at how happy she felt hearing his voice. It took away the chill and made her feel warm all over.

"Hi," she said back. Glad he couldn't see her because she thought she might be flushed. She knew she was grinning like an idiot.

"Did I wake you? I wasn't sure what time to call." He was a little nervous, calling so soon. But he had been thinking about her. He knew that there was something between them. Recognized it, had felt it before. With his wife. He had been trying to ignore it, but that wasn't working. He was too old to be playing games, and had been out of the dating game for twenty years. Could he even compete now? He'd find out.

"Oh. I fell asleep on the couch. Reading," she said.

"I stole one of your books," he admitted.

"Guess you will have to return it." Was she flirting with him?

"That's kind of what I'm calling about." He had forced himself to wait until he went home from work to call her. He had caught himself numerous times watching a wall and thinking about her. Had reached out to call her more times than he could count. He could say he was wondering about her physical progress. Any friend would be concerned. Not that he was calling himself a friend. "Maybe I can trade it for another." Added, "Tomorrow." He had meant to say Friday. Tomorrow slipped out.

"Um. Tomorrow?" He wanted to borrow another book? Tomorrow?

"Yes, we could work together on your cases. I kind of liked having you nearby to answer questions."

"Well. Um, sure." That's it? He wanted to go over her cases?

This wasn't going the way he planned. But then again, he had a dozen different plans and he hadn't been able to decide on a single one. He just knew he wanted to see her again. "I want to see you again. The book, the cases are just excuses." He waited a moment and then filled the silence with, "If you don't feel the same way, I can snail mail the book and the tablet. Work your cases from here and text questions." There he had said it. Laid it all out.

"No. I mean yes. Stop. Wait." She drew a deep breath and took the plunge. "I want to see you again, too. I was glad when you took the tablet because it meant you would come back. I'm glad you took the book and that you want to return it in person. You don't have to work on my cases. But you could come tomorrow to see me." To see me! If he could own up, so could she.

"I was planning on staying."

"Yes. Please stay." Okay!

They both sighed with relief. And laughed together. It had been hard. He changed the subject. "How did your day go? Did you eat?"

That was cute she thought. He was worried about her eating. "Yes. I ate. And before you ask, I did my exercises."

"How about working with Jake?"

"He has quite an operation. I didn't realize how much he does or how big his business is. Background checks are different on the civilian side."

"He does good work for us. Thorough. If there is anything to find on Tom, Jake will find it. Or you will. I should finish my review of your cases tonight. I'll call if I find anything."

They talked about their day and then he ended with, "I'll be over after work tomorrow. Stay for the rest of the week. I checked with Cilla. She said my room is empty." His room. John's old room. Four bedrooms for the gang of five. Kevin slept in the main house. They seldom spent a night here now since each was married or in a serious relationship. "She is going to text Annie and let her know I'm coming." Ryan had a feeling that Cilla and Annie would be comparing notes on Ryan and Becca. Because, oh yeah, there were some sparks there.

"Good. Ha, I'll be here." She laughed as he hung up.

He felt lighter. Her voice made him smile. Couldn't help it. He'd frozen when she didn't respond right away. But she'd said he could come. To see her. To stay. He felt like a school boy. So, tomorrow. After work. He could wait. He had things to clean up at the office. The meetings had all been today. Wrapping up the cases. He had filed all his reports from the gatehouse. Tomorrow he would be filling in any holes. Attending follow up meetings. Then he would take leave. Vacation time.

Maybe not. The last time he had taken leave he had gotten mixed up in multiple cases. Be brave, he told himself. Take leave. He'd been brave enough to tell her he wanted to see her again. Be with her. He smiled again. She'd said yes. He'd take leave.

**

Becca was grinning. Silly girl. But she couldn't help herself. And why shouldn't she grin. A nice guy was going to come and visit her. A guy she liked. A lot. Stop, she told herself. Time to get a TV dinner and go back to her case files. Maybe Annie left food. She had. One of her favorites, meatloaf with directions to heat for ten minutes. Mashed potatoes and a salad were there too.

She'd barely finished when Kevin and Annie walked over from the main house. Followed shortly by Cilla, Sarah, and Penney. Without their significant others. She was surprised to see Penney. She had the impression that she didn't leave Daffy much. Penney! A one man woman! Hard to believe. But Becca was so happy for her. Happy for all of them. Except for Kevin, they each had found someone to be with. All within the past year. Becca watched Kevin, because for a while he and Penney had found comfort in each other. But there were no signs of jealousy. Kevin seemed happy for Penney and satisfied with himself.

The gang had wandered in to fill in the gaps left by Ryan's debriefing. They had a lot of fun with the telling. Embellishing. Laughing. Becca told them of her day working for Jake. She took a moment to praise Jake's software. She knew Cilla and the gang had tweaked all of it, because it raced now.

They didn't stay late and after they left, Becca got her tablet, turned on the voice commands, and worked until midnight, stopping every hour to limp around the room. It had been a good day. She cleaned up her dishes. That reminded her of Ryan. She was going to have a romance. Giggling, she headed for bed. Ryan would be here tomorrow. Was it coincidence that her family came on a night he wasn't here? Did they suspect?

Tuesday

She did her off day exercises, showered, and made toast. Jen wouldn't get her until one; she wasn't tired, so she went back to work on her cases. She was more than half way through and had some questions for her Captain. How to ask them would be the problem. Just tell him she was reviewing her own case files she guessed.

And as it turned out, that was the perfect approach. Her Captain was both happy to hear from her and able to resolve her issues. She worked for an hour more, renewed by his friendly assistance, and then stretched out and took a nap on the couch. This time with the quilt. When she got her life back, she was going to buy a pretty couch. Pretty and comfortable. A soft quilt too. Maybe a yellow one. Somehow pretty made her feel better. Happy. How did that work? Maybe she was getting better.

She was waiting for Jen, just inside the door. Jen raised her eyebrows at her.

"You waited."

"Yes, I can follow orders. I wasn't feeling too well yesterday. Wait. Let me try that again. No excuses. I was ugly yesterday, an ass. Today I'll try not to be. I understand what you are doing and I appreciate it. Coffee? I have to-go cups."

"Sure, cream and sugar this morning." She let Becca get it adding, "You weren't that bad. No need to apologize, but apology accepted. I'll put the cups in the car and come back for you."

The procedure was the same as the day before. Becca got through most of the third landlord's data and his references. It was easy because the references were the same. Though this time the apartment was out of state. But then they were in a nexus. Four states within a half hour drive. Apparently Tom moved every six to eight months. That was strange. Maybe her little liaison with him would have been over anyhow. Still something calling for some reflection?

When she got home, she finished her case review. She had been through all her files and compared them to the official files. They matched. She had found nothing that looked like someone would want to harm her.

Security announced Cilla. Perfect timing. They could discuss her results.

Cilla was disappointed. "Ryan is coming tonight. Maybe he has something. If not, could it be from your past? One of your fosters?"

"I've been thinking about that. Twisting and turning it around in my mind. Trying to remember. Didn't want to follow that path until I had eliminated my case files which are the most obvious. But who? And why now? Why after all this time? It doesn't make any sense. But I know I'm going to have to look at them."

Cilla spoke slowly, hesitantly, "You are probably not the one who should do the sifting through your foster families."

"With you there girl. But I'm the only one available and I'm the one who knows all the players." She really didn't want to go digging around among the monsters of her childhood. She wasn't sure she was that tough. Emotionally. Physically; tough was her middle name. But her childhood memories left her weak.

"Okay. I should be the one to look at the fosters," Cilla said. "Don't forget, I know all the players too."

They were still talking about Becca's fosters when Ryan arrived. He hugged Cilla and walked over to Becca. Her body responded again with that physical reaction. Had she known him before? Always? Always. Her body was saying that she had known him always.

She thought he might kiss her. Surprised at how much she wanted him to kiss her. She settled for his hug and he rested his face against her hair for an extra moment, breathing in her scent.

"Why the sad faces," Ryan asked.

There was a long silence. Probably deciding what or how much to tell him, he thought. Becca answered. "I finished going through all my case files. No one there would do this to me. I compared my notes to the final versions of the police department; they're the same. I had one doubtful, but my Captain resolved it. Unless you found something?" she asked hopefully.

"No. One maybe that I want to run by you." He got out his notebook.

"That's the same one I wondered about. My Captain says the guy is dead."

"Nothing then,' he said. "You went through all your cases? And found no one else?"

"That's what I said."

"How about what you were working on when you got shot?"

"I just finished a major case. Everything was wrapped up for the district attorney."

"Do you have any unsolveds?" He was asking about any old cases that might still be open.

"I was going to take a look at my one old open case." She stopped and then continued thoughtfully. "Wait. Wait. The Captain had just dropped two cold cases on my desk. I had contacted the families that morning to notify them that we were reopening the cases and would be setting up appointments to come out and talk to them. That's it. That has to be it. The shooter has to be one of those people I contacted. I'll call the Captain and get them."

"No." Ryan stopped her from dialing. "Wait. It doesn't have to be one of them. It could be anyone they talked to. And it might be better if no one knows you're thinking of following up."

She paused, considering, "I can go get them."

"No, again. No one should know that you're planning to look at them."

"I can get them," Cilla said. "What is your unsolved? I'll get that too." She got up and walked back toward her bedroom. It wouldn't be cool for Cilla to commit the hacking in front of an FBI agent.

"Is she doing what I think she's doing?" he asked Becca.

"You don't need to know." She held her breath, waiting to hear what he would say next.

"I can help. Look at those cold cases. Off the books, not officially. I'm on leave again. I do some of my best work when I'm on leave."

"Jake can help." Was she actually suggesting she'd rather work with Jake then Ryan? She waited again to hear what he would say.

"Jake's not a cop. You need cop eyes."

"Okay. You can help with the cold cases." She saw he was ready to say more and she added, not graciously, "Nothing else." She didn't want him to know about her life before.

Cilla came back, "The cases are printing now. Three copies of each. I figured we could all look that way." She went over to get them.

"Let's read and compare notes."

Becca got done first. She had already skimmed through them the morning before the shooting. She made notes as the others read. Coincidence that two of the three were armed robberies? Why hadn't she noticed that before?

Ryan was sitting at the table. He read through quickly once and then again more slowly taking notes.

By that time, Cilla had finished her first and only run through. Ryan knew she had what passed for a photographic memory. Cilla wouldn't need notes. She said, "I don't know much about investigation, but only one of these, your old case, looks properly investigated. You guys are the experts. I'll be the gofer."

"I want to think on these a while longer," Ryan said. "But the Donavan case is a kidnapping, murder, suicide across state lines and we were called in. I can get our files. Let's eat and come back to them." They all agreed.

Annie had left chicken and side dishes warming along with cold salad in the refrigerator. As they sat down Becca said, "You know, I finally figured out what has been twitching in the back of my brain." She explained, "We have been looking into the jerk, his landlords, and his references on Facebook. All the activity on the Facebook pages came within two days of each of his moves and job interviews. And that was weather, or parties. Never anything personal. Other than that, nothing on the wall, or timeline, or whatever they call it. Isn't that unusual for

Facebook?" She stopped; Ryan had a horrified look on his face. "What? What? You're scaring me. Tell us."

Ryan thought about putting his face in his hands and shaking his head while screaming, no, no why me? Why can't I take leave without becoming involved in a major case? But that wouldn't be manly and this wasn't about him. It was about Becca. Becca and her ex-lover, who was not what she thought. Becca wasn't going to like this.

"Give me a minute here." He needed time to put his thoughts in order.

They watched him think. Waiting.

He went with the facts. "OK. Let me run this back by you. You have traced Tom through three landlords in less than two years. Tom uses the same references for each landlord. Right so far?"

"Yes," Becca agreed.

"All the activity on the social media pages happens during the week that the references are being checked for the job or his apartment. Nothing personal on the web pages. And then nothing until Tom moves again? Right?"

"Yes," hesitantly this time. "You know something, don't you." Not a question.

He did wipe a hand across his face. "Typical undercover operation. Not us, I don't think. We learned the hard way to put fake personal information on line and update the social websites regularly. It's either an undercover operation or a con. Though cons usually keep their websites active."

If Becca hadn't been sitting she would have sat. Her legs felt weak. She didn't generally misjudge people. Tom running a con? As fantastic as Tom being undercover. And she missed all the signs?

"If Tom is running a con, he's good. He never made a false move with me. I thought he was exactly what he said, a low level personnel manager. I didn't think he was that smart. Same goes for undercover." She stopped to think about that and if, now that she knew, she could determine which it was.

"Either way, we never went anywhere. Never met anyone. But that was the same on my side too. I never introduced him to my friends or family. Never even talked about them. I was the perfect sidepiece. The perfect cover." Not bitter. It had been over a long time ago. A lifetime ago. "A typical short term affair, for a normal guy, living a normal life."

Cilla sat beside her and asked, "Can I hurt him now?" That got a snort from both Ryan and Becca.

"Better call Jake and tell him what you found, Becca." Ryan suggested. "He needs a heads up, though I'll bet he already knows."

Becca had Jake on speed dial. As soon as he answered she began, "Jake um…," But he cut her off talking over her. "I'm glad you called. Tony found a problem after you left. We were going to tell you tomorrow. I wanted to do it in person, so we could talk it over."

"I was just telling Ryan about lapses I found in the social media. Is that what you mean? I didn't realize what I was seeing until just now. He says Tom may be involved in an undercover op or a con."

There was a moment of silence and then Jake asked, "You were talking to Ryan?"

"Yes, he's here."

"I'm coming over."

Becca looked at her cell. "He hung up. He's coming over. Better set another place."

Jake came with Mary Lee. Spoke her name for the security camera at the gate. They set one more place at the table.

Jake kissed Cilla on the cheek, shook hands with Ryan, and introduced Mary Lee. Becca was surprised. Mary Lee was plain. There was no other word for it. Even the makeup she wore couldn't make her pretty, let alone the beauty that Tony had implied. And she looked, well, normal. Blonde and blue sure, but average face. Maybe a little short but average weight. She did walk like a dancer. Light on her feet.

Jake headed for the table saying, "We can talk as we eat."

Becca saw Cilla smile and remembered her comments about these men and food.

"I've stopped your research," Jake said.

When Becca looked as if she would object he said, "Had to. I don't mean permanently. I mean that we need to redirect our actions. Tony found those lapses. He called Mary Lee, called her off, and brought her in. Then he notified me. I didn't want to tell you over the phone, I was going to wait until tomorrow. We have protocols for dealing with undercover operations and we need to implement those procedures. We'll start long distance surveillance, electronically. Mary Lee has been on him since you hired us. I'll let her tell you what she has found." That would give him time to eat, Becca thought.

Mary Lee flipped through her notebook. "I did an open surveillance on Tom. Each time I drove by his condo Saturday night, his car was in his parking spot. Sunday I had breakfast at the eatery down the block. He came in and ate while reading the newspaper. He didn't meet anyone or converse with the wait staff and he went back to his condo. His car didn't move all day." She turned a page.

"Monday morning I called his office complaining that my elderly mother had gotten a garbled message Friday afternoon, to call a Tim or Tom at their number. I had them identify their business name and type of business and then had them search for someone named Tim or Tom whom my mother insisted she was supposed to contact. They only had one Tom, Tom Farwood, an assistant in personnel. We both agreed that he would have no reason to call my mother and that my Mom was confused. We gossiped a little about the trials of having an aging relative before I rang off. So we know that Tom does work there in personnel."

She looked up from her notes, "He went straight home after work Monday and did not come out by midnight when I left. Today he stopped off at the local bar, The Brew, for happy hour. I didn't follow him in. Jake will get another operative to put on the inside if we need to. He was home when Tony called me in," Mary Lee finished up

Jake picked it up then. "Now that we know that he might not be what he seems, we'll follow his cell, spot check that he is where his cell GPS says he is. I've got an operative I can put in the bar, but even if we can identify his contacts that won't necessarily tell us what he's up to. We have to be careful, we don't want to blow an undercover op or get anyone killed. If it's a con, that's a different story. But it doesn't feel like a con."

"Wonder what would happen if I showed up back in his life. I met him at The Brew," Becca said. They all looked at her. "I could go there and bump into him."

"No," Ryan said immediately. He didn't want her anywhere near the jerk. And it would be dangerous, for both of them, whether it was a con or not.

Jake was nodding agreement. "Ryan's right. Not you. At least not now, he didn't slip up in the three months you were with him. He's not going to just volunteer the truth because you show up. Don't forget, he didn't step up when you were shot, either."

"Not ever," Ryan corrected. "She doesn't go in the bar ever. She's not trained for undercover and you of all people know how badly that can work out."

"Hey, I get a say," Becca injected, almost standing. It was hard to be assertive sitting down. Harder still when she had to brace herself and struggle to stand.

"Yes, you do get a say," Jake granted. "When I decide we need you. Not before. Wait, don't get angry. Ideally we can do this without you. If we can't, then we'll look at our options. All of us will look at all of our options. The timing and circumstances would both have to be right. We're not going to act on emotions or pride. We need to know if he is a cop; or if he is a con. Or he could be a private investigator. We sometimes insert an operative into a business to find a leak or a thief. For now, we'll put on the long tail. GPS tracker on his phone. Spot check that he is with his phone. Right Cilla? He won't be able to see us electronically?"

"He won't see you," she said positively. "And neither will anyone else who might be doing the same thing. We'll look for that, too." No one needed to be told that the gang had worked on the software.

"I've got an operative from the other coast already registered at the hotel with a solid cover, ready for insertion. I'd like to give us another few days of trailing before we select the bar as a contact point for him. It doesn't sound like the lunch shop would offer any opportunities." He looked at Mary Lee for confirmation, getting a few more mouthfuls while she talked.

"No, he didn't interact with anyone. He wasn't watching anyone either."

"It will be hard to put out feelers to law enforcement. We're in a junction with four states plus DC, all with multiple local towns and counties. We can't check them all."

"Think maybe federal?" he asked Ryan. "Because his last operation was in Pennsylvania, across the state line, implies we could be dealing with the feds. Can you check with your people?"

"I will, but I don't think it's us. Sloppy social websites. We don't do that."

"I want to go down one more level on the social websites. Very carefully," Jake said. "I'm hoping they might have been sloppier near the beginning and we find something we can trace back to them. I'm hoping for a break there."

They all ate while thinking about that.

"Cilla's going to check my fosters," Becca said in a low voice. She had her eyes closed as she said it. As if, if she couldn't see it, it couldn't hurt her.

Jake looked at Cilla who said, "We were talking about it when Ryan got here. I'm the best one to do it, since I already did it once, ten years ago. Back when I was too young to understand invasion of privacy. I looked at everything. I'll go back and look at everything again in conjunction with the shooting."

Mary Lee looked as if she would ask a question and Jake just shook his head at her. He didn't know the whole story himself. "OK. We'll leave that part to you. If you need us let us know."

Ryan wasn't sure what 'the fosters' were or why Becca hadn't told him. Maybe the subject changed before they got to it. He said, "I have the cold cases." And explained to Jake what he meant.

"Let me recap. You found nothing in Becca's cases. But you have two cold cases to investigate and Becca's unsolved from when she first joined the force. We have Farwood. Cilla has the fosters?" He looked around and got assents. "That's it then. You know Cilla, Cavanaugh might be able to help you if you run into any stumbling blocks. The fosters were all local weren't they?"

"Yes. That's a good idea, not everything was put on computers back then." She wasn't sure she wanted to include Cav though. Some things she and the gang had done were a little iffy legally.

"Becca, Jen will pick you up the same time tomorrow. I'll tell her what's happening. Mary Lee, I'll take you back to the office. Ryan, we need to get together. And Cilla," he smiled at her, gave her a kiss on his way out, "I'll see you back home."

Cilla and Becca said goodbye as Ryan cleaned up. When he came out of the kitchen, he sat beside Becca on the couch. She looked lost and alone. He tugged her into his side, pressed her head to his shoulder; without any resistance from her. Put his arm around her and just held her close. He could think of any number of things they had discussed that might make her look this way.

"What's wrong sweetheart?"

Sweetheart? He called her sweetheart? She was enjoying being close to him. Too much. The comfort and warmth. She turned her head to look up into his face and saw concern, tenderness. *Sweetheart.* That was good. Sort of. Did that mean she had to tell him? She started obliquely.

"Let me see where to start. You already know that I am disturbed that I didn't tip to Tom. Didn't have a glimmer of suspicion that he was playing me."

"But you wouldn't Becca. Couldn't. That was his job. And he was good at it. We know he's been doing it for at least two years. He'd have to be good, very good, at deception, to last that long. He would be very good at staying in character. Being with you, well that could be both being in character and being himself. He could honestly like you. That wouldn't have to be part of his con. That could have been real."

"I guess, that's possible. At least that would make me feel a little better."

"Another thing to consider is that you did break it off. Maybe you did sense something not quite right. Some little tell. A gut feeling. A feeling that let you understand you could end the affair without much damage to yourself."

"But I didn't know he was lying" she argued.

"Your gut did. Think about it. You are a good cop. Your gut knew. It was talking to you, telling you something. When you found an excuse to end it, you did. Otherwise, wouldn't you have found a less direct way to approach taking your relationship up a notch? Meals out, theater?" he reasoned.

It did make sense. She had surprised herself when she'd bluntly told Tom she wanted more. It was a comforting thought that her gut might have felt something off. But was she fooling herself? "I think... I think I would have tried a less confrontational method. I knew what I was doing would end it. I think. Maybe."

She looked at him again, "That idea does make me feel better." Then, daring him to come up with an excuse or explanation, she said, "But I forgot the cold cases. Explain that."

"So you screwed up," he said pleasantly.

She pulled away from him. He was laughing at her. She punched his arm.

"Think about it," he told her, pulling he close again. "You break up with your lover, and then get shot in a dark alley, and almost die. Big surprise you forgot. The cold cases didn't seem relevant. We still don't know if they are important. Your boss forgot didn't he? Did he mention them when he said he reviewed your cases and decided it was a random shooting? Or when you called him about that one case?"

"No."

"But you think you were supposed to remember after all you had been through? I think you can give yourself a pass here."

She relaxed back beside him. He'd done it again. Made her feel good. He'd given her back some faith in herself and her ability. "That makes sense."

He pulled her closer and held her, waiting. Finally he asked, "It's not Jake is it? I got the impression you had forgiven him."

"Yes, I have, almost. But I'm still going to make him pay a little. He doesn't deserve to get off that easy. And it makes me feel good to see him nervous around me."

Ryan laughed at that. "That's my Becca," and gave her an extra hug. Then waited some more, wondering if she would trust him with the truth. When she pulled away, he thought that she was done confiding.

But she was only moving away so she could face him. She took a deep breath thinking this was it; this would be her first step. She was going to tell him.

"You know I am one of Cilla's rescues?"

"Yes. But not much more."

"There's a lot more. Some of it is pretty ugly. I don't like to talk about it."

"You don't have to," he said quickly.

"Yes. I do. If you are going to help find the person who shot me, you should know. If we are going to have a relationship, you need to know. We are going to have a relationship? That's what you're planning, right?"

"Oh, yes."

"Then before you get involved with me you need to know about my past. So you can decide if you really want to get closer." She took another breath.

"When I was seven, my parents were killed in a freaky accident. I survived, barely. That was my first time in a hospital. Spent some time in foster homes, some of them okay, a couple not very good. The first foster family was good. I stayed there almost two years. Just long enough to almost get comfortable. The second family was about the same, but they moved me out quickly. I never knew why they moved me. Or when they would move me again. I stopped unpacking my sack. When I was twelve, a brother of one the foster parents raped and beat me and I got my second trip to the hospital."

His face had gone still, but he was still listening.

"After that Family Services moved me to a group home. Cilla found me there and befriended me. She was a rock for me. Then when I was sixteen I was placed in another foster home. My new foster drugged me, dressed me up, took me to a bar, and sold me to four men. I came to while they were taking turns holding me down and raping me."

She saw his anger. "Don't get angry. And I'm not looking for sympathy. Just telling you my story. It was a long time ago. And Cilla took care of it." She watched to make sure he was still listening. She didn't want to explain how Cilla took care of it.

"They hurt me bad. Not just the rape. But the beating. Because I was fighting them. They seemed to enjoy causing pain. I don't remember it all," She paused considering. She would have to say something about Cilla if she was going to tell him everything.

"You're an attorney, right?"

When he nodded, puzzled, she said. "I need to hire you." She couldn't stand easily to go get her purse. "Give me a dollar, I can't get up." He reached for his wallet and pulled out a ten. Handed it to her. "Smallest I have."

She took it and handed it back, "I want to hire you. For me and Cilla. And the gang. Before I tell you anything more. It will be privileged, right? You don't have to tell your FBI self?" she asked for his assurance.

He took the bill back. "Privileged. I won't share. And my first meeting with a client is always cheap."

She breathed a sigh of relief; she hadn't been sure it would work.

"So I woke up in a hospital again. That was the first time I woke to find Cilla by my bedside. She had come looking for me. Found me. Called an ambulance. The EMT's called the cops. Cilla got a good cop; he listened to her. He listened to a kid. That didn't happen too often back then. She told them about my foster. Told them what she thought had happened. Where to find the four men. The cop went looking and found them right where she said. Bragging. Like it was okay to rape and beat a drugged sixteen year old, because they bought me from my foster. The cop arrested them all and notified Family Services."

She took a breath and slowed down. This is where things get a little murky. "They searched the guys at the jail and found drugs. Searched their residences and found more drugs and money. The guys, of course, claimed they had never seen the drugs or the money." She looked to see if he was buying it. She'd always thought the gang planted the stuff. She continued.

"Seems that the cops found out lots of other stuff about these guys. Enough to easily convict them of drug trafficking and put them in jail for a long, long, time. I was left out of it. If you look, you won't find anything about me. About the rape or the beating. It's all gone. And somehow, Family Services lost track of me. When I was released from the hospital, Annie was my guardian."

"Cilla told me that she would keep track of those men for me and I would never have to worry about them. I believed her. I lived here, in the gatehouse, for a year. I had a part time job and the gang and Annie helped out. I lived here, hid out here, until I graduated and turned eighteen." She took a breath. That was the hard part. And he was still with her. This next part was easy.

"I got a scholarship and enrolled in criminal justice and law enforcement. Commuted. Graduated. Got this job. That's it."

He just looked at her. "What about any of that would make me not want a relationship with you?" he asked. "That only makes you more amazing. The first time I saw you at Penney's wedding I knew you were special. Brave. Admirable. The more I see you the more amazed I am and the more impressed I am at what you have accomplished. You are a remarkable woman. You are by far the bravest woman I have ever met, and I have met some very brave women." Cilla and Penney. May, back in Florida, who went up against two stone cold killers with no weapon but her wits. He paused; he knew she wasn't ready to hear him say how he felt. He needed more time himself. But he had to put it out there. "I don't mean to scare you; I know it's too quick. I'm not planning on walking away. Ever. Don't say anything now. When this is over and you are safe, we'll talk again. For now I am a friend helping out. And your attorney."

"OK. A friend and my attorney. About the other? I'm not scared. Later. We can talk later, I'd like that."

He changed the subject. "What time do you want breakfast?"

"Breakfast? Um, Lori comes at eight and then I shower. Jen picks me up at one. So. Are you cooking?" she asked hopefully.

"Yep. Breakfast at nine thirty. I'll work on your cold cases and go with you and Jen at one. I need to talk to Jake, and I haven't seen his new place yet.

Wednesday

Lori came in with a cane!!! "If you have been good and measure up today, you can trade the crutch for this cane," she promised. She set up the portable infra-red, the ultra sound, and the E-STIM. All passive procedures to help healing. Which meant that Becca could just lie on the table while Lori and the machines did all the work. Becca had made Lori explain that electrical stimulation therapy helped to re-educate the muscle, which helped it heal. Then Lori went into massage mode. Becca hated the actual massage. It hurt. She was thankful when it was over and she got to work through her exercises.

Then Lori handed her the cane. Walked her, literally and figuratively, through the rules for cane use. Who knew that canes had rules? Same side as the crutch. Guess it was a good thing all the rounds had hit her on one side, otherwise it would have been difficult to walk with either the crutch or the cane. Make that more difficult.

"I think you have been slacking off on your shoulder exercises. Probably the crutch was, um, handicapping you. That shouldn't be a problem anymore. You need to get your right arm strengthened. That's your gun hand. It's important for you to regain your flexibility. You need to work on both your leg and your arm equally. But don't overdo. You can take the cane in the shower if you want."

Becca was giddy. She would be walking without the crutch now. OK, maybe not far or fast, but she'd graduated to the cane. She could now get herself a cup of coffee and carry it to the counter without spilling, maybe. That was almost exciting. She couldn't wait to try.

Ryan tried to concentrate on the cases, but Becca was a distraction and he was half listening as she and Lori discussed dust bunnies.

Becca caught him watching her. Probably because she was watching him. He'd surprised her. When he'd said she was admirable, amazing, and brave, she'd felt her insides go cold. And then thaw quickly and freeze again when he said he wasn't leaving. Even though it was too quick. Was he right? Was it too quick? She knew she was attracted to him. Her body certainly was. Who wouldn't be? But it was too quick for love, commitment. Wasn't it? He was giving her time to adjust to the idea. She wasn't sure she needed it. But they would take it slow.

When Lori left, she showered and, feeling silly, picked out a colorful top to go with her sweat pants and went out for breakfast.

Ryan had talked with his boss and gotten permission to work on the kidnapping case officially. His boss had pulled the file himself and e-mailed it. Ryan allowed himself a smile. Cilla could have done it, but she had asked him before she hacked into the FBI network. Thank goodness. They could get around Cilla hacking the local files because Becca had access to those anyway. But he didn't want Cilla anywhere near the FBI database. He knew she'd have been successful and would have left no trace of her activities behind. But still. There was no telling what she'd decide to do once she was in there. Anyhow, it would be better to go through channels if the case ever went to court.

As he read through the kidnapping murder case again, he made notes of the relevant data, names, and addresses of witnesses and family members. People to contact and interview. The kidnapping cold case was interesting. Because New Madrid considered it open even though the FBI thought it was closed. From what Ryan could tell, the FBI Agent went into that case believing he knew what happened and hadn't looked for any other explanation. The kidnapper/killer was dead. Case closed.

Since New Madrid thinks it was still open that would mean they were not satisfied by the FBI closure. Gibbs would have to retrace the steps and see if he could find proof that would close the case for the locals. More accurately, he corrected himself; he and Becca would retrace the steps. It was a good thing she would be using the cane. He wondered if she would let him lift her in and out of the truck. He glanced over at her and she caught him looking.

The other open case, the detective hadn't really tried to solve. Cilla was right. They had a lot of work to do there.

Becca's open case though, seemed to go nowhere. It looked like she had followed every lead. It had been her first case when she had come onboard. Could they be connected? Was it a coincidence they were both armed robberies?

Once they started contacting people, they wouldn't be able to keep the investigation a secret. Not from the shooter, not from the cops. They were on solid footing with the kidnap case; that was his, but they might run into trouble with the locals. Probably would, he thought. There was a problem in New Madrid. They had forced Becca into retirement even before they knew her long term prognosis. Normally, she should have been placed on extended sick leave, and then if the prognosis was bad, they would consider retirement. So why the hurry? Someone wanted her gone and was afraid if he waited he'd open himself up to an investigation? So he jumped the gun? Ryan would have to ask her again if there were personal problems on the force. He should probably wait for that conversation before jumping to conclusions.

He asked her over breakfast. At first she was hesitant to get into it, but he told her it could be important, maybe critical. She could understand that.

"No. The men I worked with were great. No one begrudged me the job. I was good at it. The Captain was fair. It was someone on the Board who had a problem with me. I don't know who or what the problem was. The Captain wouldn't tell me. But he had my back and ran interference. He didn't want to retire me; he didn't have a choice. It wasn't his decision he said and I believe him. That made it even harder for me."

So there was another thread. Another direction for their search for the shooter, as if it wasn't complicated enough. "We'll have to find out who doesn't want you around, and why," he said. But she already knew that.

**

He rode with Becca and Jen and sat in on Jake's meeting reviewing the status of the inquiry.

Tony began with the steps he had taken. "I reran all the names with dates to see if I could find anything that made the news or the web. Nothing. That could point to a private rather than an official investigation. Or a con. It starts, or stops, depending on how you look at it, just about two years ago. I'm running the IPs, internet addresses, for the Facebook entries; so far it looks like they rotated around using free public Wi-Fi areas." His tablet buzzed. He looked down at it and started typing.

"Here's something. One of the first, oldest, Facebook comments is from a private IP. They might have screwed up here, they were just starting. I'm searching for a name. Here it is, Camden Investigations." He looked around.

Jake said, "Yeah, I know them. Didn't know they were into undercover work. And it's not recent if this guy has been out there two years. I know Phil, the owner; we share some operatives and sometimes data."

"What type of operation does he run? Would you work with him?" Ryan asked.

"Maybe. He sometimes wanders close to the line." Jake made a note and then said doubtfully, "I'm not sure if we should give him a heads up now."

"He could tell us if Becca stumbled into something. But I think you're right. Might be better to know for sure what we found before we tell anyone we found it. Let's wait," Ryan agreed.

"Tony, you and Becca see what other avenues you can follow. Maybe find somebody who worked with Tom on that job two years ago...."

"Got you, Boss, come on Becca." They left with Jen following.

Ryan told Jake about Becca's forced retirement. "I don't like the sound of that. A Board member? Tony can work on that too. Cilla was up half the night going over the fosters. She feels a little responsible there. She doesn't talk about her rescues beyond the basics." He laughed, "You know; name, rank, and serial number. She's like a mother lion.

I'm not sure I even know all of them. I don't need to know. Probably better."

Ryan agreed and then said, "Ah, I'm Becca's attorney. She hired me last night. I was also hired to represent Cilla and the gang."

Jake considered him a minute, "So there is something fishy in her rescue. I wondered. But there isn't any evidence; I know Cilla and the gang that well. They left no tracks. Even back then, they wouldn't have left tracks. Becca doesn't really need an attorney. Besides, both John and Kevin are attorneys."

"I think it made Becca more comfortable to know that whatever she told me would stay with me. I don't think I'm violating attorney client privilege to tell you that."

Jake laughed out loud. "You know just when I begin to think of them as kids, or naïve, they do something to make me stand up and take notice. I think Cilla is always at least ten steps ahead of me. Hides it so I won't feel inadequate. Ah, well. Let me get Tony working on the Board; he'll know how to do that. Maybe find someone privy to the local gossip. And Cav might have some insight on that through the Sheriff's department. He might have something on the cold cases too."

"I hadn't thought of that. He was a big help taking Sheri down."

"I'll call him." Jake got Cavanaugh on speaker phone.

"Wondering if you might have some information on Camden Investigations or New Madrid, that you might want to share,"

"Maybe. I'm busy now but I could make a late supper at the gatehouse, especially if Annie is cooking. What are you after?" he wanted to know.

"Gossip, anything you have. Current or otherwise? Maybe some stuff two years old?"

"In reference to what?"

"Becca."

"Hmm. How's she doing?" he asked, delaying for time.

"She's home. Here at the gatehouse."

"Good to hear. I can understand New Madrid, she worked there. Got shot there. One of my men worked there. He talks a lot. So I might have something you need. But I don't understand why you want information, gossip or otherwise, on Camden."

Ryan spoke then, "Gibbs here Cav. We might have a connection."

"Ryan, you in town? How do the Feds fit in?"

"I'm on leave, helping out."

"Yeah, I remember the last time you helped out. It was wild. How does Camden fit in?"

"Not over the phone. Tonight." He disconnected.

"Hmm, hope he has something we can use," Jake commented as his phone buzzed, he hit the speaker button again, "Talk."

"We got something more, maybe. Come on down."

Tony put up the information they had found on the three businesses. "You can see that we don't have anything but name, address, and phone number. Not a web page or an email. No owners. Nothing. I've started an in-depth search on all of them. Corporate papers, finance…" He let that trail off and continued, "But we might have found something else." He motioned to Becca.

"Becca speculated that Tom uncovered problems at his jobs. She wondered if it would be in the newspapers? Would there be arrest records? Or maybe they handled it in house?"

"She did a little research on Tom; and the business owners." Now he looked triumphant.

"We found an obituary. When Tom was working at the level second company, we have a suicide. That might be a result of whatever he was looking for. Two relatives of the deceased are mentioned. This is the first time we've seen any mention of individuals at any of the businesses."

They all looked at the obituary.

"We'll run all the names. See if we can find a link. If we can find an online guest book, we'll have more names. Somewhere we ought to be able to find a story. There's always one person who has to put everything they know on line. It's a start. It might just be a coincidence, but we thought you'd want to see this."

"Yes, good work, keep going. Ryan is going to work on the cold cases. I've got to go out on a job. We'll meet at the gatehouse, you too Tony, at seven. Sheriff Cavanaugh is coming by with some information."

**

They worked through the afternoon and then Ryan rode home with Becca and Jen. They found Cilla waiting for them busy at her computer. "I've finished looking at the fosters," she told Becca. "I didn't find anything connecting to your shooting, but I can give you a current status." She looked at Ryan and Jen.

Becca said, "Ryan's okay. I told him. Jen won't tell my secrets. She's here to protect me, she'll protect my secrets."

"Right," was all Jen said.

"Okay. The uncle, in the first violent rape, wasn't really any relation. He lived in the same building as your fosters. He was a convicted and released pedophile who had stopped checking in. He went down for two other children. Not you. You were only mentioned as an unidentified underage minor. He's in prison for life, no parole. No one misses him."

Cilla continued, "Those fosters, the uncle's friends, moved to Ohio and are now living high on federal and state SSI. No children. They don't even remember you."

Cilla continued, "Of the four men," she was a little circumspect, but Becca would know who she meant. "They were all arrested for trafficking in drugs. Even though the cops went after them because of what they did to you and they were overheard bragging about it. They were arrested, tried, and convicted on the drug charges. You were never mentioned. They served their sentences, plus some time. No good behavior for them. One guy died in prison. A second OD'd shortly after his release. The third got in a scuffle with the fourth and killed him and went back to prison for life."

Ryan asked angrily, "How come? How come no one was ever prosecuted for what they did? They were overheard bragging about the rape weren't they?"

Becca answered quietly, "I made a choice, get justice for me personally which meant going back into foster care and showing up in court every day. Or disappear from the system. I wanted those creeps dead, I settled for long prison terms. Prison where they could be raped every single day. I didn't need to be part of that. I wanted freedom. I wasn't going to let them take anything more away from me. I wasn't going to spend another second worrying about a trial. I knew they were going down for the drugs and that was enough." Cilla was nodding agreement.

"The creep that sold you to them went up against the wrong crook. He was tortured and left to die as an example and warning to everyone else. His wife left before he sold you. She's an addict and dying of aids. No one misses any of them. No one cares or mourns them"

"Your other fosters are old or dead. No one there looks suspicious," Cilla finished

"God," Becca said. "Good. I don't have to think about that anymore. So what's the problem? You don't look happy."

"I want to look into the freaky accident." Cilla said it quietly and waited. Not sure what to expect.

Stunned, Becca stopped breathing, started to fold. Ryan caught her. Helped her sit down. Jen was right there with a supporting arm, turning to Cilla with a silent angry question.

"Take a breath," Ryan said anxiously to Becca, who had turned white. "Take a breath. Sweetheart. Cilla doesn't have to do it. She doesn't have to look." He wasn't sure what Cilla meant, but whatever it was Cilla didn't have to do it. He was patting Becca gently on her back. Brushing back her hair. Eyeing Cilla, he demanded, "What just happened?"

Becca caught his hand, "I'm OK. I'm OK," she said as she drew in a deep breath. "Give me a minute. It was a shock."

They waited while her color came back into her face and she was breathing normally. And then she said to Cilla, "Cilla it was a freaky accident."

"I know. That's what everyone has always said. We say it. You say it. But what if it wasn't? And what is a freaky accident? No one has ever said. What happened to your parents? What just happened to you?"

Becca put her head back down and took more deep breaths. She moaned, "I don't know. I don't know. I woke up in the hospital, alone. That's all I know."

She looked up. There were tears in her eyes. "I never asked. How could I not ever ask what happened to my parents?" she wailed.

"No one ever asked. I never asked. We all just say, freaky accident," Cilla reminded her soothingly.

"You mean none of you know what type of accident killed her parents?" Ryan asked in amazement.

"I never even wondered," Cilla said. "How come I never asked? How could none of us ever ask? I guess we just assumed that Becca knew and didn't want to talk about it."

"I didn't. Didn't know. Didn't want to talk about it. Never wondered," Becca said in a quiet voice, closed her eyes for another minute. She had never needed to close her eyes before when she spoke, but now the darkness helped her gather her strength. In a stronger voice she said, "Find out Cilla. Find out what happened. What happened to my parents. To me. Please. How could I never have wondered?"

"Leave it," Ryan said. "You accepted what you were told. There was no reason to doubt it. Still isn't. Cilla doesn't need to look."

"No. Ryan. I do. None of us wondered. I'm not suggesting something was wrong. I just want to go back and look at it. Look at Becca. Her reaction alone should tell you that. Something is there."

"Yes, do it," Becca said, "I'll deal with it. Whatever you find, I'll deal." And she would too. She hoped. She'd dealt with the rest of it. "Just give me a few minutes here, please."

"Sure, we'll get food and drinks out and the table ready," Cilla said to give everyone some time.

"Jen's staying," Becca made it an order when it seemed that Jen was going to leave. Jen nodded. There was a lot she didn't know about Becca, but she knew Cilla. If Cilla questioned the circumstances of an accident, Jen thought that accident needed scrutiny. And she wanted to be here. She agreed that Becca's reaction meant the accident needed further investigation.

As they were getting ready, Jake, Mary Lee, and Tony walked in together with Cav right behind them.

Cav was heading for the table when he stopped short because there were new faces in the room. He hid his shock when he saw Mary Lee. Becca was having the same reaction. Here was the beauty queen whom Tony had been talking about. Mary Lee with her face scrubbed clean of make-up was stunning. Becca now knew why Mary Lee looked so plain before. She'd used the make-up to tone down the cheekbones, wash out her coloring, and minimize her eyes. Most women used make-up to beautify, Mary Lee used it to make herself look ordinary and blend in.

Tony was walking around the room, looking at the electronics the way Cav was looking at Mary Lee. "Wow, this is some setup," he said as he turned full circle. "I brought my laptop; can I hook into the large screen?"

"I'll do it. Our security is tricky," Becca said, as she took the tablet thankful for something to occupy herself with. She set up a link through a separate network.

Cav remembered his manners and stopped staring. He walked over to Becca, "I'm glad you're doing OK. We were worried about you for a while there."

"Thanks." What was one supposed to say? She motioned to Jake's people, "This is Mary Lee and Tony Parker. They work for Jake."

Cav shook hands with both and then clapped Ryan on the shoulder, "Let's eat. I'm starving. And Jake, you can explain what's going on here."

Becca let Ryan pull out her chair, noticing that Tony was doing the same for Mary Lee. "Mary Lee has been tailing my ex-boyfriend and Tony has been back tracking his work history on line. I've been helping Tony."

"You think your boyfriend shot you?" Cav asked surprised.

"No. It doesn't feel right. But I want to know for sure."

"That's why you're investigating him then?"

Jake answered for her. "We need to eliminate him from our possibles' list. We're looking at anything and everyone." After he'd passed the platters, Jake continued, "Becca reviewed all her cases and didn't find anything that would warrant a shooting. As did her Captain. He says random shooting. Ryan looked at her files and concurs. Becca also compared her notes to the official versions. Cilla insisted because of the Sheri affair; and everything matched."

"Right. The reason isn't in her case files," Ryan added.

Jake took over again. "While she was doing that we started a normal background check on the ex. We didn't expect to find anything. He broke it off, not her. And their relationship ended five days prior to the shooting." Jake paused, "We discovered last night he is probably undercover."

Cav stopped eating.

"Don't worry. We shut down the tail operation immediately. Called our operative, Mary Lee, back in," he said quickly. "We wouldn't do anything that might interfere with an official investigation. This morning Tony tracked Tom, the ex, back to Camden Investigations. He has been working for them for two years. Probably undercover that whole time. Tony, you find anything else out?"

"No, nothing new. We're still researching the names in the obituary."

Jake picked it up, "We tracked Tom through three different work histories and addresses. The oldest job has the link to Camden. I didn't know they were running this sort of operation. We thought you might be able to help." He stopped to give Cav a chance.

Cav was chewing on a fried chicken leg. "This is great," he said around a mouthful. He looked around the table and decided he could trust them. They had kept some high level government secrets. "Camden does do undercover work. Two years sounds about right. They go after embezzlement, drug use, theft, all kinds of things." He took another bite.

"As I hear it, Camden works it both ways. Some of his clients want to keep the problems in house and quiet. Some want to prosecute. Either way, we still get rumors. One case I know. Liquor store. Camden put a woman in as a switchboard operator for eight months. Everyone was stealing. The guy unloading booze at the back dock was taking a case here and there. The guy making up the delivery schedule was having a few cases dropped at his house every week. The delivery driver was drinking on the job. The pay roll supervisor was paying two people who didn't exist and pocketing the money. The advertising executive was submitting bills for non-existent advertising. He was paying bills for his brother-in-law who was in jail. Rent and electric were paid separate even though the landlord included utilities with the shop rental. The cashier was stealing from the till. A secretary was taking petty cash, stamps, and office supplies. Someone was even stealing toilet paper out of the bathrooms." He stopped to shake his head. "Camden turned that case over to us. The owners wanted everyone prosecuted. After everyone went to jail, one of the employees turned the owner in for bribing the state tax collector. Sometimes you just got to laugh."

He stopped and decided to go a step farther. "You got a name or a picture of the ex? Picture would be better. I know two or three of those men."

Tony passed it to him.

Becca held her breath. She didn't know if she wanted Cav to recognize him or not.

"No, this one isn't familiar, but can I pass it to someone I know?"

Jake looked at Ryan, and asked Cav, "He keep a secret?"

"Yes."

"OK then. We'd like to know if Tom Farwood is his real name. Not sure if that will help cross him off our list or not."

"What about New Madrid? If Becca and her Captain both agree that the shooter isn't in her files, why are you asking about New Madrid?"

"A couple of things. They retired her on full disability."

"So, she looks disabled."

"They did it the week after she got shot. They didn't know how severe her injury was or if it would be disabling. They didn't wait for a prognosis. The prognosis is full recovery. Her Captain told her he was against it, but it was decided by the Board."

"Humph. I can see where that might make you curious."

"Tony, you get anything on the Board?"

"The same five people have been on the board for twelve years. Each one has something a little borderline. I've listed their photos, addresses, phone numbers, and web info. Underneath are the marginal decisions. None has ever been in legal trouble. None is squeaky clean. Your task will be easier because one board member died eight months ago and another is on an around the world cruise. The remaining three decided on the disability. Didn't discuss it with anyone."

Cav was nodding, "You got most everything there that I know. But I can tell you a little bit more about each of them." He took a minute to put his thoughts in order.

"Chloe Rummel. She is for anything that appears to be pro women. Doesn't matter how stupid it is. She believes there is a war on women and it's her job to fight it. If she had known Becca had applied for a position, she would have pushed the Captain to hire her. Her Captain told me Rebecca was hired because she was the best man for the job." Cav nodded at Rebecca with a smile. "He also told me he promoted you because you are smart and intuitive. He didn't need to go to the Board for approval and he wasn't pushed into it by them. Becca was his first female hire, but he has added more to the ranks whenever one proved to be the most qualified. It's hard to believe that Chloe would vote to put Becca on disability without waiting for her prognosis. She's a reasonable woman in everything else and this decision doesn't make sense, especially from the women's movement point of view." He paused and moved on to the next.

"Sergio Nadeau, the Chairman, is letter of the law. Black or white, no in between. Only gray he has is the steel grey of his hair. He's a pain in the butt. Used to be a real ladies man; the type they like. Not much gossip since he got married, but there are rumors of a lover. No one knows who she is."

"Charlie Scott. He's a bail bondsman. I'm not saying this, but he can be bought by anyone with enough money. At least that is what I've heard. No one can prove anything. I'm surprised you didn't find any gossip on him Tony."

"Missed anything that even looked like that. But I intend to go back and look at all of them again and in depth." He didn't offer any excuses.

"Now that I know what you are looking for, I have one more source. Give me a minute," Cav pulled out his cell and tapped in a number. "Hey sweetie. Couple of months ago the Board agreed to put a cop on full disability. You know anything about that?" he asked. He listened a moment, "Yes, I would love to take you to dinner." Another short pause, he rolled his eyes, "Yes, I would love to take you to Lorenzo's. I'll pick you up at seven thirty. Now give." He took mental notes looking at Becca and nodding occasionally. The others continued eating and talked quietly until he put down the phone and grabbed another bite of chicken.

"Guess I have a dinner date." He looked around the table and said, "What? She's seventy if she's a day. Parties hard and late, can't call her before two. But she knows all the gossip, the stuff you can't print. And she can keep her mouth shut." He took another couple of bites.

"Here's how it worked. Scott made the proposal to Chloe. She could be the first one to give a woman a full disability package. A giant step for women's lib. Nadeau went along when he saw they were both going to vote for it. No one asked you, Becca, because you are the symbol, the token. Of a greater cause. No one worried about the money it would cost the county."

"And just like that, I'm out of a job I love?" Becca was fuming.

"Yep. Scott convinced her that this would be an important step for women. Remember I told you she's a little crazy on women's issues. What you wanted didn't count. It's a done deal and can't be undone."

She let that settle and then, "So someone knew he could buy Scott. And the same someone knew the lever to manipulate Chloe to get me removed from the police force. But why?"

"Why and who," Ryan added. "Guess we'll just have to find out," he said glancing toward Cilla meaningfully. He saw her exchange a smile with Becca and then she immediately started working on the tablet beside her plate. He was pretty sure Cilla was hacking into bank accounts. He should have felt more upset about it, but all they needed was a name. Once they had a name, then the investigation could be transparent. If the name was the shooter, they could come back at him legally with warrants.

Or Cilla could just be working on the game sequel. Probably both. Cav was still talking.

"You said something about cold cases?"

Becca explained.

"The Donavan kidnapping case. I remember that. It was FBI wasn't it? Didn't you guys close that?"

"Yes, we closed it. Michelle Donavan was kidnapped and killed by her boyfriend, B. J. Fanning, who then killed himself. But New Madrid didn't close the case," Ryan said. "I have the case files, ours, and New Madrid's. We're going to run our own investigation."

He pointed to another file.

"The other cold case was an armed robbery which wasn't really worked. Becca also has an unsolved armed robbery. Becca worked hers hard, did everything right. It's interesting, two unsolved armed robberies in five years. I don't like the coincidence of two unsolved armed robberies. My gut says there's a connection, that it's not a coincidence."

"I hadn't even made the connection. The cold case with my unsolved. We didn't even know about the earlier one when we worked ours," Becca said.

"Yeah, I don't see that you looked at it, at the cold case."

"I didn't think of that when I reviewed them that morning. I screwed up again. I never followed through."

"You would have. You can't do everything. You don't need to do everything, that's why you have us. Besides, I was looking at three cases, two of which were armed robberies. Of course they stood out. The methods are the same but the payoff is very different. One a jewelry store, the other a home invasion."

"You really think there might be a connection?" Becca asked Ryan.

"They have the same MO and both netted close to a half million dollars."

That had everyone's attention now. "If Becca and her partner followed every lead, it could be the crooks perfected their techniques after the first robbery. There might be a lead in that early case," Jake suggested.

"You know, I think we had one of those. Hold on," Cav got his cell out again and they heard him ask the dispatcher to search for armed robberies, cold cases. He waited a few minutes and then told her to email the results to his cell.

When he hung up he continued, "New Madrid has two. We have one. She'll send the file. I'm betting we find more if we look around to other counties. Or states, we're on the borders of four states and if I were a smart crook I would spread my robberies around to different jurisdictions."

Ryan saw Cilla go back to work on her tablet and said, "No, Cilla, this has to be legal. No hacking."

"I'm shocked and outraged," she said with a smile, "That you would accuse me of hacking. I'm doing Google and Bing searches on news articles on armed robberies going back ten years and within fifty miles and over half a million dollars." There was laughter around the table. It was a tossup what Cilla was actually doing and everyone knew it.

"Here we go, um New Madrid has two. My search didn't restrict to open cases. Two more in Camden. Two here. Eight, nine, fifteen. Here I'll just put the results on the big screen." By this time, Tony was standing behind Cilla. Watching her screen.

"Can you restrict to open cases, Cilla?"

"We can try, but newspapers aren't too good at reporting good news or solved cases. No, not here. Can't do anymore here. Can I write a program?" she asked herself, already seeing it in her head. "Do I have a database?"

"Try this search engine," Tony said and gave Cilla the address and his password.

"Two. These two are solved." She deleted them from the list. "Culprits caught a day later with the goods. That leaves um, thirteen. And this one. Here in Bear. You actually took them down during the robbery. So you only have the one open," as she removed another. "Back to twelve." Cilla was grinning to herself. Neat site. And now she had a password. She wondered if Tony would think to change it.

"I'll be changing the password in about ten minutes," Tony told her.

She tried to look chagrined, but knew that would be enough time to get herself a doorway. Jake was shaking his head.

Cav's cell buzzed. He read the printout. He handed his cell to her to download the case. They were silent as they compared the list of three crimes on the big screen. Bear's was a big box warehouse, six years ago, mostly cash. Same methods for all three. Compared them to the longer list.

"If these are all the same crooks, looks like one or two every year or so for the last, what, eight years? Spread over four states, multiple counties. What would we find if we went out to New York and Virginia?" Ryan wondered.

Cilla hit the keys. "Nothing. But that doesn't mean there aren't any. Just that I'm not pulling them up. And I might have extra ones in this list."

"Look at the timing. Can you sort by dates?"

"That fourth one doesn't fit the time schedule or they had a special two for one that year."

"Shit." Cav looked around the table. "You people. I swear. You attract the most complicated crimes. I barely know where to start with this."

"Wait a minute, we're not responsible. We're not the ones who didn't know there was a serial armed robber out there. All we did was point it out to you," Becca said. "I didn't ask someone to shoot me. We don't even know if these robberies are the reason."

"How could it be anything else?"

"Easy. Look at Tom. Look at Camden. Look at the freaky accident." She stopped there at Cav's surprise. "Forget that last one. Look at the kidnapping; we haven't even started to investigate that. I agree that the robberies could be the reason. But it doesn't feel that way," Becca insisted.

"Cav!" Cilla exclaimed outraged. "We drop a serial armed robber in your lap and you chastise us? We show you a crook who has been stealing for seven years. You should be thankful someone finally discovered a problem."

"I know. I know. I didn't mean it that way. But this is a mess." He looked around to Ryan for support. "Tell them."

Ryan was almost laughing. He could sympathize. "He's right. It's not a one time, simple crime, in a single locality. It's all over the map; it covers four states, about six local jurisdictions. Been ongoing forever. FBI will definitely lead on this. And coordinate the operation. I got to call my boss; he is going to be at least as happy as Cav." He looked at his watch. "Now, I guess." He got up and left the room.

Cav caught a look between Cilla and Becca. "What?" he grumbled.

They both burst out laughing. The others joined in.

"So what are we going to do?" Becca asked.

"Wait for Ryan. Then look at our options. Then make a plan. We don't touch any of this yet. Meanwhile we eat."

Ryan came back ten minutes later. Cilla was working on her tablet. That would have made him nervous, but Tony was still watching over her shoulder so she probably wasn't hacking anyone. "We need to shut down everything on Tom. Just temporarily." He looked around the table, "We don't want to put anyone in jeopardy." Meaning Tom. "We can leave Mary Lee on him. My boss will look into Camden, see what he can find. Get back to us."

"We'll stand down. We've done all the research. Mary Lee can still run a long tail. And I want Jen to stay on Becca." Jake said with Cilla nodding agreement.

"OK. I agree," Ryan said. "We keep Tom, the armed robberies, the kidnapping and the Board, but we'll use the FBI database. My boss will forward anything we might have. No locals. We don't contact any local jurisdictions. We don't know if the crooks have inside information. So we don't use any local informants or databases."

Becca spoke up, "We have my files on two of the cases. And Cav's files on another one."

"We'll look at them. I don't expect to find anything new. But we'll still look at them."

"My cold case. The old one, that was never really worked, we might find something there. And why didn't we work it back then? I've worked with these guys for five years. No one has been sloppy."

"She's right. If we do find anything it's going to be in one of those early cases," Cav agreed. "We worked ours to the bone. Never got a break. It was a perfect crime, no one slipped up. But I never tied it to any earlier robberies either."

"I was pretty raw when I worked our case. But my partner covered all the bases. We tried," Becca said to Ryan.

"I know. I'm hoping we get lucky with that first case of yours. Or by tying them together."

Before he could say more, Tony said, "You need Cilla and me. We might not know the law enforcement stuff, but you need us to dig through the files digitally. We'll use a 'board' for the results," he finished eagerly.

They all looked at him.

"Well they use them on TV. Murder boards. You know where the cops tack up pictures of the victims and persons of interest? Where they keep a time line?"

Becca came to Tony's rescue. "I use a board. It helps me visualize. And I don't think we're going to find the common denominator with the computer. Be too much to hope for that one name turns up in all the files. It's probably going to take some leg work. Nothing pops out from those cases on the screen."

"I don't know how you decide what to put on the boards; you'll have to help with that. I didn't mean to sound so eager, I know this is hard for you," Tony apologized.

"It's okay. We'll probably need more than one board. We have more than one investigation."

"Boss?" Tony just realized that he was working for Jake.

"Yes, it's a good idea. Especially with Mary Lee staying on Tom." Jake turned to the Sheriff, "Cav, how about assigning Jones to us. Can you spare him? Keep an eye on things here?"

"I was thinking the same thing. He has a good eye and he did good work with us before. Here though. The gatehouse. He doesn't go to New Madrid on the armed robberies. If it looks like we need leg work, we'll make a decision then."

"We don't want anyone to know we're looking into these robberies. We don't want to forget that we don't know who shot Becca or why. That's our priority. We can't afford to get sidetracked. And that's all these robberies are until we know better," Ryan reminded them. "We still need to follow up on the kidnapping and Cilla has her project. I'll start setting up appointments to interview the family, witnesses, and investigators in the kidnapping case."

"I'm going with you," Becca said.

"Never for a moment thought you wouldn't. I'll set up interviews for late morning. After therapy. You'll be an important liaison to the locals, Becca. I can interview the FBI agents over the phone. We'll start from the beginning and review everything we have."

"We need a board for that case too," Becca said, smiling at Tony. "And another to keep track of Tom," she added.

"Where do we get the boards?" Tony asked.

Cav was shaking his head. "I'll have Jones bring some. Let's finish dinner and clean up. Then I want to take a closer look at those robbery case files." He called Jones to give him a heads up for the next day.

Mary Lee was the first to leave, saying she wanted to check on Tom. "Can you get a ride back to your car Tony?"

"He can take my vehicle, I'll ride with Cilla," Jake said.

"I'll get some searches started on my tablet. You guys should trade in your boards for tablets," Cilla suggested.

"No, there is something about a hard copy. And a pen and notebook. Helps the brain think. Writing with a pen and sticking a picture to a board gives a whole different feel. Not even a giant screen can replace that. No, I'm not ready for a big screen yet," Becca declared.

They laid out plans for the next day and then Jake went home with Cilla as Tony headed back to the office, and Cav went back to the station.

Becca was sitting on the couch; Ryan put the quilt over her. She looked up in surprise.

"You looked cold. And I know you're tired. Rest a bit. Want me to get you a book?"

"No, I'm just going to sit a minute and then head to bed. It's been a long day."

"I'm going to get my notes organized and a contact list for tomorrow. We can tell the family the FBI is reviewing the case. We'll leave your current status vague. They'll recognize your name and assume you're local still. Jen can be my partner. See how long before someone contacts New Madrid if at all. But I am going to call your Captain and notify him. We don't want him surprised. My information says he's a good man. And he was the one who gave you the cases." He was waiting for her reaction.

"Good. I don't want to go behind his back."

Thursday

Jen picked them up promptly at ten. "I drive, Ryan is shotgun. Becca backseat. Same rules apply. Ryan can go first, but I'll still take a quick look around before you get out of the vehicle or go into a building. You behind Ryan, in front of me, Becca."

Their first appointment was with the victim's great aunt, Lydia Donavan. Becca expected a McMansion but they found an ordinary house in a quiet upper class neighborhood of large homes. This was a white colonial with an ell. They parked in the U-shaped driveway. Ryan identified himself to the housekeeper when she answered his knock. "We're expected," he told her. She nodded and led them back to what was probably called a sunroom. The walls and ceiling were mostly glass, the furniture a white wicker, plants were everywhere. The room was toasty, almost too warm. An elderly lady lifted herself awkwardly out of a chair. Becca could identify with that.

"Please have a seat," she motioned to the other chairs. Becca sat as Ryan went over and introduced them. "Ryan Gibbs, Special Agent, FBI, Mrs. Donavan. This is Detective Rebecca Anne Travis, and Jen Garrett." He sat and began by saying, "The FBI wants to close out the case on your great niece's murder. We have a few questions."

After she quietly asked her housekeeper to bring coffee and scones, she snapped angrily at Ryan, "You should have a lot more than a few questions. You people never even investigated in the first place."

"What do you mean," Ryan asked gently.

"I called the FBI because my great niece was kidnapped and she was dead before you even got here. Those detectives in New Jersey said that B.J. had kidnapped and murdered her and then killed himself. I told them he would never do that. They were in love. He'd never hurt her. I told your agent that too, but he treated me like a senile old lady. Took a quick look around Michelle's room, talked to my great nephew, Steven, a few minutes and left. No one else ever came back. When I called the local police, they just said the FBI was in charge. All the FBI would say was the case was closed. It's about time you got around to investigating."

"You are entirely correct, Mrs. Donavan. Can you help us now? Can you tell us what happened the day your great niece disappeared?" Ryan was at his best when trying to get information.

The coffee arrived then and they helped themselves. Jen stayed in a corner, watching.

"I thought she was off with B. J. They were planning something. They both were giddy. It was so much fun to watch them. They were so in love. Like they had invented it. They left early that morning saying they would have a surprise for me later that night." She stopped and tried to hide a tear. "You know, she moved in here when I fell. To help take care of me. Said I shouldn't be alone. Hired Jane, my caretaker slash housekeeper. Used her own money, from her trust, because she didn't want to worry about me when she was in school or at work. She was so sweet. I miss her so much."

"Yes ma'am," Ryan said.

"Anyhow, that's not what you asked. They left around seven. Steven got the e-mail around three when he got home from golfing."

"Steven being your great nephew," Ryan inserted. "He lives here too?"

"He moved into the west wing when he found out Michelle was upstairs. He got the email when he returned home and came racing in to show me. I called the FBI immediately. I've never done that before. When the agent arrived an hour later he broke the news that Michelle and B .J. were dead. He said it was murder suicide and wouldn't listen to me when I told him that would never happen. He had a local police-man with him, but never let him say anything. Like I said, they spent about five minutes in Michelle's room and then had that talk with Steven. And that was it. They were gone."

Ryan looked at his notes. The agent had relied on the N.J. cops, but nothing in the notes said murder suicide. The bodies and later, the autopsy, showed that Michelle had been shot running away and B. J. had died from a gunshot wound to the head.

"Who inherited Michelle's trust? Steven?"

"No. He expected to, but she made a will. Left it to me. I was surprised. Steven was incensed."

"Do you suppose we could look at Michelle's room?" he asked gently.

"It has all been done over. Steven had it cleaned out that same week. Took all her things to Goodwill. Even her furniture. He kept her laptop. Then he had the room painted. There is nothing of her left."

Becca couldn't stand it. That was the saddest story she ever heard. She went over and held the old woman while she cried.

When Mrs. Donavan wiped her eyes, Ryan asked, "Is there anyone else we can talk to? A friend? Someone who might be able to tell us what your great niece was planning that day? Would Steven know?"

"Not Steven. They didn't get along. But her friend Dana, Dana Lincoln, she might know. Dana tried to get the police to listen too. But she got the same treatment I did. And B.J.'s roommate, Slim Turner. They both still come to see me. And call. We stay in touch." She pulled out her cell phone, "I'll call them and tell them you want to talk." As she did that Ryan was wondering about Steven.

"Tell me about Steven. He moved in after Michelle came to help? What does he do?"

"He golfs. He goes to the night clubs. He lives in the ell, I don't ever see him"

"We have an appointment with him after lunch. At the golf course. Meanwhile we'll go talk to Slim and Dana. Where do they want to meet us?"

"B.J.'s old apartment. Slim was his roommate. He married Dana. They live there," she said it with a soft smile. And then added, "How come it took so long?"

"What took so long?"

"Some woman called about two months ago and said you were going to reopen the case."

"What woman? Did she identify herself? Say who she was with?"

"Yes, but I don't remember. Some secretary. Said the detectives were going to reinvestigate and would be in touch with me. How come it took so long?"

"Sometimes it takes time, but we're here now," Ryan said gently. "We'll get back to you. Thanks for your help."

Becca gave her a hug as they left.

When they got back in the car Becca said, "It wasn't this case. I didn't get shot because of the kidnapping."

"Doesn't look that way right now. But we still need to work the case," Ryan said, "We need to look at that autopsy report again. I have a feeling we might have missed something. On paper this case looked open and shut. But our case files only show part of what was done in New Jersey. Just a few notes on that interview with Lydia. Pages of notes with Steven's version. It will be interesting to see what Dana and Slim have to say. Lydia doesn't come across as senile."

Both Slim and Dana backed up Lydia's version. "No one would listen to us," Dana said. "But those two were so in love. They were so happy. I can't believe that B.J. even owned a gun let alone that he used one."

Slim backed her up. "He called, that morning, he called. Said they were eloping. He was so happy. But the FBI said that Michelle must have decided to back out, so he shot her. That would never have happened,"

"But they found the ransom note sent from his cell phone. They thought he must have decided if he couldn't have her no one would," Ryan said.

"No way man. No way. Those two? Didn't care about money. Well, of course they cared, but it wasn't a driving force for them. Sure Michelle had access to her trust fund. But only a limited amount. She used it for her aunt. B.J. thought she should. She didn't come into the full amount yet, not for five years. We were all going into business together. We had it all planned out." He reached for Dana's hand. "We did it ourselves. Took a little longer without them. And longer too because the murder was so awful we almost didn't go through with it. It was tough. But we're doing okay now. We'll do better if you find out what really happened."

Everyone was quiet for a few minutes. "Do you know what happened to B.J.'s stuff? Did his parents come and get it?" Becca asked.

"His parents. They didn't want anything to do with him. Told me to dispose of everything. Never even questioned that he might not have done it." Slim was disgusted.

"His stuff is in the closet. We couldn't just heave it out. Some of Michelle's things are there too. Here I'll show you, if you want to go through it. Not much here. We were all students. We didn't have much."

There were two suitcases, and a sack of items.

"Can we take these? We'll return them after we look through them."

Dana looked at Slim. "Sure," he said shrugging his shoulders. "I guess. Especially if you're going to look at the case again."

"Tell us about Steven," Becca said when it looked like Ryan was done.

Again a look passed between Dana and Slim. "He's a jerk. A stuck up freeloader. He hated that Michelle would get a trust and he wouldn't. He lives in Mrs. Donavan's house, eats her food, and never even checks in on her. He makes me so mad."

Ryan carried the suitcases down and came back for the sack.

"Most of the things in that bag were Michelle's except the cell phone. That was B.J.'s. The cops returned it when they were done. A lot of his stuff is still in evidence bags in the suitcases. We never opened them," Dana explained.

"Mrs. Donavan might like some of Michelle's things. She said she didn't have anything because Steven took everything away."

"I didn't know that. I hate him. Mean. Spiteful. Ghoul. When you're done with those, I'll take them to Lydia."

"That would be good."

Slim saw them to the door. "You'll let us know? Right? What you find?"

"When we bring his belongings back."

As they walked away, Jen said, "I think I agree with Dana. I'm mad too. I don't think I'm going to like Steven."

"We'll judge for ourselves. Meanwhile, we're meeting the New Madrid investigator for lunch. This cell phone might be a find."

Detective Khalen wasn't waiting for them. He had already started on a pastrami and rye. He stood up when they reached his table, a smile on his face for Becca. He hugged her close. "Good to see you walking," he said. "Actually a relief. How are you feeling? You didn't look so well the last time I saw you."

"Wasn't doing so well then. But pretty good now and it is a relief to be walking even if it is with a cane."

"How come you left? Looks like you could come back," he asked her.

"I didn't leave. They cut me loose. Didn't give me a choice."

"The Captain?"

"No. The Board. Some kind of women's lib equality thing."

"Jerks." Then he looked at Ryan. "Not the only jerks though."

"You're right," Ryan acknowledged. "But maybe we can work together. It was good of you to meet us."

"Only meeting with you because of Travis." He said still hugging her. "You jerks don't rate a meet. Don't ever listen to the locals."

"Paul," Becca said calmly. "We need your help."

He studied Jen. "Who's this? You look a little familiar but FBI is not ringing any bells for me."

"Jen Garrett, I'm with Becca." She didn't explain but shook hands.

Khalen regarded Jen speculatively, "Jen Garrett? Wife of Ron Garrett? Bodyguard?" he asked. "You're acting like a bodyguard." It was a statement; he'd watched her enter.

"Um, yeah," Jen admitted reluctantly.

"You hired Safe Keeping?" he asked Becca.

Becca sighed; she supposed she would have to explain. "Sort of. My sister is married to Ron Garrett's partner." She wasn't able to say brother-in-law yet.

"You don't think that was a random shooting." Another statement.

"No. Doesn't feel that way."

"You involved with that stuff that went down in Delaware? Near Bear? All the front page news? The white slavery?" Paul asked Becca directly.

"No. But Jen was. And my sister. And her husband, and Ron; Ryan here. A whole bunch of people."

He thought about that for a minute, "Ron vouch for Ryan?" he asked Jen.

"Sure will. He's a good cop. Can we eat? I'm hungry."

"Order at the counter. They'll bring it over."

"Pastrami on rye," Becca said, just assuming Ryan would order. Jen seconded it, as she motioned Becca to the inside seat. Becca and Paul talked local gossip until Ryan came back.

Becca started. "We need your help Paul. But you have to keep it quiet."

When he hesitated, Ryan added, "I talked to your Captain; he knows what we're doing. Becca means quiet from anyone else. You can tell him everything we say here."

Ryan waited for acknowledgement and continued, "We're looking into the Donavan kidnapping."

"You think that had something to do with your shooting?" Paul asked Becca.

"Maybe. We don't know. It's one of a couple of cold cases I caught the morning I got shot."

"Well we were pretty much cut out of that one. The kidnapping happened in Jersey. The ransom note was delivered here in New Madrid. The FBI took over even before we heard about it." He looked at Ryan when he said that. "They let us go with them to interview the aunt. That's it. We didn't get to say anything."

"We read your report. What we want is what you thought. About the aunt, the cousin. Anyone else you talked to."

"The aunt was broken up, distraught. Not just at her niece's death. The great niece. She didn't believe that the boyfriend did it. She was the one that called the FBI when the great nephew showed her the ransom note on his laptop. She made sense to me. But your agent already knew all the answers. He wasn't listening to her. He did listen to the cousin. Thought the cousin sounded more reasonable. At least what the cousin said fit with his version of the facts. The guy was real scum. Called the girl a freeloader. Said the boyfriend was using her. A lot more along that line. The fibbie didn't want to take it any further. Said it was wrapped up, he'd just wait for the autopsy and file it. Didn't want to talk to anyone else."

He looked at Becca, "We didn't have any authority to talk to Jersey. Didn't have anything to work with. I filed it as turned over to the FBI. But I left it open. Felt open to me."

"Feels that way to us too." As they ate Becca filled him in on what they had so far. And then added to Ryan, "I know this is five years later, and that cell has no chain of custody, but we need to dust it."

Ryan nodded, "You're wondering if we might find some unexplained prints on it?"

"Yes. I'd like to know whose prints are on the keys. And I think I remember that the gun used in the shooting had a couple of unidentified prints," she was talking as she was thinking. "I wonder if we can get Steven's prints during our interview this afternoon."

Ryan was still nodding, "Khalen, can you run the cell? We have it in the car. I can forward the FBI file to you with the unknown prints found on the gun. Can you run a comparison? With those and with B.J.'s?

Paul was interested. "Yes, I can. I'll run it by the Captain first. But our case is still open, won't be a problem. If you get prints from the cousin, Travis, we can run those too. Wouldn't that be something if they came up a match?"

"It makes more sense. Steven is jealous. Follows them. Realizes if they get married he will never see any of that trust money. Threatens them. Shoots Michelle as she tries to run away. The boyfriend jumps him and gets shot as they struggle for the gun. Could have happened that way. Then Steven decides to make it look like a kidnapping murder suicide and sends that email ransom note from B.J.'s cell. His prints really could be on that cell and the gun. No one tested the cell for prints. Just assumed they would be B.J.'s." Becca was getting excited now. "Pull up the autopsy, Ryan. Seems like the coroner said something funny about the gunshot residue on B.J.'s hand. The residue had voids? Like maybe, someone else was also holding the gun. Let's see if there are pictures."

They all peered at the pictures on the tablet.

"Could be. That void could be caused by a second hand."

"Let's not jump to conclusions. We don't want to be like the guy who did the first investigation," Ryan cautioned.

"This feels right though, Ryan, admit it."

"Yes it does, but just the same, keep an open mind. Will you do it Khalen? Run the prints?" Ryan asked again.

"Oh yeah, we can do it. Give you guys a black eye. Happy to. Let's go get that phone and you send that file to the Captain."

"I'm happy now," Jen said after Paul left. "I like the idea of Steven being the bad guy. How are you going to handle him?"

"Depends on his attitude. Just follow my lead."

They got into the golf club by explaining that Steven Donavan was expecting them. Donavan, tall, thin, well dressed, arrogant, petulant, Becca thought, was waiting for them in the lunchroom. He didn't bother to stand when they came in. Ryan recognized that as a power move and introduced himself not bothering with his two companions. Let him think they were insignificant. Jen was doing her job, staying close to Becca, and taking a cue from Ryan's attitude making it seem as if she was a little bit in awe of the situation. "Well, sit down. Tell me what this is all about. My cousin was killed five years ago."

"We're going through files and discovered that your statement was unsigned. Before we can put a final close on the case, I need you to sign it. I know it seems unimportant but you're dealing with a bureaucracy that must have all the i's dotted and t's crossed." He acted a little nervous.

"My tax dollars at work, three agents for a signature," Donavan grumbled.

"Training," Ryan said derisively, dismissing his companions as unimportant.

"Did you lose my original statement?"

"Hard to say what happened. Let me just go over this with you. And then you can sign." He pulled Donavan's original statement out of his briefcase, the one he'd made up without a signature just for this purpose. "Let's see," he put on his glasses. "I'll just hit the high points. You state that Michelle and her, um, boyfriend, by name, Bernard Jacob, were taking advantage of your great aunt Lydia. Taking money. Stealing items from the house." He looked up, "Doesn't say what items. Can I insert a few in here? Do you remember?"

"That was a long time ago. Are you sure it's not in there?"

"No," he replied with a frown. "Just one or two will make this look better. I can add them at the bottom with today's date."

"Well, a lamp, tiffany, from the spare bedroom. And goblets from the dining room."

"Good, good," Ryan said writing down the items. "You also say they were always fighting. What about? I don't see anything here."

"They fought about the time of day, I don't remember."

"OK. Not important. Now, let's see," he continued. "Oh, here, you say they were arguing about money that morning. You heard them when they left. That's good, that's good. You ever hear them talk about anyone else? Mention any names?"

Donavan thought about that, "No, I don't think I ever did."

"Ever hear them call someone? It would be good to eliminate any chance that there might have been someone else involved. They both had cell phones, right? How long ago is five years? Everyone had cells back then, didn't they?"

Becca held her breath. If Ryan could get Donavan to state that he never touched B.J.'s phone, and they found his prints on it…

"How would I know? That was five years ago," Donavan said crossly.

"Well that's okay. If you don't remember, we don't need to put that in."

"Michelle had a phone. I saw her use it. I don't know about B.J., I was never around him. He might have had one or not. I never saw it. I guess he could have sent the ransom note from a phone. I had always assumed he used a computer. But I never saw his phone."

Gotcha, Becca thought. Ryan was good.

"How about a gun? Any idea where he would have gotten a gun?" Ryan asked as if unconcerned as he wrote the cell information at the bottom of the statement.

"I've wondered about that too," Donavan said and asked, "You guys couldn't find where he got that? You lose statements, can't find guns, not as good as the papers make you out to be," he taunted.

"Well, that was the old FBI," Ryan said defensively. Becca hung her head because she couldn't keep a straight face. Donavan was going to walk right into this trap.

"No idea huh? About the gun?" Ryan asked as if really wanting his help.

"Well I bet he would have gone to a different state to buy it. No one would think to look in New York or Delaware. You can't have a gun in D.C. right? But then he probably would need a state driver's license to get a gun. You guys only looked in Pennsylvania because that's where he lived; bet you didn't find anything here. I'll bet he just bought it on the street. He was the type of person who would know how to do that. I'd have no idea how that works."

Becca had to turn away. Him? Donavan? Had he shot her? He fit her profile. Slimy, cowardly. But no, she didn't think so. He thought he was safe and that the FBI was stupid. He didn't even know about her.

"Right, I'll bet you're right. Too late to check it now of course. Doesn't matter, the killer is dead. Okay, read this over, initial the additions, and sign and date at the bottom." He handed Donavan his pen. They watched as he read every word, making them wait. Then initialed and signed.

Ryan handed a different pen to Jen. "You two sign as witnesses."

And now they had fingerprints. All over the document and Ryan's pen. Ryan carefully put the document and pen into a folder in his briefcase. "Sorry we had to bother you. We had your aunt sign a statement this morning too. We can put this case to bed. Thanks for your time."

They were out. Becca could barely contain herself. Jen put a hand on her arm. "I'm still guarding. Stay aware." Then to Ryan, "Think it's him? Think he shot them? Is it really too late to check gun sales?

"Yes, I think he shot them. No one looked at Donavan back then. He just admitted he didn't know how to buy a gun off the street, but he knew he couldn't buy one out of state. Isn't it interesting that he knew that. Let me get someone looking at Pennsylvania records. Could he be that dumb? To buy it here, using his own name? And let's get these prints to Khalen. Donavan is the only one who said that Michelle and B.J, argued. He made the case against B.J. If his prints are on the phone we have his statement that he never saw it."

They drove to the station. Becca phoned and asked Khalen to meet them outside. "I haven't heard back yet on your fingerprints," he said annoyed.

"We have more. We have Donavan's. Come on outside and we'll explain. Bring evidence bags."

He brought the Captain. Ryan got out. Jen too. Becca was to stay in the car. The Captain looked in, "Becca, how are you doing?" he asked.

"OK, Captain. Paul fill you in?"

"Yeah." He turned to Jen, "I know your husband," he said. "Heard he married a biker chick. Can't say you are quite what I imagined."

"I'm in disguise. The tats are under the long sleeves. I left the leathers home." She shook hands laughing.

He turned to Ryan next, "I checked up on you after you called. People say you're fair. A good cop. What have you got?"

"Need an evidence envelope for this. It's Donavan's old statement with a few additions he made today. And signed today. We told him we lost the old one. Note the last few sentences, which he initialed."

The Captain skimmed the print part. Read the last initialed comments." His gaze jerked back up at Ryan with the beginnings of a smile. He dropped the document in a bag that Khalen held open. "You think these are going to match what we find on the cell and the gun." It was a statement not a question.

"Oh, yeah. That document and this pen," Ryan dropped that in another bag, "Have his fingerprints all over them."

"I like the way you think," the Captain said.

"I have our people checking gun sales here," Ryan said. "You can probably do it quicker. He would have used his own ID. No one checked five years ago."

"Go, Paul, see what you can find. Any problems call me." Turned his attention back to Gibbs. "So how did the FBI decide to get involved in a five year old kidnapping?" he asked Ryan.

Becca answered, "Ryan's a friend of my sister's husband, um, Jake Jayden."

"Ron's partner. Jake Jayden is your brother-in-law?" he asked.

She wasn't sure she wanted to claim him, but she didn't see an escape. "You know him too?"

"No. But he made a good name for himself when he made that white slavery bust. Fibbers took that sting over too, but everyone knows Jayden did it. Paid a steep price for it. So you're related? Guess you two can compare bullet holes and leg wounds."

She could just picture that. It startled a laugh out of her.

"You going to work for him? He has a good rep in the field."

Her Captain liked what he knew about Jake? Becca was going to have to start calling him her brother-in-law. She sounded like an idiot saying sister's husband. She glanced over at Ryan, but he just appeared curious.

"I don't know. He hasn't offered me a job. I think I want to stay on the official side. Moot point until I get one hundred percent." she added to cover her awkwardness. "Ryan's a friend of my sister's too. He came to visit over the weekend and invited himself into our, uh, investigation of my shooting. This kidnapping is one of the cold cases you dropped on my desk that morning."

He considered her silently, "OK. Forgot about those. I'm not going to ask about the other case." He changed the subject, "I guess we are out in the parking lot and Becca is inside an armored car because you think this might be tied to her shooting? You don't want anyone to see her."

Ryan was surprised the Captain noticed all that, but Becca had said he was good. "You could see if Donavan has an alibi for the night she was shot. If you bring him in, if you get a match on the prints. But our gut feeling is it's not him. Doesn't feel like it."

"You're just giving us this case? You can't tell me you don't have your own evidence bags."

"We screwed it up the first time. You and Becca got it started. She's yours. You're doing the work. You'll interview the same people we did. Get statements. Probably get some stuff we missed." Though he doubted they had missed anything. He knew the Captain would decide to run the serial number off the gun themselves. And ballistic fingerprints if they could find shell casings from when the gun was sold. He didn't need to suggest it. Becca kept quiet too.

"Thanks. It rankled when the feds ran roughshod over us." His phone buzzed. He listened a moment.

"I think you folks are going to want to see what we found. We'll go in the back way. Put Becca in the middle. She can keep her head down."

When the forensics technician saw Becca he broke into a wide grin, ran over, and hugged her. "Girl, how you doing? You look fine. Don't know about that cane though. You going to keep that thing?"

"Hey, Johnny," she smiled at him and hugged him back. "Thanks for the flowers and toys. They kept me going. And no I'll be walking without the cane soon."

"Anything for you, girl. Sorry you got shot. You brought us these prints?" he asked excitedly.

"She did, along with these guys. FBI Agent Ryan and Jen Garrett, bodyguard. You never saw Becca today," Khalen instructed.

"Okay. Okay. I got it," he told Paul and then turned to Becca. "Miss you girl. Come on over and see what we got. You're going to love this."

"Here's Donavan's prints. The right index and thumb match the two on the weapon. So he handled it at some time. The gun is good evidence since we have a chain of custody on it. And look here," He pointed with his pen at images of the dusted cell. "We have multiple prints from the owner, B.J. On top of his prints, partly obliterating some, we have Donavan's. On most of the letters. On top of some of Donavan's prints we have the FBI agent who handled the case. He checked the phone for the ransom note, found it there, and didn't do anything else. Never dusted it for prints. With this we can prove conclusively that the ransom note was typed by Donavan's fingers. Ta Da!!! Unfortunately we don't have chain of custody."

"If the fibbie had just gone one step further five years ago," Khalen started. "Well, we got it now. We checked gun purchases and you were right on there, Gibbs, Donavan purchased the same model gun two weeks before the shooting. I know the serial number was filed off but no way is that guy smart enough to remove it completely. Your people should be able to pull it up. Then we'll have him cold with that also. Can you run interference for us?"

Ryan smiled as he pulled out his cell and called his boss. He walked into a corner to explain what had happened with the FBI's closed case.

When he came back he heard Khalen saying that they were going to check the golf club, see if they had records back five years. He was pretty sure they would not find Donavan's name there. And check the EZ-Pass. He'd bet Donavan used it on his trip to Jersey. Ryan smiled, because he hadn't thought of either of those. They had found something he missed

"I didn't even think of that," Ryan admitted, "Good work. And my boss is putting a rush on that gun. Here's his number," he handed it to Paul, "Go directly to him. He's expecting you. We have B.J.'s gear in the car. Want to send someone for it? There's a laptop too. Might be something on it. Return it to Slim Turner. We promised they would get everything back."

The Captain told them, "We're going to take our time with this. Call Jersey, see what they got. If they want to work with us. Get all our forensics together. Not going to repeat the mistakes made the first time. Thanks for your help here."

"Becca did it. She was just finishing the job you gave her. Glad it worked out so well. Let us know when you get him? How it goes down?"

"Sure. And if you need anything on that other case, give us a call. We'll leave it alone till we hear from you."

They all shook hands. "Let me know where you end up? We can always use a new contact," he said to Becca.

Becca slept on the way back, woke when the car door opened. Took a minute to orient herself and realize she had slept all the way home. She moved to get out but Ryan, who was outside her door, motioned for her to wait. Oh, right, Jen had to clear the gatehouse. Like that made any sense. No one would get through the gate. And Jen would have checked the security system to see if anyone had stopped at the entrance. But they were only doing their jobs. She could wait. Meanwhile she played back the day with a smile. Ryan was good at getting people to tell him what he wanted to know. Good at getting along with the locals, too. Probably why he had moved up in the ranks. She wondered for a moment what happened to the agent who had originally worked the case. Promoted or fired? Either one was possible with the fibbies. She might think to ask. Or wait and see if the information just came out. She decided that she would practice using brother-in-law for Jake and drop the term fibbies, it was insulting.

Jen came out with the all clear. "Call Jake if you need me tomorrow I can bring my knitting and see how you set up your boards this was fun can we solve another case tomorrow?" All that in one breath as she climbed in the car and left.

"Is she ever going to come down?"

Ryan laughed, "She thinks we're Starsky & Hutch. Or Holmes and Watson. She didn't say who was who though. I told her that cases don't all come together like this one today."

The boards were set up around the perimeter of the room with neat stacks of paper on the table. Three large stacks, a double stack, and multiple short stacks. She went over to look, with Ryan close behind.

Two of the tall stacks were her open armed robbery cases. The third was Cav's. The double stack was the Donavan kidnapping; one pile was the New Jersey file; the other was the FBI file. Need to change that she thought, not a kidnapping, or a murder suicide, but a double murder. "I need to put this up on the board. Even though I'm sure we resolved it today, I need to see it on the board."

"Me too. Make sure we got it right this time. See if we missed anything. I hadn't thought of checking the golf club for an alibi. Or the EZ-Pass," he admitted. "Don't want to do what the first agent did. Decide it's solved before it is."

"Paul's good. Thorough. He won't overlook anything. I told you."

"You were right. Your Captain is sharp too. He didn't miss a trick."

"They're good cops. Good men too. I was lucky to get to work with them." She yawned. She was beat even though she had slept all the way back. Wiped her eyebrow with her finger.

Ryan noticed. "Let me check the fridge for food. Might be something we can get quick. You rest."

She walked around the table, looking at the short stacks. "These are the other armed robberies." She fingered through a pile. "All off the web from multiple search engines. Google, Bing, DuckDuckGo. Oops, these look like official departmental files." She looked at him guiltily. How much would he overlook?

She read some more, "Huh. They are the official files. But they got these cold cases from official public online websites." She looked over to Ryan, "There's information on cold cases on the web? I didn't know that. I'll bet Cilla was disappointed she didn't get to hack into the files. More than ten of these cases though. And here's one from Virginia. Tony and Cilla have been busy. I can work on the robberies tomorrow," she decided out loud.

"What did you find?"

"A salad of greens, tomatoes, strawberries, and blueberries." He held it out.

"Mine," she said snatching it away.

"Yes, it has your name on it. And one here for me that is chicken, pepper, and potato salad. And pie for dessert." He put both on the counter then went back for paper plates, and napkins, and plastic silverware.

"I like the way you think. No washing."

"Been a long day, we don't have to add work."

They ate in silence for a while. "You're pretty good," she announced.

"Hmm?"

"Interrogation. You knew what you wanted him to say and you led him into it. Convinced him to tell it to you like it was his idea."

"Well, that's my job, interviewing."

"How do you do it?"

"Just encourage them to go where they want. Show them the way. Let them tell me. Of course, it's easy when they're arrogant and stupid. He told us exactly how he did it."

"You had him eating out of your hand from the very beginning. Not introducing us worthless underlings did it. Made you the man. How did you know?"

"Body language. You saw it too. Superior, important, smarter than the rest of us. But I had another reason. I didn't want him to know you were from New Madrid and I didn't want to lie. He could use that subterfuge later as a defense in court."

"Well, it sure worked."

"Go set up your board on Donavan. I'll do the cleanup." He threw the trash away, put leftovers in the fridge, making a mental note to thank Annie. He pulled out his own laptop and typed his report, watching as Becca worked on her board. Intense. Talking to herself. Sorting, arranging, rearranging. When she was done, she stepped back and they both studied it.

"I think we're right. It was Steven. I wonder if there is anything on B.J.'s computer." She circled laptop on the board and then wrote laptop under Michelle's name. "Do you suppose he still has Michelle's laptop? Could he still be using it? I guess we'll find out soon enough."

He sent his file off. "Let's hit the sack. You got all these other boards to do tomorrow."

She considered them longingly. Wanted to do them now. "You're right. I should do those when I'm fresh. Tomorrow will be time enough."

Friday

She wanted to start on her boards immediately but she had to do her exercises. She'd decided overnight to arrange the boards chronologically with four cases to a board. The New Madrid cases and Cav's case would rate one board each. She had another board labeled summary. Here she would have a list of the cases by date, another list by type of theft. Each would have a column to show the source for the information, search engine, or official web site. She'd have a map with each location marked. Maybe she'd see a pattern

Ryan had read through the stacks while Becca exercised and made a few notes. He cooked a light breakfast while she showered. He wondered how she would like the oatmeal, but was disappointed when she just poured cream over it, added some strawberries, and dug in. He used cream and brown sugar.

He cleaned up and then watched again as she went to work on her boards. She worked slowly taking the cases chronologically, numbering each one. He had wondered how she would set up the boards. He was as curious as Tony.

"Looks like Cilla and Tony went back twelve years and lowered the minimum value to $100,000. That makes sense. And they found more cases. A lot."

Meanwhile, Ryan checked his e-mails and found projects from his Director. Files he was to review and forward. Plus one FBI file on an armed robbery of a casino near Philly. Nothing yet on Camden Investigations.

He printed out the file. Put it beside the stacks on the table. "Here, we had this robbery. That makes four we have case files for."

He called a lunch break at one; hot chicken soup and BLT's. Becca might be eating, but her eyes kept going back to the boards and stacks of paper.

"Let's take a walk. I need to stretch my legs. You need to get away from your boards," a suggestion or an order? But she did need a break.

They followed the paved path in the garden. Her leg had stiffened up and needed the workout. She had mostly been standing on the good leg and pivoting between the table and the boards. Had he known that? The fresh air felt good.

"Cilla did the garden," she said. "It amazes me that a woman so skilled and tied to inanimate computers can make nature beautiful. This was all overgrown when I lived here. She started then. Funny, the things you remember. One day she brought a thistle she had dug up by its roots. Said she wanted me to have it but couldn't kill it by cutting it. It reminded her of me, all thorny points with a beautiful fragile center. Another time she brought a yellow daisy, a kind of Black-Eyed Susan she said. She called it a Rudbeckia and made a joke of the play on words. Rude Becca. She planted it by the door. Over there, that's her daisy garden. I laugh whenever I see them. They remind me I'm loved."

"She is a remarkable woman. I like rude becca. Makes me jealous that she got to make that comparison first." He was laughing.

Becca didn't want to discuss herself or them, "Tell me about the Inn."

He got a grin on his face. "The Inn belongs to my daughter-in-law and has been in her family three generations. It's in a pretty, quaint, town in Florida. Right on the Gulf. Marina across the street has shops owned by local artists. Maybe someday I'll show you." And here they were right back to them again. But he realized that was not what she wanted to hear. She was backing off.

So he told her more of the Inn. "People down there, Cougars Cove, it's called. It's like an old time community. People look out for each other, like the gang. Take care of each other. My daughter-in-law's employees are third generation too. They ran the place. Ran it around me. Posing leading questions like "Tomorrow's Saturday," they'd say. "It's always busy. Should we come in early? We generally do." Or gently reminding me how to do things, "Rosy always goes home early on Wednesday, remember?"

He laughed, "After two days of that, I just told them to give me a job and tell me what to do. They put me on the desk and in the office where I wouldn't get in the way. Gave me detailed instructions. They even did most of the caretaking with my granddaughter." As they strolled through the garden he entertained her with funny Inn stories. She laughed hard at the last one and said, "You are lying. That never happened. Snow in Florida?"

"Well, yeah, that didn't actually happen at the Inn. I got it from a book called "The Bread is in the Bed". It's a good tale and I've always wanted to tell it."

Becca worked on her boards while Ryan made notes on the files his boss had sent.

When she was done she stepped back, sat on the couch, and studied the cases. "What do you think?" she asked him.

"The early ones, before the home invasion, don't match."

"Right, those were totally different. But Cilla and Tony included everything." She erased them, waiting.

"And numbers three and eight don't belong."

She was nodding, "Because?"

"Number three is just a week after the second crime. None of the others came that close together. Pretty clear the way you set up the boards."

"And?"

"Number eight? People were hurt. All the others were pulled off without any injuries. Except the first and those were minor injuries."

"I think so too. And number nine doesn't fit either."

He looked at that one again. "Right. The payoff is too small. Would have fit eight years ago, but now eighty grand is chicken feed. Someone else did it."

"Right. That leaves us with seven. Seven in eight years. We have complete case files on four of them. The first, that's New Madrid's, the second is the FBI file on the casino robbery, the third robbery, the warehouse store in Bear, and my cold case, the jewelry store. If they made a mistake, it's going to be in the beginning. It's going to be in one of those first three files. We can have Cilla and Tony search every name mentioned in the newspaper articles. Run a comparison. So far I haven't seen any name twice."

"Well, should you? Why?"

"If the same people did the jobs, then I would expect a name to repeat. The newspaper articles say five of the eight might be inside jobs. None of the official information says that. But if the first jobs were inside jobs, a name should match. I want to add everyone on the payroll of the first three targets. I want to know where those people are now and what they are doing. Is someone rich? Or did someone just vanish. Is someone still a guard?"

"If a guard was a retired cop, he could be old now, or dead," Ryan argued.

"Then I want to know that. And I want to know who owns the establishments that were hit; is there a common denominator there? Or in the security firms hired."

Ryan looked at the boards some more. That all made sense. His cell beeped signaling a text. Becca's also. "Everyone is on their way over here again. I just got a text from Jake."

"Same here, only from Cilla. They will catch us up on their day over dinner and afterwards we can do a couple of hours work. They'll bring Chinese."

He looked at the timeline list. "Cross out those other three cases that don't fit while you're there, please." He thought he saw something. His eye went up and down the list slowly. Again. But he didn't see it.

Security announced Cilla and Jake with the food, the others right behind them. No one sat; they got plates, filled them with food, and walked around the boards. Tony was thrilled to see them set up. "This is what you did with our printouts?" he asked. "Sure look different laid out like this. Awesome! What are the empty boards for?"

"For information you're going to add, Tony," Ryan told him. "We've started a list on the last board. One board is for Mary Lee. We're going to work on those after dinner."

Tony passed the kidnapping board, now labeled a murder board, on the way to the table. "Oh. Wow. We didn't know this did we?"

"No, new yesterday."

The board drew enthusiastic approval and demands for the story, which they supplied over dessert.

Ryan took them over to the robbery boards. "We started a list of what we want to do next. Backgrounds on the personnel at the businesses hit. As well as the owners of the firms. Who insured the goods and took the losses. Which security firms were hired, if any, and if any of the guards show up on more than one list. Does anyone show up more than once? Becca also wants to know if any of them are rich now. Or missing." He checked and Becca nodded.

"And think about this: Why all over the map? It's unusual for crooks to go so far afield. They generally stick close to home and places they know. Or why hit in one town more than once? Do they live there? Does one of them live there?"

"This doesn't appear to be a static gang. The number of crooks varies with the robbery. Sometimes five, sometimes six. Is there a reason for that? Does it depend on the crime? The place?" he paused. "Tony, add the number of crooks to each crime so we can see it."

"And I want columns detailing what's stolen, the value, and location."

Tony was already busy copying it down. "I'll total it all up when I'm done."

"Tony," Jake said, "You need to be careful when you run the guards. We don't want anything to leak. But we do need to know if any of them has a current record." He looked at Ryan and Cav, "If we run them, it will be at best borderline legal. Is there any way to get a warrant for it?"

"I have it," Ryan said. "Based on what we have and the fact that one of the cases was submitted to us. Anything else, anyone?" he asked looking around, stopping one more time to look at the list Tony was making. And there it was. Plain as day. Ryan saw what was bothering him. "Son of a bitch. I'll bet the next one is going down soon. Very soon."

He was right. The dated list showed a robbery every year. This month every year.

"Great. Just what we need, one more crisis," Cav declared.

Everyone agreed the timeline was a cause of concern. They gave it more thought.

The map indicated that the robberies radiated out from a point midway between New Madrid and Bear. Did that tell them anything? Did that mean the conspirators lived in the vicinity?

The type of robberies didn't seem to mean anything nor did their locations. The first was a home invasion in New Madrid netting about $150,000. It was the only one with injuries. Minor injuries, the home owner had been slapped around.

Next was the casino, near Philly in Chester on a Sunday morning, which netted at least $300,000. Third was the big box warehouse near Bear in Delaware, $320,000.

Then a coin expo in Wilmington, netting gold coins to the tune of about $450,000.

A jewelry store, again, in New Madrid. That was followed by another near Cherry Hill. Netting $350,000 and $400,000 respectively. Was there a reason for two jewelry stores?

The seventh and most recent, a race track on race day in Camden, New Jersey, got them half a million.

"OK. Mary Lee next." She was already at her board. Had Tom's name written at the top. "Boards are not really my specialty," she admitted.

Jake was walking her through it. "List his previous employers and the positions he held. Another list for his references. Addresses on each one of those."

As Mary Lee wrote on the board she reminded them that she could do the Boots on the Ground research. "That is my area of expertise. I can chat up employees and get the gossip. On that suicide or if there was a shakeup in the company, they'll talk about it. It would be something that happened within a few months of Tom quitting. Not right before or right after, that would be too obvious. Maybe I can get with Cilla and we can figure out a way to look at his cell."

"Anyone see anything else there? Have we missed anything?" No one offered any further suggestions.

"What about the three board members?" Jake asked.

They were all studying the board; it only had the three names listed with a short description. But they had nothing to add here either.

"I might have an idea," Ryan said. "Give me some time to think of a way to approach Scott. Get him to tell me why he wanted Becca to be off the force."

"I have nothing new," Cilla said. "Or very little." She went to a blank board after getting a silent nod from Becca. She wrote freaky accident on the top. "Twenty one years ago here in Bear, a car veered off the road and careened into a park, narrowly missing two large groups of people. It ploughed into a small family, immediately killing the parents and terribly injuring their small child. The driver jumped out of the car and ran off. People in the park were trying to help the injured and didn't chase him. Turns out the car was stolen. That's all I can get from newspapers on line. I can use your help, Cav. Your office will have hard copies in storage boxes. Can you access your stored files?"

"You would have to do it yourself Cav." Ryan injected quickly. "Or maybe send Jones. No one can know we're looking into that accident."

Cav looked at Cilla and then at Ryan. "I've been thinking we need to look at some cold cases and that Jones needs some experience there. It will be good training for him. He wants to be a detective. Three cases, I think. Three cold cases. And maybe one should be a hit and run." He looked at his patrolman. "Maybe Becca can help you. Since she is a detective, she'll be a good mentor. I'll find three cases for you to look into. Take a camera when you access the files. Photograph everything, from multiple angles. Work all three cases."

Then he turned to Cilla. "Do you want to explain why you want me to look back twenty-one years at a hit and run accident?"

"It's always been called a freaky accident. I don't believe it was an accident. A feeling. Nothing solid."

"Can you give me a hint," he said gently.

Becca spoke up. "My parents. Richard and Anne Travis."

Everyone was now looking at Becca. She shut her eyes for a minute, and then she continued. "Cilla thought that the shooter might be someone from my past. She has eliminated everyone who might want to harm me. That leaves the hit and run." Becca looked down a moment to gather her courage. She said weakly, softly, "I didn't even know what kind of accident killed my parents. No one ever told me. I never asked. Now it's time to look." She spoke this last sentence with strength.

She stood straight and said determinedly, "Cav, I appreciate that you are willing to help, with barely a question. I can work with Jones and we can review all three cases, not just mine." She took another breath. "But if I am going to be working with him, can you tell me his first name?"

Everyone laughed at that, breaking the tension.

Jones turned red. "Ken, call me Ken."

Cav nodded and stood, "I'm calling it a night. Come on, Jones. I'll have those cases for you tomorrow. Make copies, bring them here, and work with Becca. Ryan too if he wants."

"We're going too," Jake said and ushered Tony and Mary Lee out ahead of him, taking Cilla's arm.

And just like that, they were alone again.

Ryan sat on the couch and pulled Becca over beside him. They just sat for a while, her head on his shoulder. He was gently stroking her arm. Relaxed. Then Becca asked, "So how are you going to do it? How are you going to get Scott to tell you why he decided to put me on disability?"

"Us, I think. You and me. We'll go talk to him."

"And he just volunteers the information? Because we go together?"

"Well, yes. I'm going to help him decide that he wants to tell us."

"What do you mean? How do you do that?"

"You have to make the guy want to tell you. Beg to tell you what you want. So first, you show him how tightly you have him wrapped. Then you allow a small glimmer of hope. Let him see a clear pathway out. Give him enough room and he thinks the idea is his, that he can use it to get out of the box. Almost like a carrot and a stick, but the mark never sees the stick. Never knows he is being conned."

"How? How will you do that?" She knew Ryan was considered an expert interrogator and she had watched him with Donavan, but she didn't see any way to approach Scott.

"I'll let him think we will subpoena all his files. Once we have his files, we might stumble on things he doesn't want us to know. That's the box. I'm going to let him believe he is boxed. You will provide his way out, his doorway to safety."

"Oh, how do I do that?"

"You'll do it. Just by being there. The only question is if we should do it tomorrow at his home or Monday in his office. I'm thinking his home. The threat will work better in his home. He'll feel more secure and protected there. And I don't want you walking into his office." He finished with, "We'll drop in unannounced."

"You're not going to tell me the details, are you?"

"Not yet. It's still gelling. Tomorrow, after therapy, we'll go see him. And I'll call your Captain. We need authority. And a case number for lab work. I'll have your Captain contact my boss and officially call the FBI in on the case. On your shooting."

Then he changed the subject.

"How are you feeling, tired?" he asked

"No, my brain is fried but my body is jumping."

"OK, I want to show you a couple of moves."

She smiled at him brazenly.

"Self-defense moves," he said. "Get your mind out of wherever it is. Two moves, techniques that work well with one weak arm and one weak leg. Two moves that include the use of a cane. We'll work out that excess energy. You game?"

She was almost disappointed, almost. But she'd feel better, safer, if she could at least defend herself. Right now, if anyone came at her, she would probably fall over. She was surprised that Ryan realized that.

"Thank you," she said. "Let's do it."

Saturday

Her morning session with Lori should have worn her out, but instead it left her invigorated. She showed Lori the moves Ryan had taught her. "I'm still a little clumsy and awkward," she admitted.

"Cool, I love them; here let me show you a way to make it smoother." She demonstrated and then supported Becca's weight while she practiced a few times. "Okay, try it on your own now."

This time she was not quite so awkward.

"That's better. You can keep practicing. As you speed up, the moves will smooth out." Lori was nodding her head and laughing. She said, "I can use these with a couple of my other patients."

Lori finally called a halt to the session suggesting, "I think you should be using the pool. Start with only one or two laps. Don't overdo," she warned sternly and turned to Ryan.

"You make sure she doesn't overdo. And use the spa, the hot tub. Doing laps will help both her shoulder and leg, and stomach muscles; she needs to strengthen them also. The hot tub after the swim will soothe the muscles.

Jen arrived as Lori was leaving. They exchanged greetings and spoke in the parking lot.

"Go shower," Ryan instructed Becca. "I'll get cereal ready, and we'll leave as soon as we eat."

**

Ryan knocked on Scott's front door and flipped his FBI credentials when it was answered.

Scott said, "FBI? What can I do for you? And this is Rebecca Travis. Not FBI. Who's this?" he asked looking at Jen.

"My bodyguard," Becca said not giving him a last name or explanation. Ryan had said that would give them an edge. Knowledge is power, refusing to share knowledge is power.

"Thought we might talk," Ryan said. "Do you mind if we come in?" he asked when Scott didn't back up or invite them in.

For a minute it looked like Scott would refuse, but then he waved them in and led them to the front parlor. He waited.

Ryan and Becca sat, though it took Becca a little longer. Ryan had said sitting would make them appear friendly, non-confrontational. Jen stood beside Becca.

"Thought I would give you a heads up. About a possible investigation," Ryan began. "Let me emphasize, possible investigation. We, the FBI, have been called in to look into the attempted murder of a police officer. We have discovered a connection between the attempted murder of Detective Travis and a Board vote on her permanent disability. If someone was bribed to vote on that disability, they could be indicted as an accessory to attempted murder after the fact." He paused to let that threat settle in, and then went for the carrots.

"We'll be looking into the attempted murder charge anyhow, of course. But not necessarily the bribery. I thought that it might be possible that you have some information to volunteer? If we have some answers, we might not need to look at bank records and assets." The reminder that the stick was still there.

"I don't know what you are talking about," Scott said, still standing.

"Well, I brought Detective Travis with me because I thought seeing her sitting here might jog your memory. You might remember someone asked you to propose the disability to Chloe Rummel. Maybe as a joke. A joke that just got out of hand. Maybe if you think back, you would remember who proposed the permanent disability."

Ryan waited. It was a simple straight-forward ruse. And none of it was a lie. He'd always found it easier and smarter to stay with the truth. Often the mark could sense a lie. Ryan added to it.

"And maybe there was a mysterious appearance of money, just before and or just after the vote? Maybe you were wondering where that came from?" he paused again and said, "You know, I have changed my mind." Purposely misleading Scott. Apparently pulling away the carrots.

"What?" Scott said in what sounded like desperation. "What do you mean you changed your mind?"

"I think I would like that coffee you offered." He looked at Becca, "You too Detective?"

"Yes," she said nervously. "Coffee would be good."

Scott appeared startled when she spoke as if suddenly aware she was there. Then nodded and said, "Yes. Let me get you some coffee."

"None for me," Jen said to his back as he made his escape.

Ryan leaned back and seemed to be resting, waiting for the coffee. Jen stood quietly. Becca was fidgety. She distracted herself by wondering what Jones was finding out about her parents. It still scared her that she had never wondered.

They could hear Scott first in the kitchen and then in a room near the back of the house. It seemed a long time before he came back with a cup for each of them saying, "I'll just go back for mine."

He returned without his cup but instead was holding two large USPS express mail envelopes.

Ryan smiled to himself. Scott was going for the carrot. He wasn't going to take the chance that Ryan might change his mind about seizing records. Ryan got out his notebook and prepared to take notes.

Scott started by saying, "You know Detective Travis, seeing you reminded me of a strange thing that happened a few weeks back. Let me tell you. I got a call from a voter who suggested that you deserved a disability pension. He wanted me to mention it to Rummel as some type of breaking edge women's issue. I thought it was a joke. But it tickled my fancy because with Rummel you never can tell when some women's issue will take control of her brain. It can be fun to watch. No disrespect to you or your sex, but Rummel is crazy on the subject."

He stopped a moment and then continued. "She acted as if it were the best idea since prohibition. Couldn't be stopped. She proposed it during the meeting and we didn't laugh at her, just tabled it for a week.

Hoping she would come to her senses I guess." He shook his head acting as if he didn't understand Rummel.

"What I'm going to tell you now? I never even connected it back then, not till I saw you sitting here. I got an envelope in the mail with five thousand dollars in it. Hundred dollar bills. I didn't know what to make of it. You know I'm in bail bonds and it really isn't unusual to get envelopes with cash, but generally they contain a note or explanation." He said that with a straight face. "I checked the return address; it was to a post office box. I called but they wouldn't tell me the name of the owner. Probably you can find out.

"The next week, when the disability retirement came up for a vote, Sergio had decided it was a good idea and I just went along with them. For no other reason than that they would both owe me a favor. Nothing more than that. But then the following week, I got another envelope in the mail. Another five thousand dollars. No note. I just put the envelopes in the safe. Here they are. All the cash is still in them. I haven't touched them except to count the money. Write me a receipt and I will be glad to turn them over to you."

Becca worked at keeping her face straight. Staying quiet. She was sidelined because he took a bribe. She wanted to scream at him. Jump up and punch him. She sat. Wouldn't solve anything. And he might have more to say.

"Thank you," Ryan said, "I'm glad we decided to talk to you. Did you recognize the voice on the phone?"

"No, just that it was male."

"And the date, can you narrow that down?"

"You can check our minutes. It was the day before we tabled it. I thought it would be such a joke. Egging Rummel on. Never thought she would go for it. I didn't think it would hurt anyone. Ms. Travis got a pension, free money for life. That couldn't hurt. And I never connected the two packages with that vote. Not until just now when you mentioned money and our vote on Travis. Wait, I have a copy of the minutes on my computer, I can get you that date." He jumped up and left the room, returning shortly with a piece of paper with the date on it.

"Thank you Mr. Scott. Can you count the money and I'll write you a receipt. I'll get your statement typed and have someone bring it over for you to sign later today."

As Scott counted, Ryan wrote the receipt. He pulled out and labeled an evidence bag with both the New Madrid and FBI case numbers.

"Just drop those envelopes in here please and sign and date the label," Ryan instructed him. "We would appreciate it if you didn't talk about this to anyone. Remember it is connected to an attempted homicide. You don't want to mention it to the wrong person," he warned.

He handed Scott the receipt.

Scott thanked him and laughed, "You know I'd charge a lot more than $10,000 for a vote. Wait, that didn't come out right. Joke. That was a joke," he added quickly.

"Yeah, well, your vote did hurt someone. It hurt a career cop who got sidelined."

Back in the car, Jen said, "I don't believe that. First you convinced him he was dead meat and then told him exactly how to squirm out. You totally conned him. It was all I could do not to laugh in his face when he recited your words back to you. *'Oh, it was a joke. I didn't know the money was connected to my vote.'* What hogwash." Jen regarded both of them as she continued. "That was smooth. You never actually said there was an ongoing investigation into the bribery. Just implied it. Told him exactly how to avoid it."

"Had to. No way could we ever get a warrant to examine his records. There is absolutely no proof of any connection between his vote and this cash. If we had the phone call recorded, we might have something, but even then the bribe was probably disguised. Scott would skate on it. No jury would ever convict him on what we have."

"Does it bother you, Becca? That he won't be prosecuted?" Jen asked her.

"No. And I'm a little surprised at that. Probably I'm just jaded, but he was only doing his job as a politician. Acting on a suggestion from a constituent. That's the way politics works: a little money, a little influence, a small favor. And he wasn't alone, all three of them voted on it. I wonder if Sergio got his own phone call and his own envelopes.

Rummel did it without any payment, I'm sure. I'm almost angrier at her. Idiot."

"Interesting concept, buy all three votes. Or just the two you think might vote against? A little money for a vote that doesn't seem to hurt anyone. Except maybe the county coffers and who cares about those. The county has to pay you, forever. And they lose the benefit of your expertise," Ryan declared.

"Could I get the Board to readdress that vote?" Becca asked. "He'd have to get the other two to go along. They would have to explain why they retired me before the doctors gave them my status." She paused thinking and then asked, "What about me? Could I be prosecuted for accepting a full disability when I'm not disabled?"

"The way they did it, while you were still in a hospital bed? No," Ryan said. "But when you get back to ninety or one hundred per-cent, you could walk into one of their board meetings and ask them to reconsider. Show them your medical file. Tell them the miracles of modern science permitted a full recovery. That could be their out. A miracle."

She mulled that over some, "Yes, that could work. A win win for me. Or maybe not. They could decide I don't qualify for the disability, but by that time, they might have filled my position with someone else. No disability, no job. That would be lose lose."

"There's that. But you would know if you had been replaced ahead of time. You could decide not to talk to the board." Ryan offered as an option.

She thought about that. "No. It wouldn't make any difference. I don't want their money. Once I get back on both my feet, I won't need it. That can be my goal, to walk in on two feet and confront the board," she decided.

Ryan brought her back, "Call your Captain; tell him we're on our way with some evidence. Ask him to meet us in the parking lot again."

It didn't take them long to get there and the Captain and Detective Khalen were just exiting the building.

Ryan and Jen were standing by the car when the two men reached them. "What you got?" the Captain asked.

Ryan handed over the evidence bag. "Two envelopes with five thousand cash, each. Given to us by Councilman Scott." He filled them in on the situation.

The Captain just held the bag, staring from it to them and back. "You did all this in one day? And you can't work for me anymore?" he asked Becca shaking his head. "Everyone knows you can buy Scott, but I never had an inkling he set up your disability."

He handed the evidence bag to Khalen. "Get this to Johnny. Maybe he can pull up some prints."

"This is another case we need to keep quiet," Ryan said quickly.

"Remind Johnny, lips sealed, same as last time," the Captain told Paul as he trotted off with a big smile.

He turned back to Ryan, "Sure wish I could have been there to see you work him."

"It was beautiful. Smooth and easy," Becca said.

"I'll type my notes and email them to you. Along with a copy of his statement. That will need his signature," Ryan said. "It's got to be someone local. Someone who knows Rummel is crazy and would jump on the women's lib issue. Someone who knows Scott can be bought and how much he costs."

They all thought about that.

The Captain regarded Becca. "Um, Becca," he began uncomfortably, "I had to replace you. Did it yesterday. Filled your position. I'm sorry."

Becca gave Ryan a look, shrugged her shoulders. That was it. Any chance she might have had was over. "It's OK. I figured you would. You don't really have any choice. You can't run shorthanded." Now she was making his excuses for him.

"Well, sorry."

Then he asked Ryan, "How do you want us to handle this?"

"Do as much as you can in your lab; give the rest to my people. Find where it was mailed from and when. If you get a warrant, Becca and I will check it out. I'm thinking it was mailed in person, not on the net. And not in town here. The guy would have gone out of town. Some postal employee might remember. We can check the box number on the return address too."

"I'll bet it's closed. He would have left it open just long enough to make sure his cash didn't come back," Becca said."

"Okay, we'll let you know when we get the warrant. Paul already met with the Jersey cops on the Donavan murder. They had plaster casts of shoe prints. A third person, a man. And casts of tire treads from a second car. Five years ago. No one would still have the same shoes. Would they? But he still has the same car he had then. We'll run a comparison to the tire treads Monday. They'll be more wear and tear but we might be able to match them up." He was grinning.

"Paul's bringing in Donavan next week for a talk about the supposed kidnapping." He was still grinning when he said, "The FBI is going to look really bad when we break this case."

"We deserve it. We did sloppy police work."

"But you broke it too," the Captain insisted.

"Only because you gave the case to Becca. We broke it working together. You should get the glory."

"You want to be here? When we bring in Donavan?" he asked Ryan.

Paul got back just in time to hear that. "You inviting the fibbie to my interview?"

The Captain nodded.

"Well, you're in if you want. Based on what you did with Donavan and again today with Scott, you're welcome to attend. You might even want to be lead interrogator. That was mighty fine work. Becca, you too."

"I don't think you need me. I think Donavan will tell you everything with a little encouragement. Once he understands you know that Michelle was stealing his inheritance. He's kept his success hidden for years; he's ready to brag. Probably all you have to do is mention how he outsmarted the FBI and the Jersey cops and he'll spill everything."

Jen was smiling. Ryan was setting up Khalen the same way Ryan had set up Scott.

"I'll email the paperwork on Scott and the money," Ryan finished as they got back in the car.

"Let's drive by the two crime scenes here in New Madrid," Becca suggested. "I worked one, but maybe you should look at it. We could hit the rest of them on the way home. It's still early."

"You feel up to it?" Ryan asked her.

"Sure, I can always sleep if I get tired. We're right here, maybe we'll see something."

"You could Google them. Man in the street. Google Earth," Jen suggested.

"How could we not have thought of that?" Becca grabbed her cell and texted Cilla.

"Are we going to solve more crimes?" Jen asked hopefully.

"No, we're just going to look at sites," Becca said. "The first is the home invasion. Guess what? Two blocks away from Scott's house. Coincidence?"

"Yes, probably," she answered her own question. "That's a wealthy section of town."

Jen drove by the house, Becca snapping pictures with her cell. Then they went to the jewelry store, downtown. "Drive down the alley and around to the back door," Becca instructed, still snapping pictures.

"Oh, this is so cool," Jen said.

"That's the way they went in. Two through the back door, three through the front. We never did know if they had one or two get-a-way cars."

They drove around the block one more time.

"OK. Let's go. Find a spot for lunch," Ryan suggested, "Then we'll check out the casino near Chester and the Camden race track, zip over to the jewelry store near Cherry Hill and Collingswood, come back to Wilmington and the coin expo, and home to Bear."

"Let me just call it in," Jen said turning on her Bluetooth. "Hey. It's Jen, we have a change in our itinerary." She paused a moment. "Sure put me through to Ron." Anther pause and then a smile and, "Hi, sweetie. I'm just calling in with a change of itinerary."

She listened, turned to Becca and said, "Two things. Jones made copies of all the files. He and Cilla are going to look them over and have everything ready for you tomorrow night?" She made that a question and when Becca nodded continued, "The Google thing, was there a reason you want them to get maps?"

"No special reason. We didn't do it and we can do it, so we should do it. Same with the tour today."

Jen repeated that into her headset and added, "We're going to look at the crime scenes. Heading north on I-95 to Chester, Camden, Cherry Hill and then South on I-295 to Wilmington and home. I'll call in at each site. You still have the tracker on the car, right?" She waited and then said, "Good."

"Tell them I'll post picture files on line for each crime scene," Becca said quickly.

Jen repeated that and ended, "See you later, Sweetums."

**

They stopped for lunch and then one more time again for Becca to stretch her legs during the four hours it took them to make the loop to the sites and back to the gatehouse. The only thing they learned was that all the sites were near the highway. They could have seen that by looking at a map. Made sense, Becca thought. Quick getaway.

She was relieved when they finally drove up to the gatehouse and she could stand. She ached from the long ride and couldn't stop the limp as she walked inside.

Ryan sent Jen off and then came inside and said, "Let's walk over to the pool. I feel stiff after all day in the car. We'll sit in the hot tub twenty minutes; follow that by a couple of lazy laps in the pool, and another twenty minutes in the tub. Might be just what the doctor ordered to work out the kinks from sitting all day."

Her whole body hurt and that made her testy. She'd been dreaming of just walking the few steps to collapse on the couch, not going to the pool. "Don't have a suit," she grumped.

"Hmm, me either. Guess we'll have to skinny dip."

"Not happening."

He was laughing at her. "Kevin keeps suits at the pool. As I am sure you know. You need some time in the spa to let the heat take the edge off the pain. Then one lap in the pool. Twenty more minutes in the spa. The walk over and back will be good for your leg. If you're a good girl, I'll make supper."

She thought about it. Looked at him sideways.

"What?" he asked.

"Are you conning me? Is this my version of what you just did to Scott?"

"No. I wouldn't con you. I will never con you. I'd come right out with the suggestion. That's what this was."

"Do I look that bad?" she asked.

"Yes. You look in pain. I'm stiff. I can imagine how you feel. The hot tub is a perfect antidote. Warm up in there, ease out the stiffness. Then exercise in the pool. It will feel good after sitting in the back of the car most of the afternoon. Then back to the hot tub. I know the short stop we made for you wasn't enough to ease the stiffness."

How did he know that? And she did need some exercise. And on second thought, the spa did sound good. She could just feel the hot jets easing the pain. Her body was screaming to move and she could use all her muscles in the pool. But she couldn't just capitulate. "Scrambled eggs with ham. Side of mashed potatoes with lots of butter. Toast."

"Done. And then the couch and books. No work." He'd emailed his report and Scott's statement during lunch. Heard back that Scott had already signed it.

Sunday

She woke late. She was still stiff but there was no pain. She didn't hurt for the first time since she took the bullets. If she could, she would have done a happy dance, but instead she settled for a luxurious, but careful, stretch and danced in her head. The pool and spa had really helped. She planned a repeat tonight. She got up and did her exercises, including the fifteen minutes on defensive and offensive cane techniques Ryan had taught her. Then she showered and dressed. Her pretty normal morning routine.

She smiled when she saw Ryan at the stove. Yup, she really could get used to this. "Leftovers? Scrambled eggs and ham?" hopefully.

"You are so predictable. I heard you showering. You want to get the juice? This will be ready in five."

"How come four place settings?

"Cilla is on her way over. With Jones. Check your phone."

"Huh? I thought they were coming tonight," she checked her phone. "Must have come in while I was in the shower."

"It did."

She finished just as Cilla came in and gave Becca a hug. Let's go into the bedroom."

"Is it bad? It is bad. That's why you're taking me to the bedroom."

"No. I just thought you would want privacy for this."

"No. I have to face it. I should start now. We can find another way for you to protect me. Tell me now. Before I eat."

"We don't have much. It was treated as an accident. There are some pictures." She added quickly, "After you were all transported. None before. Cells with cameras were just coming out then. The pictures might be disturbing."

"I've seen crime scene photos before. Show me."

Cilla handed over her tablet and both she and Ryan watched nervously as Becca began to scroll through the information.

Becca stopped almost before she got started. "Did you send a copy to Ryan?"

Cilla looked worried, "Yes."

"It's okay. I'm not a baby. Ryan, stop watching me," she ordered. "Look at your own file, you're making me nervous." She waited till he turned and got his tablet and opened the file. Then went back to her own.

It wasn't so terrible. Especially because she knew she wouldn't see any bodies. And she didn't remember. Didn't remember any of it. She could barely remember her parents. She remembered them as happy, laughing, and loving. Her Mom's face? She didn't remember her Mom's face. Didn't have any pictures. Didn't have anything from back then. She remembered her Mom singing to her, hugging her. She remembered her Dad as a warm smell, a clean smell. Probably a soap smell. She'd always felt safe in his arms.

The photos showed the car; after it had been dragged away from the building. The front end was smashed in almost to the windshield, the hood folded up. It had hit the building, a cement block structure, with enough force to plow right through the wall, causing extensive damage. The people, correction, her parents, must have been killed immediately. A wonder she had survived.

She looked at the schematics. The car had driven between two large groups of people, well away from either group; that was different from the newspaper reports. It smashed her parents into the cement wall. She read the report. High rate of speed, no brakes, passing between the other people in the park to strike her parents. Oh, someone saw her Dad try to jump on her and cover her as the car hit. She couldn't help it; she felt her eyes tear up. Both adult male and adult female dead on site. Child barely alive and transported to the County Hospital.

A quick follow-up two days later, the child was still critical.

She read through it again, this time slowly. Giving herself time.

"I don't remember. Just a little from the hospital. Being alone mostly. No one ever visited. No one ever came. Or sent a card. It's strange; you'd think there would be someone who cared. A coworker. A neighbor. A school chum. Who was responsible for me? I know there was no next of kin. Family Services told me that. Seems so strange."

Cilla said, "I want you to go to the hospital Monday and get your records. Jones and I couldn't do anything on the weekend except to determine that you are the only one they will release the records to. Sarah said for you to get both the medical records and the billing records. They should say who the hospital notified. What attorney oversaw your care. Sarah has a contact and will call her to see if she can expedite the matter for you. Here is her contact's name."

Becca's brain was working again. "Jen will take me."

"I'll take you," Ryan declared.

"Thanks, I appreciate that. Today, after breakfast, I want to see my house if it's still there. Maybe I'll remember it. The address in the report is in Dover. I didn't even know I lived there. Another thing I never asked. Maybe we can check with the neighbors, see if anyone remembers my family." Did she want to do that? Meet with people who knew her parents. Knew her as a child. Knew her but didn't visit her?

"Jones suggested that. He ran the addresses and found two houses with the same families still in residence," Cilla handed her the names and addresses.

Ryan said, "I'll take you. Jones will come with us. Me as FBI on an active investigation, Jones as local support, you as vic… ah, um, family member."

"I am not a victim," she said angrily.

"You know what I meant," he said quietly. "You, as a child, were a victim. You, as a cop, were a victim. You, now, are not a victim. I am not calling you a victim now. We can't forget that this is a part of a criminal investigation; we have to be careful and follow procedure all the way. You will be talking to people who will believe the child was a victim."

Jones arrived then and seemed relieved that Becca had already been through the file. Pleased that they were following his suggestion to go visit neighbors. "Today will be a good time. Most folks will be home. Tomorrow they might be working," he said.

They left right after breakfast, Jones driving his Rav4, Ryan riding shotgun. Becca in the back. Again. They cruised up and down the street twice and then stopped across from her old house.

"It's pretty," she said. "But I still don't remember it. How long did I live here?"

Jones checked his real estate records and said, "Your parents lived here nine years. So all your life."

"The house," Becca said, "What happened to the house when my parents were killed?"

"It was foreclosed. The bank took it back," Jones told her.

"I don't even recognize it." She searched her memory but nothing involving this house was there. Everything from her childhood was fuzzy, foggy. Nothing was clear except the warm safe feeling she associated with those early years. Her first memory was the time she spent in the hospital. Alone.

"Let's do it," Ryan said. "Start right here," motioning to the house they were parked in front of, just across the street from hers. Jones went first with her boxed between him and Ryan. Becca was looking back toward her house when the door was answered with a hesitant, "Yes, can I help you?"

"Yes ma'am. Mrs. Jackson?"

"Yes," the woman replied. "I'm Mrs. Jackson."

"I'm Deputy Jones, from Bear, Delaware. This is FBI agent Gibbs," he motioned to Ryan. "We are interested in anything you might be able to tell us about that house across the street."

"Well, like what?" the woman asked puzzled. "Why?"

"We're working on a case that might tie into the death of the family that lived there twenty years ago. Do you remember them?"

"Oh, Anne and Richard Travis. It was so sad. Anne was my best friend for nine years and my daughter played with her little girl. They were best friends. A shame what happened to that family. I don't know how I could help you after all these years. Come in." she moved back as Jones stepped in. Ryan touched Becca's shoulder. She was still look-ing across the street at her house. Mostly because she was afraid. Afraid to look at this woman who was best friends with her Mom but never came to the hospital, never visited her.

She turned to face the woman who looked to be about mid-fif-ties dressed casually in slacks and shirt. That was all Becca had time to notice when the woman looked into Becca's face and went white. Actually white. Her eyes went wide and round. Her hand went to her mouth. Both Ryan and Jones grabbed her as she seemed about to faint as she whispered, "Anne."

They helped her back into the house and onto the couch. "Can I get you some water Ma'am?" Jones asked.

She nodded her head. She still had her hand covering her face, star-ring at Becca. "But you're dead," she moaned. "You're dead."

"No, I'm Becca, Rebecca Travis. My Mom is dead."

The woman seemed to still be in shock. She looked to Ryan and then back at Becca. "But you're dead. You're all dead," she said again. Firmly. "Rebecca is dead too."

"No. I'm not."

Jones came back with a glass of water and placed it in her hand. "Drink this Mrs. Jackson," he said gently.

Still staring at Becca she drank the water. Gave the glass back to Jones, shut her eyes. When she opened them again, she seemed to be stronger. "You're Rebecca?" she asked.

"Yes, I'm Rebecca Travis, Anne and Richard were my parents."

Mrs. Jackson stood up, reached out a hand, and touched her. "You're real. You're Becca?" she asked again.

Becca just nodded.

The woman put her arms around Becca and held her close, crying into her shoulder. "They wouldn't let us see you. We weren't family. They wouldn't let us in to see you. They wouldn't tell us how you were doing." The woman was sobbing. Becca reached up hesitantly and held her, unsure what to do. But this woman said she'd tried to visit her in the hospital. Someone had tried.

"We tried, we called everyone. But the hospital wouldn't talk to us. I cried so hard when your Mom died, and then I cried every day you were in the hospital. You poor little girl all alone in the hospital, no one to hold your hand or talk to you. I cried every day." She was still sobbing. "And then they called and said you died. You were dead. That's the only thing they ever told us. They said there would be no funeral service. Just like your parents. I never got to say goodbye."

She finally stopped sobbing, "Why did they say you died?" And then, "What happened to you?"

"Who told you, Mrs. Jackson? Who told you Becca died?" Ryan asked gently.

"The hospital. Someone from the hospital called. They called Lucy across the street too. Oh, my God. I have to call her. What is she going to say? And Tricia. My daughter Tricia. I have to sit down again."

She sat and took a few deep breaths. It was obvious that she was trying to compose herself. She took Becca's hand, pulled her down beside her on the couch. Held Becca's hand tightly in both of hers as if she were afraid Becca would disappear.

"You are beautiful," she said. "Of course you are. You look exactly like your mother. But you know that." She was now softly stroking Becca's hand.

"No, I don't know," Becca admitted. "I don't remember what she looked like."

"But surely you can see the resemblance in pictures," Mrs. Jackson said.

Becca swallowed hard. "I don't have any pictures."

The stroking stopped and Mrs. Jackson looked into Becca's face. The pain there was obvious. "I do. I have pictures." She pointed at Jones and told him, "Bring me that white picture book on the bottom shelf, please. I don't think I can stand up yet. And bring me my phone so I can call Lucy. She lives across the street."

"Is that Lucy King?" Ryan asked. The other neighbor they planned on talking to today.

"Yes," she replied absently as she faced Becca, "She lives next door to your house. Do you remember Lucy?" she asked her.

Becca was shaking her head as Jones handed over the book and the phone. After he had gotten the go ahead from Ryan.

"This was your Mom's book." Mrs. Jackson opened it in her lap and pointed to a picture on the first page, "That's your Mom. And your Dad. With you. You were six."

Becca gasped and looked up at Ryan. Both he and Jones leaned over to look. The picture took up the full page. A woman who looked exactly like Becca. With a handsome man and a young girl. All smiling at the camera.

"My Mom? That's my Mom?" Becca asked softly, wonderingly. She couldn't see the picture anymore because her eyes were full of tears. And she wanted to see the picture. Oh, darn, was that her sniffling? Must be, because Ryan was handing her a box of Kleenex from the end table. She wiped her eyes and blew her nose and looked again at the picture. Touched the woman in the picture. My Mom, she thought. This is what she looked like. And then she looked at the man. "My dad?" she asked and needed the Kleenex again.

"You want that picture?"

Becca looked up at her, "Can I?"

"Sure take it out. I have all the negatives. Turn the page, there's lots more. You look while I call Lucy and tell her to come over."

As she picked up her cell, she seemed to suddenly remember there were two men in the house. "Oh, my manners. Sit down, sit down," she told them.

"First I'll call Lucy, then I'll get tea." she said as she hit speed dial. "Lucy, come over right now. Are you alone?" she waited and then said, "Bring him. Rebecca is here. Rebecca is alive and she is here. Come now." She shut the phone and leaned over Becca, looking at the pictures.

"That's me and Malcolm," she pointed. "He passed last year. That's us, with our Tricia. I think the next pages are mostly of you and Tricia and then more family pictures. Oh, I can't wait to tell Tricia. But she's traveling now. For her job. Tonight she'll call."

She looked up at Jones and Ryan, and asked, "Why did they tell us Rebecca was dead? Why?"

At that moment the door crashed open and another woman dashed in with a young man right behind her saying urgently, "Mom, wait."

The woman, about the same age as Mrs. Jackson, went right to her ignoring the men. "Nancy, my goodness! Are you all right? I thought you said Rebecca was ali…" that's as far as she got when she stopped short, starring at Becca. "Anne!"

The young man behind her couldn't stop and almost knocked her over. Only quick work on Ryan's part kept her on her feet. The man also grabbed her as he bumped into her. He looked beyond her, but he didn't say Anne, he said, "Rat?" like a prayer. "Is it you Rat?"

And like that Rebecca remembered him. "Teddybear? You're Teddybear." She jumped up and threw herself at him. "How could I have forgotten my Teddybear?" Teddybear, her protector and confidant. How could she have forgotten? She hugged him. And hugged him. And then laughed with happy tears. She wiped her face.

Ryan handed her more Kleenex. Gave a few to 'Teddybear' also. Everyone was talking at once.

Finally things quieted down and Mrs. Jackson introduced the new arrivals as Mrs. Lucy King and her son Ted. "We were all friends. Back then we did everything together. The three families. The three kids. They were all so close, like brother and sisters." She was explaining to Ryan and Jones.

"This is," she turned to Ryan and said, "I don't remember your name. But you're with the FBI and this young man is a Deputy in Bear?"

Everyone turned to look at him, except Becca, who was looking at the picture of her mother while holding Ted's hand tightly. A lot of hand holding she thought.

Ryan had a moment of jealousy, but then got back to business.

"I'm Ryan Gibbs and this is Deputy Jones. Rebecca has been threatened," a light version of the truth. "We're not sure, but we think there is a possibility that the threat might stem from her parents' death." That was all Ryan was willing to share for now. How much to tell them was up to Becca.

Mrs. Jackson gaped. "Threatened? Why? How come?"

"We're not sure," Becca said. "I am mixed up in a couple of things. We're looking into all of them. My sister thought we should look into my background; that's why we're here. I don't remember very much."

"Sister? What sister? You have a sister?"

"Not a blood relative, a sworn sister, a sister of circumstance. Like a blood brother. Cilla, my sister, she looked into my um…" Becca took a minute. She didn't really know these people. Though she felt instinctively that she could trust them. But she wasn't ready to share her story yet. She didn't want to talk about her fosters. She started over. "Cilla wanted to check into my parents. She wanted to know what happened to them. I couldn't remember and Cilla thought we should know. If only to cross my parents' death off our list."

Lucy King cut her off. "But how could you not know?"

"I don't remember anything from before the accident. I had a head injury," Becca admitted.

"But what happened to you? Who raised you? I was supposed to get you. Your Mom and I, we decided, I would get you if anything happened to her. You should have been mine." She almost wailed.

"My Mom wanted me to be with you?" Becca asked.

"Yes, of course she planned for your future. She would get Ted if anything happened to us. We would get you. Because you and Ted were so close. He always watched out for you. You always went to him with your problems. We thought it was all worked out."

"Did you make it official?" Ryan asked. "Sign papers for guardianship?"

"Yes, yes, we did all that. Ted Sr. and I are her Godparents and Anne and Richard were Ted's. We didn't know until Richard and Anne died, that the paperwork was lost. That we were not legal guardians. It didn't make any difference. We still expected to take her, wanted her."

Silence hung in the air.

Becca broke it finally. "My sister was right then. Something went wrong. Very wrong." And Becca had another of those moments when a window cleared in her memory. Like having windshield wipers clean the condensation off the glass. She looked at Ted. "I remember, you came into my hospital room and you held my hand. You sang."

Ted looked embarrassed.

His mother said, "You were in her hospital room? You went to Bear? How did you get there? You never told me."

"Well, I hitchhiked. And then I hung around until I located her room. I snuck in. No one saw me. Someone had to be with her. I couldn't leave her by herself. So I snuck in. A couple of times."

"And you sang silly songs. I remember," Becca said softly.

"Yeah. I couldn't think of anything else to do, so I sang songs and some kids' rhymes. And then the third time I went back, you were gone."

"Tell us again. How you found out Rebecca had died," Ryan said to Mrs. King.

"Some woman called. Said she was from the hospital and that Rebecca had died overnight. She said there was to be no funeral. And that was it."

"Didn't you contact any of the Travis' family? Other friends?"

"They were both single children of single children. Their parents were dead. The only other person was Richard's business partner and he was out of the country. He'd been called up in the Gulf War. He was still overseas. His wife just said she didn't know anything. Stonewalled us," Lucy said. "We hired an attorney, but then, when we were told that Rebecca was dead, there didn't seem to be any point. So we let it go."

"What do you know about the accident?" Ryan asked.

"Just what was in the papers. Anne and Richard took Becca on a day trip to Bear. Some person stole a car and ran down the whole family. He was never caught. Nothing else."

Ted added sheepishly, "I went over there, to Bear, down to the park the next day, on my way to the hospital. But there wasn't anything to see. I didn't even try to talk to the cops. They wouldn't talk to a fifteen year old. Some people said they saw the accident. They said the car went across a wide open field at high speed. There were no people even close to its path. The newspapers got that wrong."

Ryan looked at Jones. This guy would make a good cop.

Becca still seemed to be a little in shock, so Ryan asked, "What did Richard do for a living? Who was his partner?"

"They had a niche industry. They were remodel architects. Fred was the designer; Richard did all the structural changes, the engineering. Fred's wife, Sylvia, ran the office, did all the paperwork, and pulled all the permits. The three of them were partners. When Fred got shipped overseas, things got tough. Richard got a second job, a part time job, with a big architectural firm. Richard and Sylvia tried to keep the business running until Fred came back. Richard kept saying that Fred would be back next month. Anne worked at the school, as a teacher's aide, so they were doing okay. Things were tight, their niche business was floundering, but they believed they could hang on until Fred got back."

"Does the partner still run the business? Did he take it over?"

Lucy looked at Ted, they both shook their heads. "No, we don't know," she said.

"The partner's name? And the name and address of the business? Would you have those?"

"Fred Smith. His wife's name is Sylvia. The firm was called "FSR Associates. That was their initials, Fred, Silvia, Richard." She told them the general area where the business was located. She didn't know the exact address. "They took out key man insurance. Right before Fred left. They took it out on both Richard and Sylvia. A little late. They were able to take it out on Fred too," she added.

"I have pictures of them. They were around a lot, well Fred more than Sylvia, she didn't really try to fit in. The pictures are in that picture book." She pointed at the one Becca still held. Noticed the way Becca was holding it.

"Do you want that book? Rebecca. You can take that book with you if you want. You should take that book. Then you will have a reason to come back and visit. And you must come back and visit. We don't want to lose you again."

They were all talking again and looking through the book. Ryan excused himself to call Jake and Cilla and fill them in. Get them started on locating the Smiths. He wanted this initial search to be off the record. He didn't want to do this officially yet. They needed to find and examine the business. Find the guardianship papers. Find the will. Had it been filed officially? Was there a copy at the County Register of Wills office?

When he walked back into the room, Lucy was about to call her husband. "You can't tell anyone that Rebecca is alive," he said, putting a damper on the group.

Lucia said, "My husband," at the same time as Nancy said, "But Tricia".

"No one can know we are here, that Becca is here," Ryan said.

"Well it's too late now. My wife is back at the house. She heard my Mother say that Rebecca is alive. And there is no way you will be able to stop my Mom from telling my Dad. They tell each other everything."

Ryan digested that. "Call your wife and explain that she can't tell anyone," Ryan instructed him. He turned to Lucy, "You may tell your husband. No one else." He gave a quick glance to Becca and got a nod and continued, "Becca's life may depend on it. The more people who know she is investigating, the more danger Becca will be in."

"Rebecca's life is in danger? Why? What is going on?" Lucy asked.

"Someone tried to kill me," Becca said.

That brought gasps.

"Why is someone trying to kill you?" Ted asked as he closed his phone.

"We don't know. It could be any number of things I'm involved in. We just don't know which one. That's why we're looking at the accident that killed my parents. It's one of the unknowns."

"What other things are you involved in?" he asked, a little wary.

Becca gave Ryan the nod. "She was shot down while on routine…" He never finished.

"Shot? You were shot?" Lucy asked aghast.

"Yes. She's a cop. She was shot down while on routine patrol," Ryan finished. "She had just closed a big case and had taken on three cold cases that morning. So we are not sure if it was any of those. And there are another couple of things she is involved in. Personal things which might be a reason. We're trying to eliminate alternatives, but everything just gets murkier. Like this accident." He paused as he thought about the big case she closed. *Did we look at that? Did someone see her picture in the paper? Her name?*

"I saw that," Ted exclaimed. "A Detective Travis solved that double murder case. I thought the name was a funny coincidence. Assumed it was a male detective. The article didn't have a first name or mention if it were a man or woman. There wasn't any picture of you. I would have recognized a picture. There was a picture of the guy doing the perp walk with a bunch of cops around him."

"There was a lot of coverage. Remember when you Googled me?" Becca asked Ryan. "There were a couple of pictures of me, and my name. Someone could have seen that and got worried."

"Yeah, someone who had nothing to do with the case. A complete unknown. Damn. The list just gets longer and longer. Cav is right; your gang of five attracts villains. If it is someone who recognized your name or face in the newspaper… then it's a mess."

"Doesn't matter. If they did find me through the news, it's still going to be someone we are already looking at," she stated. Cilla had eliminated the fosters. That just left the armed robbery cold case, Tom her ex-lover, the guy who bribed the board, and her parents' death. She shook her head. Just left those few cases? They still had a lot of avenues to follow up. She suddenly realized people were watching her. God she was losing it. She had almost said that out loud. She'd only just met these people and already she trusted them. Because they liked her? Was that all it took? Someone is a little caring and she tells everything? She was a cop, dammit.

"It's not us," Ted said. He must have thought that Becca was suspicious. "We didn't even know you were alive. If we had, we would have been on your doorstep."

"I know. On some level I know that. I can feel it. Ryan?" she asked him. She was looking for support.

"Yes, I think you can be trusted. But we can't take any chances. We have to keep everything contained in this room."

He turned to the two women, "I know it's been twenty years, but is there any chance one of you kept a copy of the will?"

"I probably did," Lucy admitted. "I'm a pack rat. I keep everything. And that will had special meaning. Where I kept it though is another matter. Cellar, attic, safe deposit box. I'll have to look."

"Here's my card; call if you find it. I'll come and pick it up. One of us will. Now I hate to break this up, but we need to be going. We have a meeting."

Jones offered his card too, and Ted made sure they each had one of his.

"You'll be able to keep her safe?" Ted asked.

"Oh, yeah," Ryan answered.

"Don't worry Ted, I can take care of myself," Becca insisted. "I'm not helpless." When everyone looked at her she thought about how stupid she must sound and amended the statement. "Well, okay, right now maybe I do need a little extra help until I am back to 100%. I have a bodyguard and Ryan is with me all the time."

Now she saw the speculation in Ted's eyes. "Not that way," she added with just the proper amount of indignation. She wasn't going to explain the gatehouse or her relationship with Ryan. Like she even understood it herself. She looked at him and saw him smiling at her discomfort. That made her angry. "I have plenty of protection," she insisted and groaned when she heard how that sounded.

This time Ryan came to her rescue. "She means that we have a team of professionals on her, protecting her, 24/7."

"Private?" Ted asked.

"Both private and official. She has a lot of friends in law enforcement. And in the private sector. Some of the best men in the business."

"Okay." He touched her arm, "Stay in touch. Don't let us lose you again."

**

The meeting started while they were eating Thai takeout. Tony was first with the armed robberies. "There is no connection. Nothing. Of the seven armed robberies, there are three security services. They have four different internal monitor systems. The jewelry stores have the same monitoring system and agency. But it's a specialty system and it is reasonable that they would have the same one. Four different insurance agencies are used. None of the owners overlap. Nor do their spouses or siblings. No one has come into a lot of money. No one has disappeared. A couple are dead from what appear to be natural causes. Three security guards have moved out of state. Different states, different jobs. There is no connect. Nothing. Nada. We listed all the overlaps on the last board. They are irrelevant. How deep do you want us to go?" Tony asked.

"Well, of course it wouldn't be easy," Cav said disgusted. "I'm not sure we'll gain anything by digging deeper into relationships. It could be a girlfriend or a neighbor. Someone we would never find or recognize."

"I've been thinking," Becca said. "When we drove past the sites, I noticed they have a lot of windows. The jewelry shops have a lot of glass; I saw a man washing the windows when we drove by. Can we check who cleans the windows? Who has the janitorial services? They have landscaping and some shrubbery. One shop had what looked like live plants on the inside. Can we check lawn care? And what do you call the people who provide live plants. Not just flowers, though maybe florists would be another thing to check."

Tony and Cilla were tapping their tablets even before she finished speaking.

"And, you know," she continued. "Google has this new thing for shop owners, so it wouldn't be relevant for the older crimes. But shops can put an interactive 360 degree tour of the interior of their business on line. The whole interior is on line. Have any of our crime scenes participated in that? Have we been to their web sites to see what they do have? How long their websites have been up? Did they advertise high price items? An online video has got to be a bonus for anyone planning a robbery. Do the web sites show exits? Security wall controls? Something you can't see just by walking around the shop? Again, it won't be a factor in the older crimes, but it could have been in the most recent one. Or even for the one they are planning this year."

"We need to be thorough," Cilla said putting down her tablet. "I want to set up steps and procedures. Otherwise we might miss something. Tony, let's get together after the meeting and sketch it out. What about Tom?" she asked."

"Mary Lee is still on Tom," Jake said. "She has two associates working with her. She says, and I quote, *There is something funky going on.* She doesn't *feel*, that's another quote, that it is related to Becca. Anyhow, she says that Tom worked at the first two jobs for about six months, leaving the first shortly before arrests were made. He has already hung into this job longer than that. He hasn't gotten back in contact with any of his fellow employees from the previous jobs. She'll let us know when she gets something solid."

Ryan took over, "New Madrid should have the post office that the bribery money was mailed from tomorrow. Also tomorrow, Becca is going to the hospital to get her medical records. Find out what happened there." He told the rest of the group about the trip to her old neighborhood.

"So we have another mystery. It never occurred to me not to take Becca along. Or that she would be the spitting image of her mother."

"Not your fault, Ryan," Becca said. "No harm done. It never occurred to me either. You took me there because I asked you to. I don't think it's a problem. What we learned made the risk worthwhile," Becca argued. "Not that it makes anything easier. It's more loose ends."

"Doesn't really change anything," Jake said. "We did background checks on the neighbors and they all came back clean. Your investigation would have come out anyhow since you were going to interview the neighbors. The interview yielded more with Becca along. She got to meet her parents' friends. That's good, right?" He looked at Becca.

She wasn't so sure about that. She still felt a little, tipsy? Twenty years not knowing what her parents looked like. Not knowing there were neighbors who cared about her. And it was obvious that they did care. For twenty years she had forgotten her sidekick, Teddybear. How was that possible? How had she blocked all that out? It was a little scary. And why was so much still hidden in the fog of her brain? Should she talk to Sarah? Did she need a psychologist? She was going to think about that. She wasn't ready yet to talk about the fog. Would it be dangerous to wait? Ryan could help. He had good instincts. She'd ask him after everyone left. Maybe.

"Whoever tried to shoot me knows I'm alive. He must know that I'm looking for him. But it's not any of the people we met today." She looked to Ryan for confirmation.

"I agree. They were devastated by the deaths. Wrung out by Becca's reappearance. They weren't faking that."

Cilla spoke up with a change of subject. "Tomorrow, you need to see a Ms. Bennet at the hospital. Sarah spoke with her today. If they still have your records, she'll get them for you. She wasn't sure if they might have transferred the records from that time period from microfiche to digital. When you're done there, you go to the Division of

Family Services. Sarah's paved the way there also. Matt Warren will be expecting you. You'll need to sign multiple forms before he can give you your records. Sarah has already signed and faxed what he needs from her. And Michael's dad, Michael is Sarah's fiancé," she said for those who didn't know him. "Michael's dad knows some doctors who worked at the hospital back then. He'll check, quietly," she said before Ryan could object. "Doctors can keep secrets. Michael's dad will see if any of his buddies might remember anything. Sarah will text you with the information if one does. You still might run into walls. Even with Sarah facilitating. This is hospitals, doctors, and the government you will be dealing with. None of them part with anything freely or in a hurry," she warned.

They decided to call it a night. Tony and Cilla would text whatever they found. Jen would go with Becca and Ryan to the hospital in the morning.

Cilla stopped and talked to Becca. "I am so happy that you found family friends. These people sound solid. Good people. How are you doing?"

"I'm hanging in."

"Do you want to talk with Sarah? Can she help with what you're dealing with?"

"Not yet. I need to digest it first. I need to think about it. Maybe later, I'll see if she can help with why I don't remember. Haven't remembered. Later, not now. I'm okay, Cilla," she said again. As if saying it would make it true.

"Call if you need me. Call Sarah and talk." Cilla hugged her and left with Jake. He looked worried.

Ryan suggested a repeat visit to the hot tub and pool. Since it was what she planned anyway, she agreed. She let her mind, her emotions, wander while she worked on the physical aspects. She swam two laps, let the hot tub soak out the aches. But it wasn't until after her shower when she was settled on what she now considered her couch that she worked up the courage.

"Can I ask you some questions, theoretically?" She knew she wasn't kidding anyone; it just seemed easier to come at it from that direction.

"Go ahead," he said closing his laptop to give her his full attention.

So where to start? All that thinking and she wasn't sure. "Give me a minute."

He waited for a few and then suggested, "Maybe I can give you a hand?"

"Please, I don't seem to know where to start."

"You fell down the rabbit hole today."

She looked at him startled, "Yes. Yes I did."

"Let's try taking things one by one. You learned what your parents look like. That's a blessing. Most of us know our parents all our lives. But for you, seeing their pictures was a major jolt to your psyche. Just let it be, leave it alone, you'll get used to it and the pictures should blend with what is hidden in your brain. Okay?"

He waited for her to nod, hesitantly, and continued, "You look exactly like your mother. You didn't know that, but it makes you happy. You met people who, I think, love you. Another jolt to your psyche. But I think that will resolve itself too."

Now he hesitated. "You don't remember. I think that is scaring you. For some reason you have it blocked. I don't think you just forgot. I don't think it was caused by the head injury, although that certainly complicated things. You have it blocked. That's why you never asked yourself what happened. When your mind is ready, it will free what you have hidden. You need time to adjust. Don't try to force it or worry about it. It will come on its own." He was pretty sure.

"So far, I think I agree. Why is it blocked? They look like good people and yet I buried them."

"Maybe the accident was too monumental for you," he paused again and then said, "Maybe you saw the driver. Recognized him. And your brain couldn't handle it."

"I hadn't thought about that twist. Some rabbit hole." If she'd seen him, who would that be? Didn't appear to be too many choices. "If so, that would be Fred Smith?"

"We don't know and you can't jump to that conclusion. There might have been other people in your life. Give it time. It will come."

"Yeah, but meanwhile, I'm Alice. My life right now is almost as confusing as Alice's in Wonderland. Nothing makes sense."

"You know that Sarah could help you with that. Maybe help you understand better what's going on in your head. I'm not an expert."

"No. I'm not ready for Sarah. Cilla suggested I talk to her too. For now, I want to just let it marinate for a while. What you said agrees pretty much with what I've decided. Thank you. I think I'll try to read. Get lost in dust bunny land. Things make sense there."

Monday

She hadn't slept well. When she did sleep her dreams were all about confusion and loss. No surprise. Though she had hidden the picture book in the bottom dresser drawer it was in front of her all the time. She realized that she was burying the book physically the same way her mind was suppressing her memories. But in this case it wasn't out of sight out of mind. She knew the book was there and she could retrieve it. Knew she would have to take it out and look at it. Just not yet. She wasn't ready.

She moved through her exercises in a haze, a lingering sadness left by the last dream. She tried to occupy herself with how she would deal with the new people in her life. How would she fit them in? Did she want to fit them in? Yes, she knew she did. She wasn't going to turn her back on them. She couldn't put them in a drawer like the book. And she was curious about them, she wanted to know more. She wanted to hear their stories about her parents. She wanted what they offered: the love and caring of a family.

She was worried how that would affect her relationship with the gang, her real family. That's where she was having trouble. How would she handle that? She knew she was being silly, but how did one mesh two families?

Like marrying into a family she guessed. That would work. That's how she would think of her parents' neighbors, they could be like in-laws. Okay, she was feeling better with that idea. The gang would still be her immediate family; they would accept anyone who was good to her. Time would tell if the *in-laws* would be able to accept her chosen family. If they couldn't that would be their loss. So why was she still worrying about it? *Leave it alone, Becca,* she told herself. *Get on with today.*

And today she would be taking more hits. She would have to review her medical records from the accident, her file from Family Services. She better start fortifying herself now. She put more energy into her workout.

She finished her last exercise with the cane in a better mood and before she went to take her shower, she took the book out of its hiding place and laid it on the bed. Tonight she would go through it.

It was only when she was in the shower that she realized that her parents' neighbors were not the only new family she may be gaining. Ryan. Where was their relationship going? Ryan had a family. Stop, she told herself again. Deal with today.

She was ready when Jen drove through the gate. Ryan looked as if he wanted to comfort her, but settled for a gentle, "Can you do this?"

"Yeah, let's go." She was a cop. She'd look at her records as a detached impartial cop. Leave her feelings and her subconscious out of it. Deal with those feelings later. She laughed at herself. The things she would deal with later were piling up.

He saw her take control and promised her, "It will be okay."

**

Their contact was waiting for them in the lobby of the hospital and took them directly to Records where Becca had to fill out what felt like a hundred forms, but was actually only a dozen. It was the first time Becca had been in Records, though she had been in most areas of the hospital as a battered and abused child. She'd never been to Records or the cafeteria, or the morgue. It was clean, neat, and shiny with seating for three people in a small room that was backed by a counter. A clerk was standing behind the counter and Becca could see rows and rows of files stored in bookcase after bookcase.

Ms. Bennet apologized profusely and explained that both government and hospital forms were required before she could release anything. "But we'll do anything for Sarah," she said. "I had Records pull everything, copy it, and fasten it into a two pronged folder for you. The newest record is on top. I've already been through the file to check and everything is here. The first years were in microfiche, the latter were digital."

Becca sat with the folder on her lap in the back seat of the car. Just holding it. She was aware of Jen and Ryan exchanging looks. Finally, Ryan suggested softly, "I could do it if you want. What we need is probably on the bottom two or three pages. We don't have to look at the whole thing."

Becca took a deep breath reminding herself she was a cop. Skimmed the bottom page which listed the injuries the child presented in the emergency room. They were horrendous. That was obvious even in the medical jargon. She shut her eyes a moment as she turned the page, read it and turned to the next.

"No, nothing here about next of kin, or relatives or power of attorney. Only what the medical staff did. They made all the medical decisions. We really need my file at Family Services. They take over as guardians on page three."

She put the book on the car seat and sat back. "Let's go," she told Jen.

Family Services was exactly what you would expect to find in a government office. Rows of battered gray metal desks, each with a chair behind and a visitor chair beside. Harried government employees sitting behind piles of files entering data into outdated computer monitors or talking on phones. Much like her detective office.

Becca introduced herself and simply identified Jen and Ryan as friends. Warren led them to his office and although he appeared curious he didn't ask any questions, but was apologetic. He had the file. It was large, about five inches thick. Becca really didn't want to look at it.

"This is everything. But I can't give it to you, I'm sorry."

"I'll fill out whatever forms you have."

"Sarah already faxed me her forms. Once I have your forms, the whole package has to go to the division head to sign off. He'll be gone all week. There is no way I can give it to you without his signature."

"I have to wait a week?" She was looking at Ryan, he was shaking his head. "That's too long."

"I know and that's one reason I started the process so quickly. I didn't know my admin would be out of town this week. But rules are rules I can't give it to you or even let you look at it."

He stood and then continued, "Complete all these forms, I think there are only about thirty or forty. While you are doing that I have to go to the mailroom to get more forms." He laughed, "You have cleaned out my supply. While I am in the mail room, I am going to show the guys pictures of my roses. I have a few dozen on my cell phone. I promised them next time I came down they could look at my roses." He didn't wait for a reply as he added, "I'll be gone about twenty minutes and if Ms. Travis is not done with the forms, I'll show the pictures to you guys. You can take great pictures with these cell phones you know. Too bad about the file. When you do get it, the oldest data is on bottom. Sarah implied that was what you were most interested in." He stood and walked out closing the door tightly behind him.

Jen was agog. "Did he just tell you to look at your file?"

"Becca, you fill in those forms, and keep a watch on the door, though I think he will knock before he comes back in," Ryan said. "I'm going to take his advice and take pictures of the pages. Jen come hold them for me we'll get through more that way."

Becca could hardly concentrate on what she was doing. Fortunately the forms were almost a duplication of those she had filled out at the hospital. Two asked detailed questions and she had to be careful how she answered them. Probably nobody read them anyhow. Just filed them away. An air of tense excitement filled the office as Ryan quickly snapped each page. She was surprised at how many pages he was getting through. Probably they only needed the first two or three sheets but more was better.

Warren did knock on the door and as he started to open it he paused, saying, "Oh, I'll be right back I need a word with my secretary."

Ryan was sitting beside Becca pointing to a blank line she had missed. Jen was standing against the far wall when he returned.

"You got those forms all done for me Ms. Travis?" he asked.

"Almost."

"Let me show you my rose bushes, they are awesome." He pulled out his cell and made Ryan and Jen look at a dozen pictures of roses.

"Ms. Travis, I am really sorry about the delay. I promise to call you immediately when my boss signs off on this; he'll sign as soon as he gets back to town. Sarah is an important emissary for us; we like to see that whatever she wants, she gets," he laughed.

They said their goodbyes and headed back to the car. Ryan handed her his phone to look through the pages. Somehow it didn't seem quite as real or as personal looking at her record on Ryan's cell.

"Nothing here. It doesn't mention how I became a ward." She'd almost said, the girl instead of I. The cell pictures were that impersonal.

"Well, that just leaves Michael's dad. Let's have lunch," Ryan suggested.

Jen knew a place, "I love going out with you guys. I get to do such neat stuff. I've always wanted to take pictures of secret files. 007 used to do that. Never have I seen a bureaucrat help out a citizen. Sarah has some powerful mojo."

At that moment Becca got a text. "Michael's dad found a nurse who remembers the little girl brought in from the hit and run in the park. She is willing to talk to us and can meet us in the cafeteria at the hospital." That was spooky. Only a couple of hours ago she was thinking she had never been in the hospital cafeteria and here she was heading there for a late lunch. Hoped the coincidence didn't stretch to the morgue.

And they hit pay dirt.

"I'd just received a promotion. Charge nurse. You were the first patient brought to my floor that shift. No sooner were you brought in from emergency then a woman showed up claiming she had POA, power of attorney, for you from your father. Not even an Advanced Health Care Directive/Living Will. Just a simple POA. She was one of those syrupy sweet women. I disliked her on sight. When I told her you were struggling to survive with the help of machines, she immediately insisted I take you off them. Said as how your parents would never have wanted that. Would never have authorized life support. She wanted me to discontinue it. Saying it was cruel and unusual punishment to this poor sweet little girl to make her suffer and be in pain for no reason since you could never survive. When I refused, she threatened me. She didn't have the authority to order us to discontinue life support. I didn't have the authority to do it. But I wouldn't have anyhow. That little girl," she turned to Becca, "You honey, you were fighting so hard for a chance to live, that I wouldn't do it. She went over my head. Demanded to talk to the doctor. Tried to intimidate him. When that didn't work she marched down to administration. Almost convinced them too. But the doctor, did I mention that I married him? The doctor simply said that it was very possible that you would survive without the artificial assistance and it was just making it easier for your body to deal with the terrible injuries. To take it away would result in more pain for you and a longer recovery."

Irma smiled. "It felt so good to watch her stomp off. She never came back. I guess she was the one who called Family Services. She could do that with her power of attorney. They moved you out of my ward, but I kept an eye on you. I didn't trust her not to try the same type of intimidation in your new ward. Although it wouldn't have worked there either. You were breathing on your own by then." She put a hand over her face to cover a smile. "Don't tell anyone. But I let a young man into your room. Well, I didn't let him in; I found him in there and let him stay. Two times. He was holding your hand and singing you a silly song. I think he was making it up as he went along. I almost kicked him out because we could only let family members in, but you seemed more at ease with him there. And if no one knew what difference could it make."

And then anger. "That woman said no one but family could visit you or get information on you. But you didn't have any family. Your parents were killed in that accident. There were some people who came when we first got you but we couldn't let them in. Or even talk to them. And then Family Services moved you."

"Wait a minute," Irma pulled out her cell and hit a key, said, "Can you break free? I'm with some people in the cafeteria. Come on down."

"He'll be down in a minute."

Becca had her back to the entrance and so didn't see him come in, but she did see Irma's face light up. They all stood and Irma did introductions. "This is Ryan, and that's Jen," which was the way they had introduced themselves. He shook hands with both of them.

Irma pointed to Becca. "This is Rebecca Anne Travis," and waited.

He reached out to shake her hand and then stopped and looked questioning at Irma who was nodding with a smile. "Well," he said with a broad grin, "This is a surprise. Don't you look well. How are you feeling?"

Becca stammered, "Um good?"

He pointed at the cane, "That's a new injury. That's not from before. What happened?"

He seemed to become aware of the confusion around him. "What? What did I say?"

"You know me?" Becca said baffled.

"I thought that's why Irma called me down, to meet you. Wasn't it?" he asked Irma.

"Yes, but they don't know who you are dear." She turned to the three and finished her introduction, "This is Dr. Ashton. He performed your emergency surgery after the accident and was your doctor though your recovery and convalescence. He can probably answer your questions."

"You remembered me? My name? After twenty years?" Becca asked surprised.

"You were one of my first successes. And you were back here again remember? Didn't have time for introductions but I recognized your eyes."

"When was that doctor?" Ryan asked.

"Maybe you should tell me a little more," Ashton said. "I know Rebecca. So let's start with you young lady. Who are you?"

"I'm a friend," Jen tried.

"More than that, or less, the way you're watching her and everyone in here," he waited.

"She is a friend," Becca said. "And my bodyguard."

"OK. Have something to do with that cane? And the way you are holding your shoulder?"

"Yes," said Becca.

"And you sir? Who are you? And remember that I have spent a lot of time in emergency rooms with cops," he warned.

"You're good Doc. Not too many civilians make me," Ryan said impressed. He pulled out his ID, "FBI. But I am also here as a friend."

"Good, now that that is out of the way, let's eat; I missed lunch a long time ago."

They went through the line and came back with their food and sat at a round table. "What is it you want to know?" Ashton asked Becca.

"Who did the hospital deal with in lieu of my parents? Who made my medical decisions?"

"Who was it?" Ryan asked. "What was his name?"

Ashton said, "Tell me why that is important."

They explained simply that Becca was searching out her past.

It had taken some work to get Irma to tell them what happened. She wasn't sure she was breaking a rule, even after all this time. But when they explained that Becca was the patient, showed her Becca's driver's license, she'd started to talk. It took more proof for the doctor; he wanted more, so Ryan gave him the whole story.

"The name was Sylvia Smith. I'll probably never forget her. In all the years I've worked, she was the most radical person I have encountered. She had a legal power of attorney, signed by the deceased father. But that didn't allow her to make any medical decisions, I did that. I made the medical decisions. She would have needed medical power of attorney for what she wanted to do. Even if she'd had that, I wouldn't have let her take charge. Becca was doing fine; pulling her off the machines would have caused a slow painful recovery. Smith never had a chance. When she turned you over to Family Services, Becca, she told them to take me off the case. But of course she had no authority. She was out of the loop as soon as Family Services got you. I stayed on."

"This the same Sylvia Smith who was a partner in the father's business?" Ryan asked.

"I wouldn't know. That's about the only contact I had with her. She was bizarre." He looked at Becca speculatively and asked, "What about your foster parents? Have you looked at them? They sent you back here."

"My sister looked at all of them. They are all clear on this."

"Your sister? I didn't know you had a sister. Is she a cop too?"

"No. She's not a blood relative. But she is my sister in every other way. She is not FBI, but, um… I hired her husband's firm to help. Jen, my bodyguard, works for him."

"I think I got that. Did he also find Irma for you?"

"No that was my other sister. Again not a blood relative. A sister only through adversity. Her fiancé's father found Irma."

"Now I am really curious. Sister's, fiancé's, father. Do they have names?"

Becca considered for only a moment. "You have been fair with us. My sister, Sarah Woods. She's ..."

He cut her off. "I know Sarah. She's a child psychologist. An excellent one. And I know Michael and his Dad." He considered her a moment. "That's an interesting family you have. So that time you came in here all beat up? You were sixteen? Seventeen? That scum who beat you isn't the guy who shot you?"

"He's dead. Most of my fosters are dead or dying. One's in prison for life. No one cares about them. None of them came after me."

Ashton winced. Irma patted her hand. Both reactions gave Becca some degree of comfort.

They didn't get anything more. Becca's medical condition had claimed Ashton' complete attention. All he knew about Sylvia was the name and that she had a power of attorney.

They finished eating and were leaving the cafeteria when Ryan's phone rang. It was Lucy King; she had found her copy of the will.

"It's been a long day," he told Becca. "We can go home and pick up the will tomorrow. Or send someone else tonight."

Becca was weighing her tiredness and stiffness against a long trip. "I could nap on the way. Can we get it now? We'll still be back in time for dinner and the meeting. I'll think of hot tub therapy to get me through."

"You sure?" Ryan asked at the same time as Jen offered, "I can drop you off and go get it."

Matter of pride now. "I'm fine." She lied as she rubbed her finger across her eyebrow. He was still watching her skeptically, "What?" she said plaintively.

"You have a tell."

"I do not have a tell." And then immediately, "What tell?'

He ran the back of his index finger knuckle down his eyebrow.

"That's not a tell," she asserted. Was it? Did she do that when she was tired? Had she done that at work?

"I've never seen it except when you're among friends," he said as if he was reading her mind again.

She looked at Jen. "Yeah, you do that when we're alone and no one else is around and your body is tired. It's a tell. And it's not the only one." She shut up quick with a sorry glance at Ryan.

"What? What else do I do that you've seen?"

Jen looked at Ryan and shrugged her shoulders. "You always look toward Ryan for confirmation before you say something that you think he might want to keep quiet."

"Do not!" Becca was outraged. "No one tells me what to say."

"He doesn't tell you what to say. Why am I on the defensive here? Ninety percent of the time you go your own way, but on the other ten percent of occasions, before you speak you check with him to get his agreement before you share. You do the same with Cilla," she added. "It's subtle. He does the same with you. Partners do that. Good partners."

Becca remembered doing that very thing a few minutes ago. And again they did it earlier with Warren in Family Services.

"I just do that because he's running an investigation and I don't want to mess it up."

"Maybe. Whatever. It shows respect and trust on both sides. I might be able to see the tell but most times I don't have a clue what you are asking him about. But he always knows. And that's another tell. I'm being quiet now, I have to drive."

It struck Becca what Jen was implying. She opened her mouth to argue, but no words came out. She did respect him. She did trust him. She trusted his judgment and his nod always agreed with her gut. She didn't have to voice any concerns about why or why not. They never compared notes. She closed her mouth. Did that mean that he was taking a spot in her heart, her brain, like Cilla had? Well not quite like Cilla. She peeked at Ryan. He was looking back at her with his eyebrow raised. His tell for, do you get it? Do you understand?

She fell back in the seat a moment and then leaned forward to argue, but all the air seemed to have gone out of her. Ryan nodded with a small grin. He knew she got it.

"Who else knows?" she asked in a small voice.

"Just everyone who knows you. That's everyone who has been around you and you know they shared it with each other. Discussed it," Jen said happily. And then remembered that she was driving and closed her mouth.

Ryan wasn't trying to suppress his grin now.

She sank her head into her hands. Was doing that a lot lately. Was it another tell? Well of course it was. A tell everyone understood. And now she was procrastinating. Deal with it she thought. You and Ryan do trust and respect each other.

She was tempted to start a new argument that it didn't mean anything, but that was so obviously wrong she settled for a small, "Okay. I'm napping now." Which didn't fool anyone, but it gave her the whole ride to think about the implications.

The next thing she knew they were parking in front of Lucy King's home. She sat up and just stopped herself from wiping her knuckle down her eyebrow.

Lucy must have been waiting because she opened the door as they came up the sidewalk and ushered them into the house. Ryan introduced Jen as a friend and Lucy said, "Oh, I love the tats. I keep threatening Ted Sr. that I'm going to get one. Or at the very least color my hair. I've always wanted to try bright green or the deep blue."

She led them into the kitchen adding, "I made Rebecca's favorite, chocolate chip cookies with cinnamon."

Becca recognized the smell. A combination of cinnamon and chocolate. A warm loving smell.

"I recognize the smell," Becca said in wonder.

"When Agent Gibbs said he would come right away and you would be with him, I whipped them up. Sit down and I'll get tea and milk."

Becca was motioned to the side chair; Jen took the one with her back to the wall, and Ryan sat facing both doors at an angle.

Lucy set out tea and milk and the cookies. The glasses were already on the table.

"I'll get the will. It was in my reminder box, the first place I looked."

When she brought it back she wasn't sure who to give it to, but Becca was nodding at Ryan. "He's an attorney."

While Ryan was reading it, Lucy told Becca, "Put sugar in your tea dear, it will give you energy."

"What?" Becca said confused.

"Anne, your Mom, had the exact same habit, that mannerism, when she was tired."

Jen choked, Becca put sugar in her tea. Might as well take advantage of the situation. "Can you tell me more about her, another time maybe? After we get through this. Can I come back and talk with you and Nancy?"

"I'd love that. Nancy would too."

"The will is legal. Too bad they didn't register it, though it might not have made a difference."

"But Anne told me they had registered it."

"We've checked. It's not registered." Ryan was skimming the document.

"But she said, Anne said, that Richard had sent it with Sylvia. Sylvia did the legal work for the firm and ran errands. She was supposed to take it to the, I think it's called the Register of Wills Office."

Becca was looking at Ryan and nodding. Both Jen and Lucy saw the silent communication.

Lucy finally got it. "Oh, she didn't do it did she? She kept it. Or destroyed it. Why would she do that? Why wouldn't she want Rebecca to live with us?"

"Did you read this," Ryan asked Lucy, passing it to Becca, not answering the question.

"No, just the part where I could have Rebecca."

"There's a trust fund mentioned inside the will. It's done that way sometimes. Might be something inside that, inside the trust fund. The certificate of trust is missing. Excuse me while I get someone to see if they can find a record of it. Tough, if the will wasn't filed there's a good chance the trust wasn't either. Depends on the type of trust, too."

By the time Jake came on the line, he had thought it out a little more. "We need to see if the trust was filed or if it's in Richard Travis' tax returns. How do we find a trust? Who did his taxes? I'm not up on tax law, but I think that Becca can request a copy or a summary if we need it. How do we find the trust, how do we get copies?"

"I sure don't know. But we have a financial guru in the family. I'll call Penney; if she doesn't know,; she'll know someone who does. How's Becca doing? She looked a little distraught last night. Cilla says she'll be fine, but I'm concerned. I don't want Becca to go off the tracks like I did."

"She's strong. Strong as Cilla. She'll deal. We don't have to worry about her."

"That's just what Cilla said."

"Jake, she'll ask for help. Okay?"

"Also what Cilla said." He sighed.

"If you were female, I would say that you are being oversensitive due to your past idiocy," Ryan commented.

"Yeah, I know. Must be because I'm going to be a dad," he added.

Ryan stood up; he had been leaning against the door frame keeping an eye on the kitchen. "No shit! Congratulations."

"Aww shit, I wasn't supposed to tell anyone. Cilla wants to tell the gang herself. I must be half female if that slipped out. Hell."

Ryan was laughing out loud now. "You better just say good bye and hang up before you start crying."

Jake took his advice, laughing at himself. "Bye."

Ryan was still chuckling when he came back into the kitchen. "Nothing. Later," he amended. "We better be leaving; we have another meeting tonight."

They said their goodbyes. Ryan again told Lucy they would get back to her if they learned anything and grabbed some cookies for the trip.

Jen checked in when they got back to the car and then said to Becca, "Lucy knows."

"Knows what?"

"She was watching you and Ryan. She knows."

"How can she know anything? She doesn't know either of us," Becca protested.

"But she knew your Mom. And apparently you have the same mannerisms. She knows. I was watching her watch you."

Becca just settled back grumbling to herself. But she did it with a little smile. So Lucy thought she was in love with Ryan. Better yet, thought Ryan had feelings for her!

⁕

Jake was already at the gatehouse. Cav and Jones came in right behind them with the food. Food and Cav always made Becca smile. Because it so puzzled Cilla. Which came first, the chicken or the egg? Cav or food? And here they were arriving together.

Jen stayed. Jake announced that Cilla and Tony were running late and that Ryan had two FAXs from the New Madrid Sheriff.

"Why does he get a FAX?" Becca complained. "Are you sure it's not addressed to me?"

"Donavan confessed to murdering Michelle and J.B. He says he followed them and flagged them down. Argued with them and shot them both. Says it was an accident. He used J.B.'s phone to send the ransom note to himself. It will be in the papers tomorrow," Ryan read from the document. "There will be an acknowledgement that you helped them solve the case. This FAX is my thank you." Ryan grinned at her and handed over the first FAX.

He held up the other. "Warrant," Ryan said. "For the post office in," he glanced through the document quickly, "Bridgeport, NJ. Just down the highway and across the state line from New Madrid, if I remember correctly." He passed the warrant to her and told her, "Sit down; eat something; you're tired and hungry and testy."

She was about to say something angry, but he was pulling out a chair for her and pushing her into it. "I'll be right beside you here," he talked over her, "You can punch me in the arm every few minutes. It will make you feel good."

Becca heard Jen choking and looked up to see the others apparently very busy opening the cartons of Chinese and passing around plates, chopsticks, and silverware. She couldn't think of anything nasty to say so she punched Ryan in the arm. Jen broke up. Becca just glared at her, but she felt better.

Penney came in with Daffy who shook hands all around. But he kept hold of Penney with his left hand. And she let him. They looked silly in love still. Becca cheered up just looking at them. She hoped Penney had news.

Daffy was telling a wild tale about one of his clients, between mouthfuls, when Cilla and Tony arrived.

Cilla, being Cilla, couldn't wait with her news, announcing excitedly as she walked through the front door, "We got 'em. We got them." She was almost dancing.

"We got the common denominator. It's the landscaper. We had to go to the jewelry stores, both of them. That's why we're late. The floral section of the landscaping company, run by a Martha White, provides the live interior plants and floral displays. Everything fits except the first theft, the home invasion. I know we all decided it was the crucial crime, so you guys can figure out how it fits."

"Wait, wait, give me a minute." Becca put her fork down; she'd never learned how to manage chop sticks. "Six out of seven have the same landscaper or interior plant provider?"

"Yes, the same. The company provides landscaping on one side and White, the florist with floral interiors, is on the other. The landscaper has three crews working on new landscapes and about another fifty to seventy-five employees working on lawn services like mowing and trimming. Mostly illegal aliens," Cilla said as she and Tony were loading plates.

"How did you find that out," Jake asked with an edge to his voice.

"Calm down Jake, we just walked around looking at the plants and listening. Neither one of us is a detective nor am I particularly brave. We didn't do anything stupid," she admonished him.

"And, you didn't let me finish, we got more. We left there and went to one of the jewelry stores to look around," she started.

"I thought you just said you didn't do anything stupid," Jake growled.

"Stand down, Jake," Daffy said calmly. "Give her a chance here." Daffy was one of the few people who could reach Jake.

Jake glared at Daffy apparently getting ready to share his anger. He took a breath and swallowed his anger instead. "You're right, again. Cilla, I'm sorry, please go ahead."

"Remember, neither one of those shops has any landscaping, they're right on the street. Tony and I looked at watches, just under a really pretty floral display. But they didn't have the watch I wanted for my husband. When I commented on how pretty the display was the sales clerk told us all about it. She was more excited about the flowers than the watches. The florist, White, comes by once a week, checks with her to determine the type and color of flowers for the next week. She replaces the display every week." Cilla handed a note to Jake and told the others, "The second shop has a display in the window, the same florist's name, Martha White, is easily readable. Ta Da!!"

"You're talking one person here? At both jewelry shops? She works at the floral half of the landscaping business," Daffy said. "The geek did it!"

"It was Becca's idea. She suggested we look at interior plants," Cilla gave credit to her sister.

"Good work Cilla, really good work. Tony, you too. We'll run background checks on the landscapers tomorrow," Jake responded.

"Finally we have a link, but I still think that the first robbery is the one we need to examine. Somewhere in there, you'll find an overlap or connection to the landscaper." Becca caught herself looking to Ryan for agreement and punched his arm when he grinned at her. She saw Jen out of the corner of her eye mouthing, '*told you.*'

"We need to find out how the home invasion fits with the rest of the crimes. It's there. Family, friends, neighbors, it's there somewhere," Becca finished.

"We'll find it, "Tony said.

"It might be more important to figure out where they're going to hit next," Cav said. "That's critical for me. Even if we find the connection, we need to predict the next robbery. Cilla? Can you do that?"

Cilla had her chin in her hands and was looking out above her fingertips obviously examining her computer options.

"There is no pattern. We have established that. Except that the robberies are all along the corridor, during this month of the year. Wonder why this month?" she said almost to herself. "So we need to come at it from the other direction. Maybe we could look at what would give them the biggest payoff?"

She glanced at Tony. "Did we check to see if there were any promotions or advertisements by the shops before they were hit? TV or radio commercials? Flyers or posters? I don't know if we can do that all the way back. But we could look at current advertisements, make a list, and try to narrow it down. Guess?" She turned to Cavanaugh, "We'll work it out tomorrow, Cav. See if we can get it down to a manageable number."

Jake took over, "Next is Mary Lee. She can't make tonight, but she has asked for a meet with me tomorrow. She has sub-let a condo in Tom's building. I don't know how she did that, I'll find out tomorrow. She has some ideas. Ryan you want to be in on that, Daffy?" Jake asked.

This time it was Ryan checking with Becca, as Jen snickered. "Depends on when you meet. Becca and I want to get to that post office clerk. It's already been too long and the chance of anyone remembering anything is slim, but we need to try."

Daffy said to count him in. "Mary Lee has good instincts. If she has a gut feeling and wants a meet, you can be sure she already has a plan of action. Sure I want in."

Ryan looked at Becca again, "We'll head over when we get done at the post office. This sounds like fun." He turned to Penney. "You have any luck with that trust?" he asked.

"No. I'm thinking maybe Becca's grandparents. I want to check their maiden names. It might be hidden there. Can you find those names for me?"

"Tony, add that to your list for tomorrow, bring in whoever else you need." Jake instructed. "Next, Tony and Cilla came up with some interesting stuff on the Smiths. Three months after the accident, Smith ceases to exist. He doesn't re-up in the Reserve. He doesn't go back to work. He has no checking account, no charge cards, no email, cell, or Facebook. He is just gone. No missing persons. The architecture business, FSR Associates is dissolved. After," he paused. "After five million dollars in key man insurance on Richard Travis is paid to it."

Ryan whistled. "He's dead."

"No record of that. No death certificate. He must be another of those only child of an only child people. Tony is going to do more tomorrow. But it is a mighty big coincidence that two of the three key people die, one is killed, and the other just disappears. This might be a dangerous woman to be around. She now lives outside of D.C. where she bought a condo."

Cav was shaking his head. "You people never ever do anything the easy way. Can't just have an innocent widow here, you have to have a serial killer. Man," he whined. "The accident is in my jurisdiction. I can look into her some."

"You drive again tomorrow, Jen," Ryan said. She grinned happily. Especially when Ryan looked at Becca for agreement after a moment's hesitation.

**

When everyone was gone, Ryan walked Becca the long way to the pool through the garden. "You don't have to look at your medical records," he began.

She looked at him dispiritedly. "I have to. Because I have them, I have to review them. They are part of my case."

"No, you don't. I don't think you want to and you don't need to. There is nothing that says you have to see them. You lived through all that already. There will be nothing new." He pushed his points, "If you were on this case with your partner, would you both have to read the records?" he asked her.

"No. One of us, whoever knew the most medical jargon. He'd summarize it for the other."

"Well, same situation here. Cilla reads them and if she finds anything you don't already know, she tells you. You don't have to do it."

"Are you conning me?" she asked. "Are you running one of your scams on me? Telling me what I want to hear? Showing me a way out?"

He looked shocked for an instant. "No. You can think for yourself and make your own decisions. But you are so close to the case that you need a reasonable explanation of why you don't have to look through that file. Did you do the research on the robberies? No. Are you tailing Tom? No. You're letting others do that. You can't be everywhere, doing everything. You can cut yourself some slack on the medical records."

She was considering that when he added, "Tell you what. You don't need to decide today. You don't have to look at that file now. Or even tomorrow. Give yourself time to give yourself distance. Make a decision later."

She thought about it and didn't see where putting off reading the file was too cowardly. She could read it another day.

"What about the picture book?" she asked. "Would you tell me the same thing about that?" This would be critical she thought. If he said the same thing, then she would know that he was indeed conning her. Because she did have to look at the pictures.

"No. You need to look at the pictures. They won't hurt you."

"Is that a con? Because you know I want to?"

"No, the con part would be to suggest that you look at them with Nancy. Or Lucy. Or both of them."

And that was exactly what she wanted to do.

"If that's the con, what's the reason I should do that?" she asked.

"Because looking at the pictures with them, while listening to their stories might shake something loose. Your mind has shut out that part of your life for a reason. Granted the trauma might have been enough to do that."

"And you think it could be more than trauma?"

"I don't know. Either way, looking at the pictures might be a path through that door. You need to take it."

He let her think about that for a while and then offered other options, "Or I could sit with you here while you look through the book. Or you could take it into your room and look through it by yourself. But the con is you do it with the women. Because it will help reestablish a relationship they seem to want and you deserve."

Huh, that was sweet. "Now explain your reasons why I shouldn't look at my records."

"There lies only desperation and despair. When you walked away and let your attackers be tried for other crimes, you chose your future. That was a good decision. You know that. This is only a continuation of that decision. A strong, brave decision. That's almost the con. But it was, and still is, the best decision for you."

She agreed with that. She agreed with everything he'd said but she'd needed more confirmation.

"You can always talk to Sarah. Ask her," he suggested.

"No, I agree with you. I just wanted to hear what you thought and why. I'll hold off on reviewing the hospital records and meanwhile you can give them to Cilla. The same with my state records when we get them. I can always change my mind later, but this feels right." And if Ryan gave them to Cilla, she wouldn't have to touch them; somehow her skin felt dirty when she touched the files. She was afraid her inner self might become tainted if she read through them. She knew that was silly, but it was the way she felt.

Tuesday

"Nothing, we got exactly nothing," Becca complained as she and Ryan left the post office.

"No less than we expected. A clerk can't remember everyone who comes to his window. And the envelopes could have been prepaid, though I think our guy did use the window. Wouldn't take a chance on dropping it in a mail chute."

It was disappointing but Ryan was right. And he had used about two dozen methods in an attempt to make the clerk picture his customer.

"No, he didn't come here four times." The clerk was adamant on that. "Maybe I talked to him twice, but I'd remember if he came to my window four times. I look at my customers. And look around, it's only me here. He'd have had to come to me."

When Ryan had asked if he could check his records for any other express mail envelopes he'd found none. Just those two.

"It's interesting that he didn't mail four express envelopes, though," Ryan said. Becca waited for him to explain the remark, but he didn't.

"What do you mean?" Jen finally asked.

"Think about it," was all he said.

"Now I need to go to Mary Lee's meeting. You two can go help Tony and Cilla. They have a lot on their plates. And Becca, Cav wants you to work with Jones on his cold cases. Lord help us if they become infected with the gang version of complicated, instead of nice simple felonies. We'll never hear the end of it."

When Becca didn't complain about being left out of the meeting he asked, "No complaints?"

"No. I don't think so. Not this time. Jake didn't invite me. I thought about it last night and decided it's okay. You guys are probably going to talk procedures. You will tell me when you make a decision about what to do next. If I don't like it, or if I have additional ideas, I'll let you know then." She knew that was a fairly professional stand on her part.

Ryan continued to stare at her.

"What?" she said, protested, "I can't be reasonable?"

He laughed.

**

"I want to brace him," Mary Lee said. "Me, and Daffy, since he's here, and one other operative. I think I know what's going on, but the only way to be sure is to brace the guy and get him to tell us." She waited patiently.

"The third man should be me," Ryan said. He didn't question what she wanted to do, just who should do it.

"Why?" Mary Lee asked.

"Because when three strange people brace him, he's going to panic and fight."

"Daffy and I can handle that," she said flippantly.

"No doubt. But you need the guy on your side if you want him to talk. Bracing him and beating him up isn't going to make him want to talk to you. But if I stick an FBI badge in his face he should be interested and it should take all the panic and fight out of him"

"That could work," she said. "But this is not an FBI investigation."

"It's tied to an FBI investigation, the shooting of a law enforcement officer. A shooting he might know something about."

"Tell us what you think you know," Jake ordered.

"Farwood has been following the firm's limos the past three nights. Different drivers from those they use in the daytime. They look like bouncers, hired thugs, probably body guards. The limos pick women up at a building owned by a company called Consortstoo and drive them, singly, mostly, to hotels and go inside with them. The women go upstairs; the guards wait in the lobby. An hour or so later they come back out and go to a different hotel. Or a driver and shotgun take a flock of girls to a party generally at some McMansion. They stay most of the night. They're running some kind of prostitution call girl ring.

"I think Tom has only just figured this out since up until Friday he went to work and went home. Saturday, he started tailing them. I've been following him, my team members following the other limos. I don't think this is what he was sent to expose. I think it's something he stumbled upon and I think it's making him nervous."

The three men were listening. She had their attention.

"I think if we let him know that we can help with the call girl problem and if we tell him we know he's a plant, we can get him to spill what he's doing. There has to be money changing hands somewhere. Fleet maintenance at least. Who's paying for the gas? Who's tracking the miles driven and the mileage? How about maintenance? Someone's fudging the records."

"It would be better than following him for the next three years to see if he goes after Becca again," Ryan agreed. "Mary Lee is right. She could follow him forever."

"How do you plan to do it? Brace him?" Daffy asked, settling back to listen.

"I catch him in the elevator, in my sexy streetwalker getup with my wrist splint. Get him to help me take my groceries to my condo. You guys take him when he walks in the door."

"What about his place? Have you been in it?" Ryan asked, he was curious. "Not that I'm listening with my cop ears."

"You don't have to worry about your cop ears. He has it secure. Double bolts and I heard him turn off an alarm one time when I went up in the elevator with him. While he was at work, I slipped a camera under his door and took a look around. He has a motion sensor with cameras set up so I haven't been inside."

Jake was nodding, "It could work. When did you want to do it?"

"Tomorrow. We're spinning our wheels following him, but we can try one more night. I don't think he went after Becca. Everything I've heard about him says he would do a face to face shoot. Granted he's undercover, but some form of unbalance would show through and from what I've seen personally, and learned from the people I've talked to, he is a total professional."

"I'm assuming that these limos went across state lines too?

"Sure. Philly, of course, Camden and Wilmington. So both New Jersey and Delaware."

"That gives us another point with Farwood. Prostitution across state lines. We can take over that case. He doesn't even need to get involved. Tonight, I ride along with you, and then I can get a warrant. We take him tomorrow night," Ryan suggested.

"We need a couple of practice runs before you brace him; let's iron out the details," Jake said.

"I got video of the building. Entrance, lobby and my floor."

"Becca is going to insist on helping. She is being reasonable about this meeting, but she'll want to ride along tonight and be with us tomorrow," Ryan advised.

"Yeah, you're right. I was kind of surprised she let you come here alone," Jake said. "I'll get her." He called her to come up.

"We thought you would want to be in on the planning," Jake informed Becca after he explained.

"I want to go tonight," she insisted. "And I want to be in the apartment tomorrow night."

"Tonight's okay." Ryan agreed, "But tomorrow? I don't think so."

Before she could argue, voice of reason Daffy spoke up. "In a back room. You can listen and be available in the bedroom in case we need you. But he shouldn't see you; it will just confuse things. We want him to tell us about the limos. That will be easy because we already know. Ryan can con him with what Mary Lee has guessed about vehicle maintenance costs and mileage logs to get him to tell us what he has found at the firm. We also want to know how the firm will handle the embezzlement, in house or in the courts. But the prostitution will be Ryan's."

He looked at her. "If you're there, we lose all that. He'll focus on you. If he is focused on you, we won't be able to feel him out on your shooting. We might need to bring you into the room after we get the rest settled. So you should be there."

The other men nodded agreement.

"Okay. I can see where you could be right." Becca gave Ryan that *I can be reasonable* look again. But then added, "You can't trail crooks in New Madrid without telling my Captain. You're making this official and you're going to use it for a warrant so he needs to know."

"She's right," Jake said. "You have been working closely with him and it is his town. It will be even better if we have the locals along. We could use them on the surveillance. Think you can get them onboard by tonight, Ryan? Becca?"

They both looked at each other, "I'll call, then you can talk to him," Becca said. She got up and walked to the corner of the room as Jake's phone rang. He listened a few minutes and then spoke to Ryan, "Penney has the trust. Cilla and Tony got her the maternal grandmother's maiden name. Penney can contact the attorney who is holding it if you want."

Ryan saw Becca was listening; he nodded yes. "Have her find out what she can. We'll set up tonight with New Madrid."

**

The surveillance went as planned. Detective Khalen rode with Becca and Ryan with Mary Lee driving. Becca noticed Khalen couldn't stop staring at Mary Lee. They were to follow Tom who was following one of the drivers. Three other detectives were riding with Jake's three operatives, each following a different limo. It was to be a night of observation with video recordings. Gather enough proof to back up a warrant to arrest the girls, the drivers, and the johns the next night. Also warrants to search the buildings both at the pickup point, and the destinations.

Tonight all the limos returned at the same time. Two drivers came out and got into their own cars and drove off. Jake's teams would follow them. A third walked out and the driver Tom had been following exited and headed toward a car parked behind Tom. But then everything went south. Suddenly, the driver made a quick turn and busted out Tom's window with a baseball bat, hitting Tom in the head. He pulled open the door and dragged Tom out onto the street where he began kicking him, screaming, "Why are you following me?" emphasizing each word with a kick.

Tom was trying to protect his head and body, curled into a fetal position, bleeding profusely from the head. The other thug reached down and grabbed Tom by the shoulders and then pulled his head up by the hair. The first thug was just getting ready to hit Tom in the face with the bat when Daffy tackled him knocking him back against the car. Almost at the same time Mary Lee charged into the other guy.

Daffy easily leaned back out of the way as his thug came out swinging, leading with a right he telegraphed all the way. Daffy hit him in the belly folding him up and followed that with a right to the jaw. As the thug quietly slipped to the ground, Daffy flipped him over, checking on Mary Lee as he pulled flex cuffs out of his pocket.

He smiled and winked at her. She had the other driver on the ground with a choke hold. Subdued. He could see the guy's face; it was red and terrified. Mary Lee seldom needed help. She was a martial arts expert. Even Daffy had never been able to put her down.

Detective Khalen was just getting there. There wasn't much for him to do but check on Farwood. Mary Lee was already cuffing her guy. She hadn't broken a sweat.

Back in the car, Becca was struggling with Ryan. "Let me go. I'm a cop, I can help," she snarled as she tried to pull her arm out of his grasp. She realized he was trying not to hurt her but she still couldn't get away. She had the door open but couldn't get her arm free. She tried to elbow him, but couldn't get any leverage. Suddenly she flashed back on her 'uncle' when he held her down, helpless. She straightened her leg against the door and shoved herself hard against him, hoping to break his hold that way. Turned to face him when that didn't work, and bent her knee to kick him. Her frustration at being defenseless and immobilized brought tears to her eyes. "Let me go," she wailed. "Please let me go," she begged, punching him with the weak punches of a child.

"Listen," he said grabbing her hands. "Listen Becca. Honey, look at me," he ordered. "You can't. You can't go out there, sweetheart. Stop." He'd been gentle. He didn't want to hurt her but he heard the terror in her voice. The pain. She'd stopped breathing. Now he was talking to her gently. Bringing her back to the present. "Breathe honey. Breathe."

He let go of her hands and reached out to tilt her jaw up and toward him and saw the tears leaking out of her closed eyes. His stomach rolled. He saw the fear.

"Honey. Sweetheart. Look at me. Open your eyes."

She heard his voice. Sweetheart? Honey? Those words brought her back to now. She took a breath.

"Oh, sweetheart. It's okay." He leaned over and kissed her gently. "It's okay, sweetheart."

Her world went white with the kiss; she saw it flare through her eyelids, a bright explosion. At the same time a silence descended on her.

She opened her eyes to see what had happened. Saw only his face an inch above hers. She didn't see anger in his eyes as she had expected. She saw concern, worry. Love?

"What?" she asked. "What happened." She wasn't sure what she meant. The terror that had grabbed her. The explosion of light. The silence. A kiss that melted her insides?

He didn't answer, but kissed her again. Longer this time. Not as long as he wanted. Not as gentle. Didn't do the things he wanted to do to her. Not here in the back seat of a car. Besides they were in the middle of an op.

He let her go. His tongue tasting her on his lips. Smiled at her. Ran his fingers along her jawline. Over her lips. "The world just tilted," he said. "For me at least," looking at her questioningly.

She was nodding her head, looking at his lips. "Me too," she whispered. "Me too."

He cleared his throat. It felt like days had passed. He looked through the windshield. It took a moment to realize everyone was looking at them. Oops, mic on. Saw Becca realize the situation. She surprised him and smiled. Laughed.

"Khalen?" he said. "You gotta make it look like you all just happened by and witnessed a run of the mill mugging. Get Jake's people out of there. Otherwise there won't be anyone to arrest tomorrow night."

"Yeah, we're on it. Got a squad car coming for them and an ambulance for Farwood. Looks like they did some damage. We'll let the

EMTs deal with it." He paused and then added with a smirk, "You folks got it all squared away in the car there?"

"Yeah, I think so. We don't want anyone to see Becca. She's staying in the car. Someone could be around gunning for her. I'll stay here with her." He knew he wasn't fooling anyone. They'd been watching, listening.

He turned off the mic. "I'm sorry. I didn't mean to grab you, but you sort of freaked. We don't want these thugs to know we're following them. We don't want anyone to see you."

"I got it. I understand. I lost it I guess when you grabbed me. I'm sorry."

He hugged her. Held her tight. "We'll talk. Later. When we are alone." For now it felt good to just hold her.

**

"How did you get there so quick?" Khalen asked Mary Lee on their way to the hospital, following the ambulance.

"I'm a bodyguard," she said simply. "I move quick."

"Yes. But I was seeing the same things as you. Yet it was all over by the time I got there. You were out of the car before that guy even broke the window." Sounded like a complaint. Mixed with admiration?

"It's my job. It's what I'm good at. And what I saw wasn't working for me. Something was off. I could sense that. I thought maybe I could head it off. Daffy did the same. Call it a bodyguard's sixth sense."

Khalen nodded. "What was that you used on him, to subdue him? I don't think I've seen those moves before."

"Brazilian jiu-jitsu. It lets a smaller weaker person like me, put my stronger, larger opponent on the ground and use joint locks and choke holds to subdue them. Simple. I'm a black belt. I can teach you if you like," she offered with a grin.

Becca was only half listening because she was pleading her own case in the backseat. "I want to go in with you. I want to be there when you talk to Tom. I can be on the other side of the curtain or behind a door. But I want to hear what he says."

Ryan scratched his ear. "We might be able to do it. We can talk to him in the emergency room. Mary Lee and Daffy can stay with you." Daffy was following in his car and would meet them there.

Ryan raised his voice, "Mary Lee, can you change Becca's appearance? Something quick and easy?"

"That's my other area of expertise," Mary Lee said looking in the rearview mirror. "I got a wig in the trunk, a tacky shirt, and a makeup kit. I can flatten her cheekbones and put some pads in her cheeks. That will change the shape of her face. Simple. No one will recognize her."

That's the way they worked it. Becca became a frumpy blonde with a flat fat face in a shabby shirt.

Ryan and Khalen went in to talk to Tom when the doctors were finished with him.

Ryan started by introducing himself and Khalen. "We know about the call girls. New Madrid is going to bust them tomorrow night. We know the ring is using your cars. Well your firm's cars. We think you stumbled on those guys and followed them."

Farwood didn't say anything. It was obvious he was in pain. The doctor said two broken ribs, possible concussion. They didn't think so, but were going to send him for x-rays.

"I can repeat all of that if you want," Ryan offered. "Or maybe you think you need a lawyer?"

"No," Tom started. Stopped and drank some water. "No, I got all that." Paused again. "Yeah, I was in the garage early one morning and saw those men drive in with four, five of our limos. Not any of our drivers. I knew the cars weren't rented and if they were bringing them back, they weren't stealing them. I came the next night and waited and followed one of them to see what they were up to." He stopped again.

Ryan was smiling. He had him talking now. A trickle maybe, but he would get it all. "You figure out what they were doing?"

"Well, it was pretty obvious."

"What were you going to do about it?" Ryan asked. Again he had to wait while Farwood decided if he would answer.

"I was going to tell my boss. I got some pictures last night. My camera. Did you get my camera?"

"Probably still in your car. Khalen is having it towed to the police compound and he'll have someone take your camera into safe keeping."

"Good, I need those pictures for my boss."

"Which boss?" Ryan asked.

Now Farwood looked at him considering. "Which boss?" he asked puzzled. "My boss in personnel. Is that what you mean? He'll take it to the company manager."

"What about Phil? You going to tell him?"

Farwood started and then groaned from the movement. "What do you mean?" he bluffed.

"Phil, your boss at Camden Investigations."

There was a very long silence, Khalen was getting edgy. Ryan sent him a warning look.

Finally, "What do you know about Phil? And why would the FBI be interested?"

"The FBI is interested in a lot of things. Right now, I'm looking at prostitution across state lines. Don't really care about your job at the limo firm or with Phil. Just trying to clear up a couple of points. Let's concentrate on who is running the call girls." Not a lie.

"I'm a personnel assistant," Farwood tried.

Ryan just waited.

"Okay. Phil inserted me. The owner said he was losing a lot of money and couldn't figure out how. Took me a long time to narrow it down to maintenance. But I couldn't figure out how they were working it. Everything I checked seemed OK. I knew it had something to do with maintenance. Not a stretch, that's where most of the money was spent. Their main costs are maintenance, new vehicles, and drivers. Then I realized that I never saw the original logs, only summaries of time in time out, and beginning ending mileage for each trip. I went in at night and checked the glove boxes where they keep the logs. But all I found were individual sheets. One sheet per day, per car. That was strange. Most logs are bound booklets which include fuel, maintenance, and down time. That was suspicious. But even those looked accurate." He drank more water.

"I went over and over them. Nothing. How long was I working there? Finally I went in at night and counted the vehicles. I came up short. I figured, well some were still out. Tried it three more times. Each time I came up short. Fewer cars than they had purchased."

He was shaking his head. "Can't believe it took me so long. I compared license numbers. I had four numbers that didn't have a car. So now I was looking at the head of maintenance who submitted files for work never done and the purchaser who bought imaginary cars. I went inside and pulled the files for the four cars. All the sheets were photocopies. What they were doing is randomly taking a sheet from another vehicle and copying it. Then they would white out the license number and mileage and put in the fake number and mileage. So everything looked legit, except there was never any income from those vehicles. They had maintenance records though. They spent a lot of time in the shop. Down time."

"Then I checked the drivers. They were all fictitious and none ever earned enough that the firm had to submit a 1099 or notify the IRS of the drivers' incomes. Best of all, the embezzlers got to keep each driver's monthly check. Those checks were going into special accounts. There were also monthly payments on four imaginary car loans. The guys were pulling in thousands of dollars a month."

"I went back and checked very early the next morning and I was sitting in my car trying to figure out why I was ten cars short. That's when I saw those guys I didn't recognize bring back the cars. Six cars. I was still short four."

"That's when you decided to follow them?"

"I thought about it a few hours. But yeah."

That matched what Mary Lee had seen. "What did Phil say?" Ryan asked and waited again.

"The firm is going to handle the embezzlement in-house. The guys are both relatives. We are still trying to nail down what is happening with the limos. But both Phil and the manager are going to take that to the cops. After they get with their attorneys."

"Well you don't have to worry about that part now. New Madrid and the FBI will take over." Again the truth. Ryan had contacted his boss who had assigned a special agent to work with Khalen. They'd make the bust tomorrow night, which would be tonight now.

"Tell me about Detective Travis," he said.

"Rebecca? Rebecca doesn't have anything to do with this." He leaned forward with a groan. "You don't think Rebecca had anything to do with this. No way. She's straight as an arrow. You can't be thinking that." He leaned back, taking shallow breaths. "How do you know about Rebecca?"

"You're seeing her aren't you?"

"No, we broke up about six, eight weeks ago. She doesn't know anything about what I do."

"Why did you break up?"

"It's personal."

"Is there some reason you don't want to share?"

"She's not involved in this," he said again and then capitulated as Ryan waited. "She wanted to get serious. My job. I can't. I never know who I'm going to be tomorrow. Or where. Letting her walk out was about the stupidest thing I ever did. But it would have happened sooner or later anyhow. Better for her for it to happen sooner. She's not involved in any of this," he said again.

"You know she was shot?"

"It was all over the news. But there's no way it's connected to me or what I was doing."

Ryan believed him. Khalen was nodding.

"You go to visit her in the hospital?"

"I thought about visiting her, but then I realized we'd still end up the same way. I kept up with her progress with the newspapers. She's retired now."

"Do you know where she is?" Ryan asked.

"No. I tell you she is not involved. Leave her out of this."

The doctor came back in saying they were ready to take Farwood to x-ray if they were done. Ryan and Khalen left, picking up Mary Lee and Becca.

"It wasn't him," Becca said. "I told you it wasn't."

"We had to eliminate him. And this way Khalen gets another case solved. One he didn't even know he had. So everyone is happy."

Becca thought that Khalen might be even more happy since he had met Mary Lee. They were making arrangements to meet for some Brazilian jiu-jitsu. Becca thought about snickering, but she was too tired. They had worked all day and through the night. It was eight in the morning. Did she have therapy today? She was trying to remember. Yes. She did. Lori was going to be pissed.

Wednesday

Lori was pissed. She was waiting with Annie, the housekeeper. Not patiently. "You are a little late," she stated. "How can you be late? You live here."

"My fault," Ryan said. "I kept her out all night."

Becca had slept on the way home, her head on Ryan's lap. He'd thrown a comforter over her. "Set up your table," she told Lori, "I'm going to wash my face and then I'm resting while you work on me." She had already stepped past when she said, "By the way, I bent my knee all the way and never even noticed. No pain, no ache. I put my full weight on it, by accident, and it held. It was an hour later when I realized what I had done." Smiling, she went to the bathroom.

It was the truth. Mary Lee had made a comment about kissing noises coming from the car while she and Daffy were checking Tom. That was when Becca realized her leg had taken her full weight when she was pushing against Ryan. And she had fully flexed her knee before she kicked him. Way to go. She was getting better. She'd have danced if she could have danced. She danced inside her head again.

Lori went easy on her, happy to see her progress. "Keep up with your exercises," she reminded on the way out.

Ryan had showered and made breakfast. She was half way through her French toast when she froze. Staring.

"What's wrong?"

"You told me to think about it. I forgot. You said that. I just remembered it. But I couldn't remember what it was I was supposed to think about." She guessed she was going to tell him every step she took. "The postal clerk. He said he would remember anyone who came to his window four times. Based on what we found, no one did. The guy making the bribe only went there twice. So the other Board member wasn't bribed. But he voted to put me on permanent disability anyway, which makes no sense. It was him. It was Sergio Nadeau. He bribed Scott. He knew what would work with Rummel. Mr. straight and narrow did it."

"I knew you would get it," Ryan said.

"What took me so long? You knew it right away," she griped.

"You have a lot going on. You're too close. You got there just the same. A day didn't make any difference."

"He'd know about Chloe Rummel and her women's lib hang-up. He'd know Scott could be bribed. It's perfect. We need that clerk to look at a photo lineup. See if he can pick Sergio out." She was getting ready to stand up.

"Khalen's getting one together. One of his men will take it down. Today. But don't get your hopes up. Even if he recognizes Sergio, it won't prove he mailed the envelopes. Or even that any envelope he might have mailed was the envelope with the cash. Khalen is going to include pictures of Scott and Rommel in the lineup too. It's possible the postal clerk might just be recognizing a face he has seen in the newspaper or on TV."

Becca had been doing another mental happy dance. "Drat. Every time we get an answer, three more questions pop up. Was Sergio behind it or was someone behind Sergio?"

"We're getting there, sweetheart. Little by little we are narrowing it down."

Her insides got warm when he called her sweetheart. She was thinking about the last time he called her sweetheart and sobered.

"What just happened?" he asked her. "I could almost see you doing a happy dance and then you got serious. You okay?" He watched her waiting.

"Yeah. I freaked on you."

She saw him trying to figure what she meant. "Last night, I freaked on you."

"I'm sorry about that. I couldn't let you go out there."

"I know. I know that now. You were right. But last night I was out of control." She had to explain, he had a right to know what happened.

"No. It was me," he said.

"Stop. I need to explain. To put into words, what happened. I've been so helpless."

He snorted, "Not you. You are never helpless."

"Let me finish," she insisted. "Just be quiet." He sat back and indicated she should continue.

"Right now, I am not in control of my life. Since that creep shot me, circumstances have dictated what I do, where I go, and when I go there. It's like I'm back in the system. I don't get a say. I've been the boss of me since Cilla rescued me. Up until now. Oh, sure, I got to decide to come to the gatehouse. But there was no other option. I got to decide to work with Lori. But how else would I get better? You walk into my life and flip it upside down."

He started to interrupt but settled back when she gave him that stare. Right, she's helpless, he thought.

"Don't take that wrong. I'm happy you are in my life. Confused, but happy. But back to what happened just now, where I went. My mind went back to the last time you called me sweetheart. Last night."

She took a breath. He was listening closely. This was it. "Last night, I flashed on my foster uncle. That's what happened in the car last night. I flashed on my uncle and I lost it. My instinct was to go help. You grabbed me and I couldn't get loose. I freaked and for a moment it was my uncle holding me and I was helpless. I couldn't get away. A flashback. I know what it was but for that minute it was real. I was back there. I don't understand why that happened. That makes me scared.

He's still listening, she thought, thank goodness, he is listening. "And I think, maybe, its tied to this blockage in my mind. I keep seeing, I'm not sure, little glimpses, like I'm looking through a foggy car windshield. But not from the driver's seat. From outside, looking in. I'm not sure. That's all I see. And when I see it I get scared. I want to see more, but I'm afraid. It's only been happening just these last few days. Never before. Only since Cilla asked about the freaky accident that killed my parents.

"Wait," she said again. "You'll get a chance. I'm scared of what I'll see when the fog clears because I know it will be bad. And I'm scared because I can't see. I don't want to see, but I know pretty soon I won't have a choice. I am not in control. My sub conscious mind is in control. Somehow my subconscious substituted my foster uncle, a horror that I can handle, for the fog which I must not be able to deal with yet? That makes sense to my conscious mind. I think?" She was asking for help. She knew it. She knew that he did too.

He was nodding, agreeing. "There was more to it last night, not just the attack on Tom. Sarah is the one you should talk to. She is the expert. But I'll tell you what I see. I see a strong vibrant woman handling everything that is being thrown at her. The shooting, the pain, the weakness. Circumstances boxing you in. But you are still in control. The fact that you can analyze last night so accurately proves it. That you can ask for help proves it."

Now she was listening to him, hopefully.

"Give yourself a break. That's what your mind is doing. It's getting ready to show you what it has kept hidden all these years. Searching for the best way to do that. The safest way for you to see behind that fog. You're right; it's not going to be good. It's not going to be pretty. Meanwhile, your subconscious brain protected you last night by putting you into a different bad place."

"It wasn't me who fought you, the *Twinkie made me do it?*" she asked him bitterly. "Please don't say that."

He took her hands in his. "You had a normal reaction to the circumstances. Don't read too much into it."

"Huh. I had a little girl reaction," she said disgustedly.

"Exactly. For an instant your mind made you a helpless little girl. But Becca took over, gained control. The strong Becca that I know took control."

"Um. I think it was the kiss," she said softly.

He smiled a wicked smile, "I did help. I shut your mind down. Pulled the plug on it." He was laughing at her. Thrilled a little that he had been able to do that. But then he recognized the shock on her face and wondered if he had gone too far.

"Do it again," she ordered him because she wanted to know. It wouldn't be the same. It couldn't be. Could it? "Please."

"You're the boss," he said as he put his hand behind her head.

She watched his eyes laughing, with desire. It seemed to take him forever as he leaned down.

But then she felt his lips and the world stopped. She shut her eyes. Bright lights flashed behind her eyelids, with colors today. Then her mind went blank. But parts of her body came alive. Thrummed. Today she heard music. She tried to listen, but he was doing something with his tongue in her mouth which distracted her but which she was thoroughly enjoying.

It was her. The not silence. It was her. Humming! The music she heard in the silence was her humming. She gave in to the feeling and kissed him back.

What he had meant to be a soft kiss turned into promise. Just tongues, no urgency, just sweet promise.

It could have gone on forever, but she was still healing. He broke it off. "Yeah, soon you and me," he promised. "When you're healed."

"There are other ways."

"I know. But our first time is going to be all about pleasure. No one holding back. Neither of us should be worried about you hurting. Nothing but mutual desire and enjoyment."

"Oh." He took her breath away.

She wanted him to know the worst, before he heard it from others. She made another confession. "I've been with a lot of men."

He considered that comment. "Rape doesn't ever count as a sexual liaison. The other men don't matter. Just no one else while you're with me. And you are with me now. Forever. I'm a one woman man and I don't share."

She could see that he was serious. "I can't have kids." She spit it out. Guess she was just going to share everything. She must really be tired.

He laughed at her. He really did. "I'm forty eight years old. I probably don't want kids. Unless you want to adopt?" What had he just said? "I never considered adoption before. But that idea could work with the right woman. Whatever you want." He was thinking about kids and how much fun his granddaughter was. Changed the subject. "Finish eating."

She was still working on adopt. She'd never even thought of children beyond that it would never happen for her. Never went beyond that thought. But she had one more thing to say.

"I have another confession."

He waited.

"I lied."

"Okay. About?" he couldn't imagine. It had all sounded true.

"I haven't been with a lot of men. Tom was only the second, since the rapes don't count. I've exaggerated my promiscuity on purpose. It keeps the good guys away and the bad guys are intimidated."

"Well, that makes sense, maybe." He was pleased that she told him. Pleased that she didn't sleep around. "It doesn't make a difference to me," he told her.

"I know. But it does to me and I wanted you to know."

She smiled, comforted somehow, and ate.

They finished in silence and she helped him with the cleanup. Daffy called to say that plans were in place to take down the call girl ring. He and Mary Lee would be riding along. Jake had OK'd it. Mary Lee probably with Khalen. Daffy with Cav. And Becca's Captain would ride with the FBI agent. Or maybe the FBI agent would ride with the Captain.

Becca laughed at that and turned to Ryan, "I know I should be tired, but will you look at the picture book with me. I think I want to do that now. First with you. To see, you know, my, um, my parents." The words scared her. She couldn't believe she was having trouble saying parents and family. She was nervous about looking at pictures of her family. "Later I want Lucy and Nancy to tell me about them. But first I just want to look. With someone, well someone not related to the people in the pictures. They'll be strangers to both of us."

"Well, I'm probably going to make funny comments then. Get comfortable on the couch, I'll fetch the book."

She left room for him against the arm of the couch. She had it all planned, he would hold the book and turn the pages; she would curl up beside him and look, like the pictures were of strangers. She could draw comfort from his nearness and put a little distance between her and the book. And the pictures.

But he didn't make funny comments. The pictures were of a happy family. He pointed out objects in the background, guessed at a beach scene, a car, a bedroom. The woman looked so much like Becca now; it was uncanny. He was sorry he had never met her. He could imagine the pain Becca must be feeling.

She was laughing at something he said when he turned a page. She gasped. Grabbed his arm and squeezed hard. He looked down and saw her face disintegrate. Saw her struggle. Her right hand was raised palm out as if to stop something. Her mouth was open, a scream forming. And then she did scream. "Sylvia!! No Sylvia!! No. Nonononono." She turned white. Collapsed with a moan. Stopped breathing. Gasped in a breath. Wailed, "Nooo. Daddy? Daddy, no."

He grabbed her. Pulled her into his lap. Wrapped his arms tight around her. Stoking her head, her arms, her back. "Shhh, Shh, it's okay, it's okay. It will be all right. Take a breath. Sweetheart. Breathe."

He wasn't getting through to her. "Becca!" he commanded in a loud stern voice. "Look at me! Look. At. Me." he ordered. "Becca. Breathe."

She gulped, hiccupped. Grabbed for air like she was drowning.

He held her tighter. God what had just happened? At least she was breathing. The picture. Sylvia? Was that Sylvia? Yes. There was her name under the picture. With Fred Smith.

He concentrated on calming Becca. She was breathing, moaning. Started wailing again.

He got his cell, speed dialed Cilla.

"Becca," he said. "I think she's had a breakthrough. I need you. Get Sarah. Hurry." He knew Cilla could hear Becca crying in the background. She'd be here in five minutes. She'd call Sarah on the way. All he had to do was keep it together for five minutes.

"Hold on sweetheart. Hold on. Shhh." Holding her.

She was almost convulsing she was crying so hard. Choking. Coughing. All he could do was try to comfort her. Let her know he was there. What was taking them so long?

Right then the security announced Cilla. She came charging into the room. Went straight to Becca.

Put her hands on Becca's head, "Honey" she whispered. "Honey, I'm here. It's okay. It's okay. I'll make it right, honey. I'll fix it."

Becca leaned into her, keening. Cilla rocked her back and forth. Cilla had saved her more than once.

Jake came in with Daffy right behind. Sure, they'd been at work, Ryan thought. The gang would probably all show up. They stuck together, protected each other.

"What happened?" Jake said to him.

Before he could answer Sarah was there.

Sarah was all business. Every bit the child shrink. "Breakthrough? Cilla said you thought a breakthrough, what do you mean?"

"We were looking at a photo book of her parents. Turned to a page that had her father's partners. Becca totally melted down. That's Sylvia. She melted down when she saw Sylvia. Screamed in a little girl voice. No Sylvia. I think Sylvia ran down her family. I think she saw Sylvia do it. I think the picture brought it all back."

Sarah nodded once. "Get me ice. In a plastic bag," she ordered. Both Daffy and Jake jumped.

She rubbed Becca's arms gently as Cilla held her still speaking softly. "Rebecca Anne," she commanded, "Look at me. Look at me Rebecca," she demanded. As Becca turned her face toward her, she took the ice bag from Jake and put it behind Becca's neck. A shock went through Becca and she inhaled sharply and opened her eyes. They were vague and unfocused. "Look at me Becca," Sarah demanded again.

Becca became aware of arms holding her, someone was yelling at her to look at them, she was freezing.

"What? What happened?" Becca saw Ryan and Cilla and Sarah looking down at her. "What, what, what happened? When did you get here?"

"Oh my God," she wailed remembering. "The blood, it was everywhere. She ran down my Dad. He tried to throw me out of the way. But she ran him down and he fell on top of me. He, he, he… Oh my God, Ryan, she killed him. She killed my parents. I saw her. Behind the windshield. She had this grin on her face and she ran us all down. That's what my brain was hiding, her face behind the fog. Her insane grin." She turned into his shoulder and now she was crying normally. Crying for her parents, herself.

Ryan just held her, rocked her.

"Becca, honey," Sarah said gently. "Honey?" Sarah turned Becca's head, the tears streaming down her face. "Honey. Do you want a pill? Something to ease the pain?"

Becca choked and shook her head. "No, no don't give me a pill," she managed to say.

Sarah nodded, "But you'll drink some water for me honey?" she asked.

Becca nodded, the tears still streaming down her face. Sarah sent Jake to get her a glass of water. And held the glass as Becca sipped, catching her breath. She drank a few sips and then curled back into a tight ball on Ryan's lap with her eyes closed.

"What did you give her?"

"Nothing. The water is enough. Let her rest while her mind copes with what she has learned. She'll sleep. A couple of hours will be good for her." Sarah patted Becca's head and told them, "This is normal. Well, normal for the situation. This is the healthiest reaction we could hope for. She's dealing with it. She is dealing with this breakthrough in the best way possible."

"What will she remember?" Ryan asked.

"Everyone is different. She'll remember what she told us. Any more, I don't know."

"What do we do when she wakes up?" he was totally out of his depth.

"Let her talk it out if she wants. But knowing Becca, she'll deal with it internally first. She'll probably be more vocal about having melted down and gone into hysterics."

Cilla was nodding agreement.

When Becca drifted off, Ryan breathed a sigh of relief. Her cries had torn him apart. Cilla was still patting Becca's hair, whispering. Ryan saw she was crying too, softly. Not making a sound, the tears running down her face.

"That's good. Sleep is the best medicine now. It's good," Sarah said, "It's a good sign. Let her sleep."

Sarah's cell rang quietly. "Michael," she told them and answered it. "We're fine. No, you don't need to come. We have it under control. I'm coming back in a few minutes and I'll tell you then."

"I think she'll be okay. Sometimes these breakthroughs are easy. She's strong; she should be able to absorb this. She has really known all along. It's just been filed away until she was strong enough to handle it. Now tell me in detail what led up to this."

He told them about last night and the way that Becca freaked. About their conversation this morning. He spoke quietly because he didn't want to wake her. He looked at her curled in his lap.

"Just hold her," Sarah said to him. "She feels safe with you. She's drawing comfort. I think she'll be fine."

"I have to get back," she told them. "I'll call Penney. You guys can probably go back to work. Becca will not be happy to wake up after this and find you all staring at her. Becca and Ryan will be fine by themselves." Then she told Ryan to call if he needed anything.

Cilla was crying in Jake's shoulder. Ryan had never seen her like that. She was one of the strongest people he knew. Brave and strong. Then he remembered that Jake had let slip she was pregnant and looked the question to Jake. "I got her," he assured Ryan.

Two minutes later, they were all gone and Ryan was alone with Becca asleep on his lap. Humph, he thought, the gang really trusted him. Then he reached over, grabbed the quilt, threw it over the both on them, worried.

He awoke when Becca moved. Opened his eyes to find her starring into his face. She was smiling. "How do you feel?"

"Tired, drained, ache all over. Like I got beat up by an elephant." She didn't tell him her brain had felt like mush with bright flashing lights and piercing discordant sounds. Now it had settled down but it felt like a sore muscle that had been overworked.

"You okay?" he asked.

"I think so. I've been lying here in your lap for a while, just thinking. Going back over everything. I think I'm OK. Thank you for holding me. I could feel your arms around me all the time I slept. They made me feel safe and protected. But I need to get up and pee." She kissed him then. "Thank you," she said and got up and walked off stiffly.

Made him think he needed to do the same thing. When he came back, she asked, "How many people saw me melt down? I know I saw Cilla and Sarah? I think maybe Jake and Daffy were here too?"

"The four of them."

"So now everyone thinks I'm a wuss," she muttered.

He laughed and said, "Sarah said that would be your main concern." He walked over to her, got in her face, and said, "Those four people know you are a brave, strong woman who has faced and overcome terrible hardships. They are so sure of your resilience that they left you alone with me without a qualm. And they are right. You are one tough lady. Besides, those men don't talk. They have seen enough human misery to recognize real pain. Your tough guy reputation is intact." He let that sink in and added, "I don't know about your virtue though. Daffy winked at me when he left. You sleeping in my lap. Men do talk about sex."

She pushed him away.

"Do you remember what happened?"

"I think so. It hit me so quickly. The memory was like a tidal wave washing ashore, overwhelming everything." There was so much feeling; she couldn't handle it all. She still had tears, but she could control them now. She would cry again later. Now, she just wanted to lie down.

"Tell you what. Let's take the rest of the day off and laze in the sun, soak in the hot tub. The team won't get back together until tomorrow and Cilla and Jake are following up on Smith now," he suggested.

"That will help. I can do that."

She let the warm water of the hot tub seep into her aching bones while the jets massaged her sore muscles. The quiet rumble of the jets occupied her mind. She closed her eyes and saw Sylvia again. She saw Sylvia every time she closed her eyes. Most of the time when they were open too. But it was just that one frame. Sylvia's insane grin. She vegetated in the womb-like environment of the hot tub, a pain in her heart. Later she moved to a chaise lounge and slept, again knowing Ryan was always within reach.

Later she would think. About Sylvia. Her parents. Her memories. Right now, she couldn't. Since the hysteria, she had found a few new memories. Or maybe she was tacking memories onto the pictures she had seen in the book. But she thought the memories had always been there, hidden.

**

She came awake slowly, feeling that she had slept well. When she opened her eyes she saw Ryan swimming lazy laps. He looked so good. Strong. Later she had to think about Ryan too. How was she going to fit Ryan into her life? She would take it slowly; otherwise she was afraid she might drown in all the new emotions. She watched thinking, mine. All mine. All I have to decide is if I want him. Who could not want him? But was it love? Shouldn't love be intense? Raise her heartbeat. Make her mouth go dry?

Huh. Her heartbeat was raised. Her mouth was dry, but that was because she was thirsty. She was sure. So she felt something for him. But was it love? Like for sure. And respect. He was a good cop with good instincts. An excellent interrogator. A good man. A passionate man if she could judge by the way he looked at her and kissed her. A compassionate man. And he could cook.

He said he loved her and that made her feel special. And kept her heartbeat up. Oh, stop worrying she told herself. Enjoy. He wasn't pushing for commitment; he wasn't hurrying her into a decision. She got up and slid into the pool to do some lazy laps with him.

Back at the house, she found the counter was set for dinner when she came out of the shower. He put what he called strata in front of her.

"What is it?"

"You might call it a meat quiche. I call it strata, because real men don't eat quiche. But it has the same ingredients, milk, eggs, cheese, onions, chunks of bread, and beef."

"You made me a quiche?" she snorted, laughing at him. "Ryan, real men don't *make* quiche, either."

He let her laugh at him. Her cheerfulness convinced him that she was going to be fine.

They cleaned up together again. Like an old married couple. He settled her on the couch with her book and set beside her with his. "Those dust bunnies, do you suppose they are the remnants of the original advanced settlement?" he asked as he sat beside her.

She laughed at him again, "It's a romance novel, anything is possible." She scooted over and snuggled into him. "It would be a simple answer. But I've been thinking about that. It would be too simple a solution. And how would they have adjusted. I'm leaning toward pet of the original settlers. They thrive in all sections of the planet and seem to be a little telepathic."

He looked at her in surprise, "Wow. You have given this some thought."

"Well I am a detective and it is a mystery. Detectives solve mysteries. Most likely though, it will be a story line that is never revealed. I wouldn't reveal it if I were writing the stories. Meanwhile each book has a few tasty bits of information and I keep buying them." She yawned.

Jake called with an update. Ryan put him on speaker phone. "Mary Lee just checked in. Khalen turned one of the hotel employees; he admitted the girls were turning tricks while the bodyguards waited in the lobby. That tied up the whole package and gave us all the probable cause we needed for the warrants. While your agent got them, the Captain called his counterparts in the other counties and we had a meet. New Madrid is running the operation with an FBI agent riding with each district. They'll wait until New Madrid follows a limo into their territory and then they will supply backup for the takedown. Daffy and Mary Lee will be riding with the Captain and Khalen. Everyone is heading for some shut eye now. Mary Lee will call when it's over."

"Thanks Jake. We'll wait to hear."

Becca yawned again and put her head down and closed her eyes.

******

Her trembling woke him. And then the trembling turned to thrashing and she struck out moaning, "Nooo."

He grabbed her wrists gently, "Becca, Becca. It's okay honey. It's okay. Wake up. Wake up sweetheart. Come on honey." Why hadn't he asked Sarah about nightmares? Should have been a reasonable question. He'd always heard you shouldn't wake someone from a nightmare. Or was that a sleepwalker you shouldn't wake? But he couldn't bear to watch her in discomfort.

"Wake up honey. It's okay."

She stopped. Her breath caught. Her eyes opened. At first they were terrified and then she recognized him. "Oh," she said. "A nightmare. I saw her. That single moment. Her insane grin. I knew what was going to happen. I knew I couldn't stop it." She rested her head on his shoulder. He wrapped his arms around her and held her tight. They sat that way until the trembling stopped.

"How about I get you a glass of milk," he suggested.

"Yes," she murmured.

He got her the milk, a drink for himself. He was still shaking. He sat beside her and pulled her over into the protection of his arm. Rested his chin on her head.

"Talk to me. Tell me about your granddaughter," she said.

"Did I ever tell you about the tutu? No? She had a tutu. She wore it all the time. Loved it. But she was outgrowing it. Just since my daughter-in-law had gone to her mother's. It was dirty and raggedy and coming apart. She was crying. I told her that her best grampa would fix it. But I tell you. I don't know anything about tutus. Do you know about tutus?"

"No, I think I know what they are. Ballet dancers wear them. Those little skirts that stick out all around. That the dancers rest their hands on?"

"Yeah. Except hers is the kind that hangs. Flounces, I think is the word. Apparently there are different types. But it wouldn't be manly for me to know that. One night I was sitting in the Inn office trying to fix it. Every time I got a hold of it, it would squirm out. I was ready to go get my gun and put one of us out of his misery. And I wasn't sure which one it would be. Me or the tutu. I had promised her she could have it in the morning." He stopped.

"Don't stop, finish it."

"I was threatening it with mayhem and begging it to behave at the same time. If I could just get a good hold of it, I was sure I could fix it. And this angel walked in. She offered to grant me any wish."

"That's a fairy godmother, I'm pretty sure wish granters are fairy godmothers," she corrected him.

Good. He had her distracted. "It's my story and she was an angel. You'll get to meet her. Anyhow she offered to fix that slippery eel for a cup of tea and a room for the night."

I left and went to make tea. And it took me a long, long, time. When I came back she had everything under control; the eel secured. It was tied. A tied tutu."

"Huh? What do you mean? She tied it up?"

"No. Those flouncy things are tied onto a waistband. I know this because the next day she took us out and bought fabric to make a new tutu. So ask me anything you want. I know everything about tutus."

She was laughing at him now. "A manly man who makes and eats quiche and can make a tutu. Big tough FBI agent."

"I'll deny I ever said anything about tutus. And that was strata, not quiche."

"OK, tell me another one."

He told her about a community where people took care of each other. A community that raised thousands of dollars auctioning a worthless ugly frame. Money to fly a sick little girl home to her family. A family too proud to take charity, but able to accept auction proceeds with honor.

"Sounds like a nice place."

"You'll get to see it."

He told more stories until her eyes closed and she went back to sleep. He made himself as comfortable as he could and did the same.

Thursday

Her trembling woke him again around three AM. This time he carried her gently to the bedroom and lay down with her on the bed keeping her safe and secure, tight against him. Stroking her until the trembling stopped. And that way she made it through the rest of the night.

She woke around sunrise and was surprised to find Ryan still holding her tight. She felt safe and warm. And loved. She thought the night hadn't been as bad as it could have been. It was just that one snapshot of that grinning wicked face that had shattered her sleep. Not the aftermath. Not the killing. And Ryan had been there for her. To hold her. She snuggled in closer, her head on his shoulder. She could hear, feel? his heartbeat. Geez, when had she become so needy?

She must have said that out loud because he replied, "When your parents were killed in front of you." He pulled her closer.

"That happened twenty years ago," she complained.

"Chronologically, yes. But for you, it happened yesterday. Give yourself a break." His thumb was rubbing gentle circles on her breast. That felt good. But she rolled away so she could look up into his face. She saw concern.

"I'm OK. I can deal with it. Part of me knew it all along. That part of me is okay. The other part? It's like an old injury which aches in the rain. I can't use any of the exercises Lori taught me, so I hurt a little. I can handle it. Fits right in with the physical pain. I keep telling that part of me, it was a long time ago."

She reached up and kissed him. A short soft kiss. One of encouragement. "Lori said I could lose the cane this weekend. That I should do whatever I felt I could do. I can do this."

"You sure? You're not just saying that? You're ready?"

"Yes. Now. I want to make love now."

He pulled her on top of him. Her knees were on either side of his hips. Her body on top of his erection. He kissed her long and slow while doing things with his hands.

She opened her mouth and let him tease the inside. Tangled tongues with him. His hands caressing up and down her back. Reached inside her jeans and squeezed. She squirmed her hips trying for a better fit. Something was wrong.

"No, this is all wrong. Take your clothes off. We still have our clothes on." She was whining. "And I can't do it this way. Not on top just yet. Maybe next week. Put me on bottom."

He rolled her over and stretched out beside her. "OK. Let's get these clothes off you." He started with the shirt. Kissed her again as he undid the buttons. Kissed and licked along her jaw, down her neck. Along her collar bone. Got caught in the hollow there. Finally moved down. He had her shirt unbuttoned and off. He found the angry scar on her shoulder. "I'm sorry," he said. As if it were his fault somehow. He touched it gently. Rubbed his thumb over it. He kissed the spot softly. He pulled her bra off and lapped a breast till it was firm, and then moved over to the other. All the time his hands were doing those things to her body. She could only reach his head so she ran her fingers through his hair.

He hated to pull himself away but he wanted to see her. Feel her. All of her. Without the clothes. He moved back.

"What? Why did you stop?" Her eyes were a little glazed over. He smiled at that. He'd done that.

He stood and took off his shirt and pants. Moved over to her and undid her belt and pulled her jeans down. Stopped when he saw the scar on her abdomen. Treated it with soft kisses. Pulled her jeans all the way off. Kissed the red wound on her leg. Licked it. The undies were next. He slid them down her legs and off.

He drank her in as she lay there stretched out, her hands palm up by her head. "You are beautiful," he said.

He pulled off his briefs and pulled on a condom. Climbed onto the bed and moved on top of her resting his weight on his upper arms. She raised her knees and lifted her hips, inviting.

But he slowed down. He laced his fingers with hers and the very intimacy of the act jolted his already overcharged system. "You are amazing," he whispered as he looked down into her eyes. He kissed and licked, touching everywhere until they were both on edge. Finally he kissed her once more, gently, as he slid inside. All the way.

"Okay?" he asked because she had drawn in her breath sharply.

"Oh, yes." She pulled him down and crushed him to her breasts. "I want you touching me. All of me," she breathed, panting now.

He wanted some of that and took her mouth, making her breathe into his. She clenched her muscles. "You feel so good."

He groaned. "I won't last long if you do that," he warned.

"Quick this time. Please. I'm ready. Slow next time." And she squeezed again. He pumped three times and felt her explode as she called out. He came with her on the next thrust and they lay holding each other tightly as the contractions spread through them both.

She held him tight to her. Wouldn't let go. They were both breathing heavily. She nuzzled his ear. Licked the lobe. He felt a reaction in his groin.

"Ohhh, good," she murmured as she felt that response. "That's the way." And she tightened some muscles to feel him better. "Yes. Please. More."

"Oh, you'll kill me," he gasped, as he pushed further into her and began all over again. Slowly this time. "We're taking it slow this time. I want to feel everything. Touch everywhere." And he proceeded to make good on the statement as he rose up on his elbows. Slowly licking and sucking while maintaining a slow, in and out rhythm. Very, very erotically slow. This time he ignored the wounds. This wasn't about the old injuries. This was about the two of them together.

When he reached her breast again, he sucked it in and she squeezed tightly around him.

"Ohh, that's it baby," he moaned and raised his head.

He was looking directly into her eyes when she opened them, only slightly distracted by her tongue poking out between her lips. He lost his place and leaned down to suck her tongue into his mouth. Emphasized the move with a couple of hard thrusts. He brought her to the edge and paused.

It was her turn to moan. She closed her eyes and rubbed her hands frantically up and down his back.

He cupped her face with his hands and kissed her eyelids gently. Moved back to her mouth, drinking in her moans as he bought her to the edge again. It took all his control to slow down. He didn't want it to end.

"It's so good. So sweet. But I can't last much longer sweetheart. One more time maybe."

He went back to her breast. "You're beautiful," he said as he lapped first one and then moved to the other. He licked his way back up her collar bone and ran kisses along her jawline. Bit her earlobe gently. Smiled with satisfaction when she squirmed beneath him and dug her fingers into his back tightening around him. He worked along her jaw to the other side and repeated the nip with the same response. He lost his control and pumped hard, thrusting deep, the friction sending her over the edge. He went over with her.

Much later, when he felt he had enough energy to speak he groaned, "Oh, God, That must have killed me, I'm in heaven."

He opened his eyes and looked down at her. She glowed. "I am in heaven. You are so beautiful."

"Sweet," he sighed. "I love you. You know that, right? I love every part of you."

She found her voice, well a soft whisper. "That was, maybe, the best sex, I think I've ever had," she whispered. A whisper that was all she could manage. She wasn't sure about love yet. Lust and like, yes. Love? She wasn't sure. She felt dizzy. Lying down. And her brain was fuzzy.

"No, not just sex. Lovemaking," he told her. "That's what making love is like." But he saw the panic in her eyes and put two fingers on her lips. "Shh. It's OK. You'll get there. I can wait." And then replaced his fingers with his lips, kissing her gently. "We'll get there together."

It wasn't until then that he thought, not smart with a used condom.

"Didn't need that condom," she said, knowing exactly what he was thinking. "Remember, I can't get pregnant. And I don't have any STDs. We can lose it the next time."

"Tonight," he promised. He rose up on his elbow to look at her one more time. He wanted to remember her like this. Sated. Satisfied.

"Sleep for now," he said as he lay on his side and spooned her in front of him, still holding her tight.

**

He woke her later with a cup of coffee. "Come on, it is time to get up. The team will be along soon."

She smiled at him, "The way to a woman's heart," she took the cup. "God I feel good," she said with a secret, smug, smile as she stretched. "Thank you."

"Anytime, just let me know. Up now. Get dressed," he kissed her one more time, a quick one.

She thought about showering, but did her exercises first.

When she came into the main room, Ryan and Kevin were helping Annie set out a breakfast buffet. He watched her with a look of total pleasure and satisfaction. As if he had just achieved a great triumph. She recognized the look. It was similar to the one she had just seen in her mirror. She gave him a brilliant smile and then noticed Annie watching her. She'd better tone it down or the whole world would know what they did.

Tony came in first and the team straggled in behind him. Penney came in with Cilla and Jake. They both came right to Becca to check on her. Becca saw Jake send a questioning look at Ryan who nodded. She caught his eye and smiled. She knew he was nodding because she was okay, not because she was compromised.

Good natured joking accompanied the food and a few worried glances came her way. Along with some speculation? She felt normal, almost told them to stop worrying, but she wasn't sure if that would convince them or make them more nervous. So she would just let her actions speak for her.

When everyone was settled with a full stomach and a cup of coffee or tea, Jake got the meeting started. "Mary Lee called in early to tell us that New Madrid, in conjunction with the FBI and Safe Keeping, and Cav here, busted the call girl ring last night. Three states, three counties. They are still processing prisoners, and searching offices and homes. It's early yet, but it looks like they got everyone. So good work all of you." He included the whole room. "Daffy and Mary Lee represented us. We're making a lot of good points with the locals and the FBI."

"Penney, will you start?"

"I contacted the executor of the trust. He agreed to talk with me when I convinced him I represented Becca. The trust was set up by her grandmother before she remarried. It was part of a prenuptial agreement mandating that her money flow to her family. It was made using her name from her first marriage which is why we couldn't find it. When she married the second time both she and her daughter took on her new husband's name because he adopted her daughter." She stopped and said, "Let me write it on the board, a couple of you just glazed over."

"Everybody see? It was set up with enough income for the trustee to pay taxes and through his management, the trust has appreciated greatly. He is pretty incredible, almost as good as I am. They had started to look for you Becca and found the news reports on your shooting. They were in the process of ascertaining that you are the same Rebecca Anne Travis mentioned in the trust." Penney handed Becca the forms.

"So, Becca's shooting could be the Smith woman not wanting anyone finding Becca. Only it backfired. She fits the profile of someone who would shoot from a dark alley. And she wouldn't want anyone to know how she abandoned Becca to the state," Cav said.

"Maybe," Tony said. "That's where I come in. She might have an alibi."

"Every time we answer one question, more pop up," Cav complained. "Nothing is easy with you guys."

Tony laughed at him. "You haven't even heard the next part. Remember we determined that Fred Smith disappeared three months after the accident? Well, he didn't. He was gone long before that. It seems that he actually did come back to the states with his division; we checked with them. That's when he disappeared."

He dropped that bombshell and explained, "Apparently she made up that story of him being stationed overseas. Then we went back and talked to Nancy and Lucy. They didn't know he was back."

"Oh no, you're not going to say *body buried in the back yard?*" Cav warned.

"I don't know," Tony continued. "Can cadaver dogs find human remains after twenty years? The online sources seem to be in disagreement."

"Arggh. I guess I'm going to find out," Cav said. He reached for his cell.

"Wait," Tony ordered, "I'm not done."

Becca was laughing at Cav because he was shaking his head and muttering, "Of course you're not done. It can't be a simple murder. With you people, that's not enough."

Becca knew that Cav was grumbling for effect. He was a good cop and she was sure he couldn't wait to get his teeth into this case.

"Okay. So Smith disappears almost immediately after he comes back. Seven years later, she has him declared dead and gets his three million dollar life insurance policy."

"And you guys never deal in small numbers either," Cav added.

"Immediately after Smith is declared dead, she marries a very wealthy elderly gentleman who dies six month later. One year later, she marries his best friend. That marriage lasted four years when he died suddenly."

"Geez, tell me these are all natural deaths," Cav begged.

"No suspicion. No autopsies," Tony finished.

"Maybe we can use some of that goodwill we earned last night to get the locals to take another look," Ryan suggested.

"Worth a try, I can call over," Cav said. "No way are we going to be able to get her for the first three murders," acknowledging that he believed the two spouses were also murdered.

"No D.A. and no jury will accept my suddenly recovered memory," Becca agreed. "And even if you do find remains in her backyard, there is no way to prove who put them there or when. She is going to get away with all three of those."

"Hmm, I have an idea on a way to get to her. Let's go through channels and see what happens first," Ryan told her.

"What's your plan?" she asked.

"Yeah, what have you got?" Jake asked curious. Ryan's plans were generally creative and well thought out.

Ryan just smiled. "Not yet, it's still marinating and we might not need it. It can be Plan B."

"What? You're thinking we just walk in and brace her and she feels so guilty she confesses?" Becca asked derisively.

"Not us," he said, "You."

"Sure, right. That changes the whole scenario," Becca was her testy self now. "She sees me and…" She stopped and an evil grin covered her face. She started again in a positive manner. "She doesn't see me. She sees my mother."

Ryan was nodding and smiling at her. "Mary Lee can add some touches to make you look more like her. After twenty years, you should pass."

"Damn. Now that is devious," Jake said in admiration. "Maybe add in a couple of preliminary sightings. Shake her up, make her uneasy."

"Like I said, it's marinating. We have to decide on dialog too. But I bet we can come up with something to get, if not a confession, then maybe a lead."

"First Cav will check with the locals on the spouses. We haven't come up with anything on Sergio Nadeau, the Board member. We're still looking. And that brings us to the armed robberies. Cilla, you're up next."

"We divided this up between Tony, me, and Jen. We each looked for likely hits in the next five weeks. Anywhere along the corridor plus fifty miles. We each found fifteen possibles; here are the lists on the screen. We have included dates for any special promos, advertisings, or campaigns. We then merged the lists; you can see we had many of the same events. If we drop out the low end, keep anything above 100,000, we came up with ten likely sites, and we narrowed that down to three.

All use Blooms-n-Trees. Of the three, one uses the landscaper, two use the florist."

"Let me have a copy of the complete list," Cav said. Ryan wanted it also.

"I'll email it."

"Can we see the list by date?" he asked.

"The Expo, starts tomorrow. The other two sites are having special deals Sunday.

"Not much time."

"We have today to get some sort of surveillance set up. We're looking at; well that's convenient, The Expo's here in Bear and the jewelry store on Sunday is in New Madrid. That makes it a little easier. We can get Bear set up. Becca can help with both Bear and New Madrid until Khalen breaks free. And Jake, we might need your people again."

Mary Lee and Daffy came in then. Mary Lee gave them a summary. "Khalen had five New Madrid cars in place to follow the limos and two cars to stay on the office. The two drivers we put in jail last night were back out and working. We notified all the jurisdictions and alerted the locals as soon as we moved into their districts. The locals made the busts at three hotels and two private homes. We got the girls, drivers, and johns. At the same time they busted the office building and are inventorying the records and computers. We also seized the GPS units in the limos to trace previous trips. Tom's firm was willing to share, but Khalen felt better with a warrant. Some of the girls are already singing as well as a number of johns. The New Madrid station house has almost as many attorneys as cops. It's a madhouse. Your Captain, Becca, has called in all hands and the FBI is sending extra agents. Auto theft is the least of the charges. They'll be sorting things out and interrogating people all day."

She looked at Jake. "The really neat thing is everyone knows we broke it. We shared. And the FBI is letting the locals have the glory. So everyone if happy," she finished with a grin.

"And ML is sweet on Khalen," Daffy added.

"Sure am," she agreed with a stunning smile.

Becca wondered if she should warn Khalen. But he was notorious on the force, got all the women he wanted. Maybe she should warn

Mary Lee. She really liked her. Maybe she'd just stay out of it. Or ask Cilla. Yes, first chance she got, she'd ask Cilla.

"OK. Back to Blooms-n-Trees, Ryan said bringing attention back to the newest problem. "Cilla? Tony? Did you have more for us?" Cilla and Tony looked at each other with grins and Ryan knew they had some good stuff. Cilla nodded to Tony to go ahead.

"The Expo this weekend is a book, coin and gem show. Many high quality dealers will be coming. We found the floor plan online," He brought it up. "Shows entrances, restrooms. This entrance is for vendors, with parking reserved for them. Inside, you'll note that the vendor areas are already labeled. And the labels are hotlinks to the exhibitors' home pages or websites. Some of the sellers have complete searchable databases and some of the links just identify the vendor. We have some estimates of value from the vendors who are advertising."

"Over here," he pointed to the left of the building. "This is rare books. Books have very detailed provenance covering who owned them and for how long. So we don't think they'll hit there. Besides, books are bulky and hard to steal."

Ryan agreed, "Books would be hard to resell without the provenance. Though some people don't care if they buy stolen property even though they would have to keep it hidden. No bragging rights."

Tony clicked on the comic books link. That brought up a list of comics for sale. "This is one of those searchable databases. You type in the comic you are looking for and if the vendor has it, you'll find a picture of the cover, the grade, which includes how it was stored, maybe the quality of the paper, and selling price. This vendor has two books that are similar to one that just sold for $150,000. That one was found in an abandoned house. Anyone could 'find' a comic book. There's not any provenance."

He clicked another link at the opposite end of the building. "This one is interesting. No website, a partial list. An old lady selling her deceased husband's gem, crystal and rock collection. Pictures of some of the stones with a ruler so you can judge size. There is some interesting stuff in here. Colored diamonds. The guy collected them back in the 1960s and 1970s. No one wanted them then. Now, there is huge demand for colored diamonds. She's looking at $100,000 to $250,000 for some of those stones. She knows it. None of the stones are certified. That means they can't be traced. She also has some rare crystals. She has hired extra security with two experts to help her sell. They come on Saturday and Sunday. She is doing minimal advertising and that is restricted to jewelers and people who design jewelry. I want to see this collection myself.

"I called a friend of mine who was collecting in the same time frame. He said he has three of these colored stones. He has a pink and a blue appraised by a gemologist for over $250,000, each. The blue is a little more valuable. He has a yellow that is still considered worthless at $10,000. The stones were pretty junk when he got them. Now they are insured and in a safe deposit box while he decides what to do with them."

He pointed to the monitor. "She's in a protected corner, but you can see she is near two exits. Step in, grab a handful, and walk out the door? I don't know."

He next pointed to a third site near the cafeteria. "This is gold coins. This is not the only coin dealer here, but they are advertising some rarely seen early American gold coins. But here again they have provenance. The coins would be hard to sell without it."

"The rest of the sellers have a variety of collectibles, dolls, autographs, baseball cards. We sent everything to your tablets including inventories and the values where we knew them." He passed out hard copies.

"The Expo starts tomorrow, Friday at three PM. The vendors set up beginning at noon tomorrow. Some of them will be arriving tonight and sleeping in the parking lot. Most of them have RVs. The parking lot has two entrances, both will be manned. Parking costs a dollar."

He stopped, grinning.

"What else do you have Tony? I can tell there is more," Jake said.

"Another interesting thing? Starting Friday, there will be live feeds from the Expo. You can view the vendor areas on line. It's one of those new Google virtual 360 degree photo tours Becca mentioned. Except these won't be interactive. And at five Friday and Saturday nights, a local group will be performing in front of the snack area."

"If I was going to rob a place, I'd do it before all the good stuff was sold. So the first day of the Expo. And a concert would offer a really good noise diversion," Becca suggested.

"Can we be ready?" Jake asked.

"Gonna have to be. Don't have any choice," Ryan said. "Be hard though to get my people together that quickly.

"We always supply some backup protection to the Expo," Cav said. "But we can't use my people inside. They would be recognized. I can offer extra patrols for the parking lot. We'd do that anyhow. I'll talk to management and see if they'd like another car outside while the vendors unload." He looked around.

"That might work." Ryan was nodding. "I can bring in a couple of teams Saturday."

"I can help tomorrow," Becca said.

Both Jake and Ryan said no at the same time. She started to argue when Jake cut her off. "It's possible these people know you. It's possible they are the ones who shot you. Because you were going to look at the two cold cases," he reminded her. "You can't be on the inside."

How could she have forgotten that?

Ryan added, "They might decide to abort if they see you. So you can't be there. We don't have time to set up our own cameras. But we should be able to get into the security office with Cav's help."

"Tony might be able to hijack the Expo security feed. Becca could watch that at my office," Jake offered. "She might even see someone she recognizes."

Ryan looked at Jake."

"If all you want is people on site walking around looking for anything suspicious, we have them. They'd be you, Ryan, me, Ron, and Jen. Maybe Tony, he has done a little field work. That's seven. I'd like at least eight inside. Mary Lee, what about the team you used on Tom?" he asked her.

"They're still in New Madrid. Four of them. They'd fit right into this scene."

"I'll get with Ron on that. Set up a schedule. We'll be okay for Friday. Then Ryan, your people should be able to take over."

"It's going to go down Friday. I agree with Becca on that," Ryan said.

"What about the spycar?" Kevin asked. Everyone looked at him and Jake said with a laugh, "Oh yeah, we might have a rig. Kevin and John have been outfitting an RV for Safe Keeping. For surveillance. How about it Kevin, is it ready for a test run?"

"Oh, man, is it ever. We were just waiting for John to get back. He is gonna be so jealous if he misses the maiden voyage. Wait until you all see it," he said excitedly, looking at Cilla, Annie, and Penny. "Electronics and comfort. We took some ideas right off the web. Looks like an ordinary RV, inside and out. But we put everything in it. Computers, 360 degree exterior video cameras, each is night-vision equipped. Wi-Fi. Listening devices. We run off long lasting batteries built into the body of the vehicle. They charge by running the engine and by solar panels on the roof. We can outfit ten people with video and sound and run it all through the van. We have a luggage rack on top to hide the antennas. Cell service."

"Kevin and John and, *my husband*, did this without telling me?" Cilla said dangerously to Jake.

Jake was shaking his head, "It was just a wild comment I made at the wedding about how handy a surveillance van would be. John and Kevin jumped on it. We kibitzed and then they decided to go ahead with it. I didn't know anything about it until they just told me about it last week. Swore me to secrecy. I'm sorry. They wanted to spring it as a surprise. So take it up with your brothers. It's their fault you don't know." He wormed out of the blame.

She transferred her outrage to Kevin. Who put up his hands and begged, "Don't hurt me. Don't hurt me. We didn't not tell you on purpose. It was a challenge at first and you were busy. You know, with Penney's wedding, your second honeymoon, Becca getting shot. You weren't around and then we just decided to finish it ourselves. See if we could get everything in there. Dare you to find something we missed."

"Bet I can," she said only slightly mollified.

"You have a drone too?" Daffy asked only half joking.

Kevin's eyes got wide. "Maybe," It was obvious he didn't but that the idea appealed to him. "We could build our own. With video streaming to the tablets or cells. That would be cool. Our very own UAV. Unmanned Aerial Vehicle," he added for those who might not know. "Or maybe they have some for sale we can modify. We could control it with a cell or joy stick."

Daffy snapped his fingers in Kevin's face to bring him back.

"Sorry. Got carried away there. I'll have to look. Later," Kevin said.

Daffy was just shaking his head, "It was a joke. I thought I was making a joke."

But Jake was laughing at him. "The joke's on you. Never, ever suggest any kind of technology to these guys. Looks like I'm going to have a drone soon to go with my RV," he said smugly.

"Where are you hiding this, um, mobile command center? The spycar?" Becca asked.

"Safe Keeping's garage. Here we have pictures," and Kevin put them up on the monitor. Exterior and interior, a 360 degree Google video.

"We could park it with the vendors," Becca proposed.

"I'll bring that up with the Expo managers; I want to talk to them in person. We might be able to move it in tomorrow." Cav got up and motioned to Jones to go.

"Kevin can man it with Tony," Jake suggested.

"I want to be there, too," Becca said. When Jake looked at Ryan, Becca got testy. "He doesn't tell me what to do," she declared.

"No, he doesn't," Jake agreed. "But he does get to say how his op works, and make no mistake this is his op."

"It only makes sense to put me in the RV," she declared, only slightly mollified.

"You're right, Becca," Ryan said. "You can back them up, work the electronics, and keep an eye out for anyone you know. And you'll be safe there. There will always be at least one team member inside." When she started to protest again, he added, "Not just for your protection, but because the teams will be using it for breaks; they need a place to rest up, get off the floor, change clothing. Get outfitted with cameras and earwigs."

Jake was nodding. "You better just suck it up girl. Looks like you will be playing Snow White to a bunch of dwarves."

She couldn't help it. The idea of anyone calling her Snow White sidetracked her. She wasn't sure if she was outraged or delighted. Delighted she realized. "Okay, but only because I am handicapped with the cane. And if I am Snow White, that makes you one of the seven dwarfs. Happy?"

"Yeah. Me Happy," he agreed with a smile as he stroked his wife's arm.

Becca changed the subject. "If we put someone on the florist, White, we'd have a heads up if she makes a move," Becca said. "Though I still like Friday afternoon during the concert."

"Mary Lee?" Ryan asked both Mary Lee and Jake.

"That's what I do," Mary Lee said waiting for a go-ahead nod from Jake.

"No, I want you at the Expo. Put two of your team on White. They can start now."

As she got out her cell to make the call Ryan said, "Anything else, people. Have we missed anything?"

"I want to be in the RV with Becca," Cilla said.

"No." Jake immediately declared.

"What?" Cilla said very quietly. Stinging him with a look. It got very quiet in the room.

"Look, honey," he started.

"Don't you, look honey, me," she said again very quietly. No one argued with Cilla when she used that tone. She waited while he squirmed.

He was looking at her belly.

"Don't," she said again. Very dangerously. "Don't you dare."

Daffy didn't snicker only because he was probably worried about how far the mutiny would go. If it would hit Penney. These were not women who took well to being told what to do. He dared to glance up toward Penney; she smiled back at him serenely.

"Let's try that again," Cilla suggested. "I want to be in the RV with Becca and Kevin and Tony. I can help with the electronics."

"Good idea," Jake said this time. "You're right. You should be there. This will be a shakedown cruise with on the job training; we need all the help we can get in case something goes wrong."

"Nothing will go wrong with my stuff," Kevin declared.

"Well let's go take a look at it and see what we'll be dealing with," Becca suggested.

She rode with Daffy in the armored car because Ryan wanted to discuss strategy with Jake.

"They are the planners, the strategists. Let them do their work. They'll come up with the best plan or plans. Run it by you, whatever they decide," Daffy said once in the car, almost reading her thoughts.

"They better."

"They need to talk strategy and personnel. Get the logistics down first." There was silence for a few minutes and then Daffy looked sideways at her and said, "You and Ryan finally got it on, huh?"

"What? What did you say," Becca yelped.

"I said you and Ryan finally did it."

"He told you? He told you we had sex?" she exclaimed, outraged.

Daffy laughed at her. "No way. Ryan doesn't talk. Everyone in that room knows the two of you got together."

"How? How can everyone know?" she was shaken

"The high intensity, sexual tension between the two of you the past couple of days singed anyone who came anywhere near either of you," he said shaking his head. "That's gone. Replaced by a kind of sexual calmness. Satisfaction." He was laughing at her. "Penney jumped me in the car last night. We didn't even get out of the compound. I have to thank you for that." His laugh was appreciative now. "Some of the best car sex I've ever had. We probably weren't the only ones. The air around the two of you was like an aphrodisiac."

She digested that. "Really? Everyone felt it?" And of course Penney wouldn't wait to get home, she always lived in the moment. "Everyone knows?"

"Oh, yeah. You might as well have put out a banner this morning."

It was quiet for a while so he filled in the silence, "For what it's worth, I've never seen Ryan look at another woman like that. Except Macy. It was always only Macy."

"His wife?"

"Yeah. He only ever saw her. There was never another woman."

"What was she like?"

He was quiet again and then said, "Sweet. She was sweet. Had a heart of gold. There was never anyone for her either, but Ryan. All she wanted was to be his wife and the mother of his children. But she took in everyone. Kind of like Cilla. Their house was always filled with people, kids, laughter. Food. There was always room at her table. A refuge of sorts."

"She sounds nice." And then, "Do you think he could ever like someone else?" she asked a little innocently.

"You're kidding, right?" He turned to look at her. "He's in love with you. And knowing Ryan, he's told you that."

"Well, yes, he did. But men say that."

"Men, maybe. But not Ryan. It's not a word he would use lightly."

"But what if, what if, it's just sex? Men say that for sex," she said. Wondering why she was having this conversation with Daffy and not Cilla. Or Annie.

"Not Ryan. I doubt he does, just sex."

"What if it's just sex for me?" she asked in a small voice.

"Oh, lady, you are confused. Only have to take one look at you and know it's not just sex for you either. Ryan wouldn't make that kind of mistake. Me either."

"What if," she paused hesitant to voice her fear, and then said it out loud. "What if, with my background, I can't love." Why am I asking Daffy?

"Your background doesn't preclude love. I think foster care, with all its misery, only teaches you to love more. Appreciate love more."

"How would you know?"

"Let's just say I know and leave it at that." He remained silent and she realized he wouldn't say anything more on that subject.

"What about you and Penney? How did you know she was the one?" curious now.

"Me?" he was thoughtful. "I always knew I would get married someday. Have what Ryan had with Macy. The minute I saw Penney, I knew she was the one. Well, once I got over the shock to my system she generated, I knew." He was smiling now. "And I could tell it was the same for her. Wasn't a doubt in my mind."

"But I'm not like his first wife."

"Oh, honey, you are nothing like Macy. No one will ever confuse you with Macy." He was smiling a different smile now. "Some of us are really going to enjoy this. You and Ryan. Ryan has met his match."

"Oh," now she was disappointed.

"Don't get me wrong here. Ryan knows you are nothing like Macy. He's not looking for a Macy. He is looking for Becca. He wants Becca. That man fell for you at the wedding. He just didn't know it. All you had to do was see how he watched you. That sexual tension started that day. That man is all wrapped up and ready for you like a birthday present. He's not fighting it. He knows what he had with Macy. He knows the feelings are the same. Just the environment will be different."

"Oh." Wasn't that interesting she thought, with a secret smile.

"While we are on the subject of Ryan. You know his main goal is to keep you safe. That is his primary objective. Running this op is secondary. Jake's main job is to protect you, keep you alive. His secondary purpose is to keep his people safe. Third for both of them is to catch the crooks. You got to give them a break. Neither one of them is going to say that to you. They assume you know it." He didn't say it sternly, more like a gentle reminder.

She nodded and tried a different tact. "My turn. You call Mary Lee, ML. You're the only one who does. Does that mean there is something between the two of you?"

He got a faraway look in his eyes. "I'm going to tell you a little. Because I just pushed myself into your business. ML and I go back a long way. But we were never more than very good friends. Not intimate friends. Probably more like your gang. Almost family. You don't have to worry about me and ML."

"Okay."

The others were arriving then and Kevin took them on a tour of the van. "We designed it from the bottom up. The deep purple color is supposed to help it blend in. It has everything a high end RV has. Four glides. That's four sections which slide out making the whole unit wider. Sleeps six comfortably. Everything can be controlled by a digital panel at the driver's seat or by one of the remotes."

He pointed to the base of the vehicle. "The undercarriage and bottom two feet are armored plated to protect the vehicle itself and the batteries. Long lasting batteries, both regular and solar. I really, really wanted a Tesla battery, but no go. The RV's engine regenerates the batteries. That two foot band around the top is a solar strip and the top has a series of solar panels. They regenerate the solar batteries. It's self-contained and can run on its own power for about thirty-six hours."

"The walls and roof are lined with Kevlar. The windows are bullet proof one way glass. I can turn on the cameras remotely," he said as he pulled out his cell. "I'm sending the video to John and Peter so they can be a part of this. Right now the cameras are stationary; I'll show you how to move and monitor them inside. Individually or as a group. Though I can also do it on my cell. There is even a camera underneath the RV."

He opened the door and led them inside. It was surprisingly roomy. And it did look so much like a high end luxury RV that Becca looked a question. Tony proudly started opening cupboards and closets, folding the doors back out of the way. Pointing out each piece of equipment as he did so.

"Cameras are here. Controls, intuitive."

One monitor seemed to come on by itself and John greeted them "You're using the spycar. Without me?" he protested.

"Becca, Jake, and Ryan need it now. So we're taking it out tomorrow. But it won't be a full test run. We'll wait for you to take it out for the weekend and test all the systems."

"Kind of glad you didn't tell us, because I might have decided to come back. But we're still having fun with Peter's family. Oh, Kev, show them the arsenal." He signed off with a laugh.

"Arsenal? What arsenal?" Ryan asked a little nervously. With the gang, you never knew what they might dream up. Kevin took them to the bedroom and pulled out a drawer under the bed to show them a dozen futuristic looking weapons. One looked very much like a weapon Ryan knew was under development. Secret development. He laughed in relief when he took a closer look. "Your internet computer game. These are plastic mock ups of those weapons used in the game and in the sequel." The computer game which had netted the gang millions of dollars.

"Yeah, they're prototypes. Peter is going into production with them next month. There is space in that drawer for vests too."

"Cav's going to have a hissy fit when he sees this," Jake said.

"Yeah, I can't wait to bring him in here," Kevin said chuckling. They all laughed. Cav was so predictable.

"This RV? What did you call it? Spycar? Is it registered?" Ryan asked.

"Yeah," Jake said. "They wanted a special tag; they wanted to call it RVSPY. I told them that would sort of destroy the anonymity." He was shaking his head. "They so wanted that name. But we got the next license in line. Perfectly normal. Registered to a subsidiary of ours set up for that purpose. All our vehicles are registered with it. Anonymous identity. So the rig is ready to roll tomorrow."

Daffy laughed out loud. "RVSPY? Seriously Kevin? That would be a great cover." He was looking in a closet full of drawers. Turned to look at Kevin.

"Well, it would have been cool," grumbling.

They were all wondering around the RV looking and touching. Becca was opening a clothes closet when she heard Jake and Cilla talking. She didn't mean to eavesdrop, but they couldn't see her.

"I'm sorry," Jake was saying. "I didn't mean to come across as a caveman. I unconsciously reverted. I'm sorry."

"Yes. You did revert," she agreed. And then more softly, "It was kind of sweet."

"Sweet? You thought it was sweet? Why did you hit me with that look and tone then?"

There was a long silence behind Becca. She didn't have to see them to know that Jake was getting a slightly different look. One waiting for him to figure out what he was missing. Cilla used that type of pause on Becca frequently. Kind of a, keep up with the action.

"Oh, right. You can make your own decisions. You are an adult."

"Right. And you know that I am not brave. I am not a cop or even a guardian. I'm a computer code writer and housewife. This RV is like Fort Knox. Some strong tough person will always be in here with me. I knew all that before I said I wanted to help. And yes, you should have known that I had already factored everything into my decision."

"I know. I know. But it was the baby that turned me into a caveman," he grumbled his excuse as he pulled her tight to him.

"Baby? Baby?" Becca spun around. "What baby?" she demanded as everyone turned to look. Oops, too late, she put her hand over her mouth.

"My baby. Our baby. I'm pregnant," Cilla said a little smugly. "That's why Jake turned into an overprotective caveman earlier."

There were hugs and handshakes all around. Becca was pretty sure there was going to be some great make up sex when Cilla and Jake got home, based on the way they were holding each other. She saw Ryan watching her and was sure he could read her mind. He smiled and winked. A promise?

Jake's phone rang, distracting them. He listened and suggested they all get comfortable in the main room.

"Cav promised the manager extra patrols and got permission for the RV to park in the vendor lot tomorrow. The Expo security people will be told it's a promotional van hired by some of the vendors. They don't keep much money on the premises; most of the vendors handle their own sales and deposits. The really large sales are all credit card and instant bank transactions, but a Brinks truck comes by at the close of business every day."

He looked around and continued, "Kevin you drive the RV tomorrow, Becca, Cilla, Tony, and Ryan will ride with you. Kevin, Becca, and Cilla are not to leave the RV while we are on stakeout. That's per Cav," he added.

Cilla snorted. And then Becca did too. The two women exchanged looks. It was such a blatant lie. They let it pass, though, because it actually was reasonable. And a fair compromise.

"We'll have three teams on the floor. Each person will be hooked up with video and sound. Tony checked the local laws, we'll be OK. There are signs all over the building advising patrons that they are being recorded. The teams will swap off every hour. Take a ten minute break. Maybe change clothes and partners. Keep it mixed up. Start with Daffy and Mary Lee, Ron and Jen, Jones and Tony. Ryan and I will fill in and wander individually. Where and as needed. We only have to worry about Friday; Ryan will have an FBI crew available for Saturday and Sunday. And they will cover the jewelry stores on Sunday too."

Jake nodded to Kevin, "I want you to show Tony, Becca, and Cilla how to operate the equipment. Then take Tony and Becca out and have each of them practice driving, backing, and parking. They don't have to be experts, but I want them to be able to move that rig if they have too. OK?" They all agreed.

"I have a backup plan using Becca and me. A gap filler. We'll do some practice run-throughs," Ryan said. "It's still in the marinating stage."

Jake nodded. "Just let us know. Any questions?"

"Will we get a chance to go inside and browse?" Kevin wanted to know.

"Yes. But I'd rather you go in with one of us."

"They won't have any drones in there," Daffy said, causing everyone to laugh.

"That's it then?" Jake asked. "Get to it and afterwards go home, rest up. Expect to be at the Expo from three to ten."

"Daffy has something," Ryan said. Everyone turned toward Daffy. "I do?' he said surprised.

"About Becca impersonating her mother. You said you had some thoughts and I sure hope you do because I'm up against a wall here. I know how I want it to play, but I can't figure out where." Ryan sounded frustrated.

"Then I will save the day. Because I know where."

When he stopped for effect, Ryan said, "Give."

"Kevin has found a schedule which has Sylvia going to an opening night at a gallery Saturday. They have hired actors to be servers. The whole evening will be recorded. It would be perfect. You can write the script. We could use the actors along with our own people and a couple of cops. Our people can also make our own recordings."

"Sounds good. Better than good. Jake, do we have anyone who can get us in? Any contacts?" Ryan asked.

He was scratching his jaw and shaking his head, "No. But no problem using my people. They'd love it."

"Maybe we know someone going to the opening?" Becca suggested. "Maybe someone on that list could be a way in?"

"I know someone," Mary Lee said into the quiet.

"Got it then," Daffy said. As if it were a done deal because Mary Lee knew someone, Becca thought. Saw Mary Lee check her watch, nod to herself, and leave the room.

It was ten minutes before she came back and they waited expectantly. "My friend will meet with us and listen. That is as much as he will commit to without meeting you and hearing the whole story. I told him you wanted to do a sting at the opening night party at the gallery and that the cops would be involved. We meet him in two hours at his place. I told him I would be bringing three men. I didn't give him any names, but that should be Jake, Ryan, and Cav. He's reasonable and should be easy to convince. And he can get us local law enforcement and the gallery owner," she finished with a smile."

"Told ya," Daffy said smugly.

The men started to get ready for the drive. Daffy was the one who went over and spoke to Becca. "You know you can't go Becca. ML knows that. We can't take a chance that Sylvia will see you before we're ready," he said gently.

"I know. I don't like it, but I know."

**

"Mary Lee's friend, Morgan, liked our plan. He even called some actors to train Jake's people," Ryan told her later. He was sitting with her on the couch. He had called her once with an update. And to check on her. It was silly, but it made her feel special. "He got the local Sheriff to go along with us. If it works, they get the credit for the sting. If we can get her to admit to the murders of three husbands, they'll get credit for that. Cav gets credit for your parents' murder. Both departments will share the spotlight.

"Tomorrow morning, Cav, Jake, and I go back to look at the gallery and lay out the plan. The owner, Barbara Walker, is thrilled with the idea of an impromptu live presentation. An improvisation she calls it. She'll work with us and the actors."

"The actors' main job will be to block you from her and, at the same time, ignore you. Mary Lee's friend, Morgan, will be a supporting actor. He will walk Sylvia into a special exhibit. Only Jake's people and a couple of Cav's will be in there. You are going to walk in and look at her and smile."

"Then what?" she asked when he paused.

He frowned, "I'm not sure. I think that will be enough to send her over the edge. It will be best if you don't speak, but you might have to. She will believe her eyes and maybe not remember your Mom's voice. If you have to talk, keep it simple. 'Hello, Sylvia. Remember me? I've come for you. Adlib. She is going to catch a glimpse of you before the party, Becca. Just long enough to make her wonder. When she goes inside the gallery, she will see you again for an instant. We're trying to make her edgy, nervous."

He made sure she was listening, "I want you to do me a favor," he said.

"What?"

"I want you to wear a vest whenever you go out. From now on. Tomorrow at the Expo, Saturday with Sylvia."

"The robbers have never shot anyone," she reminded him.

"I know. I don't want you to be the first."

"The vest didn't stop the bullets that got me," she told him gently. "The first one was stopped. The one that hit me right over the heart. The next got my leg, bent me over so the third could get down my neckline under the vest. That one spun me around and over so the fourth went under the bottom of the vest."

"I know. But I'd feel better if you would wear one."

She searched his face and came up with a compromise. "I will if you will."

"Deal," he agreed immediately.

He held her close, "I'm still working on your act with Sylvia. We don't know her well enough to know which will be the right buttons. But you can improvise. You know; you're a cop. Think of it as a simple interrogation. Whatever the situation seems to need. We'll run through some possible scenarios, though. I'll think about them."

He hesitated, "Or we can wait. We can watch her, take the time to find out how she thinks."

"No. Now. We do it now. We might never get an opportunity like this again. I want this behind me. I want to bury my parents and put her in jail"

He kissed the top of her head and pulled her closer. "Good. I was hoping you would say that. My gut feels the time is right, too. It would be nice if we could get her to admit to driving the car and running you down. If we can get her for the husbands, fine. But I don't care about them. We'd like her to admit shooting you, too. But, honey, I don't think she did that. I don't think she's the one who shot you." He felt her stiffen.

"Why? Tell me why."

"Doesn't feel right. The little we know about her. She uses cars and maybe drugs. Not a gun. And she forgot you as soon as you were out of sight. Even if she did know you were alive, I don't think she cared. And she wasn't in New Madrid that night."

She exhaled a long breath. "You can prove that?"

"Yes. I'm sorry. I know you wanted it to be her. This isn't going to end with her."

"She ran us down. She needs to pay for that. And, like you say, if we can get her for the husbands that will be good. But I agree. She never felt right for my shooting."

She leaned in to him. He was running his fingers through her hair. "That feels good."

"Yeah, it does," he agreed, lifted her chin and kissed her gently.

She relished the promise of it for a few moments and then reached up and pulled his head down so she could return the pleasure. Flicked her tongue out and licked his upper lip. Nipped his lower lip. He groaned. His hand slipped from her hair to her waist and up under her shirt to her breast. She shifted into it.

Friday

They had been on the stakeout for three hours. Kevin was bored and researching drones and the applicable laws. Apparently each state had different rules covering unmanned flight. He recapped all the information as he found it. Some of it was pretty funny and broke up the monotony. But the rest of the stakeout crew were professionals. They were bored, but they still kept watch. They knew just how long and boring a stakeout could be. And how quickly everything could change. They had to be prepared for the very real chance of a heist during the show. That kept them alert. Two teams had already circled the interior of the convention hall and switched out in the RV. On Saturday, the FBI would have teams in place to cover the Expo, but for today they were on their own.

Ryan, Cav, and Jake were back from their examination and assessment of the gallery in plenty of time for the opening of the Expo. They had met with the gallery owner, chosen the room for Becca's performance, and coached the actors in their roles. Everyone would meet Saturday morning and go through improvisations and practice the foot work.

Becca and Jones had spent the morning reviewing his cold cases. They thought they had a thread to pull on one of them. She'd come up with some suggestions for him. She was still thinking about them while watching the monitors outside the Expo.

"The lawn care truck just pulled in," Becca announced. Everyone turned to the monitors. "Towing a cargo trailer. The truck is a, looks like a dump stake truck?" she glanced at Ryan who nodded. "The trailer is enclosed, a box trailer with double wide doors at the rear, single door on the side," she told the teams inside the expo. You could never be sure which information was important, so you noted everything. Five PM on a Friday night was a strange time for a lawn company to show up to cut the grass. But they could be there to go to the Expo. "They're parking in the vendor area. Between us and the entrance."

"The entertainment is starting," Daffy interrupted. He and Mary Lee were inside near the entrance to the Rare Coins booth across from the stage and lunch area. The Expo had separate stalls set up along the outside walls of the building using portable partitions. Each stall had a door which could be closed and locked, both for security and privacy. Two double rows of booths, divided by curtains, ran down the center of the building. He and Mary Lee were angled toward each other so their cameras covered the whole area. His camera, hidden behind a flag pin on his lapel, was focused on the coin booth. Hers, clipped to the strap of her shoulder bag, displayed the stage area and the people gathering around it. Part of Daffy's shoulder, too.

Becca continued in a calm voice, "A man is getting out the side door of the trailer. He is about five foot ten; gray hoody, blue jeans, red baseball cap pulled low over his eyes. Can't get a good look at him. Or the driver, who is staying in the cab." She paused, watching. "He's stopped in the doorway, looking around. Now he is moving to the Expo door. Ron, you should see him pretty soon." The teams inside were wandering randomly, but kept the RV crew informed of their locations. And right now Ron and Jen were near the entrance. Tony and Jones were by the rough diamond room with a view of the entrance. Jake was wandering by the snack bar.

A minute later, "Second man exiting the trailer. Same height, blue hoodie. Jeans. Black ball cap. Looking around, heading inside."

"We got red cap," Ron said. "Jen will follow him. I'll wait for black cap."

Ryan was standing right behind Becca; they watched as red cap headed toward the stage area. "Red cap and Jen heading toward you Daffy," Becca said.

"I've got black cap." Ron moved out. Each monitor had a split screen. They could watch Ron and Jen's cameras on one screen. Daffy and Mary Lee on a second screen. "Looks like he's going in the same direction."

"Two more men getting out of the trailer," Becca said. "The first is about six feet. Wearing a blue jean jacket and jeans. Odd kind of cap. Almost like a military cap. The second is about five nine, wearing gray sweats. Blue baseball cap. Can't see any features. Looking around the parking lot." Pause. "Going inside together."

"Jean jacket. He could almost pass for security," Ryan said.

"That's five. Four inside plus the driver," Becca said. "Is the florist still in the shop?"

"I'll check," Ryan was pulling out his cell.

Ron spoke; he was running the inside part of the operation. "Jones, you take them. If they split up, stay with sweats. Tony. You stay where you are. Remember your instructions. Do nothing. Eat your popcorn. Watch." Both Jake and Ryan had been very emphatic and uncompromising with their instructions. "Every single order we give you is backed up by years of experience and judgment. You have to do exactly what we say. Immediately. No questions."

"Gotcha boss. I'll stay by the rock shop."

"We got red cap," Daffy said. "And see black cap now too."

"I'm heading over to back you up Daffy," Jake said.

"OK. Jen and I will hang loose here about half way between the booth and the entrance." Ron's voice.

"The last two guys split up," Jones informed them. "I'm on sweats with the blue cap. He's heading down the far side. Blue jeans is staying near the door,"

Daffy spoke, "Black cap and red cap are together and going into the coin stall. We're moving closer to them. A crowd is forming in front of the stage. Getting noisy here, too. Great cover for them."

Daffy's mic picked up one of the crooks inside the stall, "Hey folks, the shows starting. Go on out and look. There's a girl out there almost naked." The booth emptied except for the vendor.

Black cap pulled the curtain shut, looked around, and hung out the closed sign.

"Hey what are you doing," the vender demanded angrily. "I'm not closing."

"Yes you are," the other crook said.

"It's going down at the coin shop," Daffy warned.

"Damn, wish we could see what was happening inside," Ryan said.

Daffy's camera showed Mary Lee slip inside.

"Hey, mister can you stay open one more minute, I need a coin for my son. I know exactly the one I want," she said innocently.

"Didn't mean that," Ryan said quietly.

"Oh my God!!" Mary Lee cried turning so her camera picked up black cap who had a gun on the vender. "Don't shoot me. Don't hurt me." Her voice raising, heading toward a scream with each comment.

"Shut up! Shut up!" red hat screamed at her as he poked a gun in her face. Both men had pulled their caps low over their eyes and their hoods up to further conceal their features.

"Don't hurt me," Mary Lee said softly.

"Both of you. In the corner. Down on the floor," red cap ordered. Mary Lee managed to be facing the counter as she knelt on the floor, keeping her head down. The camera was recording everything.

"Where's Blake? What's taking him so long," black cap complained.

Just then the guy in the sweats walked in. "Got hung up in the crowd." And then. "What's the broad doing here?"

"Don't hurt me. Don't hurt me. Please mister, I got kids," Mary Lee begged.

"Shut her up," sweats ordered red cap. Becca held her breath for one awful moment and then red cap pulled out tape, cut off a piece, and, apparently, slapped it over Mary Lee's mouth.

"No one gets hurt," red cap said. "Just do what you're told." He tore off more tape and was binding Mary Lee's wrists.

"And you get that stuff out of the case and into our bags," sweats told black cap, as he quickly taped the vendor. Then he went and helped clean out the display case. Throwing coins into cheerfully colored cloth Expo bags. They had everything in sixty seconds.

"They are getting ready to come out," Becca warned Daffy. "Red cap seems to be talking into a mic. Either to the driver or jean jacket. Or both."

"OK every one. Stick with plan A," Ron now, a calming voice. "Doesn't look like they are going to hurt anyone. Jen and I will head outside the entrance and play the lovers. Daffy, you start back now ahead of them, wait by the door. We'll take them when they come outside." Ron paused as he and Jen headed for the entrance and then said, "Ryan, call Cav and give him a heads up, and then you and Becca get ready for your part. Anyone see jean jacket?"

Tony was the only one to answer in the affirmative. "He's outside the rock shop. Has his back to me. Doing something with his hat." Tony's camera was pointed right at jean jacket.

"Eat your popcorn! Now! Tony! Eat your popcorn," Becca commanded urgently as jean jacket turned around and looked straight at Tony. But now Tony was staring at his popcorn and picking out the perfect piece.

"Jean jacket put a badge on his cap. And jacket. Looks just like security. You called that Ryan," Becca acknowledged.

"They're leaving the coin stall, all together." Becca looked at all the monitors; saw the three men on Daffy's camera as he turned supposedly looking at the stage. They were walking slowly toward the exit.

"Jake, when the crowd blocks the view, go get Mary Lee. We may need you both at the entrance. Leave the vendor for now."

Tony's camera showed jean jacket go into what Tony called the rock shop, the booth with the rough diamonds. He had a full view through the door and picked up the voices clearly. Jean jacket said to the woman gravely, "Ma'am you have to go to the office. Right now. It's about your son. Um David or Donald? He's hurt."

"Donald's hurt?" she cried. "How? What happened?"

Jean jacket responded urgently, "I don't know; you just have to get up there now. I'm supposed to stay here till you get back. I'll put up the closed sign and wait. You have to hurry, now. Go," he commanded. "I've got it here for you."

She ran out and headed for the office.

In the RV, Becca turned to Kevin and Cilla. "Keep up the running commentary. Ryan and I are on." She grabbed her cap and stepped out the door, complaining loudly as they had practiced. "Get your ass out of there. Come on. We're late. My ass is gonna be fried." Mary Lee had changed her looks again. She didn't even recognize herself.

Ryan was yelling from inside the RV. "Hold your horses. No one cares if we're a minute late. I had to get this bet down." He was climbing down the steps as Becca grabbed the handle to the trolley, loaded with equipment, which had been left by the side of their rig.

"Come on, come on," she said disgustedly. "Grab the handle and let's get this stuff inside."

They started dragging the trolley around the lawn care truck. Ryan slightly in front.

"Bitch, bitch, bitch. That's all you do," Ryan was grousing. "Why don't you just quit?" he sneered.

Becca dropped her handle and turned to face him. Her back was turned toward the driver's door. The trolley was in front of the right bumper. She was grinning like crazy at Ryan as she called him a few bad names.

He was screaming back at her as he moved ahead of her. Neither one appeared to notice the driver yelling at them through the window. He finally got out of the car to get their attention.

Becca felt him move behind her. Too soon, she thought. He is going to get here too fast. She looked over Ryan's shoulder for red cap. She was so surprised she almost said something. But she stopped herself, thought about it. She could still feel the driver behind her, not close enough yet. She smiled at Ryan, raised an eyebrow, and exclaimed, "Oh, my God. Look at them. He's going to do her right in the parking lot. Over there." She pointed.

"What? What?" Ryan said. That wasn't part of the script. The driver was almost where they wanted him. Ryan turned around to see what she was looking at and laughed. The driver was looking too. Ron had Jen up against the column to the left of the door, holding one of her legs tight against his waist. Pushing into her. He had her head bent back under an aggressive kiss. Becca could see Jen panting from where she was standing. The three men came through the door. Stopped suddenly when they saw the group by the truck. All staring near the entrance.

Red cap turned and saw the pair. "Oh, go get a room," he said disgusted, as the other two laughed.

"Give it to her," black cap smirked. The three thieves stopped to enjoy the show, laughing.

Meanwhile, Tony's camera was documenting the clear view through the door of the rock shop. Jean jacket grabbed the tray which held the diamonds and upended it, pouring the stones into his Expo bag. He then got another tray, the rare gems, and scooped them into the bag also. He turned and walked out of the booth. Ten seconds. That was all it took.

"Jean jacket is coming out with the gemstones," Tony said excitedly. "He just dropped them all in his sack."

Red cap had stopped laughing at the lovers and took another look at the truck. Saw the driver standing and the trailer in front of the bumper. He was screaming at Becca and Ryan as he charged over to them, "What the hell is going on here? Move that trailer."

Becca saw Ron and Jen break out of their clinch. She spun and hit the driver with the cane, taking his feet out from under him. He fell hard.

"What the?" red cap started to say when Ryan pulled his gun with his right hand, his FBI ID with his left. "Put them up guys. It's all over."

Red cap was reaching to his waistband when Jen put her gun to the back of his head. "You heard the man. Raise your hands," she said quietly.

Ron was on his other side. His gun turned on the other two. All three raised their hands.

Jean jacket came out the door. Took one look and started to back up. Daffy was right behind him. "Just keep going on outside," he ordered. "Walk over to your buddies."

Jean jacket looked over his shoulder, saw the gun. Shook his head and walked over to the truck.

Jake and Mary Lee were right behind Daffy.

Cav came in with lights and sirens blaring. A second squad car screamed in from the other entrance.

"On the ground. Face down," Ryan ordered the crooks. "All of you." Outnumbered and out-gunned, they complied.

"Jake, you better check the trailer. Make sure no one else is in there. Becca, check the cab," Ryan cautioned.

Jones called in that he would stay with Tony and guard the shop. Tony's camera showed Jones with his badge around his neck.

Ryan turned to the Sheriff, "OK Cav. They're all yours. Let's get them cuffed and ID'd."

Cav was all smiles. "You feds sure know how to do it," he said to the group. "Jake, you too. I especially like the video hookup you put in my squad. Will make everything a whole lot easier when we get to court."

He raised his voice and in an official tone told the men on the ground that he was the Sheriff and they were under arrest. He had parked his car so the dashboard camera was recording everything. The individual cameras were still running.

"Jones," he spoke into his mic. "I'm sending in two deputies to relieve you. I want you to go to the office and smooth things over until I can get in there. I'll be sending two other men to the coin shop. One will stay there and guard the shop; the other will escort the vendor to the office." Then he turned back to the guys on the ground.

"We're going to start with that guy on the left, the driver," he said to his deputies. "Cuff him, frisk him, sit him up, and bring me his wallet. I'll Mirandize him and then we'll move to the next guy."

He nodded to two of his men to get started.

"Gun!" one of them exclaimed as he pulled it out of the guy's waistband.

"It's fake," jean jacket declared. "We all have fake guns."

"This isn't fake," the deputy said as he put on the safety and dropped it in an evidence bag. "This is the real McCoy."

"What, you asshole. You have a gun? Are you crazy?" jean jacket said furiously. "I told you no guns."

"Tsk. Tsk," Cav said. "Guess that adds a few years to your sentence. Your buddies too. Bet they are not going to like that." No time like the present to sow the seeds of dissent among the crooks.

The deputy pulled out the man's wallet and handed it to Cav. Sat the guy up against the trailer tire and pulled his cap and glasses off. Put both in an evidence bag that another deputy labeled. "Well Mr. Walter R. B. Grady," Cav said reading the man's name and address from his ID. "Let me read you your rights," he did so and dropped the wallet in another bag. He told a deputy to start the warrants for each of the men's home addresses. And a warrant for the landscape office. "Call over to New Madrid. Khalen is waiting to send a car out to secure the building. We'll want to talk to anyone inside, especially Ms. White."

"I'll call him," Mary Lee offered.

They moved on to the next guy in line, repeating the process, working their way to jean jacket.

The deputy pulled off his cap and glasses and Becca said, "Well, well. Mr. Board Chairman Sergio Nadeau. What a surprise."

"Travis," he growled, recognizing her. "Bitch. I knew you'd be a problem as soon as I heard you caught that home invasion cold case."

"Is that why you tried to kill her?" Ryan asked quietly.

"Kill her?" Sergio swiveled his head to look at Ryan. "Kill her?" he repeated as if Ryan were speaking a foreign language. Then shock spread across his face. "You think I shot her?" he said stunned. "Why would I do that?" he asked clearly baffled.

"Because she caught your home invasion case," Ryan said reasonably. "That's what you just said."

"No. No, that's not what I meant. I didn't mean that. God I didn't need to shoot her. I don't even own a gun. You can check." He faced Becca. "I was going to get you assigned to the courthouse. You wouldn't have had time for any cases, cold or otherwise. By the time you got back to regular duty that case would have been back in the cold files. I had the paperwork all ready for your Captain. Shoot you? Why would I shoot you? That's crazy."

He turned back to Ryan, "That's crazy," he repeated. "Besides, we have an exit strategy if anything goes wrong." He paused, looked at Becca again. "I didn't shoot you."

"Who's we?" Becca asked softly.

"What do you mean?"

"You said *we* have an exit strategy."

"Nobody," he said quickly. "Me. No one." Obviously lying now.

"Might as well tell us. We'll find out soon enough. One of you will talk. I promise," Becca said.

"No one's talking. I want my lawyer. They want theirs too." He turned to his partners and instructed, "No one says anything," he told them. "They got nothing."

"Oh, I don't know about that. We have you guys. Using a gun in a robbery. We have the stolen goods right here," Cav said. He turned to one of his men, "Let's open those Expo bags for the cameras, and then put them into evidence bags. We'll do an inventory at the station. With the owners present." He didn't mention that both thefts had been recorded, or that the cameras were still running. Save that for later. Also, save for later, that he knew they had committed other robberies besides the home invasion.

"Oh, did I forget to mention that you are under arrest for armed robbery?" Cav turned to his men, "OK. Let's load them up. Take them down and book them. Separate cells. Let them call their lawyers."

"I'll need statements from your team, Jake. And you and Ryan. Come down to the station tonight, tomorrow. Whichever works."

"Tonight," Jake said. "We'll debrief back at Safe Keeping and head on over to you with our statements."

"Works for me," Cav agreed. "Ryan? Maybe you would want to help us with the interviews?" he asked.

Becca snorted. Let him do the interviews, more like, she thought. Ryan was famous for his ability to get admissions and confessions. He wouldn't have trouble turning the crooks against each other.

"Red cap, anyhow," Ryan said.

"I'd appreciate that."

"I would like to watch, Cav," she asked politely, she thought.

"Good. You know more about all this than the rest of us. It would be a help. Thank you," he responded, surprising her. He continued, "OK, that's all set. I need to go inside and talk to management. We'll secure the two stalls for tonight and I'll have my deputies bring the vendors down to complete the inventories. I'll be about an hour. That gives you time, Jake, to get your people together, debriefed, and down to the station."

**

They met in the Safe Keeping board room for the debriefing. Becca had driven the RV and Tony had made copies of all the videos on the way back. Jake had them fill out statements and then they headed out to the station.

"You can ride with me and Daffy. In the armored car," Ryan told her. "This might not be over yet. We don't know," he cautioned.

She nodded.

"And Daffy will stay with you in the station," he said.

"I don't need a bodyguard in the police station," she said rudely. It made sense, just barely, to ride with him, but a bodyguard at the station?

"Yes, you do," Ryan said simply.

Daffy was shaking his head at her with a smug knowing look. She knew she was going to lose this battle, but she fought it anyhow.

"The place is full of cops," she pointed out to him. "Who is going to be dumb enough to shoot me inside a cop house?" she thought that was a reasonable question.

"A cop?" he said patiently.

"A cop?" she protested. "He just pulls out his weapon and shoots me?" she asked outraged.

"Yeah," Daffy said. "Puts a throw away in your hand and says you pulled it and aimed it at him. You're dead. He can explain it any way he wants."

"You're crazy. You're both crazy. The one place I'll be safe is a cop shop."

"Maybe," Ryan agreed. "But Daffy stays with you."

"He's right Becca. He's not just being bossy. This is my job remember and stranger things have happened. Someone is out to get you; no place is safe. No time. You know that. Besides, I'm fun to be with," Daffy added. "And I can tell you some tales about Ryan." Winking at her and giving her a graceful way out.

She couldn't help it. She laughed. Besides it was a good bribe.

"No stories," Ryan said sternly. Daffy just smiled.

**

"I think we should start with red cap. Anthony F. Meed," Ryan was telling Cav.

"Why him in particular?"

"He seems to be in charge. Just under Sergio. He has a lot to lose. We can't go after Sergio, he's lawyered up, won't say anything. He'll ride it out. I think I can turn red cap."

He walked into the room with Cav behind him. Sat in one of the chairs. "Mr. Meed. I'm FBI Agent Gibbs. And I guess this is your attorney?"

"Yes, I am. And Mr. Meed has nothing to say. Charge him or let him go."

"Have you met Sheriff Cavanaugh?" Ryan nodded to Cav who also sat. "Your client doesn't have to say anything. You don't have to say anything. I plan on doing all the talking. All you have to do is listen." He waited a moment.

"First, though, let me say, that Mr. Meed will be charged. He will get to decide what the charge is. You have two options and I want to make those clear. We have you on video robbing the coin vendor. You're holding a gun, Anthony. Now you and I? We know it's fake. But both the vendor and the woman believed it was real. And I got to tell you, Anthony, it looks real in the pictures."

"They were fake. They're fake guns," Meed insisted.

"Quiet," his attorney said. "Hear him out."

"Doesn't really matter if they are fake. Because your driver had a real gun. But we'll come back to that. You were also complicit in the robbery of the rock shop. You can plead to two counts of armed robbery or two counts of robbery. You get to decide. But the lighter counts come with conditions. Are you listening? Because I am going to lay them out for you."

"Go ahead," the attorney said.

"We want to know who your partners are. All of them. Not just the ones we got today. You give us a list of the other robberies and your partners in each of those."

"What other robberies?" Meed asked sullenly.

"We know you've been doing this for a few years, Anthony. How do you think we caught you? If you own up to today's crime and the other crimes, I'll see that you are charged for today only. Unarmed robbery. But we get it all. Everything. And it better include everything we have."

"How do I know what you know?"

"You don't. That's what will keep you honest. You won't be charged with the older crimes. But your partners are going down for all of them. For the full count" Cav added.

Ryan took the lead back. "So those are your choices. Admit to the past robberies. I'll give you a hint; we have eight years' worth. Tell us your partners. You get charged with only today's crimes, both unarmed. Five years. You'll probably get time off for good behavior. That's option one and it's on the table until we walk out of the room and offer it to one of your buddies. Option two: you go down for all the robberies, armed.

"Keep in mind that we are searching your house as we speak. We both know we're going to find some of the stolen items there. We'll be looking at your financials for unaccounted income. We'll be combing through your computer. Won't take us long. Even if we don't find any-thing, we still have you for two counts of armed robbery. That second robbery today comes with a mandatory prison sentence. Total time will be about thirty years. And that's just for today. You help us; we'll help you. We want everything. Who picked the locations. Who made the plans. How you disposed of the loot. Did you split the take evenly. If not, how. All of it. Everything." He looked at Cav and asked, "Did I miss anything?'

"Probably. But all and everything should cover it."

He looked at the attorney and said, "If he skips anything, the deal is off and we keep and use what he tells us. Now my friend, the Sheriff and I are going to go stand in the corner over there while you talk this over. The way I see this, its win win for both of us. We'll give you a few minutes."

Ryan and Cav walked to the corner. "Think he'll go for it?"

"Pretty sure. It's a good deal. Five years versus a minimum of thirty? How did it go with the Expo manager?" They talked quietly while they waited and watched.

"We want it in writing," the attorney called to them. "Before he says anything."

"I'll get the D.A.," Cav said.

He didn't have to go very far. The D.A. was watching through the one way glass with Becca and Daffy. Daffy was between the door and Becca. Still protecting.

"That was pretty impressive," the D.A. said. "You two are a good team. You really worked that guy. And his attorney. That's one of the best criminal attorneys in the county. I don't think I ever saw anyone get him to make a deal that wasn't his own suggestion. Certainly not one that worked so well for the prosecution. I'm going to get a lot of free beers off this story." He was laughing. Happy with the results. Even though at first he had been reluctant to cut any deal. He wanted the big splashy front page headlines. But Ryan had explained to him that he'd have to share those headlines with D.A.s in three different states. Furthermore, convictions were not guaranteed. The older crimes would be tough to prove for one thing. And in most cases were beyond the statute of limitations. Pennsylvania had a five year limit. And, besides, Sergio would drag the whole thing out for years.

His only hope, Ryan had told him, was to turn one of the crooks. Get a confession and use that against the others.

Then Ryan had explained his reasoning again for starting with Meed. They wouldn't get anything from Sergio. He'd work the system. The driver was just a grunt, a go for. Besides, he was the only one with a real gun. If they gave him a deal, they'd have to drop the armed robbery charges and go with simple robbery. Even with the fake guns, they weren't assured a conviction. The jury might be sympathetic to the defendants. After all, the robbers never intended to hurt anyone. Black cap was a hot head. Sweats appeared to be another grunt. Most likely, neither of them probably knew anything. More likely, they'd been told when and where to show up.

But red cap, Meed, he looked to be in charge in the video. He obviously had some authority. If they could get him to cooperate, they could use him to get the other two to confess. Identify the fence. And finger the missing robber. There was at least one more crook involved. They were pretty sure it was the florist, Martha White. Meed could name her. If they could turn him, he would make an excellent witness against Sergio. "His job as a county department chief gives him an aura of respectability and reliability. He'll be very good on the stand," Ryan had finished up.

That was what convinced the D.A. A chance for a trial where he could look very good to the voters. He had the agreement all typed up, waiting for signatures. Two copies.

Everyone signed, the attorney kept one copy and Cav gave the other to a deputy to make more copies. Ryan gave Meed a yellow note pad and pen, "List the locations and dates. Start with the oldest on top."

Meed looked at his lawyer who nodded and reread the contract.

"I can't remember the exact dates," Meed grumbled.

"Do the best you can. Day of the week, month," Ryan told him and watched. The first was the one he was concerned about. The home invasion. He needed the home invasion. Would red cap start with that?

He did. The home invasion was at the top of the page. Ryan sat back to watch. Meed started out slowly, hesitantly, either from a natural reluctance to implicate himself or from trying to remember. Stopping every couple of words to get encouragement from his attorney. But by the time he got to the third robbery he was writing smoothly.

He was done before the copies of the contract came back. That was not a coincidence; the deputy had been told to wait.

Cav gave the list a quick glance, nodded to Ryan, everything was there. He traded the list for the contracts. "Copy this. One for each of us," he told his deputy.

Those copies came back immediately.

"OK, Meed. Let's go through these, one by one," Cav said.

Two hours later they decided they had all they were going to get. Meed had said that the members of the ring all worked for the county.

The idea for the robberies had started at a poker game. They were talking about easy money when Sergio said he knew a guy who kept a lot of cash and jewelry in his home. Meed thought that Sergio might have had a hard on about the guy. Seemed to enjoy hitting him to get him to open the safe.

Now that Cav had a connection, they might be able to dig out more information on a relationship between Sergio and the home owner.

Meed gave them the fences. There were two of them. And he knew Sergio's ID, user name, and password on eBay, where he sold a lot of the jewelry.

The robberies were always the same week of the year because that was when most county employees and the Board were on vacation. Ha. That was too simple.

They always used a landscaping vehicle. Meed didn't know why. He thought maybe Sergio had something on the owner.

The split was 30% to Sergio, 20% to Meed, 10% each to the three others. So there was 20% unaccounted for.

The unknown person. Meed didn't know who it was.

So they still didn't have anything on the florist, except she was working late when one of her vehicles was being used in a robbery.

Cav was going to work on the other two crooks. Khalen and Jones would be busy all night supervising the search teams. They had five residences, the landscaping office, Meed's office, Sergio's office, and lockers at work for the other three men.

Sergio said nothing. His attorney said charge him or let him go.

"I'll be out by midnight," Sergio bragged.

But he was going to spend the weekend in jail. No judge was going to set bail tonight or over the weekend.

"That's it," Ryan said. "We're not going to get anything more from Meed. We're not going to get anything from Sergio we don't already have. He is not going to serve up his partner. We have nothing to offer him. He knows the law. He might go down for the count, but I doubt it, and it will take a long time. Let's go home."

Daffy dropped them off at the gatehouse.

He was watching Becca when he said, "He didn't shoot you."

"I know. His surprise was real. It wasn't an act. I wonder what he meant when he said they had an exit strategy. He gave us two things with that statement. That he had a partner and that he still has a plan. He knows he shouldn't have said that; he slipped up."

She glanced up at Ryan, "Are we checking his financials?"

"Yeah, but it will take a long time."

"Is it Sylvia then? I guess we'll find out tomorrow. God I'm tired."

"Sit, I'll scramble some eggs and ham. We'll eat and hit the hot tub."

Saturday

They headed out early for the gallery to practice scenarios. There were six actors; two had actually been in stage productions with ghost characters. They demonstrated the techniques they had learned and used. One of them suggested having a chime sound whenever Becca appeared. It had worked well in his play. But they passed on that.

They practiced walking through her, talking around her, and looking past her. She'd learned quickly not to step out of the way, but it was a long time before she mastered the technique of not flinching when they narrowly missed her. It took a while to perfect the subtle shift of hips or shoulders to avoid a collision. Becca was surprised at how much concentration it took for her not to bump into the actors while they appeared to walk through her. It also required good balance and turned into a strengthening exercise for her leg.

That hardest part was learning to keep her eyes on Sylvia even when an actor blocked her view or brushed past her. Keep her eyes focused.

Daffy, Jen, Ron, and Mary Lee were quicker studies. Becca assumed they were used to role-playing.

The actors demonstrated the presentation of phrases that she and Ryan had brainstormed the night before and ad-libbed several new versions and variations. They added hand gestures which might be appropriate. She learned how to put the accent and emphasis on different words and use body language instead of speech.

Mary Lee didn't have much to do because Becca already resembled her mother closely. But because Ryan didn't want to leave anything to chance Mary Lee fixed Becca's hair in her mother's style and found a vintage outfit.

**

Sylvia came out of her house to go to a luncheon at noon time. Becca was standing across the street, not quite looking at Sylvia as she stepped out the front door. A car door slammed and Sylvia looked across the street. Becca turned in her direction, but looked past her. Sylvia froze and stared as a large RV drove down the street. After it went past, Sylvia was still looking where Becca had stood. But no one was there. Becca was out of sight down on the floor where she couldn't be seen in a non-descript car parked at the curb. Sylvia looked up and down the street. She shook herself and allowed the chauffeur to help her into her car.

Again, at the restaurant. Sylvia was looking out the window as Becca walked by and looked inside, smiling directly at Sylvia. Sylvia turned white. It was working.

One more time; they didn't want to overdo it. Becca was in the back seat of a different car when Sylvia came out of the restaurant. Becca smiled at her as she drove by. Sylvia hesitated, stumbled before she collected herself. She was white again.

Later, inside the car, outside the gallery, Ryan asked her, "OK Baby?"

"Baby?" Becca buried her face in her hands. "Now I'm baby? That's just great." She knew she was being difficult. Ryan was rubbing her shoulders.

"The plan is working. This evening should be fine with all our practice. Just relax. We'll be nearby at all times. You'll never be alone." They had all perfected the 'look through Becca', and the 'walk through Becca' techniques.

"I'm a cop," she said straightening her shoulders. "This baby is fine." She had a feeling that he'd called her baby just to get this reaction. "I just need to be careful that I don't get in anyone's way as they walk through me. This stunt works in the movies all the time." She took pity on Ryan. It was nerves. They both knew it. "I'm fine. As long as you're near, I'm fine." That sounded a little too intimate or needy, or both. So she added, "Don't let me scratch her eyes out."

Daffy laughed, "That's our girl. Break a leg." He opened the door and they went inside.

Sylvia was to see her one more time across the proverbial crowded room. A glimpse that would be blocked immediately by the actors. Becca walked two steps through the doorway. Mary Lee's friend Morgan turned Sylvia to lead her to another exhibit making sure Becca would be in her view. Sylvia stopped short and stumbled against Morgan's arm.

"Are you all right," he asked her with concern.

"That woman, there," Sylvia pointed, but by that time the actors had moved in front of Becca and she'd backed out of the room.

"The one in the black dress? She is very lovely. Is she one of the artists?" Morgan asked.

"No, the other one."

"I don't see anyone else; she must have gone before I looked. You simply must see the exhibits in the Rose Room." Both Morgan and Barbara Walker, the gallery owner, had excitedly participated in the earlier practice. They were 'on' now. It was their job to escort Sylvia to the room selected for their play where Jake's people were viewing the exhibits. Becca would wait in the office until her curtain call. Morgan led Sylvia down the hall and into the room. Daffy was paired with Mary Lee and Jen with Ron again. Each had cameras and ear buds.

The actors were scattered throughout the gallery pretending to be customers or waiters. They were carrying trays with the white wine and cheese and crackers. A table was set up as a buffet with cold meat and bread loaves on a cutting board. Clear glass plates with silverware and cloth napkins were on one side. Condiments were at the other end.

Becca was anxious. Waiting was the hardest part. The office was elegant, but then this was a gallery. Old furniture, antiques? Modern computer, pc, on the desktop. She walked around, not touching anything, just looking. She actually felt like an actress might feel before her big first night. She forgot that everything was being recorded back at the spycar parked in the back lot. Kevin had preened when Ryan asked if they could use it. The locals wanted some way to monitor the takedown. Jake suggested his RV. So both the local Sheriff and Cav would watch from the RV. Jake would be there, as an observer. He had to remind people that he was a back office man, not a guardian. Cilla, also, was in the RV.

Finally, Becca got the signal from Ryan that they were ready in the Rose Room. "Okay," she thought, "Mom, Dad, this is for you." She took a deep, steadying breath, walked down the hall, and stood in the doorway. Inconspicuously sidestepping as the waiter walked through her. Morgan had Sylvia facing the door. She froze and grabbed his arm.

"There. She's there. That woman. By the door. See her?" Sylvia cried.

Both Morgan and Barbara turned to look. Ryan who was standing nearby turned also as Sylvia pointed.

"No. I don't see anyone, must have missed her again," he said as he looked directly at Becca.

"Are you all right, dear?" Mrs. Walker asked. "You're shaking."

Sylvia continued staring at Becca, who was still in the doorway.

"She's right there," Sylvia shrieked. "Can't you see her?"

Both Morgan and Mrs. Walker looked toward the door again, then at each other, and then at Sylvia with concern.

"Perhaps we should go to the office and sit down," Mrs. Walker suggested gently.

Sylvia pulled her eyes from Becca. Took a deep breath. "I'm okay. Just tired. My doctor said I should expect a little dizziness. I'm just getting over the flu. You two go along, I'm just going to sit here for a minute."

Morgan and Mrs. Walker stood beside her and talked quietly to each other. Morgan motioned over a waiter and sent him for a glass of water. "You just catch your breath. We'll be right over here." He led Mrs. Walker a few steps away.

Becca took a step toward Sylvia who sucked in her breath, shaking her head, no. Ron and Jen walked through Becca. They were so smooth that Ryan who was watching almost believed it.

Becca took another three steps forward and now was about five feet from Sylvia.

"Go away. Go away. You don't belong here," Sylvia ordered.

Becca smiled.

"You're dead," Sylvia growled. "You're dead."

Becca nodded, sadly. Agreeing.

Sylvia smiled at that. "That's right. I don't see you. You're not here."

"Oh, but you do see me Sylvia. I am here."

"I don't see you." Sylvia closed her eyes.

"That's okay. No one else can see me either. So I sort of am not here. No one can hear me either. Just you."

"Why?"

Becca had to be careful how she answered this. They had talked about it.

"Why am I here? Well, for you Sylvia."

Sylvia was quiet for a long time. Now Mary Lee and Daffy walked past Becca. They split apart at the last second with just enough space between them for Becca. From Sylvia's angle it looked as if they walked through her.

Sylvia put her hand to her mouth covering a cry. But then she got a gleam in her eye.

"You can't do anything," she whispered fiercely. "You're dead."

"You don't have to whisper, Sylvia, no one can hear you."

Sylvia looked around. No one was paying them any attention.

"What do you mean? Why can't they hear me?"

"Why you're disappearing, Sylvia. It's time almost. I've come for you and you're starting to disappear from this world."

"You can't. You're dead. You can't do anything to me." But her voice shook as she spoke.

"Well, you did kill me Sylvia." Becca brushed the back of her index finger across her eyebrow. Her tell. Her Mom's tell.

"I did. You're dead," Sylvia said with a smirk. "I ran you down. You and that self-righteous husband of yours. You're both dead."

Gotcha, Becca thought. Gotcha. Now for some more.

"He's here with me Sylvia."

Sylvia's head jerked around, looking for Richard.

"Not here in the room, Sylvia. He's parking the car. He'll be here soon. When he gets here, we'll take you back with us. Oh, not the same place we've been which is rather pleasant. You'll be following a different path."

"What? What do you mean?"

"Richard is very unhappy that you ran me down. You might have had a good reason to kill him. But you didn't have any reason to kill me." Becca held her breath. This was a gray area.

"He deserved to die. He told me he was going to the cops. If I didn't confess, he was going to tell them I killed Fred. It was self-defense. Richard should have left it alone. It's his fault he's dead. He is such a self-righteous prig."

"But why me Sylvia?"

"I couldn't take a chance that he hadn't told you that I killed Fred. I don't know how he figured it out. You had to die too. Two birds with one car. It was easy." A manic giggle slipped out.

"He's angry about Rebecca too."

"Spoiled brat. Suppose she's here with you. You never went anywhere without her. If you had left her home that day, she'd still be alive."

That stopped Becca for a second. She wanted to kill me because I was spoiled? Becca thought.

"No, for this we left her home, Sylvia. But someone else is with Richard."

"Someone else?"

"Yes. Someone else you know."

"Fred?"

"Yes. Fred. He's unhappy with the way you killed him."

"But I was very gentle with him. He died in his sleep. I gave him my sleeping pills in his nightcap. I even buried him under his favorite apple tree," she protested. And then looked quickly around. But no one was watching them. People were walking around the room looking at exhibits and talking. It was like she wasn't there.

Becca adlibbed. Sylvia had admitted to killing her parents and Fred. She'd try for the two other husbands.

"And someone else, Sylvia. We picked up someone else. A couple of people." Hoping she wasn't leading Sylvia.

"Charleston? Do you mean Charleston? But he went gently in his sleep, also." Charleston was her second husband. She said that as if killing him gently was okay. But Sylvia was still talking.

"Or do you mean his son?"

Becca almost said whose son she was so surprised. Whose son? Charleston's son? Did Sylvia kill him? She waited. "Charleston's son. It's unfortunate but I had to run him down. It was very violent. Like you," Sylvia said simply.

"Charleston is with Richard. But, no, not Charleston's son. Unless they picked him up after I got out of the car. Someone else, Sylvia." This should be the last husband.

"Oh. Poor Duncan. He was very sick you know. He should be happy I helped him along. Sleeping pills in his nightcap. Such a nice quiet way."

Becca almost danced. All of them. Sylvia had admitted to all of them. They should be able to exhume the bodies and do autopsies. At least on Duncan. And there might be a way to link Sylvia to Charleston's son.

"It's time to go now," Becca said.

"But the others. They're not here yet." Sylvia stated. Looking toward the door for them to enter. "I won't go with you. You can't make me. You're dead. I killed you. Go away."

Becca smiled.

Sylvia spoke to Morgan loudly "Morgan, please help me up. I need to go home. I'm not feeling well."

But Morgan came over along with Ryan and held out his hand to shake with Becca. "That was impressive. I can't thank you enough for letting me be part of this. Mary Lee knows how to pick them."

"You can see her?" Sylvia asked shocked. "You can see her?"

"Of course."

"But she's a ghost." Sylvia said confused.

Becca gave him a pleased smile and accepted his hand. "It was a pleasure." He was beaming at her.

Ryan said, "That's my girl." He turned to Sylvia. "Allow me to introduce myself. I am Ryan Gibbs, FBI, Special Agent in Charge. This is Rebecca Anne Travis. Daughter of Richard and Anne. I arrest you for the murders of Richard Travis, Anne Travis, and Fred Smith."

Becca stopped listening. Suddenly, just like that, it was over. It was almost anticlimactic. Twenty years later this evil woman was going to pay for killing her parents. Suddenly she realized that Sylvia was standing. And screaming at her. "You're the brat? You're the brat? You died with them. You're dead." With that scream Sylvia charged at Becca before anyone could stop her.

It was instinctive. Becca hit her in the face with a left hook. She had enough time to make sure she wouldn't break a nose. But she was sure it would leave a bruise. And maybe a black eye. The punch knocked Sylvia down. No one was quick enough to catch her before she hit the floor with a loud thunk.

A satisfying loud thunk. Almost as satisfying as the smack that most likely blackened Sylvia's eye. Becca didn't smile; but only because she remembered that this was all being recorded. She didn't want her satisfaction to show.

She turned away from the limp form on the floor checking her knuckles and caught Ryan's wink. Gave him a tiny smile. Showed him her bruised knuckles. Maybe he would kiss them and make them better later. Now she smiled.

The local cops came and got Sylvia. They would take over the investigation, exhume the bodies, search Sylvia's house.

Ryan got Becca out of there as soon as he could and they rode home in the armored car. The vehicle reinforcing the fact that it wasn't over. Ryan drove with one hand, cradling her bruised one with his other. Frequently lifting it to his mouth to kiss her knuckles. Each time he did that, her stomach dropped out and she smiled.

She didn't want to think about what would happen now. About her shooting. She was all out of ideas. About Ryan. She was just starting to get ideas. Long term ideas? She still wasn't sure.

"What happens now? Was it a random shooter like my Captain thought?"

"No. We have one more, maybe two more possibles."

"Well, my brain must be dead, because I sure can't think of even one."

"I might be exaggerating. Sergio's wife could be one. If she knew about the robberies. If he told her you could be a problem. She might want to stop you."

Becca thought about that. "I don't know. That's a real long shot. He doesn't strike me as the type of man who shares with his wife. He didn't even share with his fellow crooks. You really think he talked to her?"

"No, I don't. I agree with you. That's why I said I might be exaggerating when I said two people."

She considered what he said, looking at it. Turning it all around. She finally saw it.

"The florist. We know there is another person and we think the florist is involved. It makes sense for it to be White. Sergio is protecting White. He cares about her. It makes sense too, that he talked to her. Told her I'd been assigned the cases."

Ryan was nodding. "That's what I think. Now we just have to figure out how to get Sergio to talk. Or, I can think of another way, but it's dangerous and we'd need to do it soon. Tomorrow. Let me think some more. Cav and your Captain and Khalen would have to agree to it. Give me some more time. OK?"

He kissed her knuckles again.

"That makes me tingle in interesting places."

"Then I guess we better get you home and hope that the folks in the caravan behind us don't follow."

**

He woke up in the middle of the night, alone, and went hunting for her. She was in the far bathroom crying. He almost went back to bed. She was safe. She deserved her privacy. This wasn't hysteria. This was healthy weeping. But something drew him inside. Made him sit on the floor beside her, his back to the wall. Drag her over into his lap.

"Oh, honey."

She turned her head into his shoulder, sobbing.

He wrapped his arms around her, rocking her, comforting. He didn't tell her it was okay. He didn't say everything is all right. He held her, stroked her head, and let her cry.

When she seemed to be easing off, he reached for the Kleenex and passed her a handful.

She blew her nose, reached out for more Kleenex and blew again. Wiped her eyes. Leaned into him. He held her closer.

He was stroking her head. "You don't have to hide in the bathroom to cry, honey. It's okay to cry. It's healthy." He lifted her head and kissed her lightly.

She looked at him and then admitted, "But it was a selfish cry."

"A selfish cry?"

"I was crying for that little girl. The one that lived in the perfect house with the loving family. She could have grown up cherished and married Teddy Bear. That's what she planned but that woman killed her when she killed my parents. I was crying for her."

He didn't know what to say.

"I was ashamed. So I came in here to cry for me."

"You don't have to be ashamed. And it's not selfish. It's okay to cry for that little girl. Someone should cry for her. We should all cry for her. What happened to her was wrong." Again, he lifted her chin. This time so she could see the sincerity in his face.

"But from her ashes, a vibrant woman was born. A woman forged in fire. A protector of the weak. A seeker of justice for the wronged. One with a core strong as steel, wrapped in caring and compassion. That woman is the one I fell in love with. The child would have married Teddy, you're right. But the woman was designed for me. Created for me. I would never have noticed that little girl. But the woman? She makes my heart beat fast, screams *this one*. This one is mine."

She smiled when he said that. Her heart seemed to be saying the same to her.

"It's okay to cry for that little girl. But you also need to appreciate the woman she has become. You are so much more than that little girl could ever have been."

"But I would have had a normal life."

"Yes, and missed out on all you are now. Missed out on your family of equally strong people forged from adversity. You wouldn't have them. Think of how sad that loss would be. For all of you. That little girl would have been strong and sweet. Sweet, like my Macy was probably."

"I'm not anything like her."

"You are inside. You are more like her then you can realize. But different. Oh so different. Too good for me, probably. But that's okay. I'm willing to chance marrying up. You understand that I love you?"

She barely nodded.

"I love the child you were with the promise she had. I love the woman you have become. I love you." He kissed her softly. "Come on, let's go to bed."

She nodded again. She still had tears in her eyes, but these were from his words. Happy tears. He stood with her in his arms and carried her to bed where they made sweet gentle love.

Sunday

They were waiting. Had been waiting at the rest stop for two hours.

Khalen finally called. "White's here. Just sitting in the parking area, waiting. The Captain notified her an hour ago. Told her that the Sheriff from Bear would be coming in this morning, returning her stolen equipment. Told her that if she came in and signed the paperwork while Cav was here, she could get her truck and trailer back. He also just happened to mention that Detective Travis would be present. Maybe Martha would want to thank the Detective since she was responsible for capturing Sergio and retrieving the stolen truck and trailer." He gave an empty laugh, "We're all set up. It's your turn."

Ryan was driving Mary Lee's splashy red sports car, Becca beside him. "Ready?" he asked. She nodded, "Let's go get her."

They parked in the police lot, stood by the car, and took the time for a prolonged session of steamy kissing and necking. Even a little groping. Until Khalen broke them apart with a comment in Ryan's ear, "I think she has the picture guys. She knows you are a couple. You don't actually have to have sex in the parking lot. Please. It's against the law." He was laughing at them. Becca was out of breath and a little embarrassed. She'd totally forgotten herself when Ryan kissed her. It was only supposed to be an act, for God's sake.

She gave him a love slap. "You did that on purpose," she accused him.

He grabbed her hand laughing and walked her slowly toward the building. Slowly, because that was part of the plan. Becca was limping, leaning heavily on the cane. He stopped outside the door and leaned in for another long kiss. "I really like this plan." He looked over her shoulder. "Here she comes." He led her inside, brushed against Khalen, and headed for the ladies room. Looked around quickly, ostensibly to make sure no cops were watching, but actually to make sure Martha saw them.

He led her to the far wall. They both checked for the camera that Khalen had said was set up in the corner of the room.

Becca nodded at it and whispered, "Mary Lee?"

"Um," she replied from the first cubicle, standing on the toilet seat.

Ryan backed Becca against the wall. This time he only leaned in, not quite touching. She could feel the tension in him. "It's okay. It's going to work," she whispered.

Then, even though he expected it, hoped for it, Martha's voice startled him. He'd been pretty sure she wouldn't start shooting, that she would want to gloat first. Just the same his body shielded Becca.

He stayed leaning into Becca, but turned his head to give Martha his sexy grin. "Sorry, sorry. We just needed a couple of minutes of privacy." He stopped when he saw the gun. With a silencer. "Oh, you don't need a gun. We'll leave."

He turned facing Martha, still blocking any shot at Becca, waiting. They needed a confession.

"I heard you would be here today, Miss Detective Travis. I waited for you. Followed you in here. Is this your new boyfriend?"

Becca just stared.

"Answer me," Martha screamed when no one said anything.

Becca nodded. She couldn't speak. This was exactly what they'd planned and yet she couldn't speak.

"You know Becca?" Ryan asked.

"I know her. Sergio said she would ruin everything. And she did. I tried to stop her before. I'm a good shot. I don't know how I missed. My first bullet should have got you right in your heart. Today I'll make sure you're dead before I leave. But I think I'll start with your boyfriend, Miss Smart Detective. You took my boyfriend from me; I'm going to take yours." And she shot Ryan in the heart. He clapped a hand over his chest as he was thrown back and around and into Becca. Blood running down his front. She shot him one more time as he went down pulling Becca with him.

It wasn't supposed to hurt this much he thought. That wasn't planned.

Becca started to get up, but screamed, her eyes wide. Blood? There wasn't supposed to be blood. He had on a vest.

She reached out to him, "Ryan?"

Touched where the blood was. Lifted her hand and looked at it. "No. You can't be shot. No," she wailed and looked up at Martha. "You shot him," she said in disbelief.

"You're next," Martha promised as she started to pull the trigger. Becca used the cane to knock the gun aside as it went off. At the same time, Mary Lee rushed out of the john and grabbed Martha's gun hand and Jen came through the door and put her pistol in Martha's face. They were followed closely by cops. Lots of cops.

Becca wasn't watching anymore. She was leaning over Ryan trying to find the entrance wound and stop the bleeding. But she couldn't see. Why couldn't she see?

"Ryan," she was crying. "I can't lose you now. Ryan. Where are you hit?" She was desperately trying to open his shirt. Get to the vest.

He grabbed her hands. "I'm OK," he breathed. "I'm wearing a vest. A vest. Honey. God it hurts to talk. I think she broke a rib. I'm OK honey, I have a vest."

"No. No. You're bleeding." His vest had failed him as hers had. She was ripping his shirt open, unstrapping the vest, still searching for his wound. The vest had a dent in it. But no hole. No blood on the inside. She could see that much as she brushed her tears aside. No blood inside his vest. Hunh?

She pulled the vest closed and looked again. Red. Red. On his shirt. Not inside his vest.

She took a deep shuddering breath, punched him in the shoulder.

"You skunk. You have a dye packet? You have a dye packet and you didn't tell me? I'll kill you myself." She was mad, relieved, mad again. She hit him a second time, harder. He grunted.

She leaned over and hugged him close. She was laughing and crying now.

He groaned, "Broken ribs, sweetheart. Be gentle."

"Why didn't you tell me? I thought she shot you like she shot me. Why didn't you tell me?"

"There wasn't time. Khalen slipped me the die packet when we came in. I didn't even know I was going to use it. When she shot me, I grabbed my chest; it was an instinctive reaction. The packet was in my hand; it broke." He winced, "The bullet took my breath away. The second one felt like a sledge hammer to the kidneys. Ow."

Khalen came over then. "Let me see." He pushed Becca out of the way and opened the vest. "Yup. Think you're right. Broken rib. Sure is making a beautiful bruise." He rolled him lightly and looked at his back. "Yup. Took the second one in the kidney. That's got to hurt. Better get you to the hospital."

"Don't need a hospital. Just help me stand up."

"Stay where you are. The ambulance is out front; the EMTs are right behind me. You go to the hospital," the Captain ordered.

He turned to his detective, "Get White processed. Give that gun to Johnny in CSI. Bet it's the same weapon she used when she shot Becca." He turned back to Ryan who was sort of standing but leaning heavily on Becca, breathing shallowly. "We got this Gibbs. Let the EMT's take you to the hospital."

"I'm OK," he croaked. "They can strap me up. I want to see what she says. Then they can take me to the hospital."

"We're not talking to her until we get the results from ballistics. And search both her home and office. Time enough for you to get checked out at the hospital."

The EMTs came into the room and took charge. "I'm riding with him," Becca told the technicians.

"We don't generally allow that Ma'am."

"I'm a cop. I'm riding with him."

"Is he dangerous?"

"No. But I am. I'm going with him"

"Okay. Ma'am." She rode with him to the emergency room holding his hand, afraid to let go. She stood by while they checked him over and strapped him up, wrote out a prescription for pain. Another for sleeping pills, because the blow to his kidney would make sleep difficult. It took two hours. When they came out, she was again holding his hand tightly. Had not let go since they left the police station. The EMT's and the emergency room doctor smiled at her like she was an idiot. She didn't care. And Ryan? He was holding her just as tightly.

Her heart had slowly moved back into her chest somewhere during that two hour ordeal. She couldn't believe how it had seemed to stop beating when she thought Ryan had been shot. When she thought he might be dying. This was what Cilla meant. This was the way she felt about Jake. How Penney felt about Daffy.

This was love. She loved Ryan. She'd had to think she was losing him before she could recognize love. That feeling when she had first seen him, that body slam of recognition. That feeling had hit her when she was searching for his wound. She knew then. This man is mine.

She'd decided then that she would say yes when he asked her to marry him. She would choose to bury her cynicism and go with her gut. Her heart knew; her head knew. Her gut knew. She smiled to herself. She'd say yes and choose life. Life with the man she loved.

Daffy had followed the ambulance in the Rover, picked up Ryan's pills, and drove them back to the station.

"I still can't believe she shot you in my cop shop. How did she think she'd get away with it? Guess she thought she'd walk away before anyone found you. That's why she used the silencer. Leave you in the ladies room and just walk in my office and collect her vehicle. Crazy." The Captain was still shaking his head. "The gun is a match to the bullets they dug out of you, Becca. So we're ready to talk to her. You coming?" he offered Ryan.

Becca smiled when she caught Ryan checking with her. She shook her head. "No," she said. "You and Khalen should do it. If either of us is in there, it will confuse the issue."

It didn't matter. The only thing Martha would say is *Lawyer*. They kept at it, but eventually gave it up and let her call her attorney.

The Captain apologized to Ryan.

"No, not your fault. Some crooks lawyer up. Time to make a run on Sergio. He'll talk now."

"Why would he talk now?" Khalen asked. Ryan let him figure it out. Knew he got it when he saw Khalen smile.

"You should do it," Ryan told him.

"You coming?" Khalen asked. And again Ryan checked with Becca for a shake of her head. "Take the vest, though," he suggested.

Two hours later, they were all back in Cav's jail in Bear.

"I'm not talking without my attorney," Sergio said as his attorney joined them in the interrogation room.

"What's going on?" the attorney asked. "My client has nothing to say. Period."

"You don't have to talk, just listen." Khalen threw the bloody vest on the table. Everyone sat and looked at it. "We just arrested your girlfriend for the attempted murder of a federal law enforcement officer."

Sergio waited; he wasn't talking, but he looked interested.

"Martha White, your girlfriend and partner? Just gunned down the FBI agent who interrogated you."

"What?" was surprised out of Sergio. "Stupid bitch. That has nothing to do with me. I've been right here in your jail cell."

"Agreed. You had nothing to do with this shooting. But she used the same weapon on the agent that she used on Detective Travis. And guess who is going down as accessory in that attempted murder."

"No way. No way can you get me for that. If she did that, she did it on her own. I told you already, I had that all figured out. Travis wasn't going to be a problem for me." His attorney was trying to shush him, but he wasn't paying attention.

"That's what you say. But Martha seems to think that Travis was a threat."

"No. No way. You can't get me for that. I never told her that."

"We can tie her to you through the robberies. Seems she kept a bunch of the jewelry." Khalen put three property bags on the table. Each one labeled with a crime scene. "Found these in her very own jewelry box," he said with a snort.

"Stupid bitch. I told her not to keep anything." He looked at his attorney, realizing what he had just said. "Get me a deal. I'll give them her. Get me out of the attempted murder."

He gave her up. Gave them everything. Confirmed that she had helped plan all the jobs, supplied the equipment. They really had only one question.

"The first crime, the home invasion? That was her former lover. That was both personal and profitable. She'd told me about the money and the jewelry, and I got to beat the guy up," he explained.

Ryan was drooping by that time. He was being stoic, but the pain was a bitch. He was ready to head home.

Mary Lee had taken her red sports car; she was staying with Khalen. Daffy drove the Rover with Jen in the front seat, Ryan and Becca in the back. Becca had made him take his pain pills. That he wasn't arguing suggested that he felt as bad as he looked.

"You were protecting me," she accused him.

"I love you. How could I not protect you? I will always protect you."

She should have been angry, but instead she felt loved? Cherished? But he was still talking softly because that was all he could manage with the pain.

"I fell in love with you at Penney's wedding. I didn't know it until that first night in the gatehouse when you felt you had to tell me you could be testy." His laugh at that ended with a groan. He was holding her hand as he continued, "Even then it took me a few days to realize it. I love you. I will always love you."

He wanted to see how she was taking this but Daffy hit a bump, and he barely held in another groan.

"You'll ride better lying down," she said as she eased him down. "Put your head in my lap."

The picture that put in his mind made him growl in frustration. She looked at him, worried.

"I'm okay. Just sore and bruised. It will pass." He looked up at her, but couldn't keep his eyes open. He blinked. "You slipped me a sleeping pill."

"No, I didn't. It's the pain pill. Rest." Then she added, "I love you, too." But he was already asleep.

She was happy to sit and watch him sleep. When had she become so sappy, she wondered? But she was thankful he was alive. Almost losing him? That feeling had overwhelmed her. They would talk. He had promised they would talk when it was over and, finally, it was over.

She felt, relief? She wasn't sure what she had expected. Not relief. Or this elation. She had gained so much. She'd learned her parents loved her, had found missing parts of her childhood. She had been welcomed by her parents' friends and embraced as part of their families. They wanted to be part of her family, the one that had saved her.

There was more too. Almost as an afterthought, Cilla had told her about the money. The trust money. SC Digital had made millions of dollars and though most went to Sarah's Child, a small portion went to each member of the gang, as well as trusts for each of the rescues. Jake had deposited most of his share into Becca's trust. Becca thought that was just like the gang; to forget to mention that they had put money away for her. Tell her as an afterthought. So now she had two trusts. But the money wouldn't make a difference. She'd always earned more than she spent. More than she needed. She smiled to herself when she thought of telling Ryan she was wealthy.

Penney had found the perfect solution for Becca's disability pension. If the board wouldn't terminate it, Becca would give it to her Captain as a grant. For an extra position. She toyed with the idea that the position should be hers for only a fraction of a second. She'd retain control of the grant money; it would be pulled if the Board ever decided to include it in the official budget.

More importantly though, she had found Ryan. She didn't know what she would be doing or where she would end up. She just knew that wherever it was, she would be with Ryan.

He woke up as they drove through the gate. Daffy helped him inside and to the couch and left. They were home only a few minutes when Cav called with the status on Sylvia.

"As expected, she lawyered up. Her lawyer is trying to say entrapment. He's saying Sylvia can't be held accountable for anything she said to a ghost. Even though it's on multiple recordings. Doesn't matter. When they searched her house, they found a whole drawer of car keys. Apparently she collected them." He paused for effect. "Including the set from the car she used on Charleston's boy. That car is still in the impound yard. They think another set is from the car she stole to run down Becca's parents."

"She kept the keys to the cars she stole? They had keys in them?"

"I guess she took cars that had the keys in the ignition. Makes sense when you think about it. Wouldn't expect her to be able to hot wire a car," Cav said.

He continued, "She probably killed Fred when he got back from overseas for the insurance money like she did her other two husbands. The locals will exhume their bodies. Now that they know what to look for, they should be able to find some evidence; and they'll look for Fred under the apple tree."

"Buried under his favorite apple tree," Becca commented.

"Oh, I almost forgot. Sylvia's finger prints are on the inside of the car she used to run down Charleston's boy. We got her solid."

**

"That's it. It's all over," Ryan told her. "We are still going to talk. Tomorrow. I can't keep my eyes open. Help me up?"

She did and let him lean on her to get to the bedroom. She helped him undress. She helped him into bed, putting pillows behind him so he could lean back comfortably. He probably could have done all that himself, but it made her happy to take care of him. He dragged her down beside him. And then stopped.

"No. Help me up. I am not doing this from bed. I am not waiting for tomorrow."

When he stood facing her, he took her hand in his, and looked in her eyes. "I love you Rebecca Anne Travis. Will you marry me? Will you be my wife?"